Satsang with Baba

Volume 3

Questions and Answers
between Swami Muktananda
and his devotees

May 16–December 29, 1972

S.Y.D.A. Foundation

LCCN 76-670008
ISBN 0-914602-40-3 (Set)
ISBN 0-914602-38-1 (Vol.)

Published by S.Y.D.A. Foundation, P.O. Box 11071, Oakland Ca. 94611

Printed in the United States of America.

Introduction

Satsang is one of those rich sanskrit words that has no exact equivalent in English. It means, roughly, "the company of truth," and it is usually used to refer to an assembly of people interested in spiritual matters. Satsang also means "the company of saints and holy beings" especially the situations in which their teachings are imparted. The reason these volumes have been titled *Satsang* instead of just "Questions and Answers" is because satsang is the word that best conveys the feeling of the twice-weekly question/answer sessions which took place in Baba Muktananda's Ashram in Ganeshpuri between 1971 and 1974. The people who attended these gatherings came from all over the world, but almost all of them were devotees who were intensely aware that to sit in Baba's presence was to be in the company of truth. They approached him not as casual seekers, but as disciples approaching their Guru, with reverence and faith. Indeed, part of the value of these volumes is what they show us about the Guru-disciple relationship. The communication between Baba and his disciples is general and universal — meaningful to people at every stage of spiritual life — yet at the same time it is personal and specific, reflecting the concerns of particular people at a particular moment in time. From reading these exchanges, one gets a very clear picture of what life was like in Shree Gurudev Ashram in the early seventies — the flow of the seasons, the special incidents, the course of the sadhana of the questioners.

Above all, these books convey the flavor of Baba as a teacher. As one reads them, one feels the play of his personality, the interweaving of love and humor and sternness with which he guides his disciples, the balance he maintains between a traditional scriptural rigor and a revolutionary dismissal of inessential forms, his devotion, his insistence on discipline and one-pointedness, his impatience with spiritual charlatanism. One gets to know his spontaneity, his surprising turns of phrase, his way of moving freely between the universal and the particular so that in one statement he will shift from a high philosophical teaching to a graphically specific direction aimed at one or two individuals. Baba makes spiritual life a practical affair, not something lofty and abstract, but a daily process of moving closer and closer to a clearly defined and reachable goal. Over and over in these satsangs, we find him pointing this out to his disciples. Week after week he reminds them with the same demanding insistence that if they simply do their sadhana, if they simply recognize the truth of their real nature, they will naturally become everything they are capable of becoming. And this insistence, this implied certainty, is no small part of the value of these books. When we are in Baba's company, whether we are sitting in his presence or reading his words, it is easy to experience the inner reality he is showing us. It is one of the characteristics of a Guru like Baba that his words are alive. They have the capacity to enter into us, and work within us, and create the experience of which they speak. This is what was happening during those satsangs in Ganeshpuri, and this is what can happen as we read them.

Satsang with Baba is a book to read slowly, for there is something about the question/answer format which demands that we take a little bit at a time. As we get to know the book, we find ourselves going back to it for answers to our own questions for there is virtually no subject that comes up during sadhana which is not covered here. The range of these volumes is enormous. More than anything published, they give us a sense of the breadth and variety of Baba's knowledge and of his limitless willingness to teach us, on whatever level we are willing to learn.

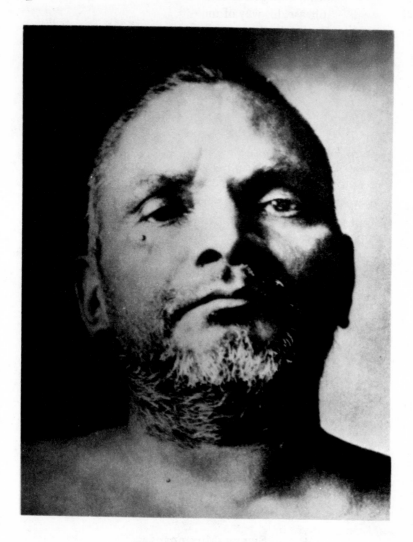

Bhagawan Nityananda

Swami Muktananda

May 16, 1972, Baba's Birthday

No one likes to even look at an old man; you would rather turn your eyes away. But everyone likes to gaze at a young person. It's really ironic that man never seems to wake up, never seems to realise that time is passing by so quickly. Bhartrihari was a great and noble king of ancient India. After reflecting on the meaning of life, he renounced everything. Then he composed some very great poetry. He wrote a poem about a bee to illustrate how days pass by quickly and yet man keeps deceiving himself.

There was a bee in the prime of his life. He was beautiful and strong, and drunk with the vigour of youth. He had a wife and many girl friends. One day, while he was flying, he happened to land on a lotus. Once he took a sip of it, he just kept drinking for hours. He would take a deep drink and enjoy the intoxication, and when he came down, he would have another sip and get high again. He said to himself, "Well, this is so good, I think I'll bring my wife, my mistresses, my children, my wife's friends and their friends, and we'll have a great time here drinking the nectar of this flower."

In the meantime night came and the lotus closed while the bee was still in it. If he had wanted to, he could have escaped by nibbling his way through the lotus petals. But he was more interested in drinking the juice of the flower, so he said, "It doesn't matter. I'll stay here for the night and keep drinking this nectarean juice, and in the morning I'll invite my wife and mistresses and friends and companions and we'll all get high together."

But the bee should have been wiser; he wasn't able to fly away while the flower was open, so how could he

1

fly away when it was closed? He had the power to cut
his way out of the flower, but he wasn't at all concerned
with that. He was only concerned with the sweet juice
of the flower and thinking of his friends who he would
invite in the morning to enjoy this intoxicating drink
with him. There are five such creatures who get intoxicated beyond redemption: the bee, elephant, fish,
moth and deer.

In the meantime an equally intoxicated elephant
went there. He was pulling up this tree and that tree
and merrily destroying everything around him. Finally he
waded into the lake, plucking this flower and that flower,
eating them all. And he also plucked the flower where
the bee was drinking the juice. The elephant munched
the flower and the bee was ground between his teeth.
While the bee was being crunched he exclaimed in great
distress, "O! O! I'm dying!" None of his friends, his wife
or girl friends could rescue him now. They were all left
behind and the poor fellow died.

This is exactly what happens with us. We keep
postponing things saying, "I'll do it tomorrow, and if
there is no time tomorrow, I'll do it the day after." And
in this way days and weeks and months and years pass
by, and one enters into his 65th year without having
done anything. One celebrates one's birthday very merrily and feels very happy when people give him presents
and he distributes sweets. But unfortunately, you don't
pause to think that birthdays mean the passing of another
year, and another birthday means that another year has
gone too quickly. And one is like the bee who after
having been intoxicated the whole day, is looking
forward to spending the whole night in the same manner.
This is exactly our condition.

Do not think that while your body is young and strong
and healthy you can afford to spend your youth gratifying
your senses, filling your stomach with all kinds of foods
that damage or cool the gastric fire. In fact, as long as
the senses are strong, the body healthy and radiant, you
should meditate, practise yoga and become immersed in
the inner Self. Do not think that you can find God after

your body and senses have lost their strength. One should not squeeze the juice out of his body like juice out of an orange. If the body is reduced to a shrivelled, dry thing, what discipline can you possibly practice?

Most people think that gratification of the senses and raising a couple of children are the only pursuits in life. Look how many people there are in the world and how few of us there are here pursuing the spiritual path. Take the case of Spotty, for instance. She has taken a husband and now has given birth to four babies and that wasn't very difficult. How can that kind of life be considered any kind of accomplishment?

As far as worldly life is concerned, everybody is already in it. You don't have to make an effort to plunge deeper into it. There was a great philosopher in this country, the greatest exponent of non-duality, Shankaracharya, and he has written commentaries on so many works. Shankaracharya has written such abstruse works that you would find it difficult to grasp even the introduction, not to mention the main text. And even after having written so voluminously, Shankaracharya said in the end, "Here is the gist of all the scriptures in half a verse." He said, "Your inner Self is the Lord Himself, the Supreme Being Himself, and never forget this. The realisation of this truth is the only worthwhile goal of life."

June 28, 1972

Kalyani: *How can one acquire perfect faith?*
Baba: Perfect faith can be acquired through perfect understanding. Faith is important; by faith one attains something very valuable. It is only the faithless who

have to turn to some other aids in order to be able to concentrate their minds on God.

I learnt to ride a horse before I became a sadhu, not during my sadhana. If I had started learning horse riding during the course of my sadhana, that would have shown that I was lacking in faith completely, or that my faith was very weak, or I wasn't worthy of faith. I learnt to wield a sword in sixty different ways, but that was before starting my sadhana. If I had started learning these things after starting my sadhana, or during the course of my sadhana, that would have shown that I didn't have faith. If after taking to the spiritual path you begin to take pleasure in childish games, to play with little balls, or to play chess, what opinion shall I have of you? Shall I consider you to be infantile or stupid? Whatever way you would like to be considered, let me know. It's just like a university student using an elementary primer to learn the ABC.

Faith is complete in itself and it doesn't depend on any other factor. The miracle of faith is that one remains absorbed in the Self for twenty-four hours every day, and one is surrounded by the Lord all the time. The Gopis had ideal faith in Krishna. They had so much faith, their faith had reached such a point, that even when they were making dung cakes, they would give them Krishna's shape, because Krishna completely possessed their eyes. A seeker should become completely absorbed in what he is doing like the Gopis. When the Gopis went out to sell butter and milk, instead of saying, "Buy butter or milk," they would say, "Buy Krishna, buy Govinda, buy Gopala." People thought they had gone crazy, but the fact was that it was the people who were crazy. If you are without knowledge of God, if you don't understand the Self, if you have no interest in spiritual life, no one is crazier than you. It makes little difference whether you are a man of high status holding degrees, or whether you are educated or not. Therefore, one's faith should become so overpowering that all one's activities are permeated by it and aimed at the realisation of the goal. Bahinabai, a great woman saint of Maharashtra, says in one of her verses that the glory of faith is such that by it God Himself ran after her.

* * *

It is good that we have resumed these question and answer sessions after two months. I am very happy to know that people from different countries all over the world—America, Europe, Australia and other places—are benefiting from these sessions through the *Newsletter*. They are able to read the questions and answers and I receive letters from them full of praise for the *Newsletter*. I was pestered by individuals with questions and gradually questions started being put to me in groups, and then the answers started being taken down in Hindi and Gujarati and other languages. Now the answers have been compiled into book form and it looks as though this has happened as a result of divine will.

Uma : *What should one do to increase one's capacity to bear the fire of meditation?*

Baba : The fire of meditation is very intense, far more intense than a coal or electric or wood fire. It is mainly discipline and self-control which enable one to bear this fire. The sages laid down discipline not for fun or masochistic motives, but to help seekers. The other day a very good meditator came and we began to talk. Soon it was time for the *Om Namah Shivaya* chant and the bell rang. I asked him to go and attend the chant, because by continuing to talk during the chant we would be violating the discipline. And he said, "I am only interested in meditation. Chanting is something very ordinary and trivial and I couldn't care less about it."

I said, "It wouldn't be good for me to call the teacher who taught you meditation stupid, because if I said that you wouldn't like it. So all I can say is that you have not learnt meditation fully from him."

He said, "How is that?"

I said, "The one who taught you meditation should also have taught you the secret of chanting; if he didn't then obviously he is imperfect, because a yogi cannot be perfect without knowing the secret of chanting."

After some time he said, "Swamiji, I have a problem in meditation, I feel as though a fire were blazing inside my head, and my hands and feet also seem to be on fire. Due to that I am not able to progress, and some people suggested that I come to you for advice."

I said, "Do you know who Shiva was? Even the best yogis pale into insignificance compared to Shiva. Do you know that when Shiva comes out of samadhi he begins to repeat the name of Rama in order to cool down the fire of samadhi? Either you are deficient in understanding or the Guru did not teach you the secret of chanting." When I said this, he immediately went into the hall and joined the chant.

You have gurus of all sorts these days, such as the business-type guru, who deals only in those commodities for which there is a demand on the market. If certain commodities were not in demand, they would be losers if they kept them in their shop. As far as I am concern- ed, I couldn't care less whether my commodities are selling or not. I would be quite content to put them away. If those gurus started emphasizing discipline and devotional practices, if they started insisting that you chant the name of God, that you live a pure life, and mend your ways, pleasure and ease-loving seekers would not go to them and they would have to close down their shops.

We should sprinkle the nectar of the name of God on the fire of meditation and that would take care of it. The divine name is meant for this purpose: it helps you to bear the fire of meditation. It is for the same reason that the scriptures emphasize purity of food. Food should be pure and balanced; it should neither be too heating nor too cooling. And it is for this reason that drugs such as ganja and bhang and other heating things have been prohibited; yoga itself heats up the system. Yogis go to the Himalayas not because they learn yoga there, not for attainment, but because it is quite cool up there. If the Himalayas could teach you yoga, then the hill people who have been living there for centuries would be the best yogis. But the fact is, if you go to them and ask, "What is yoga?" they would say, "How do you eat it?"

We already have a lot of trees in the Ashram, but we are going to have many more and the Ashram will look like a forest in times to come. And that is to help meditation, and for no other purpose.

The name of God is cooling and it bestows nectar. It cools the fire of yoga. Therefore, keep on repeating it. The father of Prahlad was entirely opposed to God. I wouldn't call him a communist because he was fabulously wealthy but he was an atheist through and through and did not like his son to think about God. There is a certain kind of foolishness which comes from an excess of pride. The king thought that he was the greatest living creature; thus it was insulting that his son should repeat the name of God. He tried to persuade Prahlad away from the name of God, but Prahlad was a great bhakta and would not agree. Then many brutal methods were tried to make him give up the divine name, but they did not have any effect. Finally, a pyre was made and Prahlad was put on it. The pyre was lit and his father said, "You are not worthy of the royal household because you just think of God all the time. It will be better for you to die."

Prahlad was repeating the name of God peacefully. The king had played this game in the hope that since Prahlad was a young boy it would be possible to scare him out of repeating the divine name. But Prahlad continued to chant the name of Rama and his father was taken aback. He said to Prahlad, "Look, the pyre has already been lit and still you are repeating the name of Rama?"

Prahlad said, "Father, can't you see how glorious the name of Rama is? One who repeats the name of Rama knows no fear. Neither earth nor fire nor air nor any other elements can frighten him. To you it appears that I am surrounded by leaping flames, yet by the power of the name of the Lord I feel that a cool breeze is blowing on my body."

The inner fire of meditation is extremely intense. It has such great power that it can consume all the accumulated karmic impressions of countless births. These impressions cannot be consumed by any other fire. And we can bear the fire of meditation by taking shelter in the coolness of love for the Guru, of devotion to the Lord, of the divine name.

Paul : *What are mental kriyas and is it possible to tell if one is performing them?*

Baba : One can certainly know that mental kriyas are occurring inside by looking at the changes taking place in the mind. There are sixteen different feelings or states which the mind experiences. Sometimes it gets acutely agitated. Sometimes it becomes completely pacified. Sometimes it is filled with wrath, other times it is filled with lust. In this way, there are sixteen different feeling states and all these are mental kriyas. Then, in certain cases, the mind seems to go blank or become empty, and that too is a mental kriya. In other cases the head begins to feel very heavy and it feels as though all the nerves inside the head are quivering very violently. That is also a mental kriya. As a result of these mental kriyas, the mind becomes pure and still in the course of meditation, and then filled with bliss. As a result of these kriyas you may also acquire the power of reading the minds of others and understanding what is happening in the world.

Kashmiribai : *What should a disciple who is living far away from the Guru do after receiving Shaktipat from him?*

Baba : After receiving Shaktipat, although you may live far from the Guru, the Guru is with you in the form of Shakti. What is your idea of the Guru? Do you think that the Guru is just a particular person who has a certain kind of hair and who wears a certain kind of clothes and chats all the time? That is very limited and narrow idea of the Guru. And what is the Shakti that you have received? In fact, through Shaktipat, it is the Guru's own energy which enters the disciple in subtle form. In other words, the Guru himself enters the disciple. Shaktipat from a Guru is not like a shot from a doctor. When a doctor gives you an injection he injects some foreign material into your body, which has nothing to do with him. But the Shakti which the disciple receives from the Guru, is, in fact, the Guru's seed. Even though a seed is tiny, it is a potential tree. It is the Guru who is entering you in his fullness in the form of Shakti.

Unfortunately, because of their lack of knowledge, even after receiving Shakti from the Guru some seekers do not understand what is happening to them, what the nature of Shakti is, or the nature of the Guru. That is why they do not have all the experiences the Shakti could bring them; they are not able to experience the fullness of bliss or attain the powers they could have if their understanding were perfect. Even after receiving Shakti, you find people who still lack faith in the Guru. They seem to have more faith in all kinds of books that they should not even read; they have more faith in the written word than in the Guru. That is one of their impediments. There are seekers who tell me that they sit for meditation in front of my picture and then they have a vision of Nityananda. There are others who tell me that as they look at me I seem to dissolve into Nityananda, and they see Nityananda who permeates every fibre of my being. It is he who entered me in the form of Shakti; Muktananda is no longer there.

The Guru's ashram has a certain discipline and no matter how far you advance in your sadhana, you must not begin to slight that discipline. Then there is a certain etiquette to be followed in the Ashram. You must remember the Australian avadhoot, Brian, who went back home just a few days ago. Sometimes, in the intoxication of a certain spiritual state, he would come and sit on my seat, and I would have to apply my stick to him. I was forced to do it, even though it would give me pain when I hit him. I did it because I wanted him to follow the proper etiquette, knowing full well that when he was sitting in my seat, he was not sitting

there as Brian, but as Muktananda; because in that state
he would completely identify himself with me. During
his earlier visit I had hit him hard two times, and this
last visit I hit him only once. But that doesn't mean
that he is crazy. On the contrary, he is an extremely
intelligent person. He was a pilot. His devotion is so
great that he did not even ask me why I was hitting
him. If he had asked me, I would have hit him again
telling him that he was sitting where he wasn't supposed
to sit. But at that time, he was not himself; he was
Muktananda.

After Shaktipat it is the Guru who enters you in his
fullness, in his perfection, in the form of Shakti. The
Guru is not left out even in the least measure. I have
thousands and thousands of students. How many of them
can come and stay with me? I have students not only
in India, but in every distant corner of the world. We
receive reports that seekers receive Shaktipat just by
looking at my pictures, by reading my book. It is only
after having received Shakti, after having meditated very
well, that they come to meet me. So who guides them
until then? During Shaktipat it is the Guru who enters
into the disciple in the form of Shakti, in seed form.
Therefore a disciple should worship the Guru within
himself.

Jon: *Do you have any recommendations for our sadhana
during the monsoon?*

Baba: The monsoon season is especially good for sadhana.
The farmers are able to do their sadhana of agriculture
during this season. The forest department people do their
sadhana of planting new trees during this season. It is
during this season again, that the Creator beautifies the
forests and landscape with new greenery. This season
is meant particularly for meditation. The scriptures say
that sadhus should not move around or undertake any
pilgrimages during these months. They are enjoined to
stay in one place and observe silence, do japa and meditate
quietly.

The rainy season seems to be especially suited for

meditation, for writing and receiving knowledge. It was during this season that I completed *Chitshakti Vilas*. One year I happened to go to Mahabaleshwar. Some blank paper was given to me. I started dictating and finished only after the book was complete.

This time is especially suited for the opening of the heart lotus, for its coming into full bloom and for the experience of inner joy and bliss. So this time is specially meant for meditation. That is why I told everyone that they should increase the duration of meditation, not the quantity of food. In this season you should try to engage the mind in meditation, in chanting, in silence, in inward meditation. Do not try to please it by taking it to restaurants, thinking of Bombay, spending days there, or by thoughts of nightclubs or movies. You don't have to entertain the mind by playing cards or chess. If you do that, you will find yourself landing in a pit one day. The mind is absolutely undependable. Beware of it. Such is the nature of the mind that it would create hell even in heaven. So grossly wicked is the mind that even when it is in heaven it sometimes begins to look for a hellish corner; it gets bored with heavenly bliss and begins to look for hellish kicks. Such is the nature of the mind, that instead of drinking the nectar which is so freely available in heaven, it wants to devour stinking shit.

During this season we do not want you to even work. I renounced 3,000 acres of family land, and I have absolutely no desire to turn you into farmers. But I would rather you utilized your spare time digging the soil than gossiping because then at least your body would get some good exercise. If you want to while away your time playing carom, then I would rather you go and pick up rocks because that would give your mind some peace. If you are given more work at a particular time, the reason is that you are being helped to stay away from certain undesirable pursuits. No one is interested in disturbing or interrupting your meditation.

So you should sit for meditation two or three times a day, and you should do silent inner japa all the time.

You can go around the gardens for walks, look at the sky, look at the trees and look at the new green grass shooting up from the earth. You can look at the beauty of nature. But you should go alone and remain silent. You can walk anywhere in the Ashram.

Keep chanting the divine name joyfully. Your mind should be occupied with pure, high thoughts; you should think the right kind of thoughts about yourself. This time is especially meant for contemplation. This season, lasting for four months, is a very special time for meditation. During this season meditation seizes me by force. And it is for this reason that I don't come out for long periods of time.

Therefore, meditate more in quiet and peace. There is so much contentment, so much beauty inside, that if you only take small doses of meditation, I wonder how long it would take you to realise all that is inside. This is the time for meditation.

June 30, 1972

Mrs. Salunkhe : *What can one do to be worthy of receiving Shaktipat and how does a person know whether he or she has received it ?*

Baba : To receive Shaktipat one has to possess the necessary worth. What after all is Shaktipat? To many people this term must be unfamiliar. Shaktipat is grace, the transmission of divine grace. Shaktipat, God's grace and Gurukripa are synonymous terms. For Shaktipat one should become worthy of God's grace. For Gurukripa a student should first bestow his kripa on the Guru. The Guru's grace will, of course, come to the disciple naturally, spontaneously. But then the Guru needs the disciple's grace, in the form of worthiness for Shaktipat.

You don't have to ask in order to know whether you have received Shaktipat or not. If you catch the flu you begin to know about it without asking anybody else, by observing the changes in your body. If you contract dysentery or some other form of indigestion, you know it directly. If you quarrel with somebody, by looking into your own mind you will know that your mind has become restless; that quarrel has left you in a very ragged, disturbed state.

Similarly, after receiving Shaktipat, certain things happen inside. By watching you can know directly that you have been blessed with Shaktipat. The moment divine grace enters into a disciple he feels completely rejuvenated. Yogic kriyas or movements begin to occur by themselves .These movements may be subtle, mental, external or internal. As a result of Shaktipat one of two things can happen. Either you will get into a very high state of meditation, a state of deep absorption, or the mind will get disturbed like it has never been disturbed before, and you will begin to wonder what has happened.

After the Shakti enters within, every day new kriyas begin to take place automatically, and in short, you could say that your life is totally transformed. A yogi attains the state of freedom after Shaktipat. Until Shaktipat one is dependent on others. For ordinary pranayama, you have to go to a teacher and learn it. For ordinary meditation, again you have to depend on some technique or some teacher. But after Shaktipat, the Shakti works freely within you and you don't have to go around learning techniques from different people, because different forms of pranayama occur by themselves and meditation follows spontaneously.

After receiving Shaktipat a seeker is able to have visions of the different worlds, such as heaven, hell, the world of death, the world of ancestors, and the worlds you have read about in stories and in the *Puranas*. You will have these visions in the waking state, the dream state, or the tandra state of meditation. These visions are of enormous importance, and after receiving Shakti, a seeker should conserve Her, revere Her, make every

possible effort to hold Her within himself. If you want
to know more about it, you should read *Chitshakti Vilas*
a few times.

Kedarnath : *Can a seeker, with the grace of the Sadguru,
achieve dispassion as a result of his sadhana? Will he be
able to practise all the yamas and niyamas? Will he be
able to master his senses and achieve full control over
his mind?*

Baba : Yes, if a seeker comes to a Sadguru, and is able
to stay with him, whatever his condition, he is bound to
achieve perfection. His mode of life with the Sadguru
will naturally include all the different qualities required
for sadhana. If the seeker has those qualities before
coming to the Sadguru, very good. If he doesn't, as a
result of his stay in the ashram, which has a certain
discipline, a certain routine, these qualities will grow
naturally, because in any genuine ashram there is no
scope for pleasure-seeking or indulgence in mundane
pursuits. If an ashram permits all these, then you can
be sure that it is not spiritual. On the contrary, it is
a house of business which has been set up with some very
mean, mercenary motive. In this Ashram there is a
wake-up bell at 3-30 a.m., and if you do not wake up with
the bell, we have the tape of the *Vishnu Sahasranam*
running. If you are not able to wake up even with that,
then you are told to go home and take rest for a while
until you are in a fit condition to live in the Ashram.
A very close watch is kept on seekers here, to see if they
get up when they should, that they have a bath, and
attend the arati, meditate and sing the *Guru Gita.* And if
anybody does not follow the routine faithfully, he is told
firmly to leave the place. Many people think that it is
the Secretary who is telling a particular person to go.
That poor fellow has no power to tell anyone to get out.
It is in fact Muktananda who is speaking through his
mouth, who is telling an unfit person to get out. After
Guru Gita a check is made to make sure that the seekers
have gone for work; they may be assigned any job:

cleaning the dormitory, or working in the garden, or making beds, or doing something else.

There is no point in coming to the Ashram and expecting that others will do your work. Even if you happen to be rich, if you happen to be a millionaire, in my eyes you are a pauper, you are utterly destitute if you have to depend on others to do your work. If you expect somebody else to make your bed, do your hair, wash your clothes—if wealth means dependence on others even for your own work—then that wealth does not indicate that you are rich, on the contrary, to my mind it is the worst kind of poverty.

This is service to the Ashram, and service to the Ashram strengthens one's detachment, one's renunciation. If you come to the Ashram and spend your time only eating and sleeping and gossiping, then what's the point of coming to the Ashram? Wouldn't the Ashram be better off if you had not come at all? This way seekers are taught to be self-reliant and to live by their own work in the Ashram. No one, however rich he may be, whatever his status, however much power he may enjoy, should depend on others for his own work. Everybody should learn to live by his own work, by his own labour. Otherwise, one falls into a disease.

After the work period, we have the chant and the arati, and after the arati, we serve pure and simple food. After that you rest for a while and again we have a chanting session. In the Ashram no one is allowed to indulge in pleasure-seeking. We don't have any shows here, or other ways of entertaining people, or helping them to relax, as they put it.

As a seeker meditates more and more, his mind naturally turns away from mundane affairs and becomes focused on God. It becomes focused on the Self. The more it becomes focused on the Self, the more it becomes detached from the world. That is true dispassion, true renunciation.

Renunciation or dispassion does not mean that you give up your clothes and everything and smear your forehead with sacred ash and then stand on the roadside and harass every passerby for a small coin or a piece of bread. That is not renunciation. That is only a different kind of bullying, the worst kind of bullying possible, and it is extremely sinful. Take the case of a thief who steals things secretly and lives on them, or the case of a blackmarketeer who through his dealings earns money which does not lawfully belong to him. That kind of renunciate is in the same class, because he, too, is living on money which he has not earned himself, which belongs to somebody else. He is living by somebody else's labour. That is not renunciation.

My idea of renunciation is that you live by your own work without depending on or using somebody else's labour for your own personal ends. Renunciation does not mean giving up one house and entering another. Generally, those people who go to ashrams or monasteries lack the qualities which are necessary for sadhana. But as they stay with the Guru, all these qualities are developed in them very easily, very naturally.

There are many different modes of sadhana described in the scriptures. However, meditation, deep meditation is the greatest method.

Susan: *I am confused about the extent to which one is responsible for one's own evolution when one has a Guru. I always think that I have to do such and such in order to change, develop, etc.*

Baba: You are upsetting your mind for nothing, and there is such a thing as addiction to upsetting your mind. Take the case of a person who has made friends with a great doctor. He made friends with him in the beginning because he was sick but now he has overcome his sickness, and still he keeps wondering how he can get help from the doctor. It is good to make friends with a doctor, it is good to take the treatment which he gives you, but to keep on thinking about it all the time, to keep brooding about it, that is what is objectionable. That is an addiction.

Similarly, after you have full faith in a Guru, then all that remains for you is to follow the path shown by him

and not to allow your mind to brood or think unneces-
sarily. Through Shaktipat, the Guru, in fact, casts his
seed into the disciple, and this seed will one day grow
into a full tree, a tree which bears blossoms and fruit. If
the disciple begins to worry about when blossoms will
appear, and if after the blossoms have gone away,
whether the fruit will appear, and after the fruit has
come whether it will be juicy or not, or whether it will
go bad, all these things indicate that one has become
accustomed to worrying, to brooding. You should give
up brooding. You should continue to meditate with deep
faith and great reverence and I can assure you that
everything will come to you through meditation, and
your worrying or brooding about it won't help at all.
If you have to think, then think how your sadhana can
become more intense. If, through meditation, you are
able to unfold the lotus of the heart fully, then you will
be able to have the entire universe in your grasp, because
the entire universe is encompassed by that lotus.
Meditation will purify your body, strengthen it, make
you new; it will give you knowledge of future events,
enable you to travel to different regions. What can't
you attain through meditation? Kundalini awakening
is, as it were, the seed of the entire universe and once
this awakening takes place, then the entire universe
begins to fall at your feet.

Stop worrying. Stop brooding. You seem to be fond
of tormenting yourself for no reason. While living your
everyday life you should have the fullest faith in
Kundalini. Kundalini, according to the scriptures, is the
power which controls everything. The only responsibility
which a seeker has after finding the Guru is to make
sure that he meditates regularly and that he follows the
path shown by the Guru.

Stan: *How may I become worthy of thy grace?*
Baba: It is a very good question; brief and to the point.
We have so many scriptures in our country: they are
full of deep knowledge, and they are full of questions.
All the questions contained in them are brief and concise.

2

One should put a question having thought about it very carefully. He should state it with great care, as precisely as he can. Otherwise, what will happen is that the speaker too will start wandering and digressing like the questioner. In the Vedantic scriptures, the manner in which a question should be put to a Guru is described. In courts of law, if a criminal or the accused has any questions, it is the lawyer who asks them. The questions relate to the criminal. Isn't it strange that the questions relate to the criminal yet it is the lawyer who asks them? The obvious reason is that the lawyer knows how to state them. A very important question is asked in Vedantic texts: what should a question be like? The answer is that a question should be phrased in the same manner in which Savitri made her request to Yama Raja. That is a very long story. Sri Aurobindo has turned it into a long poem which I understand is a very great piece of literature; and it is full of deep mystical meaning. I am not going to narrate the whole story right now.

Yama Raja took away the spirit of Savitri's husband because his life had come to an end. Savitri began to chase Yama Raja, the god of death, telling him that he must return her husband to her. He wasn't in a position to oblige her. So she said that he must take her with him also. Yama Raja said, "Even death follows certain rules and I am authorized to take away only those people whose time has come. If somebody's time has not come, I cannot oblige that person."

Yama Raja reasoned with Savitri for a long time but Savitri did not pay any heed, nor did Yama Raja accept Savatri's request. Yama Raja proceeded further with her husband's spirit but Savitri was determined and she kept following Yama Raja. Yama Raja tried to scare her away by showing her frightful sights, by putting her in extremely trying situations, but that did not deter Savitri. Finally, Yama Raja decided to try some tactful method to get rid of her. He said to himself, "I will offer her some material rewards and she will probably get tempted and go away and then I will be able to take away her husband's spirit." After going a little further, he halted and turned back and looking at Savitri he said, "I've tried my best to send you away but you seem to be bent on following me. I can assure you that there is nothing I can do about your husband. I have to take away his spirit. However, I will grant you a boon. You may ask of me whatever you like and I will grant whatever you ask."

Yama Raja was delighted. He said to himself, "Now I will give her whatever she wants and then take away her husband's spirit."

Savitri was not an ordinary woman. An ordinary woman would die of sheer fright just at the mention of Yama Raja's name. Savitri was a woman who had the courage to chase him, to follow him, and not be daunted by any of his tactics. Savitri was also very intelligent. She framed her request this way, "Yama Raj, grant me this boon that my in-laws will be able to see my children eating sweets on gold plates." Yama Raj said, "So be it," and granted the boon.

Savitri's husband when he was alive was very poor. He used to cut wood and sell it in order to make a living, and they lived a life of austerity.

Savitri said, "Now restore my husband."

Yama Raja : "I can't do that."

Savitri : "I don't have any children, and since I am a loyal wife how am I going to have children if you take away my husband?"

Yama Raja had to restore her husband to life. Then Savitri said, "You will have to give a kingdom to my husband because my children have to eat from gold plates and it is only princes who eat from gold plates. And you must also grant me children who will be eating from those plates."

Her in-laws were blind, so she said, "You have granted that my in-laws will be able to see the children, so you must also give them eyesight."

If she had put her request in an elaborate form, stating all the details separately, "Give me back my husband, give me children," and so on, Yama Raja would never have accepted her request. She knew how to frame her

request in a concise manner and as a result she got everything, including a kingdom.

To be worthy of Guru's grace, you should surrender
yourself to him. I always say that in order to receive
Gurukripa you must give Shishya kripa, disciple's grace.
Bestowing your grace on the Guru means that you
surrender yourself totally to the Guru. Even in our
ordinary life we become possessed by that to which we
surrender ourselves. We surrender ourselves to attachment and we become possessed by attachment. We
surrender ourselves to anger and we become angry.
We surrender ourselves to greed and we are overcome
by greed. Or we surrender ourselves to a particular
individual and we are possessed by that individual.
So in the same manner, if we surrender ourselves to
the Guru, it should be no surprise if we become worthy
of his grace. We suffer the consequences of the thoughts
that we hold in our mind for a length of time,
and these consequences we suffer privately or secretly.
Sometimes, as a result of our thoughts we are in a happy
state, and other times we may be disturbed. Surrender
has great power. Whatever the mind surrenders itself
to, that object possesses the mind. Therefore, you should
get rid of you, and become somebody else. Then it will
not take long. That very moment you will become
worthy of grace. The moment you get rid of you and
replace you by me, you will become worthy of grace.

Barry : *What should we do if visitors do not co-operate
or follow the discipline of the Ashram?*

Baba : All visitors should abide by the Ashram rules. I
can assure everyone that Muktananda Swami is not the
father-in-law of anybody, and this Ashram is not anybody's in-law's place where you can stay for any length
of time and make merry and fill all the shit pots. Here
everybody is treated equally regardless of status or
wealth, whether they are ministers or high officials,
whether they make generous donations to the Ashram or
do not give a single paisa. What matters is discipline.
It is discipline which is worshipped here, not individuals.

If anyone goes to a hospital—whoever he may be, whatever his degree or title—he is considered a patient by the doctor and that is his new title. In the same manner, anyone who comes to the Ashram is considered to be a seeker or a devotee or a student, and if he does not want to be considered that, why should he come to the Ashram in the first place?

We do not have any shows here. We don't run clubs here. When you come here you should leave all your titles and degrees behind and you should be ready to accept the new title that the Ashram gives you, namely, that you are a seeker.

If there are people chatting away merrily and I happen to hear them, I tell them to go to the hotel because that is the habitat in which they can flourish. All people, whether they are visitors or Ashramites, whether they are staying here for a short time or a long time, whether they are learned or ignorant, whether they are high or low, rich or poor, must follow the Ashram discipline. If they don't follow the discipline, they have no value here. If there is a person who considers himself exceptionally intelligent, but misses an Ashram programme, then he is behaving like a stupid fool. Venkappa has been with me for such a long time—thirty years—and he gets up at 2.30 every day. If he starts to get up at five, it means that he will not be treated like an old devotee or disciple; he will have to be treated like a new entrant who has to be taught the Ashram discipline. Or take the case of Desai. If, while managing different things here, he himself does not follow the discipline which he is trying to enforce, then what discipline can he enforce? So he should make sure that he himself follows the discipline which he is trying to enforce here.

It is because of your abiding by the Ashram discipline that you are honoured here, that you are valued here. What, after all, is the criterion of greatness of an old devotee? The only criterion is that you are following the Ashram discipline, that you are abiding by Ashram ways.

You can tell the visitors, "You have come to the

Ashram. Do you know what an Ashram is like, what you go to an Ashram for, and what the rules of an Ashram are? You have to follow the Ashram rules. Otherwise, the Ashram gate is not very far."

If there is a doctor who himself is sick and diseased, how can he help any patient? If with his medical knowledge he has not been able to help himself, how can he help others? If he is still giving medicine to others, it shows that he is using his knowledge to make money. It is of no real significance. If the Ashram swamis themselves have big bulging stomachs, and if they keep on snoring right till 8 or 9 a.m., how can they expect others to get up early? You will find different ashrams full of such characters. There is a verse in the *Rig Veda* which says, "He alone can command who obeys."

July 4, 1972

Pratibha : *I have seen that the Kundalini Shakti living within us generally works in accordance with our temperament, but there are many workings of Hers which are beyond the reach of our intellect. To what extent is the Shakti living within us really ours, and to what extent is it different from us?*

Baba : Kundalini lives within us all and She works according to our individual worth. Kundalini is a great power. It is the same Kundalini which dwells within you which throbs into the countless forms of this universe. Just as Sheshnag is holding the earth on his hood, in the same way, Kundalini is the support of all the different kinds of yoga.

The relevant question is not to what extent the Kundalini Shakti works within us; the relevant question is whether it works in accordance with the needs of our body or not because as far as Kundalini is concerned, She can do anything. She can accomplish any of the things which She accomplishes in the outside universe, in our body but it depends on how much our body can take. There is no limit to Her capacity or to Her work. But She will adjust Herself according to our limitations.

All the workings of Kundalini are beyond the reach of mind, intellect and speech, because ego, mind, intellect and speech came into being at a much later stage than the Kundalini. She has always existed. It is by the great power of the Kundalini that the mind, the intellect and speech acquire their respective powers. Kundalini is all-pervasive, and the more worthy you become, the more extensive will be Her work within you. If you wish to get an idea of the immense limitless might of Kundalini, you should know that when Kundalini closes Her eyes, this entire universe is dissolved. When She opens Her eyes, another universe comes into being.

When such mighty Shakti dwells within man, he should live his life gratefully. Unfortunately, man is wasting his power on unnecessary thinking, on thinking evil thoughts. Are we conscious of the fact that we are using up so much energy in evil passions such as greed, lust, delusion, jealously and wrath? It is not that we are deficient in power. What is happening is that we are misusing the Shakti which is dwelling within us. A poet, Gudli Swami, says in one of his poems, "When the transcendental force of Kundalini dwells within man, how is he so poor, how is he such a pauper? This surprises me."

If we are careful in the expenditure of our energy, if while engaging in different activities like talking and thinking, or giving or taking, we take every care not to waste our Shakti, we shall have a mountain of Shakti within us. You read about the great powers of Jnaneshwar. They say that Jnaneshwar was able to bring a dead person back to life. That is nothing extraordinary. Don't think that God is partial, that He gave more Shakti to Jnaneshwar and deprived others of it. To God, all are equal. We are wasting our Shakti every day, in fact, every moment of every day. And that is why we are living like wretched, unfortunate creatures.

Danny : *Mental hospitals are filled with cases whose symptoms resemble those of awakened Kundalini. How is it that these people are not doing sadhana with a Sadguru? Where does madness end and yoga begin?*

Baba : The kriyas which take place after the Kundalini is aroused indicate that this power is a dynamic force, while whatever is happening to mental cases in a hospital is due to madness, and that is very different. Take the case of a mad man who laughs like an idiot, who laughs not because he understands things but because he doesn't understand anything. A Kundalini yogi may laugh with equal merriment, but he is laughing out of love. Who would call a Kundalini yogi mad? Perhaps the person who calls him mad is himself mad. We shouldn't forget the important difference between the two: in mental cases, if there are any kriyas taking place, they are taking place in utter ignorance, while in the case of a Kundalini yogi, the kriyas are springing from knowledge, with a complete understanding of what is happening. So an onlooker should be intelligent enough to perceive the difference between the two.

In a mental hospital, patients who suffer from insomnia are given sleeping pills and they pass out. If you find a doctor also sleeping in another corner of the hospital, would you say that what is happening to the doctor is exactly the same as what is happening to the patient? The sleep which the doctor is enjoying is natural while the sleep which has seized the patient has been brought about by artificial means. There is a great difference between the two.

However, there may be some seekers who are somewhat mentally unbalanced and if their Kundalini is aroused they begin to behave like madmen. Their kriyas will in course of time rid them of their madness, while the kriyas which take place in the case of really mad people only increase their madness, and there is no hope that they will one day become sane through those kriyas.

It is only in a few cases that you will find certain signs which are similar to those of awakened Kundalini, but not in every case. The kriyas brought about by Kundalini rid you of delusion while the kriyas happening to a mad person happen due to certain impurities or defects. Kundalini Yoga is not a yoga of madness, it is the yoga of love. If there is anyone who thinks that Kundalini Yoga is the yoga of madness, he himself is a lunatic.

Leela : *How does one acquire faith and devotion to the Guru after Shaktipat?*

Baba : As you experience the force of Kundalini every day, and as you also understand its significance, your love for the Guru will increase automatically. Take the case of our elephant. He begins to shed tears of joy when just an ordinary mango is given to him. There is nothing especially significant about a mango. He becomes so overwhelmed that he begins to pull my hand again and again, demanding another mango. So how much should a seeker who has been blessed with divine Shakti by a Guru, surrender? He will be able to achieve this surrender only when he becomes aware of the nature and significance of the Shakti. Mainly it is knowledge which matters in every field. Without knowledge, whatever you do will not bear fruit. Without knowledge, no matter how beautiful you appear to be, you are, in fact, ugly. There is no value in beauty which is not accompanied by knowledge.

We should be able to fully grasp the power, significance and nature of Kundalini Shakti. We should reflect on this matter as much as necessary. Kundalini Shakti is the sustaining power which sustains the entire universe, which sustains all our actions. Kundalini Shakti lives in the base of our spine, and that way, too, it is the basis of our existence. As long as we do not acquire full knowledge of Her nature, of Her power, of Her potency, we will not be able to love the Guru, we will not be able to experience our inner fullness, and we will not make much headway in our sadhana either.

It is not so bad if man considers himself to be small
and ordinary but if he begins to consider the inner
Shakti to be ordinary and insignificant also, then he will
be doing great harm to himself. It is a pity that man
does not ponder over the nature and power of this great
Shakti, the Shakti that projects a universe in the pure
void, the Shakti which manifests Herself in innumer-
able forms, the Shakti which dwells within his own
being. Ignorant of the knowledge of this Shakti, he
spends his days in misery. Shouldn't such an ignorant
person be considered a dry log of a tree which has been
uprooted by an elephant and thrown away on the roadside?

Man should understand his own nature. Man should
understand what lies within him. He should not become
a victim of self-pity, taking himself to be a dry, shriveled
log on the roadside. By constantly thinking about his
flaws and weaknesses, man becomes miserable. By thinking stupid thoughts constantly he becomes almost
half mad. By harbouring all kinds of feelings and
thoughts he falls into great suffering. If there is anyone
who thinks that by thinking good thoughts he will not
become pure and good, what should we take him for?
Isn't such a person a piece of inert and dead matter,
utterly stupid and utterly worthless?

What's the beauty, what's the meaning, value and
significance of a life which is lived without an awakening
of the inner Shakti? Isn't such a life a pathetic tale?
You find people behaving in impure, corrupt ways in
different places and even after coming to the Ashram
they insist on behaving in the same way. Shouldn't these
people be ashamed of themselves, of the fact that they
are pursuing the same stupid, corrupt ways even after
coming to such a pure place as the Ashram?

Man becomes small only because he worries all the time,
because he thinks evil thoughts and feels evil feelings
all the time. Man was not meant to be so small. He
was not meant to be such a sorry creature.

After Shaktipat, when the disciple becomes fully aware
of the nature and importance of the Shakti, total devotion

to the Guru springs up in his heart naturally. If the disciple were to become aware of the fact that the Kundalini Shakti which pervades the entire universe, which has limitless power, which creates the universe, is now running through every cell and fibre of his being since the Guru has awakened it in him—in fact, it is the Guru himself who has entered into him in the form of Shakti—devotion would arise in him spontaneously. You feel so pleased when you get a degree, you even begin to dance, and you feel so grateful to the person who confers the degree on you. What would your feelings to the Guru be if you became aware of the fact that he has aroused the all-pervasive divine power in you, that he himself has entered you in the form of Shakti?

George : *If one were writing a poem about Guru Purnima, what should one say?*

Baba : If one wants the poem to suit the occasion, then one can deal with the themes of Guru and Purnima. Guru Purnima is a symbol of the perfection of the Guru. On the full moon day, the moon showers purest nectar. So on the Guru Purnima day, the Guru showers the nectar of supreme bliss. If you deal with the Guru in such a manner in your poem, then the poem will suit the occasion.

Kedarnath : *Previously I could sit in a posture throughout the swadhyaya session, but for the last month I am not able to sit in a proper posture for more than fifteen or twenty minutes because my knees begin to ache. I find it impossible to bend my knees and keep sitting in that position. That also distracts my mind from swadhyaya. What should I do?*

Baba : The fact that you were able to sit in a posture for one hour before and are not able to do it now even for fifteen minutes doesn't show that you have made any progress. It only shows that you have progressed towards laziness and lethargy. This is what is called the great disease of sloth. It would be quite all right if somebody were to tell me, "Yesterday I was able to sit in a posture for fifteen minutes and today I sat for twenty minutes, and tomorrow I will sit for twenty-five minutes." If the duration is increasing, very good. But if somebody could sit for half an hour one day and then the period came down to twenty minutes and then to fifteen, it shows that one is contracting this horrible disease of laziness and nothing else is the matter with him. Through practice you should be able to sit for longer and longer periods. It is very strange that through practice one's ability is decreased. Once I sit in a certain posture, even in a moving car, I can remain in it for six hours. I may change it once or twice, but that's about all. You must have seen me sitting for long periods on the platform outside. Through practice you should be able to sit in a posture longer. If your knees begin to ache very much, then you should sit in the easy posture, because you can sit for a long time in the easy posture.

Nathalie : *Last time you said, "Get rid of yourself, replace you by me." Would you explain this more thoroughly?*
Baba : To understand this more fully you should first read *Chitshakti Vilas* very carefully, particularly the essay in the last part on the ways of a Siddha student. I can see that you have improved very much since you came here.
   In the *Upanishads* a question is asked, "When does man attain God?" The answer given is that the moment man completely gives up the desire for attainment, he attains God. It is only as long as you remain you that you are bothered by the thoughts of either filling yourself or emptying yourself. If you get rid of you, you will find that you are already full. Man is always oscillating between two states: one is the state of bondage, the state of limitation, and the other is the state of divinity. As long as you are in the state of bondage, you always feel empty within. Once you enter into the divine state, you always experience fullness within. Man is poor not because he has no wealth but because he does not know that he has so much wealth.
   Somebody came and told me that a swami here had

made a prophecy about him. He told him that he started his pilgrimage in the moment of conjunction of the planets Mangal and Shani (Mars and Saturn) and it was for this reason that he ran into trouble. There was a barber who wanted to be initiated into sannyas, so he went to a Mandaleshwar. On the sannyasa initiation day, so many others had also come. They were made to sit in a row. The barber was also asked to sit in the same row. They were all initiated one by one, including the barber. They were given certain instructions and each one of them was also given a bath, and after that they were asked to leave. So they left. Everybody else went away and began to beg for food. The barber also went away, but he returned to his village and the next day took out his tools and began to work as a barber. When the other sannyasins saw him working as a barber, they were shocked and said, "Look, yesterday you were initiated into sannyasa and today you are working as a barber giving haircuts."

The barber said, "I am quite aware of the fact that I was initiated into sannyasa but though I was initiated into sannyasa, I never discarded my tools."

That is exactly what is happening to that swami. Though he has taken sannyasa, he still insists on behaving like a petty astrologer who would make all kinds of stupid predictions. He took sannyasa in order to get rid of himself, but even after taking sannyasa, he seems to be holding fast to himself. After taking sannyasa he should have started contemplating, "I am Brahman, I am the Supreme Being," and he should have started asking other people to meditate. Instead, he is foretelling their future like an ordinary fortune-teller.

You should not behave like that. You should get rid of yourself. If you get rid of yourself, what remains will be Muktananda. Give up your consciousness of Nathalie and then you will be filled with Muktananda. Isn't it a strange irony that man prefers to live in a state of poverty, a state of bondage, a state of chains, and he doesn't even want to listen to anything about the state of freedom?

I thank everyone for having listened to me, and I will thank you doubly if you have understood what I have told you and if you will take it with you.

July 7, 1972

Vishwas: *In Ganeshpuri, water falls on the Shivalingam in the temple near the Samadhi. Where does this water come from and why does it come?*

Baba: They say that it is the Ganges which is dripping on the Shivalingam. You find this water dripping not only in the rainy season but also in summer. What is particularly noteworthy there is that the water drips only on the lingam, not on the floor. It is enough to know this much about it.

Leela: *When I sit down to meditate, I sit quietly, repeat my mantra and think of you. But still I do not meditate. What should I do?*

Baba: Continue to do what you are doing at present and you will certainly get into meditation. Besides, meditation is something very subtle and sometimes when you are in it you may not be conscious that you are in it. Which meter do you have to detect exactly what work is being accomplished inside you by the Shakti? Therefore, continue to meditate.

It is said that meditation destroys all sins. The *Vedas* also say that through meditation one is purified of all sins, but you do not understand exactly what this purification is and how it takes place inside. However, you should continue to strive to make your mind one-pointed. What I feel is that you are not conscious of what is happening, and from looking at you I can see that you are certainly meditating.

What is meditation after all? To sit quietly, to repeat your mantra and become permeated by the mantra, that is meditation. Meditation is nothing but the state you achieve as a result of the continued repetition of the mantra in the heart, the state in which you become entirely permeated by the mantra. You probably don't know what meditation is. Some people have a wrong view of it. They think that to meditate is to become like a log, to lose consciousness. That's not our idea of meditation. If you lost consciousness then how would you know that you were meditating? In that case you would have to use some kind of meter to indicate what's happening inside, just as you use a certain instrument to get a correct picture of the heart. There are many people who say that they sit for meditation and they are able to meditate, yet they are conscious of everything. What makes you think that to lose inner consciousness is a sign of meditation? How can you stop the working of the inner Self, the one who is witnessing whatever is happening inside you, remaining apart from the mind, who is the object of meditation and who moves the mind? In meditation the mind becomes calm, it becomes steady, and finally it becomes one with the object of meditation. But how can you lose awareness of the Self who is watching what is happening inside you all the time? Those who think that to meditate is to become inert, like a log, are entirely wrong.

God within us is the object of meditation, and it is due to His existence that the seers say that we ourselves are Rama, we ourselves are Shiva. The very nature of the God within is knowledge. He is aware of what is happening all the time, so He continually sees what is happening with the mind, where it is going, what kind of thoughts it is occupied with. So how can you lose awareness of that?

In fact, we should understand what the true object of meditation is. The true object of meditation is not an image, it is neither Rama, nor Shiva nor Krishna, nor is it anyone with a shaven head or matted locks. The true object of meditation is the inner knower, inner

consciousness, the inner Self. If there is any Rama, he
lives within in the form of the inner Self. If there is
any Krishna or any Shiva, he too lives within in the form
of the same Self. And this Self is all-knowing, conscious
of everything, aware of everything and knows whatever
is happening. How can you divest this Self of its knowledge, of its consciousness? This is exactly what the
scriptures say. The scriptures say that the inner Self is
aware of all that happens in the waking state, as well
as all the dreams that you have during sleep. Even
though you are sleeping, the inner Self is awake, keeping
watch on the dream world. Not only that, the inner
Self is also aware of the emptiness, the void of deep
sleep. How can you divest the inner Self of its awareness?

Many people complain to me, "Baba, whenever I sit for
meditation, my mind begins to wander. It wanders here,
it wanders there, and it doesn't listen to me."

I ask, "Why are you meditating on the mind? Even
your mind must be sick of you because instead of concentrating your attention on God, you are concentrating
your attention on it, and that is why your attention keeps
wandering along with your wandering thoughts."

Meditate on the one who is the knower of meditation,
who is aware of meditation. Think of the one who is
totally free and who knows everyone from within. The
greatest wonder is that the inner Self knows everything
in the waking state through the senses but in the deep
sleep state, also, it knows everything without any senses.
You should meditate on the one who is aware of the
wanderings, the unsteadiness, the restlessness of your
mind. Meditate on that. Do not meditate on the wanderings of the mind. It is the inner knower who is the
greatest being, who is Shiva, who is Krishna, who is
Rama, who is Ganapati, who is everything. The inner
knower is aware of everything, and there is no way you
can divest the inner knower of awareness. It illuminates
everything, it is of the nature of pure knowledge.

Now you will be able to meditate if you focus your
attention on the inner witness, the inner knower. The

inner knower is in meditation all the time; you don't
have to put Him into meditation. He is in meditation
even when your mind is wandering. It is He who is
constantly watching all the wanderings of the mind.

Everyone should continue to meditate, because meditation is the highest tapasya, the highest penance, and
nothing else can equal it. No yajna, no other ritual can
equal meditation. The *Upanishads* say that the earth
is constantly in meditation and it is because of this that
the earth is able to stay in place. Similarly, the sky is
constantly in meditation and it is for this reason that
the sky has been able to remain in its place from time
immemorial. Water too is constantly in meditation, and
it is only because of that, that it retains its characteristic
flowing. If water were to stop meditating, it would
merge into the void. All the five elements have emerged
from the void and they are able to retain their separate
identities because they are continually in meditation. If
they were to stop meditating, they would all merge back
into the void. The mountains, the oceans—all these
things exist because they are all in a constant meditative
state.

I repeat once again, that to meditate does not mean to
engage in warfare with your mind. To keep your
attention focused on the one who is continually watching
the mind, whenever it wanders, wherever it goes, is my
idea of meditation.

Kedarnath : *If a seeker, in the course of his sadhana,
begins to think about the faults and flaws of others, if
he gets angry with them, if he is caught up in fancy and
imagination, if he is always picking holes in others, how
is his sadhana affected?*

Baba : The effect of such an attitude is that the seeker
falls from sadhana. If a seeker, during the course of his
sadhana, begins to look at the faults of others, or gets
into the habit of looking at the faults of others even
slightly, he falls. Afer all, how much poison does one
need to kill himself? One may need a lot of food to keep
alive, but to die one doesn't need a large quantity of

poison. Similarly, for progress in sadhana, you need so
many good qualities, but to fall from sadhana, you don't
need many bad qualities. Even one bad quality would
be enough to bring about your fall.

Why should a seeker be so interested in seeing what
others are doing, in looking at their dirty linen, or trying
to find their drawbacks? How can a seeker whose mind
is impure, who has given up good actions and who does
not care for the scriptural injunctions become absorbed
in Rama, in the Lord?

Isn't it surprising that the earth bears the burden of
everyone, the earth does not reject anyone? Even the
prana keeps everyone alive. And all the deities of all
the different sense organs perform their functions in
everyone. It is only man who finds it difficult to bear
others. It is only he, who even while he is at a distance
from others, keeps on picking holes in them, making
himself miserable. You can be certain of one thing: you
look at others in terms of yourself. If you have certain
qualities, you will find those qualities in others. If you
don't have those qualities, you won't find them in others.
Take the case of a sinner who commits sins without
even being conscious of it: the onlooker, who is not
committing those sins, is making himself miserable only
by looking at them. Isn't it a great pity? This is not
a good tendency at all and one should not get caught
up in it. To engage in fault finding is not good for you;
it only indicates that you are getting ready to become
a victim of those very faults.

Only today I copied a certain verse. I am very fond
of reading the poetry of poet-saints. This is a verse of
Eknath Maharaj. Eknath Maharaj is considered to be
very distinguished among the saints of Maharashtra,
particularly for his devotion to his Guru. Eknath says,
"You say that it is God who dwells in every heart. I
would like to know who dwells in the heart of the Lord?
Where do bad qualities arise from? Your body is made
up of the five elements. Some other elements come into
existence so that bad qualities may be manufactured.
You see the faults of another person and consider him

to be low, but I would like to know how you, being so high, were able to perceive the flaws which you say you are perceiving in another person?"

Such a seeker is immersed in the faults which he sees all the time, and even his sadhana becomes vitiated. The fact that we insist on such strict discipline in the Ashram shows that we try to ensure that people remain free from faults, free from drawbacks. We do not insist upon strict discipline simply because we are interested in torturing people.

Eknath Maharaj says, "A yogi naturally dwells in the sahasrar, in the thousand-petalled lotus, and he keeps on repeating his mantra inwardly like a bee which is buzzing all the time. How can such a yogi think of others' faults, how can he pick holes in others?"

My Guru used to say that wherever a crow may go, he will not cease to be a crow. So one who is accustomed to seeing others' faults will always be seeing faults. He would see impurities even in purity, even though there is no impurity in purity. And a crow can never become a swan. Similarly, a fault finder can never become a good seeker. To see faults in others is not a sign of a seeker.

Larry : *How can I get rid of the habit of seeing others' faults and learn to appreciate all in an understanding manner?*

Baba : This shows that you are not seeing even yourself in the right manner. If you were to make yourself completely pure, even once, then you would not be able to see faults in others, and this would do good not only to yourself but also to others. You have to perceive yourself as you truly are, you have to perceive yourself with great reverence.

If you start seeing faults, then who is there that is free of faults? You will see faults everywhere. If you start seeing purity, what is there in the world which is impure? You will see purity everywhere. One may make certain mistakes and there is always a reason behind it. You shouldn't attach any importance to those mistakes or

lapses. Instead of engaging your attention with the
faults of others, why shouldn't you keep your mind
occupied with yourself, with what exactly you should
do?

There is another verse of Eknath Maharaj which is
very relevant to this question. Eknath says, "I will tell
you the secret of becoming pure in a very simple manner.
You should see at least your own being as God. You
should be able to perceive the all-pervasiveness of the
Self. Instead of seeing impurities or faults, you should
be able to see the one Spirit which is pervading everywhere. If you can do that, then your own hidden Self
will be revealed to you and you will begin to feel that
you yourself are God."

The world is not really the world; the world is a
vibration of God. To understand this truth you should
give up your ego, your pride. If you can take shelter
in God from within in this manner, then you will receive
the full grace of the all-pervasive Spirit.

Man is guilty of evil when he thinks of the faults of
others. It is only your own thoughts which bear fruit.
The attitude of fault finding is a very great obstacle and
a very bad addiction of the mind. It keeps you very
far from peace. A sinner would perhaps be able to enjoy
peace, but one who looks at the faults of others will
never be able to get peace. Take the case of a person
who has committed a certain lapse today: it is not impossible for him to make amends and become pure
tomorrow. Thus, you find that a person himself falls
into certain flaws and he himself is able to pull himself
out of them. So one who is impure today can become
pure tomorrow. But a person who is seeing his faults
will never be able to get rid of this attitude. Because
today he sees this person's faults and tomorrow somebody
else's and he will never be cured of this tendency even
until his death. People, perceiving the faults of others,
think that they are very clever but in fact they are very
stupid and they will never be able to make any spiritual
progress.

Therefore, you should be able to see others as pure.

If you look for faults, are you yourself free from them? If you begin to see purity, then where is impurity? There is a very important dialogue in the Mahabharata. It is worth meditating on. During the days of the *Maha- bharata* there were two persons who had mastered their respective arts: Duryodhana had mastered the art of see- ing faults in others and Yudhishthira had mastered the art of seeing others as totally pure. One day there was a vast assembly of people; Duryodhana and Krishna and Yudhishthira were all there. Krishna said to Duryodhana, "Duryodhana, you are such a great king, you are so intelligent, please select a truly virtuous soul from this assembly and show him to me."

Duryodhana said, "Lord, what are you asking me? There is not a single virtuous soul in this assembly. Everyone here is a sinner."

Then the Lord said to Yudhishthira, "Show me a sinner in this asembly."

Yudhishthira said, "The people here are all noble and pure; they are God-like and free from taint, and I cannot see a single sinner among them."

Duryodhana could not find a single virtuous soul and Yudhishthira could not find a single sinner, because what you see is your own heart.

Therefore, make your own heart pure, and then see others through it. It is for this reason that instead of calling upon everyone to meditate on the Lord, to worship Him, to honour Him, I am asking you to meditate on your own Self, to make yourself pure, because if you make yourself pure, then you will see purity everywhere. You should change yourself.

Susan: *Baba, aside from meditating, please tell me how can I live in the middle of a family and children who are rooted in worldly pursuits, and still dedicate my life to you?*

Baba: Do not look at the world as different from me. Do not look upon your children as different from me. Do not look upon your husband as different from me. And do not consider your responsibilities and duties towards

them as different from the work that you do for me.
Just as this entire Ashram, this large Ashram, is nothing
but Muktananda Swami, similarly, the entire world is
nothing but Muktananda Swami, and your affection for
me should not affect your worldly life. You should be
able to see me in your tamboura, and then play it well.
You should see me in your children, and as you look at
them you will go into meditation. True knowledge will
not bring a split between your life in the world and God.
Any knowledge that causes such a split is not true
knowledge. If true knowledge were against the world,
then I would ask you all to get out of here. What do I
need you for? Just as I am here with you, you should
be there with your family. You should live your family
life with an awareness of God. No other pursuit of your
daily life will go against it. Therefore, while living your
life in the world, continue to meditate. And then when
you are free from your worldly responsibilities you will
get a lot of time to meditate.

July 11, 1972

Balkrishna Agarwal: *Is the effect of Shaktipat short-
lived or permanent?*

Baba: If the effect of Shaktipat were not permanent, it
would imply that the Guru would constantly be performing Shaktipat. In that case, just as the contentment
that you receive from eating food is not perfect, so,
Shakti, too, would not be perfect. How long the Shaktipat that you receive from food is going to last depends
on the kind of food you have eaten. The effect of puris
may last for eight hours. The effect of plain rice may
last for one hour, and so on. The effect of the Shaktipat
of khichari may last for about three hours.

The divine Shakti is not imperfect. The divine Shakti is perfect, and once it is transmitted into a seeker it works in him permanently. This is the Shakti which ever grows, which ever unfolds Her glory. This Shakti is not ordinary energy which depends on external factors. Take for instance the energy of heat, or the Shakti which hot water may possess: that lasts only as long as the water is hot. But that is not the case with divine Shakti. The divine Shakti is only another name of the divine will, and She has been called Uma. Uma is the divine Shakti and Uma is the eternal maiden. The Shakti is immutable. She holds Her external sport without undergoing any change, and Her playfulness never wanes. Her play is not like us: happy one moment and weeping the next. So wonderful, so amazing is this Shakti that it is as perfect in each part as it is in the whole.

Shakti is the root of all yogas. Unless the Kundalini is awakened, any yoga you practise remains merely external; it is no better than the performance of an acrobat in a circus. To learn external yoga you have to go to a teacher and put in strenuous effort to master it, which is not the case with the awakening of the Shakti. The yoga that you receive through the awakening of Shakti is absolutely natural and spontaneous. You don't have to learn it from anyone else. And there is no strenuous effort involved. This yoga arises spontaneously from within. Once you receive Shaktipat, its effect will last not only through this life, but also through all the future births that you may have to undergo—until you achieve total liberation.

Hariprasad: *I request your grace for less hunger in order to concentrate on dhyan. I am helpless in my efforts.*

Baba: Your request is very extraordinary. Even in the *Vedas* you find the seers praying, "May we have more food and may we be able to eat a great deal." You find so many people going to doctors and getting treatments so that their appetite may be increased; and they do all kinds of exercises with the same objective. And here you are, wanting your appetite to decrease. I can assure you that you are not the only one who has this problem. You have many sisters here who are in the same boat. After the Shakti awakes, one begins to eat a great deal, and there is no harm in that. Let yourself eat. In course of time it will become disciplined itself. You should meditate before eating. He who feels ravenously hungry will get very good meditation. Usually I ask meditators to eat less so that their meditation may become more intense.

It is quite obvious that you are meditating very well, which is very good. As far as your abnormal appetite is concerned, it will come under control gradually. If you have a good healthy appetite, that is an indication that the Shakti is working very well within you and even in the *Vedas*, as I have pointed out before, you find the seers praying for more food and for a keener appetite so that they may be able to eat a great deal and digest it.

It is not so very common to be able to eat a great deal and digest it. Most people have to take pills in order to digest all that they put in their systems. Food is God, the Lord Himself. The Lord Himself says in the *Gita*, "It is I who become the gastric fire which dwells in the abdomen of every living creature. And by becoming that fire, I digest the four kinds of food."

So if you are very hungry and if you digest your food, that means that God is very pleased with you. I always tell dyspeptics, that is, those who cannot digest all that they put into their stomachs, that God does not seem to be very pleased with them. It is the Lord Himself who is blazing in the form of the gastric fire in your stomach, so honour Him and be pleased about it. The two greatest blessings of the Lord are a good wholesome appetite and the power of digesting all that you eat, and good sleep. If you are able to digest all that you eat, and if you fall into a deep sleep soon after you lay down, you can be sure that you are enjoying the grace of God in His fullness. Wealth is no blessing. If wealth were a blessing, then all the rich people would be very happy, and particularly the accountants in the bank would be

happy, because they are surrounded by so much wealth;
they are surrounded by all those currency notes all the
time. But what happens with them is that they lose
their sleep, they lose their peace by keeping on counting
all the notes that they receive. And they have to keep
figures in their heads which disturbs their sleep. If you
have a good appetite and good sleep, and are digesting
your food, you are a blessed person.

Chandra : *How is it possible to be detached from the
bliss and inner contentment that seem so natural?*
Baba : Why should you want to be detached from inner
bliss and contentment? When you are in bliss and inner
contentment, that means that you are enjoying the
company of your own Self. You started learning yoga
and meditation only for inner bliss and contentment.
Detachment should be gained from outer things, from
outer obstructions: there is no point in trying to get
detached from inner contentment. Bliss and contentment are the very nature of the inner Self, and if you
feel bliss and contentment, it shows that you have reached
somewhere. This is true spiritual realisation. Spiritual
realisation does not mean siddhis or miraculous powers
or tricks. Spiritual attainment means bliss and contentment.

What is real attainment? Real attainment is one's own
Self. Real attainment is not seeking for contentment
in the outside world. Real attainment is obtaining contentment within one's own Self. And this contentment
does not depend on any outer factor. It is for such contentment that we become renunciants for the whole of
our lives. After you achieve inner bliss and contentment, it is futile to make efforts for anything else,
for anything further. Inner contentment and bliss are
like the dome we put on top of the temple after it is
complete. As long as that dome has not been installed,
it means that we are still in the process of building the
temple. But once that is done, it means that the process
of construction has come to an end. Similarly, if you
have achieved inner contentment and bliss, it means that

your sadhana has reached its consummation.

The very first question that is asked in Vedanta is, "What is the object of sadhana? What is the purpose of meditation? What is the purpose of renunciation?" The answer is, "The purpose of meditation, the purpose of all yogic methods, the goal of the path shown by the Guru, the purpose of renunciation of worldly life, is the cessation of all misery, the cessation of all sorrow and the attainment of supreme bliss." And there is no question of getting detached from that, because it is bliss itself which is supremely non-attached. You can never be detached from inner bliss and contentment. Inner bliss and contentment are themselves detached from everything else; they are different from everything else there is.

Inner bliss is the root of all pleasure. In this connection Tukaram Maharaj says, "It is absolute transcendental bliss, it is the bliss of the Lord which is the root, the source of all pleasures and delights."

For instance, the pleasure of seeing, hearing, taste, touch and so on springs from inner bliss. In other words, it is perfect inner bliss which is reflected in all the pleasures we seek through sense objects.

Yesterday I was shown a newspaper clipping which said that an international seminar was held in Israel on sex education, and the secretary of the seminar, I forget that doctor's name, is reported to have said that sex is a lot of fun and all young people should be given the experience of sex so that they may receive sex education more effectively. But no pleasure, including sexual pleasure, is perfect in itself, or complete in itself. It is only a reflection, and a very poor reflection, of inner bliss.

Our *Upanishads* say that the pleasure we experience at the end of a good meal, which lasts for a brief moment, and the pleasure that we experience at the end of a good sleep, which lasts only as long as we are waking up, and the pleasure that we get through the sexual act, which lasts for a very brief period, is just a drop of the ocean of inner spiritual bliss. It is said that the pleasure that we experience, not during sleep, not after we have woken up, but at the moment that we are waking up, the pleasure which is just like a flash of lightning, is a reflection of supreme bliss. Surely it doesn't mean that in order to experience more of supreme bliss we should continue to sleep the whole day.

Similarly, the pleasure of eating is experienced only at the moment in which you finish eating, and that too will be experienced provided that you have very good digestion, you are eating with a good appetite, and the food is also very good. This pleasure is experienced the moment you have the very first burp, and that burp indicates contentment. That burp is, in fact, the voice of inner contentment. The moment I get the first burp, I stop eating, because that is the signal that enough has been put into the stomach. Even if I have a piece of food in my hand, if I get this burp, I stop eating. But this does not mean that you should eat more in order to get more pleasure; because if you overeat, you get dysentery, and I can assure you, there is no pleasure in dysentery. Dysentery is sheer misery.

Then they say that inner bliss is like the pleasure that you experience at the end of the sex act. Does that mean that we should be engaged in sexual intercourse all the time? How many times during the day and night are you going to engage in it? That pleasure also lasts for a brief moment, and that too, you experience only if you have semen in you. If you don't have any semen, you are deprived of even that pleasure.

According to Ayurveda, the science of health, what we eat during 24 hours produces one drop of semen. If you were to eject the semen which is so precious, after listening to the educated prattle of this doctor, what will be left inside your body? The seers say that inner bliss is eternal, it is everlasting, while all these pleasures last only briefly, like flashes of lightning. Diseases such as tuberculosis and various stomach ailments arise from lack of semen. It is not the gastric fire which digests food, it is, in fact, semen which digests food, along with the gastric fire. It is semen which is called fire. If you lose this fire, what would happen to you? If you eject this

precious fluid on the enlightened advice of this gentle-
man, then what would you do? You would have to inject
semen from the outside into your body. Inner bliss is
everlasting, but it arises in the sahasrar after semen is
stored up inside. When such bliss is available, when
through meditation you can experience inner bliss in such
liberal measure, throbbing through all your nerves, isn't
it stupid to waste your most precious fluid for momentary,
fleeting pleasure?

When bliss and contentment arise within, it is an indication that you have become detached, because they arise
only in a state of detachment. It is the nature of the
inner Self to be ever-contented, and it is contented in
itself, and its contentment is eternal. For this contentment, the Self does not have to depend on any outer
factor. This contentment is totally independent. It arises
itself in the Self. You don't have to hear sweet, soothing
words from somebody else, you don't have to laugh, you
don't have to weep. It is as a result of inner contentment that you experience some contentment when you
see something beautiful, or when you taste something
delicious, or when your hands give or take gifts. This
is the true attainment, and this is what one's Self means.
One Upanishadic seer asks, "What is greater than the
Self?" It is this inner bliss, the bliss of the Self which
is the source of all pleasure. It is as result of this bliss
that we experience the bliss of seeing or hearing, of taste,
of touch. Tukaram Maharaj describes the nature of this
inner bliss. He says, "I am drowning in inner bliss and
I am seeing it reflected all around me. When this bliss
arises within, one gets beyond the waking state, the state
of sleep, the state of dreams. One gets into an entirely
different realm altogether. This supreme bliss pervades
everywhere. It stretches above and below, from east to
west, from north to south; it is lapping on all sides.
What should I do now, or what shouldn't I do? Where
should I go, where shouldn't I go? This bliss or inner
ecstasy is engulfing me from every side. This bliss is
also called Satchitananda, existence, consciousness and
bliss. And it is this very bliss which is called the Lord,

Govinda. As this bliss began to throb within me, my
ego dissolved. Now I see divine bliss all around; my
refuge now is the feet of the Sadguru."

Inner contentment and bliss arise in a state of
detachment.

Sheshi: *How can man give up his attachment to others,
except of course, attachment to God?*

Baba: It is the nature of the mind to become attached
to one thing or another. Some people get attached to the
body, to beautiful forms. Some get attached to scholarship, taking great pride in the vastness of their learning.
Others get attached to arts. There are some who get
attached to dancing and they take pride in being among
the best dancers in the state. The mind will certainly
get attached to one thing or another. Either you become
attached to the body or to worldly possessions. When
that very attachment is directed towards the Lord, you
get free from the hold of everything else. You can be
attached only to one thing, either the Lord or the world.
When you become fully attached to God, you become fully
detached from everything else. But unfortunately, our
attachment to God is not real, it is not genuine. It is
like a counterfeit note which no bank will accept. We
are always half-hearted. We are neither fully attached
to the world nor fully attached to God. As a result we
neither master the world completely, nor become attached
to God. If we were totally attached to the world, even
that would be good, because one day that attachment
would be turned to the Lord.

There is a story of the great saint Tulsidas relating
to the subject of attachment. This story must be true,
because in those days people were not interested in
concocting false tales; in those days falsehood was
rare. These days truth is rare. Tulsidas was very
passionately attached to his wife. His wife was his five
vital airs, his food, drink, father, mother. She was east
for him, she was west for him, she was every direction
for him. He used to work as a priest and sometimes
it would happen that while performing a ritual he would

suddenly begin to miss his wife, and he would leave the ceremony and rush home just to have a look at his most beloved wife. This is attachment, and in Tulsidas's case it was a very genuine attachment.

But his wife was sick of it. What is so fascinating about the body? One looks at one's body every day, so why should there be a craving to look at some other body? I could describe at length the charms of the body, but I don't want to use a certain kind of language here. You find people trying to adorn their bodies and make them look more presentable, more attractive, and they use all sorts of ornaments and cosmetics just to throw dust into the eyes of others. The other day I read in the newspaper that one so-called guru in Bombay wants college boys and girls to go around naked. This amused me very much, because once you become naked, you won't want to look at each other. So fascinating, so charming is the body, that once all its charms are fully exposed, it becomes the most repulsive thing in the world. It was that which amused me. It would be one way of making people conscious of what the body really is.

Tulsidas' wife was fed up with his continual shower of caresses and one day she decided to leave him and go to her parents' place. While Tulsidas was at the temple, she went, leaving a note for him. When Tulsidas returned in the evening he found the house completely empty and this plunged him into grief. That evening there was nobody to greet him, nobody he could look at and admire. Tulsidas could not eat, could not drink, he felt so despondent. He left for his in-laws' place immediately.

It was a stormy night, a dark night, torrential showers were falling and the river was in spate. The story-writers say it was so stormy and dark that one could hardly see one's way. Tulsidas crossed the river by riding on a corpse. He mistook the corpse for a log, and rode on it. He had become so blinded by his attachment to his wife that he could not even distinguish one thing from another. The picture of his wife had taken seat in his eyes, as a result of which he could see nothing but his wife. When

he reached the other shore there were two fishermen
standing there. They were amazed to find that Tulsidas
had crossed the river by riding on a corpse. These
fishermen were from the same village which his wife was
from and they considered Tulsidas as their own son-in-
law, and they began to follow him. It so happened that
a python had come out from the storm. A python is
not poisonous and doesn't bite, but it can swallow a
person alive. If a python were to hold even an elephant
in one of its coils, the elephant would not be able to
get free. The python was laying on its side. By chance,
it happened to raise its head, and it was so huge that
its head was as high as Tulsidas' in-laws' house. Since
it was a completely dark night, Tulsidas could not see
anything and he thought that the snake was a rope and
he climbed it and reached the first floor where his wife's
room was. He knocked at the door and she opened it.

As she came out, she was confronted by the vision
of her husband. Down below the two fishermen were
standing, knocking at the main door on the ground floor,
and they woke up her parents. The parents asked,
"What's happening?"

They said, "Well, we wonder what's happening with
your son-in-law because we saw him riding a corpse."
They went upstairs and Tulsidas' wife asked him, "How
did you get up here?"

He said, "I climbed a rope." Then they lit a light and
were terrified when they saw that the rope was really
a python.

The wife was full of remorse, and she was sorry that
she had gone away. She said to herself, "He must be
hopelessly attached to me because he was compelled to
undertake a journey on such a dark night." She said to
him, "You braved such a night, for what reason?"

Tulsidas said, "It was for you."

His wife said, "If you were as strongly attached to
Lord Hari as you are to my body, which is mere dust,
you would reach Vaikuntha without any difficulty. No
one would be able to stop you."

The words of his wife sank into him. That moment

he turned away from the house of his in-laws, away from the hopeless attachment to his wife, and became fully attached to Rama. The miracle of that new attachment was that he not only had a vision of Rama, but Rama became his constant companion. He would rub sandalwood on Rama and Rama would apply the sacred mark on his forehead.

You should not try to give up your attachment. You should only try to direct it towards Rama, towards the Lord, towards Nityananda. Just as Tulsidas redirected his attachment from his wife to Rama, you should do the same.

July 14, 1972

Swami Chidananda: *The senses vibrate with the perception of sense objects and the mind vibrates with anger and hatred, pleasure and pain and memory. What, then, is the Self? Does the Self exist? If it does, then how can we find it in pleasure, pain, anger, hatred, etc.?*

Baba: It's the Self which vibrates in all the senses and it vibrates according to the nature of the particular sense. Are the senses inert? Are they conscious or unconscious? How many consciousnesses are there after all? You are thinking in terms of the consciousness of the senses, the consciousness of the mind, and then some other consciousness. It is only one thing which is conscious, not everything. All the rest lack consciousness. It is the Self which vibrates in the different senses according to their nature.

This matter has been very well discussed in the 13th chapter of the *Gita* and you should read the commentary on that chapter in *Jnaneshwari*. The Lord says there, "It is the Self which performs all the functions of the sense organs. It is the Self which sees forms through the eyes, smells perfumes through the nose, tastes nectars through the tongue and speaks through the vocal cords." If the Self were not vibrating through the senses, making them alive, making it possible for them to perceive their respective objects, then the question of restraining the senses would not have arisen. The sense organs would have remained happy with their functions and there would be no need for us to bother about them.

We should understand why restrain of senses is emphasized. The seers were not interested in tormenting people, and they were not antagonistic to the senses as such. They did not hold the senses responsible for anything. They recommended sense control only so that we could collect the energy of the Spirit. The vibrations of that energy are pouring out through the senses and getting scattered in the external world. If we collect this energy and turn it in on itself, we experience the Self.

Whatever thoughts and feelings appear inside are the thoughts and feelings through which the Self itself is vibrating. It is the Self that becomes anger, hatred, love and lust and appears in various other forms. What makes you think that we have different storehouses inside for different feelings and thoughts? It is the Self which vibrates in the senses and in the mind. Whatever functions the senses are performing, they are able to perform them because of the Self. Whatever the mind is thinking or feeling, it is able to think or feel, again because of the Self. It is the Self which is assuming the forms of anger, lust, desire, love and so on.

The purpose of sadhana is to make sure that the Self does not vibrate in negative forms, that the Self manifests itself only as love. Otherwise, what's the point of sadhana? The way the Self vibrates in the mind or in the senses has a direct effect on the body, on all its seven constituents. Therefore a seeker strives to keep his mind directed towards love. He takes it away from all other thoughts. He is called upon to withdraw the mind from the body and the senses and from all negative

thoughts and feelings, so that it may vibrate constantly
with love and love alone. It is then that the body
becomes divine. This is what Tukaram Maharaj also
said. The question of the Self becoming divine does not
arise, the Self is already God. What is most marvellous
is that the body and mind become divine as a result of
this effort. Eknath Maharaj says in a verse, "I am going
to tell you the secret of the absolute enlightened state,
and I will say it in very simple words. The secret is that
it is God who pervades all beings. It is God, nothing but
God, who is present in everything, in every creature.
And the purpose of sadhana is to become one with the
all-pervasive God, to achieve such complete identity
with Him that you do not feel different from Him any
longer." The statement 'I am God', should not be mis-
used to ask people to worship you. If anyone says that
he has become God so there is no need to worship God,
he is an utterly wicked and depraved person and no
attention should be paid to him. This truth is being
revealed so that one may experience the inner Self, so
that one may experience the identity of the inner Self
with God. Therefore, one who claims to be in this state
should really be in this state. He should have actually
experienced the Supreme Being. There is no point in
making a tall claim.

A group of scholars approached a teacher who claimed
to be an incarnation of God, and said, "We want to discuss this matter with you because your claims go against
everything the scriptures say." He refused to have any
such discussion. In fact, he ran away from the scene.
Such a person cannot be said to be in the enlightened
state. Sundardas says, "One who claims to be in the
absolute state, the highest state, but who is not actually
in that state, must be spurned. One who only exploits
the scriptural knowledge of Brahman to throw dust into
people's eyes, who exploits Vedantic knowledge, who
sees himself as God but doesn't see the same Lord in
others, must be treated like a most wicked person."
Sundardas says, "This is not what I am saying. This is
what Vasishtha has said."

The world is the vibration of God, the Supreme Being, and this is the truth. You will realise this only when you become free of all impurities. It is the Supreme Being who vibrates into all your different thoughts and feelings. It is the Supreme Being Himself who becomes anger, ego, greed, and other negative passions, only to punish people for their evil actions. Otherwise, there is no anger in the Self, there is no lust in the Self, there is no greed in the Self. The Self is absolutely pure. The soul is one. There aren't many in the world. Eknath concludes by saying, "By Guru's grace, I achieved complete perfection."

It is the Self which vibrates into negative forms, awarding the consequences of bad actions to their doers. It is the Self which disturbs one's sleep. It is the Self which agitates one's mind with greed, or which rises up into the mind as lust. Whenever love arises in the mind, try to increase those vibrations. When something else begins to throb in the mind, withdraw the mind and turn it towards love once again. You may think about others, but do not forget that those thoughts occur inside you. You may find faults in others, and think that those faults have nothing to do with you—and that may be true—but don't forget that those faults, just because you are turning your attention to them, are beginning to vibrate in your own mind. You may observe that somebody else has made a mistake, and you start thinking about it. The moment you start thinking about it, you are vitiating your own mind. Your mind is at that time assuming the characteristics of the faults that you are thinking about. If all evil or negative vibrations could be stopped or prevented, that which would remain behind would be pure, good vibrations, constructive, creative vibrations. If you can guard against evil vibrations, if you can keep them away, then love will vibrate within, purity will vibrate within, omniscience will arise within.

You can find it out from your own direct experience, you can try it out. Just turn your attention to your Self for half an hour, and think nothing about anyone.

You will see what will happen. Try to experience the inner Self for at least half an hour every day. What's the point of thinking about others? What's the point of finding faults in them? Once you begin to find fault with others, those faults get reflected in you, and there is no point in that. If you can restrain these negative vibrations, you will find only nectar, pure nectar flowing within. If you can do that you will overcome all your physical and mental ailments.

Judith: *What brings further progress—just following one's inner inclinations, whether good or bad, or disciplining the mind and body?*

Baba: The best thing is to acquire complete control over the mind. If you completely restrain your mind, still its movements, you realise how much power it has; without that, it is difficult to realise it. You must have heard so many interesting stories about all kinds of miracles which are being performed, and you must have heard about people materialising things, about their power to send things from one place to another, and so on. All miracles are creations of the mind, not God. If you could restrain the mind, completely empty it of all thoughts, of all imaginings, then all my congratulations to you, because it is not so easy to do. Only a man who has tremendous power can restrain the mind to such a degree.

If that is not possible, you should stay as a witness to your mind, without identifying yourself with any of your thoughts. Let thoughts come and go; just keep yourself continually aware that you are not that. You are the pure witness. Keep your attention focused on yourself as the witness. Furthermore, if you could look upon all the thoughts, good or bad, positive or negative, which pass through the mind as movements of Chiti Herself, as Her throbbing, Her vibrations—that would be the best. Then you would be aware only of Chiti, not of thoughts. You would see Chiti's play in thoughts. This is the highest form of meditation, the most rewarding form of meditation, and this is possible only by Guru's grace.

It is not so easy to control the mind. The author of *Pratyabhijnahridayam* says the mind is not a concrete object which you can hold in your hand or put away, and the mind is not an independent entity. The mind is not something small and your power great, so that you can control the mind without any difficulty. It's not like that. The mind is nothing but a vibration of Chiti.

If while meditating calmly you could regard the countless vibrations of the mind as the movements of Chiti, if you could keep your attention focused on Chiti, if you could remain full of Her, then instead of your mind causing you misery and suffering, it would flood you with bliss and happiness. This is the meditation of very highly evolved seekers.

There is not much point in practising methods without understanding their basis. If you do not understand its basis, the truth behind it, then no matter how strenuously or earnestly you practise it, you get nowhere. Take, for example, the countless clouds which appear in the sky; they form and dissolve. When they form, as long as they last they are in existence, and when they dissolve, they don't affect the sky at all. And they don't affect the on-looker either. It is the nature of space to assume the form of clouds and that's about all.

Likewise, Chiti vibrates into countless forms in the mind, bringing into existence countless worlds inside you, some of which are good and others bad. Chiti sustains them for a while, then dissolves them. After dissolving one world, She brings another into existence, sustains it and dissolves it, and this process goes on. For Chiti, none of these worlds are either good or bad. For Chiti is pure play. It is only for a conditioned individual like you that a physical world appears to be good or bad. If you look at its inner nature, you would find that it is all Chiti. The other day somebody offered me a sweet in the form of a fish, then along came somebody else with a candy in the form of an elephant. Surely you can't take a candy that looks like an elephant or a fish for an actual elephant or fish. It is sugar which appears in the shape of a fish or an elephant, but it is all sugar.

The best and easiest form of meditation is to sit calmly and keep watching all the thoughts that arise, come and go in the mind. This form of meditation has enormous value. By considering whatever arises in the mind as Chiti's movement, one makes the quickest progress in sadhana. The method is more effective than that of acquiring control over the mind.

Girija: *Baba, what is the meaning and significance of one's personal, external relationship with you?*
Baba: As far as the Guru is concerned, there is no question of any distinction between external relationship and inner relationship. The character of the most rewarding relationship with the Guru is when the Guru begins to pervade your body, speech and mind; that is, you feel related to him in body, speech and mind. Until he achieves complete identity with the Guru or Lord, a seeker should practise Gurubhava, identification with the Guru.

Mohini Amma: *If for some reason one begins to feel dry in sadhana, and loses interest in chanting and recitation, does not find any joy in any rituals, what exactly is happening to him?*
Baba: First, such a person should understand that he is lacking in true mumukshutva, intense desire for liberation, that he is not a true seeker, or in any case, that he has fallen away from his seeking. The mind cannot remain in a void, for something or other will always be throbbing in it. Most people, people with so-called normal minds, are those who are interested in something relating to the outside world. But then there are two other directions that the mind could take: one is that of mental sickness, getting completely away from mundane concerns and escaping into a mental disease. The other is to become absorbed in the samadhi state. Then your mind will become completely free from ordinary thoughts. If the mind has started taking interest in sadhana, it would be quite natural for it to turn away from everything else, and if the mind turns away from sadhana

to something else, then it would be natural for it not to make any progress in sadhana. Suppose your mind is engaged in devotion and all of a sudden it is distracted by a certain addiction and loses interest in devotion. If your mind begins to wander in hotels and guest houses, it will acquire a distaste for solitude, for living in a forest. If your mind begins to turn to things which are antagonistic to sadhana, then you develop a distaste for sadhana.

There is a very funny play called 'Brahmachari' written by a local playwright. It is about a brahmachari who was a devotee of Hanuman, and he used to worship a picture of Hanuman three times a day. He would practise different postures and exercises to keep his body in good shape so that he could perform his worship without any interruption. Every day he would spend his time working in the temple of Hanuman, worshipping him, going around the picture and sitting before it. In this way he stored up more and more Shakti.

Company is extremely powerful. Then the brahmachari, who was a worshipper of Hanuman, happened to meet somebody who used to visit a prostitute. That fellow said to the brahmachari, "What you are doing is too much. You are worshipping Hanuman three times a day. Who would think of worshipping Hanuman three times a day, these days? Don't you think that worshipping him once is enough? You have made your life very dull and uninteresting by keeping yourself confined to Hanuman. You should take interest in the outside world, you should go around, spend less time on the picture of Hanuman and take more interest in other people, and occasionally there would be no harm in visiting that great soul who practises her own kind of celibacy."

They became friends. The brahmachari would take his friend to his temple of Hanuman, and his friend would take him to the temple of his prostitute every night. As time passed, the brahmachari began to lose interest in worshipping Hanuman, and began to develop an interest in the prostitute. Now the prostitute had two on her side, whereas poor Hanuman had only one on his side.

She exerted greater power, she was more successful than Hanuman. Hanuman was lonely. He was just by himself, while the prostitute had two other persons who were her worshippers. One day the brahmachari said to himself, "The worship that I have done of Hanuman so far should be enough at least for this lifetime. Now I am going to start worshipping the prostitute much more seriously." He continued to worship her. One night, when he returned from the prostitute, he covered Hanuman's picture with a screen saying, "I am no longer going to worship you."

So you can master only one thing. If you become interested in something which is antagonistic to sadhana, if your mind becomes dull, it becomes indifferent to sadhana, it becomes apathetic, it may even turn completely away from sadhana. If your interest is really strong, then you succeed in whatever you do.

I told you about Tulsidas the other day who, because of his very strong attachment to his wife, even rode a corpse. Whatever you pursue, you become addicted to it in course of time, and as a result of your interest getting stronger, you do not find it difficult to pursue it. Take, for instance, the early morning addiction to tea. You don't have to think of tea in the morning, because the desire for it arises without your even thinking. It is as though the germs of a particular thing that you are pursuing begin to inhabit you and then multiply. If the germs of sadhana begin to multiply inside you, then sadhana itself will force you to do the different practices. When it is time for meditation you will be forced by something inside you to go and meditate. When it is time for chanting you will be driven to chant, and so on. If you get addicted to meditation, it may become so powerful that even sometimes while you are walking, meditation may force you to plunge into it, and you may even fall down.

If your mind becomes interested in some worldly pursuit, it will lose taste for sadhana; or it will become indifferent to sadhana as a result of bad company. There is no dearth of such people in the world, particularly these days, who will come and tell you, "Mohini Amma,

what's the point of getting up so early day after day,
day after day? These days life is lived in a different
manner. Anybody who is sensible stays awake the
whole night and gets up at 10 o'clock in the morning."

If you begin to be influenced by such people, you
become indifferent to sadhana. Therefore, a seeker
should live most carefully, and he should avoid bad
company at all costs. Narada, in his *Bhakti Sutras,* has
condemned bad company in the strongest terms. He says
that bad company must be avoided at all costs. You
should remember that the virtues that you might have
acquired over a long period of time by earnest effort, can
be lost through a moment's influence of bad company.
It is for this reason that in the Ashram I insist that you
do not mix with people too freely, that you do not go to
all kinds of gurus, or that you do not set yourself up
as a guru—because there is a likelihood of falling away
from sadhana. Man has a wicked tendency which drives
him to advertise all that he practised in privacy. It is for
this reason that I insist that one should not talk too
much or about things which should not be talked about,
that one should keep one's speech under perfect control.
And one must avoid bad company. All this insistence
is to save a seeker from falling away from sadhana.

Company is very powerful and the impressions which
are embedded in the mind are also powerful. A past
impression can awaken at any time, in spite of all that
you might have done to acquire self-control. If you
begin to eat and drink without control, and mix with
people freely, if this kind of tendency were allowed to
spread in the Ashram, then the Ashram atmosphere
would become polluted. That is why I am so vigilant
and sometimes I have to thrash people and turn them
out of the Ashram. That is to maintain the purity of
the atmosphere.

July 18, 1972

Susan: *In meditation, I meditate on you instead of my inner Self. If I try to meditate on my inner Self, I don't know what to meditate on, as I feel no connection to myself. Any feeling that I have is one of disdain, which I can't seem to overcome. Nor can I bear to think anyone can see what I am really like, even you. How can I ever become loving towards myself and others?*

Baba: In meditation there is not the least difference between Shiva, Guru, the inner Self and the meditator. The only difference is of words; but what the words signify is one and the same. You may meditate on any one and you will reach the same place.

It is not only you, I feel almost everyone in the world is unjust to himself, and sins against himself by belittling himself and glorifying others. You find this mentality prevailing in all countries, all nations and in all religions everywhere. You find people underrating themselves, condemning themselves, while glorifying others. This attitude is not at all good.

It is of course, true that man should perform high, noble, beneficial deeds, which promote the welfare of all and which lead towards God. If you are able to perform good deeds, very good. If you are not, and if your actions are not good, well then, try to get away from bad actions and do good actions. Even if you cannot help doing bad actions, then for heaven's sake do not suffer from guilt. Do not keep the memory of them alive in you, because that memory brings pain, and that pain is very bad. I don't know whether this happens in your country or not, but in our country, women leave their babies alone sometimes, and then you find the baby playing and sometimes falling and then you may find him relieving himself and then eating his own shit, because he doesn't understand what it is. If that baby, even after growing up, were to remember that he ate shit, what good would it do him? I would not mind if you were to underrate God, I would not mind if you were to underrate religion, but to me there is nothing worse than underrating your own Self, by looking at some of your actions, or by looking at the condition of your own mind, or by looking at some of your thoughts. There is no worse hell than this: the state of self-pity, the state of self-condemnation.

I still remember the words of my Guru. I used to write them down. He would speak in a very simple, easy language, the language of everyday life, and yet he would saturate his words with divine knowledge. One day two local people went to him, one complaining about the other, saying, "Here is a chap who ate fish yesterday."

Baba said, "What does it matter what he ate yesterday, he passed it out the other end today. It is no longer inside him."

So there is no point in recollecting what you might have done at one time and suffering from a sense of guilt, falling into dejection. What should one look at? Should one look at one's past actions or should one look at the body, or the inner Self? There is absolutely no use in underrating yourself. You should understand the nature of your Self. The Self is not the body, the Self does not participate in any of the things the body does. The Self is pure knowledge, the Self is pure consciousness, the Self is the pure witness. The Self is supreme Shiva. The Self is the soul, which is ever pure. The soul never does anything.

The important question is, what do you identify yourself with? Do you consider your eyes to be you, your nose to be you, or your stomach or your clothes? What exactly constitutes the 'I' of you? So discard the memory of what you have done and think deeply about what are you going to do in the future. Leave what you did in the past alone. In fact, completely eliminate it from the mind. Never consider yourself to be small. One poet says, "God is true, the scriptures are true, and you can discover their truth only if you are true, that is, true to your Self."

We are not true to ourselves. Our understanding of ourselves is defective. The soul is pure, the soul is nothing but pure knowledge, and those that say that

the soul is this or that are ignorant. I am surprised
that you belittle yourself in spite of the fact that nobody
has taught you, nobody has asked you to belittle yourself,
no scriptures in the world say that you should consider
yourself to be small, and you haven't been given any
initiation in that direction, you haven't been given any
discourses on how to underrate yourself. You are not
looking at yourself as you are, in spite of the fact that
that is what all scriptures are asking you to do—to
look upon yourself as pure consciousness, as pure
knowledge. And that is what I ask you to do all the
time. I have initiated you in that direction. And that
is what I impress on your mind again and again.
I wonder why it is that you insist on belittling yourself instead of understanding yourself as you are,
in truth. The Lord says that the inner Self, even while
living in the body, is absolutely pure. It doesn't even
become contaminated by any of the actions that the body
indulges in. So why don't you meditate on that inner
Self, inner inspiration? Meditate on the place from
where thoughts arise and into which thoughts subside.
Meditate on the brief interval of total stillness between
two thoughts. You may meditate on the inner Self or
the Guru or God, because the three are one.

The body, too, is sinless. That is how you should look
upon the body. Why blame the poor body? If you
want it to wear a decent suit, it wears a decent suit, and
if you want it to wear plain saffron clothes, then it puts
on plain saffron clothes. Why do you get angry with
the body? If you give the body plain food to eat, the
poor thing eats that. Or you may take it to a grand hotel
and feed it with all the richest delicacies, and the body
accepts them too, even at the cost of dysentery.

Kirti : *What is the significance of seeing the Guru in
dreams and in the state following meditation, especially
if he talks to you and touches you?*
Baba : In spiritual life, the Guru that you see in dreams
is far more effective than the Guru you see in the waking
state. The mantra that you receive in the dream state

works much more quickly than the mantra that you get in the waking state. Tukaram Maharaj says, "He who takes seat in your heart also appears in your dreams," so if you see your Guru in your dreams, it means that he has taken seat in your heart. Many great Siddhas received initiation in dreams. Tukaram Maharaj was a great saint of India and he received initiation from his Guru, Keshav Chaitanya, who is also known as Babaji, in a dream on Ekadasi day. There are many other saints who received mantras from their Gurus or deities or gods and goddesses in a dream state, and that indicates that the gods and goddesses were pleased with the seeker. The mantra or initation that you receive in dream bears fruit very quickly.

If you see the Guru in the state following meditation, that indicates that you are getting into a very high state, the state which all the great saints and seers were living in, and it was in that state that they could see the whole world without going anywhere. The ancient seers discovered the various worlds such as the world of the moon, of Indra and other worlds. I also saw many different worlds, such as the world of ancestors and the world of the moon, in meditation. What you see in meditation is true. It corresponds to reality as it actually is. It is not imagination; it is not a figment of your own fancy. You can see all the different worlds through meditation. Only today I read in the paper that the Americans have released a new satellite and the Russians are keeping track of it, following its movement in their research centre. None of them have learnt meditation. If they had, they would not need any outer meditation. In ancient India, there were many people who meditated very deeply and particularly worth mentioning among them were those who meditated while living their normal worldly lives. Even in that condition they attained omniscience. On one hand they would carry out their duties and responsibilities and on the other they would meditate and travel through various regions.

Just as there is a centre of dreams inside, similarly, there is a centre of meditation, and if you are able to

reach that place inside, you will be able to see the whole
world while sitting in one place. All that is required
is that your devotion be single-minded, and your heart
pure. We should realise that the inner Self is true, the
Shakti is true, and we should love the inner Self and
the Shakti as such. It is unfortunate that man, because
of his ignorance of his pure Self, commits suicide, because
ignorance of one's Self is nothing but suicide. By judg-
ing himself on the basis of thoughts and images that
appear in the mind, he does great harm to himself.

Leela : *I am never satisfied with what I have. How can
I overcome this?*

Baba : You become dissatisfied with what you have
because you are not aware of all that you have. If you
were aware of all that you have, it would give you
supreme satisfaction, and the question of being dissatisfied would not arise at all. Everyone suffers from
this tendency. There is a centre of perfect contentment
within you. Why don't you reach it? Keep on repeating
your mantra calmly, and by the support of that repetition
plunge deeper and deeper and still deeper into yourself.
There is tremendous contentment inside. I am certain
that you will feel contented within yourself one day.
It is just a matter of time. Continue to meditate. However, learn to be satisfied within yourself. If you haven't
learnt to be satisfied with yourself, how can you be
satisfied with others? In such a case, your dissatisfac-
tion is double. So, meditate more and more and you
will certainly get satisfaction. For contentment to arise
within, you must love your own soul intensely.

Lalita : *Baba, how can one overcome the pain of separation from you?*

Baba : An incident occurred during the time of the great
teacher Ramanuja. In Kangerum, Madras, there was a
well-known wrestler. He had great strength. After he
retired from active wrestling he started teaching the
art to others. During the course of his daily travels he
would run into a certain girl in the street where prosti-

tutes lived, and he developed great affection for her. A great wrestler, if he has really devoted himself to the art of wrestling, would be incapable of any sexual performance, because in the process of mastering that art, he loses that capacity. The affection that he felt for the girl had arisen naturally in his heart. Sometimes he would even take her with him to the school where he was teaching. In spite of the fact that girls were prohibited to enter there, no one would say anything to him because he was the greatest wrestler of his time.

One day Ramanuja went to that town. Ramanuja was a very great teacher, as great as Shankaracharya and Madhavacharya, and he had just established his supremacy in religious debates. When the people came to know that Ramanuja had come, they ran to greet him. The wrestler decided to take his girlfriend with him, so she could also have the darshan of the great teacher. It was a rainy day, and he held an umbrella over the girl to make sure that she did not get wet; but he was getting wet. It was in this condition that the two approached Ramanuja. As people saw them, they laughed in amusement and waited to see how Ramanuja would comment on it. Some of them even complained to Ramanuja, saying, "Look at the miserable condition of our greatest wrestler. He has completely fallen from his glory. He has become the slave of a girl. In the rainy season he won't let her get wet but he gets wet himself. And when it's very hot and the earth is burning with the heat of the sun, he carries her on his shoulders. His attachment has made him helpless."

Addressing the wrestler, Ramanuja asked, "Oh, wrestler, sir, what are these people saying about you?"

The wrestler said, "Holy Sir, you are all-knowing. You know that I am a wrestler. I am, in fact, a master of the art, so I am incapable of any sexual performance. My affection for the girl is pure. Because I have lost all sexual capacity I don't even mind carrying her. I love her very much."

Ramanuja said, "I believe you. It is true that the girl is completely safe in your hands. I'll tell you how

to get out of the situation. Why don't you consider
yourself to be the girl? Consider your own eyes to be
her eyes, consider your nose to be her nose, consider
your body to be her body, and love your own Self as
that girl."

The words of Ramanuja sank into his heart and he sat
down on one side. So far he had been looking upon the
girl as someone different from himself. Now he started
identifying himself completely with the girl. He stopped
considering the girl as different from himself.

So why don't you do the same? Instead of considering Baba to be different from you, consider him to be
you, or you to be him. If you become your Baba, then
the question of separation does not arise. It would be
perpetual union.

Kedarnath : *Since I have been here, two Saptahs of the
Hari Ram chant have taken place. During the Saptah
time I had many new experiences, but after the Saptah
I have not been able to recover any of these experiences.
Certain experiences came all of a sudden, but they have
never recurred. What is the reason for this? I have
also felt that the chanting makes it easier for me to control my mind and senses.*

Baba : Why did you let the Saptah slip through your
hands? Why don't you hold it firmly? It is only because
you let the Saptah slip from your mind that you fell
into that condition

I have observed something extremely funny; that is,
those people who apparently go into intense states of
meditation and who have all kinds of kriyas, who shake
their heads violently and do all kinds of things, are
usually the ones who are talking big and saying things
which they don't even understand themselves. During
my secret inspection rounds I have seen that in public
these people make a show of meditation but among themselves they indulge in gossip. So I don't know how
seriously to take your words, whether to believe that
what you are saying is true, or just another pretence.
There are people who claim that they get deeply interest-

ed in chanting, but when they get free time I don't see them chanting, I see them gossiping. I haven't heard you chanting *Hari Rama, Hari Krishna* during your free time. I hear you talking about how the food is cooked in the kitchen, the ingredients, where the visitors put their shoes, what the elephant eats, where the elephant's food comes from, what Venkappa is busy with, and what these other people could be writing about. These are the different themes of your holy satsang. And that doesn't convince me that you are really interested in what you say you are interested in.

People may think that I retire to my room and I am not aware of anything. They are mistaken and don't know that I watch each little detail. Don't think that I am meditating all the time on my Self. I can also meditate on you and what's happening in the Ashram, and I can see very clearly how a certain person who happens to be writing, dozes off in the middle of writing, leans back and has a comfortable sleep. I am also aware exactly what people are doing.

I don't see people sitting in silence, indrawn. If you have really begun to enjoy the inner nectar, I find it hard to understand how your taste for it can decrease. Those poor fellows who are not able to meditate keep quiet, because they do not know that they are not able to meditate. It is only those who seem to be meditating intensely, who talk in a certain manner about meditation, who seem to be the most perturbed, the most agitated about various things.

One who has genuine interest in the divine name, in chanting, would not be a chatterbox. And a chatterbox would never be able to enjoy the nectar of the divine name. There is no point in just saying that you are having a certain experience. You should really have that experience. And if you are having that experience, if you are really sipping the inner nectar, there would be complete contentment, so much so that you would become silent and still and all actions would fall away from you.

Talk less. Don't sit for satsang with others. Do not

5

listen to anyone talking ill of others. What makes you
think that malicious gossip is as nectarean as the divine
name? Therefore, repeat the name intensely. Those who
repeat the divine name should glide into inner silence
spontaneously. For these people, taking a vow of silence
is not at all necessary. In the future, talk less and
remain by yourself. Do not sit with others and gossip,
because wrong company can be very harmful. Even if
you were exchanging good words, at least for that time
you would be keeping yourself deprived of the divine
name.

July 21, 1972

Shyama : *On Guru Purnima, the devotees of the Siddha
Yoga Dham in Delhi are installing the Guru sandals and
celebrating the occasion. In the context of this celebration, please talk about the Guru, the Guru sandals and
Guru Purnima.*

Baba : How do you know how the Delhi devotees are
going to worship the Guru sandals and how they are
going to celebrate the occasion? It is not only in Delhi
that they will be celebrating Guru Purnima—Guru
Purnima will be celebrated in so many places in Maharashtra, Gujarat, Karnataka, and even in England and
America, and we shall receive reports about these celebrations later on. You are in Ganeshpuri, and how Guru
Purnima will be celebrated in Ganeshpuri you will be
able to see for yourself. You will also be able to see
for yourself what its importance is, and what devotion
the devotees express here. It is not enough to just hear
about devotion to the Guru and then let those words
melt into thin air. This is surely not your first Guru
Purnima. So many Guru Purnimas have passed.

This question is like the story of the 100 Bhishmas of India, which goes like this : The *Mahabharata* was ended and Bhishma, the great hero, was going to leave his body in a most wonderful, noble manner.

Lord Krishna asked him, "Do you want anything from Me?"

Bhishma said, "Lord, one who is born dies, and one who dies must be born again. As long as one does not receive Your grace, this process of birth and death goes on indefinitely. It is only after receiving Your grace that this process comes to an end."

Krishna asked him again, "Please ask Me for something."

Bhishma said, "What shall I ask You for? If you are so insistent, then I will ask for one favour: that You cremate my body according to Hindu rites, but cremate it in a spot where no other body has ever been cremated."

Krishna said, "That's very easy, you may leave your body now."

Bhishma then recited a hymn consisting of one hundred verses. This is a very great hymn, full of praise for the Lord, and it contains ritual, devotion and knowledge. I am going to repeat only one verse here: "He in whom this world is, He from whom this world comes, He who has made this world, He by whom this world has come into existence, He to whom everything here belongs, I bow to Him."

Reciting the one hundred verses in this manner he left his body. In our country, after somebody has left his body, not too much fuss is made about the body. Now that Bhishma had left his body, they decided to cremate the body and they carried it to a distant spot to make sure that they would cremate it where no other body had been cremated. The moment they put the body down, the earth said, "Wait! One hundred Bhishmas have already been cremated here."

They took the body to another spot and when they were about to cremate it there, again the voice of the earth said, "Don't cremate it here, because one hundred Bhismas have been cremated here also."

This way they tried all the spots in all directions and wherever they went they heard the same voice saying the same words to them. This is exactly the case with the Delhi celebration. It happens every year.

Visitor: *What is the importance of Ekadasi in the month of Ashad, and how should it be observed?*

Baba: Ekadasi is a day which is especially sacred to the Vaishnavas. On this day they remember the Lord every moment. On this day one should observe silence for twenty-four hours and remember Lord Vishnu. One should fast, or not eat more than once in twenty-four hours. Tukaram Maharaj says, "This is the path to Vaikuntha."

This is not a question for the question and answer session. If you wish to know about if fully, you should read the *Puranas*. It will take you at least ten days to read all that is said about Ekadasi. The Ekadasi celebration mainly implies complete silence for twenty-four hours, fasting and remembrance of the Lord. Here, also, we are observing Ekadasi tomorrow. Every month we have two Ekadasi days. Many people observe these days, but in our Ashram we observe only two of them a year. One is tomorrow, and the other is Mahashivaratri day. On Ekadasi, people don't eat grain. And in the name of fasting, they eat so much that it lasts them for at least four days. So in the name of Ekadasi they become sick. Sometimes somebody comes to me and tells me that he got an acute headache due to observing Ekadasi. And I say, "People go to heaven after observing Ekadasi, and here you are, down with a headache."

In Pandharpur, on every Ekadasi everyone there has to get a cholera injection. Isn't it a strange irony that on Ekadasi one should be forced to get a cholera injection? Cholera is a disease which results from overeating. Your stomach is full and yet you eat more. You get dysentery, and still you eat more. The dysentery becomes worse and yet you insist on eating more. And that is how you get cholera. Isn't it surprising that on a day on which one is supposed to discipline oneself, one is supposed to follow very strict restraint and silence, on that very day one should get sick and contract a horrible disease?

It generally rains continuously this month and even if it isn't raining, the influence is in the atmosphere, as a result of which the gastric fire becomes weak. On this day, in the name of the Ekadasi celebration, people make very rich and heavy sweets, particularly from milk: they make barfi from cream, and gulab jamans. If you happen to be a Babaji, if you happen to be a renunciant, you may be fed first with malai barfi, followed by gulab jamans, and on top of that you get peda, which is another concentrated milk sweet, and so on. The devotees are very keen that Babaji should partake of the prasad offered by each one of them, as a result of which poor Babaji is compelled to put more and more into his stomach. Layer after layer of sweets get deposited in the stomach, and it is Baba who is the first casualty, who gets dysentery.

But on Ekadasi you are not supposed to eat too much and contract dysentery and get laid up in bed. On the contrary, you are expected to observe restraint and remember the Lord. On this sacred day you are supposed to eat very little, and what you eat is supposed to be pure and easily digestible, sattvic food. There is one variety of rice which is generally cooked on this day. We shall also cook it tomorrow. It is very easy to digest. Then we prepare a vegetable dish from sweet potato. That kind of rice does not contain any sugar, and the necessary sugar is obtained from the sweet potato. Our rishis were very scientific in their outlook, and even when they laid down certain restrictions they had definite scientific reasons for them. Tomorrow you shouldn't have any breakfast, and you should eat very little lunch—no more than half the amount you normally eat. At night you should chant intensely and dance. And eat supper only if it is absolutely necessary; the best thing is to avoid it. Pious people generally don't take supper. You have been eating for so many days, and if you don't eat for a day, it won't make any difference to you. On this day you owe your digestive organs some rest. By this time they must be awfully tired. Your stomach must be tired of digesting all that you put into it, and your anus must be tired of excreting all the shit that you manufacture. Give some rest to your inner organs at least for a day. All of you are so keen on having a holiday, you want a holiday, you want free time, you want a holiday at least once a week. People are clamouring for more and more holidays a month, more holidays a year. If you have worked for three hours, then you want two hours rest. Imagine the poor condition of your digestive and excretory organs. The poor things work constantly and have been working for years and years without any rest. One day, in sheer disgust, they also decide to go on strike, and the result is many visits to the bathroom.

So on Ekadasi you should eat very little and sleep very little and chant as much as you can. That is the proper manner of observing Ekadasi. Celebrating Ekadasi does not mean eating excessively and sleeping excessively and forgetting the Lord altogether. Ekadasi has great importance. Nowadays, of course, people are losing faith in it. On Ekadasi a special fair is held in Pandharpur which attracts about five hundred thousand to a million people. On the following day people eat their lunch early, after offering it to the Lord, and that is how the Ekadasi fast ends.

Rajen : *What should a seeker do to approach a woman as a mother?*

Baba : Everyone, whether he is a seeker or not, should look upon women with great respect. If you don't have reverence for women, and the Hindi word is nari, the same nari becomes mari, and mari means pestilence or plague. If you don't have respect for women, they turn into a plague and eat you up. That is what the scriptures say. If you have respect and reverence for women, then you insure your progress in every way. It doesn't matter whether you are a seeker or worldly person. Respect and reverence for women means prosperity, progress, and every good thing. But if you lose your respect and reverence for women, if you begin to look upon them with disrespect, with lustful eyes, that is the worst kind of death. You don't have to be killed by poison or by a bullet, or by some other method. Loss of respect or reverence for woman is the worst kind of death.

There was a great Siddha purusha called Basavanna, and his fame had spread so much that a certain king had given his throne to him. It is said that Lord Shiva used to visit him every day in the guise of an ordinary human being. Akkamahadevi was a disciple of Basavanna, and when he became king she came to his court one day. She met him in a manner which surprised the courtiers and which made them cast a lustful glance at her. Then Basavanna composed a verse, and it is about women. *Mukteshwari* has been written in the same style. Basavanna says in his verse, "When woman is pleased, she is Mahadevi; when woman is displeased, no pestilence is worse. Therefore look upon women with respect and reverence."

Our scriptures carry a commandment for brahmacharis, and that is, "Keep away from woman because she is fire. If you go near her she will burn you."

If you have discrimination, then from looking at yourself, you can get an idea of what a woman is. Then you don't have to ask a question about it. Shall I quote some spicey verses? I can assure you that they won't make you laugh. You may have to turn your head away. A man should realise that a woman has a body just like him. From a look at your own body, you can have an idea of what the body of a woman is like. "Man should first look at himself, then he would get a very clear idea of what a woman is like. She is just like you." This Sanskrit verse occurs in the *Upanishads*. A seer says, "This body excretes stinking waste matter through nine different openings, and this waste matter is of the sort which nobody would like to retain inside. When this is the truth of the body, then what is there so fascinating, so attractive, that forces you to become a slave to it?"

What is there so interesting, or so fascinating about the

body? The body is full of all kinds of waste matter, it is full of all kinds of impurities and filth; even you wouldn't like the filth which is in your own body. A body looks tolerable because it is adorned, but if the adornments were taken away, it would be absolutely horrid, you wouldn't be able to bear it. Sunderdas says, "The body is full of dirt and filth, and is like a mountain of disease and ailments. Sometimes it gets pain in the stomach, sometimes in the head, sometimes in the behind, and it is always excreting filthy fluids from different outlets. And sometimes you pass the most foul gas through the other end, nauseating everyone else. This body is full of disease, it is full of impurities. It begins to suffer from various respiratory troubles. Sometimes the breath begins to move too fast, and at other times you find it difficult to breathe. What is, after all, so attractive about the body?"

If you realise the truth of your own body, that is, to see it as the dwelling place of filth, of disease, then you would be able to realise the truth of every other body.

And if you look upon every body this way, then you would find nothing in a mere body to attract you. After all, what happiness can you get from this body?

So far we have done one stanza. Shall I give you the next stanza? I read these verses when I was a young boy, long ago during the time of my sadhana, and it was such verses that saved me. Sunderdas says that people think that they can get tremendous happiness through the body, and under that illusion they go after other bodies, making friends with them. The body is a mere skeleton of bones through which different fluids are flowing—blood and bile and other fluids. You may open it at any point and it is only one of these fluids which will shoot forth. This is the truth of the body: the body is nothing but a bag full of waste matter, full of stinking fluids and disease.

If you are able to assimilate this truth of your own body, you will be able to look upon every other body with the same attitude. Such understanding would bring peace and you would be able to meditate calmly. If you

wish to be redeemed, then you must have respect for
women, and you must also be fully aware of the truth
of the body of a woman. Only the day before yesterday
somebody said to me, "Babaji, my ego is tormenting me
very much. What should I do?"

I said, "What in you is so great? Have you ever tried
to make yourself aware of the truth of what you call you?
Look at your body bit by bit and find out what's in
it to feel proud of. Do you take pride in your bones,
your bloodstream, bile or phlegm? The nails you discard
periodically? The hair you shave off from time to time?
What in you can you feel so proud of?"

And this silenced him. There is nothing in the body
to admire, take pride in, or identify yourself with. I
would certainly admire you if you were to identify yourself with the awareness *aham brahmasmi*, I am Brahman,
I am the Supreme Being.

Visitor : *What should I do to develop self-confidence? I
lack self-confidence very much and if sometimes I become
confident it vanishes very quickly, and because of this
my personality is not developing.*

Baba : The essence of the philosophy of this Ashram is:
"Look to your Self first, worship your Self first, honour
your Self first, meditate on your Self first." And the
cause of lack of confidence is a wrong understanding of
your own Self. Lack of confidence is nothing short of
suicide: it is the worst obstacle in one's path. The cause
of lack of self-confidence is that you do not know anything about the Self, while you know so much about
what is not-Self. Unfortunately, one's sense of Self is
confined only to the body. One identifies himself with
the body which is made of flesh, and it is because of
this identification that one tries to adorn the body all
the time, to make it look attractive. Get beyond the
body and try to find the true nature of the Self. The
only purpose of coming to the Ashram is to acquire true
knowledge of the Self, to meditate on the Self, to explore
the inner world. Otherwise there is nothing in this
Ashram which could fascinate you. Here we don't have

any of the recreation or entertainment that you find in the outside world; and whatever seems to be interesting in the outside world is not valued here. If you come here you are obviously coming here to find your own truth. You should ask your own mother, who is constantly immersed in a meditative state, and she will be able to tell you what exactly the state of the Self is, and how much joy and beauty is inside.

The Ashram exists only to enable you to meditate on the Self, to explore the Self and to have faith in the Self. Continue to meditate. If you don't have any confidence in yourself, you lose confidence in others also, and your life is deprived of any quality.

Ved Amma : *Baba, you once said that meditation which you get by means of your own effort doesn't have much to it, that only spontaneous meditation is really meaningful and significant. If one hasn't received spontaneous meditation, what should he do to progress?*

Baba : As long as you do not receive spontaneous meditation you should continue to make a strong effort to meditate. Once you have received it, effort would be out of place. There are two kinds of meditation. The first kind of meditation is that which is inspired by Chiti, by the inner awakening, by divine power. The other is the kind of meditation which you try to get into by using your will power, by effort. And that kind of meditation only shows a state of bondage. It is not difficult to receive spontaneous meditation.

What is the purpose of meditation after all? You meditate in order to remove from your mind all those thoughts and images which are undesirable. You are already meditating on the wrong sort of things. In which school did you learn to meditate in that manner? From which guru did you get initiation into that form of meditation? And from which guru did you receive 'Shaktipat' for this? You accept ordinary words with faith and respect, and these words keep vibrating in your mind for hours and hours and days and days. So why don't you accept what is said about meditation, true meditation, with the same respect? How long would it take then to get into spontaneous meditation? You are caught up in so many worldly things, and your mind dwells on those things all the time. Who taught you to do that? Man accepts ordinary words, words springing from a state of bondage. He embraces them intensely, as a result of which he meditates on them all the time, and these ordinary words take the place of *aham brahmasmi*. You don't have to make an effort to get worldly thoughts in your mind. They come and throb and vibrate on their own, spontaneously. You don't have to go to school to learn the art of filling your mind with all kinds of thoughts. When you don't have to do anything special to learn that, there is no need to learn how to get spontaneous meditation either. All you have to do is move towards it naturally, just as you have become absorbed in the world. Make your heart pure, follow the path shown by the Guru and have faith in your Self, and I would like to see how spontaneous meditation does not come then.

July 28, 1972

Veena : *What is the need of other Gurus in the life of one who is truly devoted to his own Guru?*

Baba : If we understood the true meaning of devotion we would realise that the essence of devotion is the lack of promiscuity, that is, absolute fidelity, absolute loyalty. Only single-minded loyalty and devotion bear fruit. One who is promiscuous in his devotional affiliation may find it very pleasant externally, but it would not do him any good. Sunderdas says, "A person who is promiscuous in his devotion gets neither respect not any attainment."

Promiscuity does not only mean sleeping with a number

of women or having contact with professionals. Promiscuity means giving your allegiance to more than one thing at a time. Promiscuity seems to be inherent in the very nature of the mind and the senses. The mind wants to give allegiance to so many different systems, so many different paths, so many different teachers. Our sense organs are promiscuous. It is the very nature of our eyes to keep wandering from one object to another. It is the very nature of our ears to wander from one sound to another. And it is the very nature of the tongue to keep talking about one thing and another. The mind and the senses seem to be hopeless victims of promiscuity. You can get a fairly good cup of tea at the neighbouring canteen, but it is because of promiscuity that some people go to Ganeshpuri to have a cup of tea. Then after Ganeshpuri, they go to Vajreshwari and after Vajreshwari to Bassein, and then to a big restaurant in Bombay. I know of many girls here who go to Bombay only to indulge in promiscuity of the palate. They go to Bombay, not because they have work to attend to, but because they want to have a couple of days in ease and sense gratification. This is promiscuity of the stomach and the palate seeking different tastes. Promiscuity is not confined just to one sense; it seizes every sense. And because our sense organs are always mating with their objects promiscuously, it has a very bad effect on the mind. All kinds of impressions are being implanted in the mind, as a result of which the mind loses its peace. I becomes disturbed and agitated.

The devotion that one feels in the mind should express itself in all the senses. Tukaram Maharaj says, "He is a true devotee whose sole object of sense enjoyment is Narayana." That means that your eyes should only want to see the divine form, the form of the Lord, your ears should only want to hear the sound of the divine name. Only two days ago we had a two-day chant here and the chant was broadcast over the loud-speakers the whole day and most of the night. It must have cost us between fifty and a hundred rupees a day in electricity alone. Yet I know that there were people who deprived

themselves, at least for some time, of the divine name.
They kept themselves engaged in talking all kinds of
nonsense, and in hearing all kinds of meaningless chatter,
insignificant, utterly worthless sounds. That is not how
one should participate in a Saptah.

Similarly, your tongue should want to taste only the
divine nectars, the inner nectars. The nose should want
to smell only the fragrance of the Lord, the inner frag-
rances. So let your inner Self become your sole friend.
Let your sense of smell inhale the inner perfumes alone.
Let the eyes see the inner beauty alone. Let the ears hear
the inner sounds alone. That is what true devotion is.
Jnaneshwar Maharaj, while defining unpromiscuous
devotion, says that it exists "Only when a devotee forces
his sense organs to write their letter of resignation." In
other words, a true devotee is he who has renounced his
senses.

Unfortunately, most of us, rather than renouncing the
senses embrace them, feed them and strengthen them all
the time. It appears as though we have signed a bond
of friendship until death with them. But, Jnaneshwar
says, "It is only a devotee who has renounced the senses,
who has discarded all cravings, all desires, who, becoming
the Lord, enjoys the Lord. Such a devotee alone is truly
loyal, unpromiscuous." And this applies to devotion to
the Guru also.

On several previous occasions I have told you the story
of those very clever disciples who ran away with the
frying pan instead of the stick which made gold. If
such disciples had never come to the Guru, no harm
would have been done. They would not have lost anything. And if they had run away with the stick instead
of the frying pan, I wouldn't have minded. There was
a Guru who was an alchemist. He knew how to turn
base metals into gold. As his fame spread, more and
more students or aspirants were drawn to him. They
all wanted to learn that secret. But no science, whether
it is alchemy or some other science, can be learned
instantly. To learn any science or other knowledge takes
a certain length of time and you have to serve the Guru

with utmost devotion. It is only then that you get the
secret. Even if the Guru were to give you the secret,
if you haven't served him, if you haven't been with him
for a certain period of time, that secret would not bear
any fruit.

There were two students who were very clever among
the crowd of aspirants who were following this Guru.
One day the Guru asked them to roast some grain in a
frying pan. They put it in the pan and began to stir
it with a stick. That was the stick that turned base
metal into gold. As they were stirring they were also
gossiping, and they were so absorbed in their chatter
that for quite some time they did not notice that the
brass frying pan was turning into gold. After some time
their attention was pulled away from their gossip, and
they found that the pan had turned into gold. They
were so excited, so elated, that they forgot to behave
rationally, and they threw the miraculous stick into the
fire and picked up the pan and ran with it, leaving the
stick behind to burn in the fire.

So, if you have been able to get a little Shakti, what
makes you feel that you have attained everything and
you can afford to run away with it, leaving the miraculous stick?

Then why become attached to Guruhood? Being a
Guru, too, is an addiction with most people. Just as
people are addicted to chattering, they are addicted to
so many other things, and they get addicted to playing
the role of the Guru. Guruhood should come to you
naturally. You should not run after it, making yourself
utterly miserable in the process. For a true Gurubhakta,
even the thought of turning to other Gurus is promiscuous. Even an assistant Guru, until he has received a
very clear command from the Guru to start serving as
Guru, is also being promiscuous when he starts to play the
role of Guru. As long as my Guru was alive, nobody
knew me. People did not even know my name, I
would not even tell people that I was Muktananda.
If anyone asked me a question, I would not make any
attempt to answer, I would only ask that person to

remember Nityananda and thereby he would get the answer. Nityananda is as alive today as he ever was, and wherever I go he appears to me in meditation and gives me messages. When Nityananda was in his physical form, when he could talk to other people himself, it would have been utterly stupid on my part to say things on his behalf, to go around lecturing or to start serving as Guru in his place. When the Guru himself is alive, when the Guru himself is capable of taking care of all the disciples that come to him, what's the role of an assistant Guru, or of a sub-Guru? When the time comes, and you receive the command to serve as a Guru from your Guru, then you will be effective like no one has ever been. You know we receive reports from the centres being run by seekers. Quite a few come to me and ask how to run the centre, and I tell them they don't have to worry about it, they just have to get a place and the centre will run itself. A true Guru does not have to give explicit instructions about how a centre should be run, because behind the true Guru stands the divine power. It is the divine power which looks after everything and which makes all the centres run. Of course, people can help each other.

For many years people in Ganeshpuri thought that I was a fool, that I was an idiot, that I didn't know anything. I didn't read a single book. They thought I was an utterly ignorant lout, because all they would see me do was sit for a few hours and perhaps doze off and go away when Nityananda told me to go away. That was all that I would do there, nothing more. I never went very near my Guru, I never asked him anything. People in Ganeshpuri thought that I was good for nothing and they gave me up. Now, of course, they are repenting. At that time they thought that I had absolutely no worth and I was incapable of doing anything.

And this is exactly what happens in so many cases. If you have true worth you don't make a show of it. You don't wear it on your sleeve to dazzle every fool. If you have true worth you will always keep it concealed. If you are fond of display, you will only be displaying

worthless things, things which have no value. You will
be trying to make a display of the qualities which you
are supposed to possess, but which you don't possess
even in your dreams. There are so many women who
come here from Bombay, and I see some of them wearing
what look like quite heavy gold necklaces. And I ask
them "Why are you wearing such rich necklaces?"
They say, "Babaji, we are not worried at all, because
this isn't genuine gold, this is imitation gold. If we lose
them we won't lose much." Then other women come
whose ears are bare and I ask them why they don't wear
their earrings, and they tell me that these days the
trains are so packed, there is the danger of someone
snatching their earrings. And since those earrings are
made of genuine gold, solid gold, they prefer to keep
them hidden at home. Genuine gold is hidden at home,
whereas false gold is worn around the neck to impress
every indiscriminate fool. I have such boys and girls
here who have so much power that all they need is a
hint from me, and they would revolutionize the whole
world. And people would wonder where they got so much
radiance, so much power. But they keep it all concealed;
they do not keep it on display. It is said about Kalidas that
all his servants were great poets like him—the man who
washed his clothes was a poet, the maid who cooked his
food was a poet, the boy who swept his floors was a poet.
And exactly the same is the situation here. The girl who
cooks my food is a great yogini, the girl who sweeps
for me is a great yogini, the boy who washes my toilet
is a great yogi. And there are so many other great yogis
and yoginis here. When the time comes they will do
most wonderful work in the world, and everybody will
begin to wonder how so much divine power was kept
hidden for such a long time.

He who is sincerely interested in the true worship of
his Guru does not have to turn to other Gurus. In fact,
this is a rudimentary thing which everyone should understand. Those who are true Gurubhaktas will find that
their devotion to the Guru will affect even stones, water,
birds, animals, trees and plants. And they have abso-

lutely no need to turn to sub-Gurus and sub-sub-Gurus and their assistants. They have absolutely no need to turn to sectarian gurus, or to gurus who are a mere mockery.

There is absolutely no need for anyone to run after Guruhood. What you need is to make yourself more and more worthy as time goes by, and the status of the Guru will come to you itself. In fact, it will come running after you. Have more love in your heart. Have more love for everyone. Do not increase attachment, increase love. You should increase your love so much that your heart becomes absolutely soaked in it. By the force of love you should be able to eliminate all the wickedness and hatred from your heart. Then you would learn not to harbour feelings of revenge towards anyone. A Sadguru will never seek revenge on anyone.

You should make yourself keenly aware of the true nature of Kundalini. Kundalini is pure consciousness. In other words, Kundalini is pure love, and you should see how much of Her love has been manifested within you. First become your own supreme Guru. First make your heart absolutely pure. If you have nothing, if you are a pauper, if you are utterly penniless, what's the point of trying to give liberally to others? If you yourself are a burden on yourself, if you think that you yourself are the greatest misfortune for yourself, what's the point of trying to lead others, to guide them, to serve as their Guru? If you are lacking in yourself then what can you give to others? Love should be realised in abundance in the heart, and if you are still cruel, if you are still insensitive, it means that you are not even a seeker, it means that you are a wicked, depraved person.

My Guru was absolutely pure, and if he expressed what appeared to other people to be attachment or aversion, it was only appearance. If he happened to abuse somebody, that anger would not last, and when that person would return, he would find Baba all smiles, lovingly asking him, "When did you come? How are you?"

On the other hand, you have sub-Gurus who would not forgive even their mothers for yelling at them for

6

eating mud when they were children. They keep the
memory of this single act of cruelty on their mother's
part alive throughout their life and they keep complaining and grumbling all the time that their mother was
so unkind to them, that she behaved in such a manner.
What kind of Guruhood is this? What worth does this
kind of attitude show?

You should not assume Guruhood, nor should you be
play-acting as a Guru. You should have so much worth
that people begin to look upon you and look up to you
as their Guru by themselves. People, when they see you,
when they talk to you, should bow their heads to you
spontaneously, without any bullying on your part.
Acquire true Guruhood within yourself by filling your
heart with love. There is absolutely no worth in the
kind of Guruhood which is a mere show, which is a mere
affectation. Let true Guruhood grow in you spontaneously.

There was a time when people in Ganeshpuri asked
me where Muktananda Swami was, and how he lived
and how he spent his days. I would conceal myself to
that extent. I would not even wear saffron clothes while
going to Ganeshpuri. I would roll up my saffron clothes
in a bundle and go to Ganeshpuri incognito so that I
would not be pestered by people there. The more
anonymous I stayed in those days, the more famous I
seem to be becoming now. The fame that seems to be
coming to me today seems to be in direct proportion to
the anonymity which I assumed at that time. If pure
love arises in your heart, you won't have to depend on
anybody outside you, because that pure love is also perfect contentment, that pure love will keep you immersed
in its own depths all the time. If you are without love,
what's the point of your assuming Guruhood? And what's
the worth of that Guruhood?

There are so many wild beasts in the forest. Can you
call them renunciants because they are living in the
forest? The true mark of a renunciant is that love and
serenity keep flowing from all his senses all the time.
If peace and love do not flow from him all the time, he

is not a true renunciant, he is only play-acting. Now take the case of our elephant, Vijayananda. Who could beat Vijayananda in renunciation? He doesn't wear any clothes, he doesn't ask for food, he only eats when he is given something to eat. Most of you, if you don't get anything to eat for some time would start complaining, and if you have to remain hungry for two days, you would like at least this much to be known to the Guru— that you have not eaten for two days, even if you are not making a demand. But that information is only a veiled demand. You are trying to convey to him that you are starving and need food and that it should be given to you.

Without love, without serenity, without peace, Guru-hood is a mere sham. Love and attachment are absolutely different from each other. Attachment depends on the body; it is related to the body, and whatever depends on the body, whatever is related to the body cannot be real, cannot be genuine. Pure love springs directly from the inner Self, and it has no desire in it, no craving, no self-seeking in it. It is a pure expression of the inner Self. Stop taking pride in things relating to others. Stop taking pride in things which are purely relative. For instance, if you take pride in being a great renunciant, then you are no better than a sensualist, you are only the big brother of a sensualist. There may be hope of redemption for the sensualist, but there is no hope for you, because through your brand of renunciation you are only trying to accede to the throne of pleasure and enjoyment. Bhogi and yogi are relative terms. Bhogi has meaning only in relation to yogi and yogi has meaning only in relation to bhogi. A bhogi is a pleasure-seeker. What, after all, is so valuable in the external world? What is there in your body to feel proud of? This body is only full of filth, so what is there in the body to elate you? What is there in wealth to elate you?

For a true Gurubhakta, there is absolutely no need for other Gurus, and if there is a need, it is nothing but promiscuity. In America it may be quite accepted to have a boyfriend other than your husband or a girl-friend other than your wife, but that fortunately does not prevail here. Another Guru can at best be a boy-friend or a girlfriend to you. He can't be a Guru. You may be promiscuous, but you won't gain anything by that promiscuity. A prostitute who sells her flesh is better than a devotee who is promiscuous in his devotion. It is true that the Lord used to ply the grinding wheel for Janabai. It is true about Eknath Maharaj that the Lord Himself used to draw water for him. He drew water for him because of his absolute devotion to his Guru, Janardan Swami. I am very fond of the fort where Eknath Maharaj used to live and I used to spend long periods of time there, and whenever I go there I feel very strange stirrings within me, and I will certainly make another visit to that place. Eknath Maharaj says in a verse of his, with a ring of absolute finality, "The Guru's name alone is all my *Vedas* and all my scriptures. It is by the miracle of the dust of my Guru's feet that all my work is accomplished automatically." He goes on to say, "The mudra of meditation of my Guru is my yogic sleep."

There are different mudras of meditation. You must have seen Nityananda Baba in his typical mudra, in which his eyes are half-open; the lids don't blink, but he is not looking at anything. So a true Gurubhakta would not try to get yogic sleep through yogic practices. It would be enough for him to keep looking at the Guru's dhyan mudra and that would automatically produce profound yogic sleep in him. In the last line Eknath says, "I had only one mind and I have merged it in the Guru's feet, and that is my supreme attainment."

A true Gurubhakta would be totally loyal to his Guru, and he would be loyal in all senses. Purity or fidelity is not only confined to a certain hole. If you try to practise purity just in relation to a certain hole, and you practise promiscuity in all the other sense organs, in seeing, eating, hearing, smelling, then there is absolute-ly no worth in the other form of fidelity which may be so precious to your heart. A true Gurubhakta is one

who is absolutely loyal to his Guru without the least
compromise, in all his senses, in his mind, in his thought,
in his speech.

August 1, 1972

Rana : *Does one who is meditating very well need to
recite Guru Gita, Vishnu Sahasranam, and chant the
various chants?*

Baba : What does a good meditator do when he is chanting the *Guru Gita, Vishnu Sahasranam* or other chants?
After meditating for one or two hours, what are you
going to do for the rest of the day? Would even a good
meditator be able to meditate like Vyas? It was Vyas
himself who said, "You must never neglect swadhyaya,"
that is, chanting. If after meditating well for one or
two hours you doze off during swadhyaya, what's the use?
On the contrary, the samadhi which is induced by the
hearing of the sacred mantras should come very easily
to a good meditator. The *Guru Gita* recitation in particular will help you meditate far more deeply; it will not
take you away from meditation.

What do you understand by chanting, and where does
your mind get focused in good meditation? Doesn't it
get focused on God? That is exactly what is happening
in chanting. The effect of meditation may not last that
long, but chanting keeps you intoxicated the whole day.
And from that point of view, chanting is even more
effective than meditation. There are so many so-called
yogis who complain that their lives are without joy,
their hearts are dry and they haven't attained anything,
and that is because they are practising yoga and neglecting chanting. If you meditate and neglect chanting,
then your heart will remain as dry as wood. The medita-

tion scriptures say that a seeker should do japa for a
very long period of time with perfect faith and reverence,
being fully aware of the meaning of the mantra and of
the goal of the mantra. Patanjali enjoins a seeker to do
japa with true respect and reverence, with spontaneous
love. A seeker shouldn't do japa simply because Baba
insists on it so much, or because the Ashram discipline
demands it. The japa which you do under compulsion
won't do much good. Japa should come spontaneously
from the heart and it should be done with true respect
and reverence. It is because a seeker doesn't want to
chant, or doesn't like to chant with reverence, that his
heart becomes dry after some time and he loses his joy;
and after some time he wouldn't even be able to meditate.

Chanting and swadhyaya raise a seeker to a state
which is beyond the mind. Moreover, swadhyaya is a
very important aspect of our Ashram life. The Vedic
seers have declared with absolute firmness, "Never
neglect swadhyaya, never forget it." What do you do
during swadhyaya after all? Even during swadhyaya you
get into a state of shravan samadhi, that is samadhi which
is induced by the sound of the mantras. Swadhyaya is
our way of honouring the great primordial, supreme Guru.
Goraknath, Matsyendranath, and Jnaneshwar Maharaj
were among the greatest yogis, and yet in the end they
all turned to the divine name, and they found the divine
name most nectarean and joyful. What do you do during swadhyaya besides meditate? Isn't swadhyaya also
a form of meditation? Eknath Maharaj, who was a
disciple of Janardan Swami—and Janardan Swami had
received initiation right from Dattatreya, the divine
Guru, not from any human Guru—Eknath, the disciple
of that great Siddha, says, "One who gets immersed in
chanting becomes divine, becomes God Himself."

Do you think that the samadhi state is better than the
divine state? If the tongue keeps chanting the name of
Hari, the mind transcends itself, and the experience of
the mind transcending itself goes further than even
samadhi. As a result of chanting, one becomes so immersed in the divine name that he doesn't see any

distinctions such as high, low or medium, or worldly and spiritual. A bhakta sees his Lord, Narayana, in everything, everywhere. Such is the magic of chanting. Such is the influence of chanting that one becomes pure both within and without. I wonder why you don't experience the great power of chanting? A mind which gets bored with chanting and only likes to meditate is utterly impoverished. Such a mind first gets bored with swadhyaya and then it gets bored with other things and finally it even gives up meditation. Even a good meditator needs chanting very much; and chanting is nothing but meditation.

I would like to know what the experience of a good meditator is in this regard. Can you get out of a meditative state if you have really got into it? For Tukaram Maharaj, the yoga of chanting was the supreme method. Once you become immersed in this yoga, it keeps you in a state which remains the same all the time, which is completely independent of time, place or other external factors. Tukaram Maharaj was so immersed in chanting that even while going to the bathroom he would be chanting the name of God. People would get so offended they would throw stones at him. The lower organ is doing its work and the upper sense organ is doing its work. When the lower organ is active, why should the upper organ become inactive? While his lower organ was busy, his tongue would be chanting *Vitthal, Vitthal*, and for that he was persecuted. One day some people got hold of him and said, "You are a very strange character. You are insulting religion. You are insulting the Lord by chanting His name even when you are shitting."

Tukaram Maharaj replied in the most humble manner with folded hands, "I can't help it. I have become such a slave to the divine name, it is no longer in my power to stop it."

Those who are fond of creating trouble will always be thinking of fresh ways to create trouble. So there were four fellows who decided to harass Tukaram. The next day they hid themselves near the spot where he used to relieve himself. As he was sitting down they caught hold of him and gagged his mouth with a piece of cloth saying to him, "Now we'll see how you can chant the divine name during such an unholy activity."

It is said that the body of one who becomes one with God also becomes divine. So after his mouth was tied up, the divine name *Vitthal* began to emanate from every single pore of Tukaram, as a result of which they heard thousands of voices chanting *Vitthal*. Such is the effect of chanting. Chanting releases divine nectar inside and it fills the state of samadhi with its sweetness.

Once your Kundalini has been awakened, once you have begun to meditate, what makes you think the Kundalini will go to sleep again, or that meditation will stop? At a given time you may have an intense phase of kriyas, and at another time the kriyas may not be so gross, they may occur on a more subtle, invisible level.

When a good meditator needs good food, good clothes, good sleep and even gossips and chats with friends, why shouldn't he also need chanting?

Ram : *After one year at Shree Gurudev Ashram I feel that I have learned a lot. However, I feel no more able to control my emotions than before, and I am less meditative than before. I wonder what should be done about it.*

Baba : As far as complete control of emotions is concerned, that happens after a long period of time. And if you have such a temperament that you explode every now and then, you shouldn't worry about it. Try to meditate, try to intensify true meditation and increase it. As your meditation becomes more intense, in course of time your excitability will be much less.

There are only two methods by which you can increase your meditation. First, continuous japa, continuous remembrance of the Lord. And second, intense love for meditation itself. You should love meditation so much that wherever you may be you get into a meditative state, regardless of whether you are sitting for formal meditation or not. One's attention should be constantly focused on the sahasrar or on the heart. One should be constantly roving in the inner world. It is when you begin to wander too much in the external world that your meditation becomes weak.

Kedarnath : *I am witnessing a strange phenomenon. On the one hand there are some people who are young and who come from good families and who consider themselves to be pure and handsome and even strong, but they are absolutely blank with regard to inner attainment, and their hearts are callous. On the other hand, there are people who have come from distant places and who do not consider themselves to be pure, and whose past lives might not have been so good either, yet they seem to have some inner attainment. How do you explain this?*

Baba : One will always fall lower and lower if one begins to consider oneself important and take pride in things which relate to the body. It is good to consider yourself to be great with regard to your inner Self, but not with regard to your body or externals. One may come from a very good family, be very bright in his appearance, and possess all the outer advantages. All that relates to the body. Somebody came here the other day and asked me what I thought of the body, the body which is such a beautiful creation, and I said, "There are so many mills in Bombay. One mill manufactures cloth, another manufactures utensils, and a third manufactures something else. Likewise, the body is a factory which manufactures shit."

If you begin to consider yourself to be great because of your body, then that consciousness becomes an impediment. You won't be able to meditate, you won't be able to perceive the Guru, you won't be able to engage yourself in good and noble deeds, you won't even be able to do swadhyaya. In the *Shrimad Bhagavat Purana*, you find that the wives of the great seers and sages had direct visions of the Lord, while their husbands didn't have any spiritual experiences. The reason was that the husbands were always conscious of their purity and

status, thinking, "I am such a great brahmin. I am
practising all the holy rituals. I am so great, I come
from such a noble family." And it was this consciousness, this pride which kept them away from the Lord.
It is an illusion to consider oneself great with regard
to one's body.

If one is conscious of the body all the time, if one takes
pride in things relating to the body, then one's identification with the body will become stronger and stronger.
And if your identification with the body becomes
stronger, how can you meditate? How can you attain
higher spiritual states? For meditation, for higher
attainments, you need to break your identification with
the body completely. Various kinds of people came to
my Guru. There were some who thought that they were
great and were proud of themselves, and quite conceited.
And they would look down on the other devotees coming
to my Guru. They thought that those other devotees
were low-born, that their actions were impure, and that
they were good for nothing. But time proved something
quite different. In the end, the so-called low-born, the
so-called impure people gave up everything, became good
renunciants, and attained the divine state, while the ones
who were proud of being born of such high families and
of their status are still in the same position, counting
coins at their hotel counters.

There is nothing more purifying than repentance, than
a sincere feeling of remorse, nothing, not even regular
baths, not even holy rituals can purify you as much as
sincere remorse. In the *Gita* also the Lord says, "Even
those who are born in sinful wombs, who are considered
to be utterly unworthy and downtrodden, become one
with Me if they repent." It is because these people have
nothing to take pride in. It is pride, conceit, which
brings the complete downfall of a person. There is
nothing worse than pride.

In the *Bhagavat* there is a very good story, the story
of Gajendra, the king elephant. In spite of enormous
strength, he was losing a fight with a crocodile. It was
only when he became free from the consciousness of his

own strength and utterly humble, and remembered the Lord, that the Lord Himself appeared there and helped him.

Humility, lack of pride, is the greatest quality. If you are proud of your family or your status, that pride will obstruct your meditation and all your other spiritual practices. The name of the teacher who taught me Vedanta is Muppinarya Swami. I used to wash his bathroom and as a result of that I still fully remember whatever I learned from him. Nothing of what he taught me has vanished from my mind. Near Yeola there was a hill called Ankai, and near that hill a vairagi lived. He was an expert in the *Ramayana,* and I wanted to learn the *Ramayana* from him. He said that he would teach me the *Ramayana* on the condition that I did a certain job for him. He had people for all the other jobs: there was only one job for which he didn't have anyone, and that was picking up cow dung. So while I learned the *Ramayana* from him, I picked up cow dung for nine months.

Family pride is the worst obstacle in the path of meditation, the worst obstacle in the path of union with God. One should not be proud of one's body or family, or of the vows he may be observing. If one is conscious of all this, he is only heading towards a decline. However, one should be pure and clean. In your worldly life people may be impressed by your family or by other external factors, but as far as God is concerned, He pays absolutely no attention to your body, to its beauty or to your facial features. He doesn't pay any attention to your sense organs. He only values the feelings in your heart. An Upanishadic seer says that one who considers the body to be his Self is committing a sin equivalent to the slaughter of a million cows.

So this pride in the body is the worst thing that could happen to a person. It is this body-consciousness, this tendency to take pride in things relating to the body which is the worst obstacle in meditation. And not only in meditation, but in every other field. The merit of the consciousness that "I am the Self," is limitless. You

cannot measure it. Nothing that was done in the past can
equal it, and nothing that will be done in the future
can excel it. God only sees your heart and the love in
it. A big-hearted person would never be bothered with
petty things like how many chapatis or fruit salad you
ate at a given meal, or what you were doing at a certain
time. Do not think that God is so petty that He would
be bothered about such things.

What could the Lord lack? What could the inner Self
lack? And what could you give to the Lord or to the
inner Self which would please Him? The Lord does not
need anything. The Lord is perfect in Himself. So the
only thing that could please the Lord is surrender, loving
surrender. There is a Marathi poet, Krishna Suta, who
says in one of his songs, "I can say one thing for certain:
that there is nothing higher than devotion."

In the divine realm, in the realm of meditation, your
family consciousness is of no use, your vows are of no
use, your status is of no use, the power that you wield
is of no use. It is only complete humility, complete surrender and devotion which matter, which will take you
deeper into meditation. Remember that consciousness
of the body, pride of the body, attachment to the body,
will certainly bring about your downfall one day or
another.

This is a very good question. Mainly it is pride of
the body, attachment to the body, identifying with the
body which obstructs meditation. Then there is another
factor in spiritual growth also, and that is faith and
devotion to the inner Self, and the degree of your surrender to the inner Self. The law is that you look at
another exactly the same way you look at yourslf. So
if you look upon yourself as perfect, you will also see
others as perfect. If you look upon yourself as being
divine, you will also see others as divine. But if you
look upon yourself as imperfect, if you evaluate yourself in relation to other things, then you will also evaluate
others the same way. It is good to keep oneself pure
and clean and disciplined. But one should not become
attached to any image of oneself. One should be full

of love, but keep clear of attachment, because attachment and love are absolutely different. One who is attached is always dependent on others, while one who is full of love will never depend on others, because love is complete in itself. The consciousness of one who is attached is limited to his sense organs, while the one who is full of love is aware of the Self all the time. So one should be totally free of attachment, but full of great love. If you become attached, you will fall for certain.

Did I tell you the story of a brahmachari who got married in a dream? I'll narrate that story now. It is a story which has enormous significance. It is like the mantra which should be repeated continuously. You should be aware of it all the time.

Whenever a person becomes attached to his own body he is bound to fall into attachment to other bodies also. He who spreads a net to catch another person gets himself caught in the process. There was a large ashram in the forest, far away from the crowds of the cities, and it was just like the monasteries you have in the West. The ashram was full of celibates, renunciants who were quite proud of their renunciation, of their celibacy. It was summertime and the rains were about to come, and the head of the ashram sent one of the brahmacharis to the town to get the things they would need during the rainy season.

The boy went to the city and made the various purchases. After finishing his work he started looking forward to spending an evening at some rich devotee's place, and he found some devotee where he could get all the pleasures. It was summer, and summer is the season for weddings, and that very evening there was to be a wedding of the children of some wealthy people. The bride and bridegroom had been adorned very richly. The boy saw the wedding procession, which was very grand: there were bands, there were riches all around, and he was greatly impressed with the rich attire, the lights, the jewels, and all the other costly things. The rich devotee was a worshipper of Lakshminarayan, the god of wealth. The celibate said to himself, "It is much better to be a

devotee of Lakshminarayan." He asked a person standing there, "What is this all about?"

That person looked contemptuously at the celibate and
said, "You come from a forest, you live in a God-forsaken
place. How much of the world could you possibly
know? You are only wasting your life away eating plain
food and drinking water and doing practically nothing.
So what could you know about these grand things?"

The celibate was young and impressionable, so the
person he was talking to completely brainwashed him
—so much so that his mind became filled with thoughts
of riches and he became obsessed.

In the morning he packed up his things and went to
his Guru's place. He wasn't a false person. He was
basically very honest, and he gave the Guru the things he
had purchased. After handing over everything he said
to the Guru, "Sir, now I am leaving this place. I am
going to some other ashram because I am feeling quite
bored here. Sir, do not be upset, because soon instead
of one there will be two to serve you."

The Babaji said, "That's very good. I don't mind your
departing, you can leave at once. And I am quite happy
that instead of one there will be two serving me."

The celibate left the ashram. He had spent a long
time in that ashram, and he had become accustomed to
living a life of renunciation. In our country there is
usually a well outside a village. On his way there was
a village and he decided to sleep by the well.

When he lay down he began to think of all that he
would do later, of how he would get married, and how
he would begin to worship Lakshmi, the goddess of
wealth, and return with his wife to the Guru, and these
fantasies elated him. Before going to sleep, instead of
performing mental worship of the Lord, the brahmachari was performing mental worship to the woman he
would marry. As a result of such thoughts he had a
vivid dream, and in that dream he got married. His wife
was very beautiful, and he was trying to make love to
her. The wife, besides being beautiful, was quite proud.
He happened to say something she didn't like, so she

pushed him aside. He tried to persuade her but she pushed him away again. And this time she pushed him so hard that he fell into the well. The well was twenty-five feet deep. And he had to spend the night, not with a woman, but with water creatures in the well. He spent the night groaning from a severe pain in the back, remembering the Guru all the time, and calling him loudly. He thought to himself, "I got married only in a dream, and this is what happened from an unreal wedding. I wonder what would happen if I were to actually get married?"

The brahmachari cried the whole night in the well. In the morning, some women from the village came to draw water. When they saw that somebody had fallen into the well, they began to shout for help. Many people from the village came rushing; they lowered a ladder and pulled him out. Then they asked him, "What happened? How did you fall into the well?"

He told them the truth, "I got married in a dream. I was trying to please my wife while making love to her. She asked me to move aside, and in an effort to oblige her, I moved aside and found myself in the well. Now I have a broken back into the bargain."

This is moha, or attachment. This is not true love. This is attachment to the body. Love is something entirely different. Love will never land you in such a situation. Identification with the body, this 'I' consciousness, is the worst thing. If you lose this self-pride, this self-conceit, you will become absolutely pure. All your sinful and virtuous deeds spring from this sense of 'I'. Once this sense is dissolved, you become absolutely pure. You transcend both sin and virtue, and you become the beloved of the Lord. Jnaneshwar, in his commentary on the eighteenth chapter of the *Gita*, says that ignorance is the root cause of our notions of good and bad, sin and virtue, and identification with the body. If you can discard the root cause, that is, the sense of 'I', then you become completely pure. And once you become completely pure, meditation is not at all difficult, God-realisation is not at all difficult. Krishna Suta, while commenting on this very verse of the *Gita* says,

"One who has committed even the foulest deeds in the
past, if he can embrace the Lord with full devotion,
with full love, all his sins fall away and he becomes
absolutely pure."

It is the consciousness of family, pride, which is such
a bad obstacle. People who suffer from this consciousness sink, but those, even if they do not come from good
families, who are humble, swim across. Keep your body
clean and pure, but do not identify yourself with it.
Do not become attached to it. Surrender it to the Lord.
Do not let your heart remain callous or insensitive. Fill
it with love.

August 4, 1972

Shaun: *Sometimes I find myself to be my own worst
enemy. How can I overcome this tendency?*

Baba: Yes, the Lord says in the *Gita*, "One is one's own
friend, and one is one's own enemy," and this is completely true. Nobody else can be either your friend or
your enemy. It is you yourself who are the cause of
your own progress or downfall. Unfortunately, you
begin to hold others responsible for it. In the *Mahabharata* there is a very important dialogue between
Krishna and Duryodhana, where it is said that nobody
else can give you either happiness or sorrow. If you
feel that somebody else is causing you sorrow, you are
deluding yourself. Similarly, if you feel that somebody
else is giving you happiness, again you are deluding
yourself. It is foolish to think that somebody else is
causing you happiness or pain. You suffer the consequences of your own actions. The poet-saint Krishna
Suta says, "Man has become his own worst enemy. Nobody else is his enemy. He never bothers to find out

why he has come into this world, where he is going, and where he should go, what he is doing and what he should do. By not concerning himself with these questions he remains blind, and it is this blindness which is his worst enemy."

This tendency can be overcome by contemplation of the Self, by right thinking, by thinking about the fundamental questions, "Who am I?" "Why have I come here?" "What is my duty?" "What should I do?" "What should I avoid?" "How can I achieve the highest good?" "What should I avoid in order to escape a downfall?" It is by engaging oneself in these questions that one can cease to be one's own enemy.

Therefore, man should take himself across the ocean of change. He should transcend body-consciousness by right thought, by studying the scriptures, and by finding the truth of the Self through meditation. He who comes to know his own inner Self directly through meditation —the inner Self which is shining as pure knowledge, as pure consciousness in the heart—he is his own best friend. If he doesn't do this, then he passes from death to death. After taking birth in this world man should think about what he has done, what he has been born for, where he has to go, and what he has to achieve in the course of his brief existence. You should be able to expel the various passions which keep arising and subsiding inside, and make friends with your own Self. Begin to value your own Self. Know it. Remain aware of it. Then you will be your own best friend, and you will cross worldliness.

Don: *What is the correct attitude towards self-discipline?*

Baba: After understanding the nature of one's own Self, one should withdraw one's attention from the senses and focus it on the Self. In his present condition, man relies entirely on his senses for happiness, for peace, so much so that he begins to consider his senses his all in all. It is the inner Self which should be the supreme object of all our senses. If the eyes want to see any-

7

thing, let them see the light of the Self. If the ears want
to hear anything, let them hear the music of the Self. If
the tongue wishes to speak, let it speak of the inner
Self. If your hands wish to give or take something, let
them give or take from the inner Self. This should be
your attitude towards self-discipline. True self-discipline implies that you turn all your senses inward and
make the Self the sole object of all your senses. If you
don't do this, you will never be able to find peace by
seeking delight through the senses. Through the senses
one can never find peace. One can only find misery.
As a result of being afflicted with misery, one has to
turn to the inner Self and seek peace and delight there.
Even in ordinary life you get rest only by merging the
senses in some inner centre, either during sleep or during
the dream state or during meditation.

Uma : *What do you mean by a pure heart and a pure
mind?*

Baba : One who has a pure mind and a pure heart has
become fit to be a true temple of the Lord. If you do
not have a pure mind or a pure heart, whatever path
you follow, whatever sect you subscribe to, whatever
views you hold, none of these will be of any use to you;
you are just acting. You are just like the phony Ravana
or the phony Rama that you see during the performance
of the *Ram Lila.* You find a certain character acting
the part of Rama or Ravana, but there is no real Rama
or Ravana. Likewise, if you are without a pure heart
or pure mind, whether you claim to be a bhakta or a
yogi, a jnani or a Guru or a disciple, you are no better
than a mere actor.

If your heart becomes pure then the divine Shakti
will come seeking you, because the divine Shakti is looking for a proper home, and the best home for the divine
Shakti is a heart that is pure and full of love. You
know from your own everyday experience, and particularly women know it very well, that if you get a stain
on your sari, or any other garment, you try to get rid
of it by using some stain remover or soap. Even if the

stain is not harmful, even if it is not visible, and its being there is not troubling anyone, you still try to remove the stain by every available means. Likewise, God, too, would not like to dwell in your heart if there is even the slightest stain, the slightest impurity, the slightest defect there. When you can't bear any stain on your garments, how can God bear any stain on your heart? God is not far. You are far from God because of the impurity of your own heart. Man's mind is impure and poor because of its various failings. Otherwise, all the treasures of power and wealth lie hidden in it. I had an attack of flu a few days ago and it left me so weak that I could hardly do anything. After that I didn't have to go around gathering strength from outside. After the flu subsided, my strength returned by itself. Likewise, the moment your heart becomes free of impurities, you won't have to go around seeking God; God Himself will appear there. You don't have to go around gathering Shakti; Shakti Herself will come and make your heart Her abode.

Kalyani: *What is the karma that draws members of a family together, and how does that debt affect one's sadhana?*

Baba: It is true that it is past impressions which unite people in one family. One may or may not accept it, but it is God's absolutely true law. God's dispensation is such that the soul has existed from time without beginning, and the soul has connections with all the different worlds. It has connections with every particle of matter in the universe. It is past karma which brings people together in the form of a family and unites them with the bond of affection. But that lasts only as long as the karma lasts. If you look at it from the point of view of the Self, you will realise that all of us form one family, because in the beginning there was only the one Self who assumed countless forms. The poet-saint Krishna Suta says, "The world may appear to be varied and manifold, yet the Self is one."

The connection between different members of one

family is rooted in some past life. It is because of the force of past connections that different members of a family offer themselves to each other in love and affection.

There is one very important scripture in our country called *Yoga Vasishtha,* which embodies the philosophy of truth. A man of ordinary intelligence cannot grasp it. Only highly evolved people can understand it. This is a most interesting scripture. The *Gita* was given to Arjuna by the Lord, the *Guru Gita* was given to His wife by Lord Shiva. But the *Yoga Vasishtha* is the one scripture which was given to the Lord by a bhakta, by a devotee. It was Vasishtha who instructed Lord Rama. This most respected work is also highly honoured in Germany. Swami Ram Tirth, when he visited Germany, was questioned about it quite frequently by the people there. Swami Ram Tirth was one of the greatest saints of this country.

There is a very interesting story in this work. There was a seer who had two disciples. The elder was a perfect knower of Brahman. He had had a true experience of the Supreme Being, while the younger one had mastered all the scriptures but was without any direct experience. The Guru was also the father of the younger disciple. One day the Guru left his physical form. After the passing away of the Master, the other disciple calmly began to perform all the various funeral rights and rituals connected with the departed, such as fire rituals, making oblations and other offerings to the departed. But the younger disciple began to lament very loudly, and he lamented so loudly that he began to disturb the peace of everybody else. As days went by, and as various rituals were finishing one after another, the older disciple began to feel more and more satisfied and happy, while the younger disciple kept falling into greater misery. Then one day the older disciple called his younger brother and said to him, "Fifteen days have passed since our Master left his physical form and you are still lamenting as much as before. And when people hear your lamentations they get very disturbed and wonder what has happened to you. What is agitating you so? Why should you get so attached? Why should you be such a victim of ignorance?"

The younger one said, "My Guru, my Babaji has passed away and who is going take care of me now, what is going to happen to me?" As he uttered these words he began to cry louder than before.

The older one said, "He was only one of the many fathers that you have had at different times. Why should you lament so much for just one of them?" Then the older disciple induced a high state of meditation into the younger and asked him to find out by direct vision how many fathers he had had from the dawn of creation until the present day, how many wives he had had, how many mothers, and how many children. He asked him to find out in meditation what happened to all of them, how many of them became brahmins, dogs, pigs; how many were born in our country and how many abroad.

During meditation he saw that he had been born in many different places, that he had families in each of those places, and so many people from his different families were dying, and so many were being born. After he had seen all this, the elder one put a stop to his meditation. Then he said, "In this life you have known only one father. You forgot that you have had so many fathers, and you yourself have been a father to so many."

As the younger one heard these words he was awakened and he realised the truth—namely that one who is born must die, and he who dies must be reborn, while the Self remains deathless, immortal, ageless all through. And this knowledge filled him with peace.

You will have to find out yourself what karma bound you to your family, but generally it can be said that people are brought together in a family relationship because of past karma. It is the samskaras, the old connections, which are responsible for our different connections in the present birth.

The soul takes birth in so many different forms. In one birth it may be born in one form, in another birth

in a different place or form. In the course of this journey
of the soul there may come the auspicious moment when
it becomes aware of its own true nature, of its relationship with its Lord, and then it merges into its own
source.

If you are doing your sadhana properly, then your
family will not be able to affect it in any way. And
if your sadhana is strong then you may be able to affect
your family by your enthusiasm and dedication. If, however, the family is stronger than you, then the family
will affect you. We often find that after just one
member of a family comes, the others are also drawn
here, and even friends and acquaintances, residents of
the same place, may be strongly affected. And from
time to time we have been receiving the sisters, aunts
and mothers of seekers here. That is the power of
sadhana.

Virendra: *For the last nine or ten months, by your
grace I have been experiencing a great change in my
consciousness. While I speak I identify myself with
you, and I talk just like you. But meditation is not
yet coming to me spontaneously. How can one reach
the sahasrar without getting absorbed in deep meditation? Though I remain immersed in devotion to the
Lord all the time, though I have full faith in the inner
Self, without meditation how is inner progress possible?
Without Guru's grace meditation is not possible, so
please bless me with your grace.*

Baba : This question is self-contradictory. Gurubhava,
identification with the Guru, is the result of meditation; it does not precede meditation. It is just like
saying, "I can't sleep and I can't wake up." It is just like
saying, "I eat very well, though I don't have an appetite."
Identification with the Guru is the goal of meditation.
Devotion to the Guru, merging in the Guru, is the very
destination of meditation. One who lives in identification with the Guru does not need meditation. Meditation is needed for achieving this identification.

Gurubhava lies even beyond the sahasrar. Gurubhava

is achieved when you become one with the inner witness.
Then the inner witness is seen to be one with the Guru.
In the course of meditation, one sees different visions
and experiences different states, and then passes into
the maturest state of meditation. It is only after that
happens that one is filled completely with true love
for the Guru, with infinite love for the Guru. Then it
appears as though he were starting all over again. After
achieving perfection, he begins to worship the Guru
all over again. The scriptures say that you can worship
God only after you have yourself become God. That is
true worship of God. This is the perfect worship of a
perfected seeker.

One who has boundless love for the Guru does not
need any sadhana. For him, remaining immersed in that
state is enough. Take the case of the ancient seekers.
It was as the result of their continued worship of their
deity that they had a direct vision of His true form,
and it was after that direct vision that they were
immersed in total devotion to Him. So total devotion,
perfect devotion, perfect love, come after your sadhana
has been consummated. If you have devotion for the
Lord, if you have faith in the Self, you don't need meditation, because devotion for the Lord and faith in the
Self are nothing but meditation. Faith and devotion are
extremely powerful. You might have heard about a
great woman saint of Maharashtra, Bahinabai, who was
a contemporary of Mirabai. She says, "Devotion has
so much power that it can give you the fruit of your
desires." Such is the power of devotion. And if you
have devotion to the Guru then you don't need any
sadhana. Gurubhava transcends all sadhana. In fact,
all modes of sadhana are included in Gurubhava. But
we must distinguish between Gurudhyan and Gurubhava. While you are meditating on the Guru, you are
different from the Guru, but while you are in Gurubhava, you have become one with the Guru.

Veena: *The Lord told Arjuna in the Gita, "Surrender
all your actions to Me and become free from anxiety*

about virtue and sin." If one has been able to achieve
such surrender and yet falls victim to lust, anger and
egoism from time to time, will he have to bear the con-
sequences of this or not?

Baba : While surrendering to your deity, why should
you keep lust and greed and anger with you? Why
can't you offer them to Him also? That's like some
tenants who, while leaving a house, remove all the best
fittings. When you are surrendering to your Guru, why
should you keep the 'best' things, such as lust, anger and
greed with you and offer everything else to him? Why
can't you offer them to him also?

You will certainly have to bear the consequences of
your lust, greed and egoism, to a certain extent at least.
And even if there are no consequences to be suffered in
the future, while you are angry, aren't you suffering from
anger at that time? Doesn't your blood start boiling,
doesn't your mind get disturbed? Don't you start mis-
behaving with others? And don't people, while looking
at you, begin to wonder what you have done, if even
after such a long stay in the Ashram, you are still in the
same condition as you were when you came here, behaving just like the dogs Ramu or Shamu who, while
quarrelling with each other, make all kinds of funny
angry noises? Even if you don't have to bear the consequences of these things at some future time, in the
moment of anger you are suffering anger. The question
of whether you will have to bear the consequences does
not arise because anger itself is a suffering. Whether
or not you will have to suffer later is irrelevant. If you
become very angry, you may not be able to sleep at
night. And if you lose your sleep, you may have to take
a few sleeping pills, or else you may have to lock yourself up in your room and keep on crying in the privacy
of your heart the whole night through. Don't you think
this much suffering is enough? What's the necessity of
suffering in the future?

August 8, 1972

Ramesh : *What is the one question, the question of all questions, the essence of all questions, by knowing the answer to which I may become free from doubt forever?*

Baba : The question of questions is exactly the one asked by Arjuna in the *Gita*. In answer to that, Lord Krishna says, "Take refuge in Me, giving up all dharmas. Surrender yourself completely with all your heart, not just part of it." Your surrender should not be for any selfish motive, nor should you make a show of surrender. It should be genuine, real surrender with all your heart, with all your being. The Lord accepts the responsibility for the redemption of one who takes total refuge in Him.

This verse, occurring in the eighteenth chapter of the *Gita*, is most important. It says, "Give up all dharma, give up all ideas of duty, and seek surrender in Me alone." Jnaneshwar Maharaj has commented on this verse in a most beautiful manner. Surrender is the most important thing. He who becomes a slave to the Lord makes the Lord his own slave. Man only talks about surrender, but he doesn't do it. One should offer everything to the Guru. If you hold back anything, your surrender will not be perfect. In the *Shrimad Bhagavat*, the story of the elephant who achieved liberation is a most important story and Tulsidas comments on it. Gajendra was the king elephant. He remained intoxicated all the time. He would go into the forest and pull out trees and run about in joy and freedom. (You must have seen our own elephant coming to the Ashram and tugging at this branch and that. That kind of play comes spontaneously to an elephant. It is his very nature.) Once Gajendra went into a lake and began to play with the lotuses there. He was plucking this one and that one and having his sport in the lake. All of a sudden his leg was caught by a crocodile. Despite all his strength, he could not get away from the crocodile. The battle between the two went on for a long time. Gajendra realised that his last moment had come, even though he had so much

strength. Since death was so near he decided to remember the Lord at least once before passing away. He
picked up a lotus and looked upward and invoked the
Lord, saying, "Oh Govinda." As he said these words, he
surrendered himself to the Lord. When Gajendra realised that all his strength was of no avail, he turned in
utter humility to the Lord. The Lord appeared at once.
The fact is that the Lord was always there. He was
standing there between the crocodile and Gajendra, even
as the fight was going on. But at that time, Gajendra
was intoxicated with the pride of his own strength, and
he could not see the Lord. The Lord came to the aid
of Gajendra and set him free.

Gajendra did not have a vision of the Lord while
managing his affairs, while enjoying life with his friends
and his near and dear ones, while having stately banquets
and indulging in all kinds of recreation and entertainment. In the end he was able to have a vision of the
Lord when his leg was in the mouth of a crocodile. So
Tulsidas says that as long as Gajendra was proud of his
own strength, he was moving further towards death.
The moment he remembered that he was in reality without any strength or power, the moment he became
completely humble, the Lord Himself came to his aid.

Likewise, you should also surrender yourself totally,
completely, to the Lord, giving up the pride of your own
effort. You should offer yourself entirely to Him. Then
the Lord will become yours in His fullness. This is the
essence of all teachings, and the answer of all answers.
You should feel content with what the Lord is pleased
to give you. In meditation, also, you succeed only when
you take total refuge in the Shakti, in Gurudev. It is
only as long as you haven't taken refuge in the Shakti,
in Gurudev, that your inner Shakti is not awakened.
The moment you surrender yourself, the Shakti is
activated.

Mahadev: *Sometimes I love being here in the Ashram
and at other times I feel just the opposite. What can
I do to maintain a steady positive attitude?*

Baba: It is only your own understanding or attitude which is behind the two opposite feelings arising in you. It all depends on how you look at the Ashram. If you look at the Ashram with love, you will see nectar filling every direction. Compared to the Ashram, every other place will fade into insignificance. You wouldn't like to go to the Ganges, to the Himalayas, to Kashi. Even Kailas would pale in comparison to the Ashram. The Ashram will yield its secrets to you more and more. But if you look at the Ashram with a fault-finding attitude, with a wrong attitude, then you will soon get fed up with it and want to go away somewhere as soon as you can. The Ashram will appear to you to be a hell, an intolerable place. How the Ashram appears to you depends on the state of your own mind, and you should improve your own mind.

The mind is at the root of everything. The mind is at the root of bondage and liberation, of happiness and misery, of virtue and sin, and every other duality. If your mind accepts a certain place, you begin to love it, you make friends with it, and you love to be there. If the mind rejects a certain place, you begin to hate it, you become callous towards it, you lose all your feelings for it and you try to run away. So it is the mind which is its own heaven and hell. When the mind is deluded it becomes its own hell, and when the mind enjoys its own grace, it is heaven itself.

It is futile to blame somebody else for your being in hell. It was only the day before yesterday that a visitor came here and began to complain, "My boss isn't good, my subordinates aren't good, and when I go home I find that my wife is equally worthless and so are my children."

I said to him, "Is your mind in harmony with you?"

He said, "No, not at all. My mind torments me very much, my mind is very bad."

Then I said, "If your own mind doesn't agree with you, how can anybody else agree with you? If your own mind is not your friend, how can your boss be your friend, how can your subordinates be your friends?"

Therefore, first make your own mind your friend, because it is your own mind which is the source of good and bad. The way you look at a certain thing depends on the state of your mind. Therefore, make your mind clean and pure through chanting and meditation and then you will find everlasting peace.

Rana : *People who visit this place are amazed when they see it. They wonder how such a large Ashram is run, how the many residents are fed, how the various other arrangements are made and from where the resources come. Please say something on this matter.*

Baba : No matter how large the Ashram may be, how great its expenditure, or the number of people eating here every day, we must not forget that everyone who comes and stays here or eats here or makes use of the various Ashram facilities, does so because of his invisible destiny. Besides, those who live here, who eat and drink here, are not the type who are good for nothing. These are people who work purely in the spirit of service, without expecting any monetary return. This is particularly true of our foreign seekers. They have means and are not living in the Ashram on charity. They work in the spirit of service and make donations to the Ashram in return for the food and other facilities which they get here.

Anyone who has even the slightest wisdom or intelligence would not like to live off others. It would be impossible for him to be comfortable at somebody else's expense. An intelligent person would like to be self-reliant.

Most of the people who come to this Ashram are intelligent and wise. They have good sense. One comes for a day, takes food, and when he comes again, we find that he's bringing a tin of ghee. Another comes here, spends a couple of days, and when he goes back home he sends four bedsheets. Another comes a second time with a sack of wheat flour. This is how the devotees of this place behave. Some devotees bring vegetables, others bring flour, others bring oil, yet others bring other

provisions. And those who do not bring anything with
them leave gifts of money in the donation box in the
hall. Hardly anyone goes away from here having taken
charity. No intelligent person would like to live on
charity. Only a stupid person enjoys charity. This way
the Ashram is run very easily.

Besides, the people who live here are not people who
are bored with their life in the world and are looking
for a place to while away their time in comfort and holy
laziness. The seekers here are hard-working and intelligent. They have a great capacity for tapasya, self-
control and self-discipline. They are full of devotion,
zeal and enthusiasm, and they work very hard, so we
don't have to employ any servants and thus increase the
Ashram expenses. All the Ashram work is done by the
seekers themselves, whether it is sweeping the floors,
work in the garden, in the office or the kitchen, or going
to Bombay to look after publications, or selling books. A
lot of work is being done in a wonderful spirit by our
foreign seekers. And the result is that the Ashram does
not have to incur any expenses by hiring employees, and
the place is running very smoothly.

It would be quite natural for anyone coming here to
be surprised on seeing the way things are. But if he
were to understand the quality of the seekers who come
here, he would probably understand how the place runs
so well. Also, even in these times India is full of people
who are liberal givers, who have large hearts, who are
full of compassion and love. The tradition of giving
liberally that we have had in this country has not yet
vanished. So the Ashram is, in fact, running itself,
because everyone here is self-reliant, doing his own
work. We have neither bosses nor servants. The Ashram
is like the Lords' Club in Swami Ram Tirth's story. Here
everyone is a boss, everyone is a servant, everyone is a
renunciant, everyone is a worker. Everyone here is doing his job earnestly. Since the people here are wise,
intelligent and hard-working, interested in sadhana,
meditation and remembrance of the Lord, the Ashram is

running itself, and we don't face any problems or difficulties.

What goes wrong in the case of some ashrams is that the ashram tends to become the exclusive property of a handful of people who go there. We have not allowed this to happen here. This Ashram belongs to all the people who come here, and that is why this Ashram runs so smoothly. The Ashram is very large, its expenditure also is quite large, and we must not forget that the number of people who give generously to the Ashram is also large. In our Ashram everyone is a worker and everyone is a swami.

Bill : *How can I honour and love myself when I see so many faults in me, such as fault finding, jealousy, and strong cravings of all sorts?*

Baba : While honouring yourself you should lose consciousness of your faults. I may feel angry this evening but when I sit for meditation in the morning, there should be no trace of that anger left in me. I can honour myself and begin to meditate. Just as during sleep one only sleeps and does nothing else, similarly, while honouring yourself you should only honour yourself. You should not do anything else. In course of time you will begin to honour yourself for longer and longer periods.

One should lose self-consciousness or consciousness of one's weaknesses. Attachment and aversion may be there, but along with them there are so many good qualities also. You may not honour yourself for your faults, but you can certainly honour yourself for your good qualities.

Don't underrate yourself. Don't let your price fall on the market by keeping the memory of all your faults, attachments and aversions alive. Depending on the temperament of a person, attachment and aversion will persist for quite some time. You should keep cultivating and developing good qualities. Do not let the consciousness of your attachments and hatreds become constant. Hatred and attachment do not last, so why should your consciousness of them last? If something undesirable has taken place in one's life, the sign of a wise man is that he forgets about it very soon.

Uma : *How long does it take to overcome old samskaras? Does it take as long to overcome them as it did to form them?*

Baba : No. Even if it took you thousands of years to form certain samskaras, you can get rid of them in a moment. No matter how long a room has been dark, how long will it take to become lighted if someone switches on the lights? The Lord says, "Cut your old samskaras, your old ties, with the sword of detachment." It is not difficult to give up a bad habit. We must have the necessary strength. By the fire of knowledge, by the sword of detachment, we can cut out our bad habits without any difficulty. It takes just a moment to overcome old samskaras. One should firmly cut them with the weapon of non-attachment; one should acquire the power from within oneself to cut a particular samskara with firmness and throw it away. The power of samskaras is very small compared to the power of the Self.

Kedarnath : *What is the relation between music, chanting and sadhana? On many occasions during the morning chanting you have instructed us not to sing too fast. Why? What is the correct method of chanting, and what are its advantages?*

Baba : There is a definite way of reciting a mantra. It should be done neither too fast nor too slow. If you go too fast in life you lose your wealth, and become poor. If you go too slow you lose your health and become sick. So you should go neither too fast nor too slow. You should go at a medium pace. It is for this reason that I don't allow the chanting to go either too fast or too slow; I want it to follow a regular tempo. Only when it is done properly is it good for one's health. Done improperly, it is even harmful to health.

Generally speaking, we find so many people in holy

places reciting mantras so fast that only they know what
they are reciting. Nobody else can understand what
they are saying. If you look at the r condition of misery
and want, then you understand why it is wrong to go
so fast. When I meet such people I tell them, "The
reason you are in such misery is because you are reciting
your mantras at supersonic speed."

Swadhyaya should be carried on with reverence. And
it should be combined with music, because music is a
great aid to swadhyaya. But you should sing at the
right speed and in the right key. The instruments are
there to keep us in tune.

August 11, 1972

Chris: *How figurative or how real is the saying in
Chitshakti Vilas (Play of Consciousness) that to attain
realisation one needs three, six, nine or twelve years?*

Baba: In a work like *Chitshakti Vilas*, which is a
philosophical work, there would be no question of using
figurative speech in such a context. A work relating to
spiritual sadhana is certainly not like a modern movie
which is partly imaginary, partly true, which has a bit
of fun in it and other elements, and all that hodgepodge
for entertainment. That is not the case with a serious
philosophical work relating to spiritual sadhana. One
who is a highly serious sadhaka, who is completely pure
and who makes the most earnest effort would be able
to achieve realisation in three years. One who is not
as earnest would be able to get it in about six years. Then
there are sadhakas of the third category who are sometimes interested in worldly pleasures and sometimes
interested in sadhana, and who keep oscillating between
the two, trying different things at different times, some-

times meditating on the wife, sometimes on the children, sometimes on business, sometimes on some frivolous activity. They take nine, twelve, fifteen years, even twenty years. And some may have to be reborn. While one is engaged in sadhana it is quite possible that he may depart from this physical form, and the remaining sadhana is completed in the next birth. A yogabhrashta, as he is called in the *Gita,* is not one who falls from the path while doing sadhana, but one who departs from his body before completing his sadhana. And such a person will complete his sadhana in his next life.

One has already wasted so many births, countless births, in fact. No harm will come to you if you were to spend one or two lives in sadhana. The scriptural authors, the wise seers, say that the soul has existed from time immemorial and has been passing from one form to another, including the human form. So, when so many births have already passed, there would be no harm if one were to spend a few more births in sadhana. Even if one were to spend ten lifetimes in sadhana, it is worth it.

People differ with regard to the purity of their body, their mind, their heart, and the condition of the seven constituents of their body, and that is why they take more or less time to complete their sadhana. A seeker who is highly worthy, who has completely purified his body through the practice of the six purificatory exercises and Hatha Yoga, who has completely purified his mind and heart through sadhana, and whose only desire is to attain realisation, having completely overcome all other desires and cravings, will probably take three years to achieve realisation.

You shouldn't have any fear or anxiety regarding this. Your sole concern should be to have your Shakti awakened somehow or other. When your Shakti is awakened, She will take care of everything and make sure that you achieve perfection in course of time. The Shakti, once awakened, keeps chasing you through all your births, and it makes sure that you achieve liberation some time.

Rana: *There are many bhaktas who, to have a vision of Lord Krishna, practise bhajan and kirtan for a long time. They sing bhajans and weep, overwhelmed with emotion, and it is only then that they are able to have such a vision. But a seeker who has found his Sadguru, while going to sleep remembers his Guru and glides into sleep in a most natural manner, and as he gets up is able to have a vision of both Radha and Krishna. What is the difference between these two methods and which method is greater?*

Baba: Those who practise sadhana on their own have to practise for a very long time, in fact through a large number of births, to achieve realisation. Even the Lord says in the *Gita*, "One in a thousand takes to the spiritual path, and of every thousand of those, only one succeeds." As Jnaneshwar says, "Then there are some equally rare ones who are able to receive the Guru's grace and immediately purify their being both inside and outside, and are able to have realisation at once." One who is doing sadhana on his own will have to do tapasya for a long time. He will fall and rise, and fall and rise again. I am not suggesting that he will not achieve God-realisation; he will certainly achieve it one day. But the time it takes will be extraordinarily long. In any case, tapasya never goes to waste, and even if he has been unable to achieve God-realisation, whatever purity he has achieved is a gain in itself. His effort has been worth it. Even if such a seeker is not able to attain God, the tapasya which he has performed, the way in which he has lived his life, is worthy of honour, worthy of all respect and reverence.

If you try to find something on your own, it takes you a long time, but if you can get the help of somebody who has already found it, then it will take much less time. Likewise, if you are with a Sadguru who has already seen God, you will also be able to attain God easily. The poet-saint Krishna Suta says, "I am telling you a very easy method of God-realisation: if you are interested in overcoming the cycle of birth and death you should take refuge in the feet of a Sadguru. Then

you will be able to see God easily, because God dwells
within him."

However, it is true that it is difficult to have faith in
a Sadguru. There are some who find it easier to have
faith in God than in the Guru. So it is also a matter
of great fortune if you are able to have faith in the
Guru. Unfortunately one runs into so many false gurus
that one's faith receives rude shocks and can even be
shattered. But if a disciple or a seeker is able to look
upon the Guru as God, it shows that he has already
received the merit of very great tapasya. It shows
that his understanding has achieved a very high level
of maturity. If you can't look upon a Guru as God, you
won't be able to get very much from him. Since everyone is conscious of the different passions and emotions
that one is subject to at different times, such as anger,
greed, delusion and lust, he projects these passions on
to the Guru also, and he sees the reflection of his own
degraded self in the Guru.

However, after one's inner Shakti has been awakened
by the Guru's grace, one finds it easy to regard the Guru
the right way and overcome his wrong understanding. By
Guru's grace one is able to realise God within himself
very easily. Without the Guru's grace it is going to
take an awfully long time and there is no guarantee
that you will not get deluded on the path. The great
poet Sunderdas draws a contrast between ordinary
teachers and Gurus. An ordinary teacher will ask a
seeker to see God in a holy mountain, Badrinath or
Kedarnath, or will send him on pilgrimages or prescribe
some rigorous austerities, or he may ask him to have
holy dips in the sacred rivers. According to him, God
will always be outside the seeker. It is only the Sadguru,
who by awakening the inner Shakti of the seeker, enables
the seeker to realise God within his own being, to realise
the One who is considered to be far and remote, as the
closest, and the most intimate being.

Chaitanya: *There are some people who worship two
Gurus in their homes. In spite of their being with one*

perfect Guru, they begin to worship another also. **There**
are even some who are running ashrams who worship
two or even three Gurus at one time. What does this
mean?

Baba: Such a person is not a genuine seeker. He is not
genuinely interested in spiritual realisation. He is only
doing business, and his secret motive is selfishness. There
are many different kinds of gurus. There are gurus who
will tell you about horse-racing. There are others who
will give you advice in business. There are still others
who will be able to help you in some other aspect of
your daily life. But the supreme Guru, the Sadguru,
is the only one who will bring you God-realisation. So
a seeker who is interested in spiritual unfoldment would
only turn to a Sadguru.

One who has selfish motives, who wishes to be successful in other fields, would seek the aid of other Gurus
also. If someone has set up a small ashram and has
installed the pictures of five or ten Gurus and is worshipping all of them, it doesn't show that he is a seeker,
truly interested in the spiritual path. It only shows that
he is carrying on some secret business. If one worships
four or five Gurus in his ashram, then some of the
students of all of those Gurus will visit that ashram, and
it will be much easier to run the place and become
popular and successful. But this does not mean that
such a person is a true worshipper of the Guru. It only
means that he is a true worshipper of his own selfish
interests, putting on the facade of Guru worship. If you
had this attitude, it would be very difficult for you to
promote your own spiritual good. Whatever devotional
practices you resort to should be undertaken for inner
progress, for spiritual evolution. Don't forget that the
One who is always present within us, the inner Guru,
is constantly watching how genuine our devotion is, how
much true interest we have in spiritual practices and
pursuits. It is He who gives us the rewards of our
worship. And it is He who keeps us deprived of grace
if our attitude is not proper. In certain places, in the
name of meditation, in the name of Hatha Yoga, people

are trying to further their own interests, their own
businesses. It is for this reason that they have to make
a pretence of worshipping a number of Gurus at one
time. Then they are more succesful; they get more
students. Otherwise, the truth is that if you receive the
grace of just one Guru, that would be enough for you.

Deshmukh: *Many people who attend satsang at our place
ask various questions, such as, "Have you received the
mantra from the Guru? Have you had any experiences?"
I always reply, that I went to the Ashram and stayed
there and returned, and that is my initiation, and that
is my experience. Is this reply the correct one?*

Baba: There are some seekers who ask these questions
to find out the truth, to achieve certitude within themselves. So if you tell them your own experiences
honestly, you will be helping them. One wants to gain
something immediately. That is the common human
failing. So if, when somebody asks you, "Have you received anything, have you had any experiences?" you say
"Yes," that person will start following you at once in
the hope of getting the same experiences himself.

Kedarnath: *What is yoga nidra, how is this achieved,
and what is the difference between yogic sleep and
ordinary sleep? It is said that by yogic sleep one attains
pratyahara. How is that possible?*

Baba: One cannot know the true nature of yogic sleep
just by asking a question about it. One can know only
by having such an experience through the practice of
yoga. Tukaram Maharaj says, "If somebody were to ask
me, 'How is a fish able to sleep in water?' what would
I say? I could only say that you will know that only
by becoming a fish yourself, by sleeping in water and
finding out from your own direct experience."

In the course of meditation, one transcends the centre
of sleep and enters the realm of tandra. Tandra is
neither waking nor sleep. Tandra is the state one
glides into after having crossed the centre of sleep
through meditation. This is yogic sleep. This state is

not the waking state, it is not the dream state. It is like sleep, but is not the ordinary sleep state. It is a state free from waking, free from dream, full of intense joy. There are many seekers who tell me that they get sleepy during meditation, and I tell them to sleep. The reason is that I want them to have the experience of the tandra state. The joy of even one instant of yogic sleep, or of the state of tandra exceeds the joy of even one thousand hours of ordinary deep sleep. Yogic sleep is so joyful, so sweet, that even one instant of it completely refreshes a seeker and gives him new life. It is in this very state that sometimes one has visions of the past or the future, visions of different lokas such as heaven and hell and other things. Yogic sleep leads to all realisations. Yogic sleep removes fatigue completely and refreshes you for a whole day's work.

Susan: *What is the best way to learn to control your senses? In the past I have found that if I either suppress a desire or use will-power to overcome a desire, that desire is not really overcome, but only submerges to emerge more forcibly later on. Please speak about this.*

Baba: I can assure you that you can't overcome a desire by indulging it either. If you indulge it, it will become even stronger than if you suppress it. Indulging a desire is like adding fuel to a fire. The only way to overcome a desire is to keep your senses well under control. There is no other way. Talk to your mind again and again, use right discrimination and keep your senses under firm control. As long as your senses have any strength in them, they will continue to upset you, to disturb you. Therefore, it is man's essential duty to spend some time in that state which is beyond the senses. The senses are related only to the physical body, so only one who has identified himself with the physical body, whose consciousness is bound by the physical body, will be under the sway of the senses. Even in the state of ordinary sleep the senses lose their hold over you. If through meditation you are able to pass to the subtle body from the gross body, then your senses would have no power over you, just as this book lying in front of me has no power over me.

If you realise the true meaning and importance of self-control and the vows you take, you will not be so perturbed by desires. In this connection I will narrate a short story. I haven't told you a story for quite some time. There was a renunciant, a Babaji, who was quite good and who attracted quite a number of good disciples. One of them was a king. It was the king's custom to present to his Guru whatever he received, whatever gifts he received from his friends or others. I find that kind of thing happening here also. There are so many devotees and disciples who offer whatever they receive from abroad without caring whether I have any use for it or not. This place is full of such things. In fact, this place is gradually turning into a museum, and if people were to ask me, "What do you need this for?" even I would wonder. I would say, "It is here because somebody brought it." Chandra has made a couple of foot mats for me, and they are so beautiful that I'm afraid to put my feet on them for fear of spoiling them.

Once an eminent physician prepared an aphrodisiac for the king that would make him so potent that he would be able to have at least twenty-five women in one night. He got the pills from his physician and then went to his Guru. As was his custom, he offered the gift to his Guru first. The Guru took one pill, and the king took one, and then they talked about various things. After a while the king returned to his palace, and the Guru remained in his ashram. The king spent the whole night with his queens, and after his morning bath, all of a sudden he remembered, to his utter dismay, that he had given his Guru one of the pills. He thought, "What great sin have I committed?"

He got on his horse and rushed to the Guru's ashram. After having prostrated in front of his Guru, he sat down. "Guruji" he said, "I am guilty of a most terrible sin, a wicked deed against you. I beg your forgiveness. You may punish me in any way, I beg your forgiveness."

The Guru said, "What has happened?"

The king said, "That pill had such a strong effect on
me. What did it do to you?"

The Guru said, "Well, it had absolutely no effect on
me. It had no power over me. The only thing that has
any power over me is my own Self."

The king was amazed when he heard this. He said
to himself, "It had the most extraordinary effect on me,
yet the Guru says that it had no effect on him."

When the Guru saw the king sunk in thought, he
realised that the king was not convinced. He said,
"Your Majesty, I shall explain things in a manner that
you will understand quickly. Bring the famous wrestler
here tomorrow."

The next day, right in the presence of the king, the
wrestler was asked to take one of those pills, and he was
given full permission to visit anyone or any part of the
city. The wrestler was waiting impatiently for the sun
to go down so that he could start enjoying himself. In the
meantime, he heard the drum of the town crier, and he
heard him announce that such-and-such a wrestler would
be hanged at 7 a.m. at such-and-such a place. And he
was the wrestler. The moment he heard the announcement, his life seemed to leave him. He was utterly
shocked. His legs gave way and he collapsed, as a
result of which he had to be carried home. Throughout
the night he was counting the number of hours which
were left before he was to be hanged. "Now only ten
hours are left, nine hours are left. Now I will be hanged
in about four hours."

Early in the morning the wrestler was carried to the
ashram, and the king was also asked to come. The Guru
asked the wrestler, "What effect did the pill have on
you?"

He said, "Babaji, the pill had a most wonderful effect
on me, but right at sundown I got another pill, this one
in my ear, which said that I would be hanged at 7 a.m.
and as soon as I heard that, the effect of the first pill
vanished. This announcement was far more powerful.
Not only did the effect of the pill vanish, even life
seemed to leave all my limbs, and my hands and feet

got ice cold. Because of the fear of death I was as little affected by that pill as I would be by water."

So it all depends on what importance you attach to your vows. If a particular vow is of the utmost importance to you, and if its violation is like death for you, if a vow is not being used as a pill to elate you, then you will never fall from your vow. If you consider the violation of a pledge you have taken as death, then the different desires of the senses will have no power over you. This way one is able to conquer the senses and passions. And if you fully understand the consequences of your desires, you will be able to get free from their hold.

Man is a most noble exalted being because in his heart the living God is shining in all His splendour. Man should realise this and live his life in continual awareness of the inner supreme reality. I am not against pleasure, but I am certainly all for self-control. There is no harm in eating good food, but you should not forget that overeating will cause dysentery and dysentery will deprive you of even the little strength that you might have had before. So do not give up your worldly things, your worldly life, but at the same time, practise self-restraint. Understand the importance of the treasures which are in your body. By meditation try to go close to the inner Self, the Self that makes it possible for you to enjoy beautiful forms, to get delight from different foods, to enjoy different touches. Always remain aware of the inner Self. Always let your attention be focused on the inner Self. Always worship the inner Self. If you are continually thinking of the inner Self, nothing will be able to get you down, and your desires and cravings will not be able to exercise any power over you.

August 18, 1972

Janaki : *Sometimes I feel that I am being torn apart mentally and emotionally. At such times nothing seems to make sense. I get very confused and it is difficult to maintain self-discipline and not give in to despair and depression. What can be done to prevent this from happening during those times when sadhana is particularly painful?*

Baba : Many obstacles come up on the spiritual journey, but you shouldn't get overwhelmed by them, because they last only for a short while and then vanish on their own. There are so many different varieties of depression —inferiority feelings, feelings of emptiness and other negative feelings in the heart. Be aware that these emotions come up as a result of Kundalini's grace. The mind moves when it is moved by the inner Shakti Kundalini. Whether the mind is thinking good thoughts or bad thoughts, it is the Kundalini which is providing the motive power. A seeker should not attach much importance to these thoughts. Just as in the sky cities of clouds form and dissolve, and do nothing to the sky, good or bad, likewise, in the mind different universes keep forming and subsiding. Some of these worlds are quite painful and meaningless. You shouldn't attach any importance to them because they are going to vanish in natural course.

According to the seers of the yogic scriptures, countless impressions of past lives are embedded in the central nadi, sushumna. After Kundalini becomes awake, these impressions start rising to the surface. You should be aware that they are coming to the surface to be ejected from the system. If you are aware of this truth, you will find it entirely pointless to be concerned or over-whelmed by the feelings that come to the conscious surface. In order to bring you back to good health, to rid the system of impurities, doctors sometimes give you purgatives. As a result, all the parasites in your system are thrown out. If you were to look at a stool full of those parasites, you would react in one of two ways. One reaction would be to start pitying yourself, saying, "All these nasty creatures are festering and multiplying inside me," and that thought would make you utterly miserable. Or you could say, "How wonderful that all these little beasts are coming out of my system and I am becoming purer and purer."

Therefore, meditators should not look upon the mental world as being different from Chiti Herself. The mind is entirely under the domination of Kundalini. Kundalini sometimes fills it with love and at other times with anger. You should treat both love and anger equally. Look upon them both as gifts of Kundalini and remain calm, unmoved by the different antagonistic passions which arise in the mind from time to time. You should not look upon your thoughts and emotions as being separate from the inner Shakti, from Chiti Kundalini. You should not consider them to be inferior to some of Her other work. You should not think that these negative thoughts or feelings that are arising inside you are not Kundalini's work, that they are the work of some other agency, maybe some devil or some other force. If you begin to feel that way, then you will be confronted with the kind of feelings you have asked about today.

Lauri : *It sometimes happens that devotees living away from the Guru begin to act as a Guru and speak on behalf of the Guru. What do we do when such persons start giving so-called guidance?*

Baba : Every devotee should be constantly aware of this great truth: no matter how far away the physical form of the Guru may be, the Guru is very close to him, as his own innermost Self; nothing is closer to him than the Guru. It is only when students lose sight of this truth that they begin to have this kind of problem. Whenever the Guru has to give a message, he gives a very clear indication. He would either send the message through a letter or convey some other indication to the disciple living far away from him. He would not leave him in doubt. The Guru is not the kind of person who would send messages through all kinds of people in obscure or silly ways.

If a devotee comes and stays in the Ashram for a time and after returning begins to help people meditate and chant, that is very good. There is nothing wrong with it. But if he assumes any other responsibility, if he begins to suggest things that the Guru himself never did, or that would never be sanctioned by the Guru, how can you accept them? What makes you think that a disciple will act contrary to the example of the Guru? If a person is a disciple of a Guru, he will certainly follow his example. He will do those things which the Guru does and which are done in his Ashram. It is a strange irony that though your inner Self has perfect knowledge, you begin to underrate yourself, and end up considering yourself to be very small and insignificant. Then you start looking around for people you can look up to, admire, and revere, and you start getting instruction from them. It is just like men with eyes following a blind man and falling into a pit with him.

Once, when I was living in a certain village, I was told about two renunciants who claimed that they were disciples of Nityananda returning from Ganeshpuri, and that Nityananda had directed them to go to Kashi, and for that purpose they needed funds; and they asked the local people to collect funds for them. The local people came rushing to me because they knew that I too was connected with Nityananda, and they asked me for advice. I asked them to call those two persons. I asked them, "Where are you coming from?"

They said, "Ganeshpuri."

I: "Whose disciples are you?"

They: "Nityananda's."

I: "What brings you here?"

They: "We are on our way to Kashi, and Nityananda has authorised us to collect funds from people."

Then I said to the people, "Tie these two to the tree over there, because they are lying. Nityananda never begged for anything in his life, so how could he ask any of his disciples to beg?"

You should be very careful. You should be aware of my teachings, of how I treat the visitors and Ashramites, of what I do here, of what I insist upon and what I like and what I don't like. Why can't you just sit calmly, with firm faith in the Guru? If you have firm faith in the Guru, the Guru will give you a message right from inside. The other day a French couple came here. Already they had received Shaktipat, started meditating and having experiences. After all those things had started happening, they came to see me. Such is the power of the Guru. He can give you whatever messages You need right from inside. All that is necessary is that you have firm faith in him, that you believe in him.

No true Guru or saint would ever use a seeker as a means to his own pleasure or comfort. No true Guru or saint would ever try to live off his students. A Guru has a sense of shame. A Guru has a fear of God. A true Guru would be ashamed to even think about exploiting his students for his own petty personal ends. Let those devotees act as Gurus on their own. Let them speak on behalf of the Guru. But you should beware of them. You should not accept them as the Guru. You should not accept their authority. You should not become their student. Remain your Guru's students. Don't become the student of such a devotee, and nothing will go wrong.

Helen : *What is the peace that flows from the beauty of nature, and what is its relationship to the peace that arises from the grace of the Sadguru?*

Baba : The peace that flows from the beauty of nature depends on the beauty of nature. If nature were not beautiful, would you still experience that peace? Or would your mind be disturbed? But the peace that comes from the grace of the Guru is true peace because it is completely independent of all external factors. It is not the sort of peace that you feel when you give or get something from somebody, or when you see something beautiful, or when you do a good deed, or when you hear something pleasant. That peace is relative,

that peace depends on external factors. The peace that
comes from the grace of the Guru belongs to your very
nature. It is a part of you. It is genuine, it is true.
The peace that depends on external factors won't last
long in any case, so one should not depend on it. Look
for the kind of peace that is independent, that is unrelat-
ed to anything outside, that is permanent.

In fact, peace is one. Peace is not confined to one
particular place, to the region of the heart. God's peace
pervades the entire universe. The peace that you find
in nature is the same as the peace that arises in your
mind when it is full of pure feelings, when it has become
sattvic, when it is calm and bright. But you should
attach more importance to inner peace and move towards
that. If your peace depends on the beauty of nature,
then to experience peace you have to go to places where
nature is beautiful. You have to go to Kashmir, to the
Himalayas, to a hill resort, or to Paris, or some other
place where it is beautiful. But the peace that is within
does not depend on any external factors, and besides,
that peace is present every moment. Try to seek the
peace that lies within you.

Dan: *I would like to become more calm and increase
my memory and concentration. Can this be done?*
Baba: The more your mind is freed from its obsession
with thoughts or objects, the more it is filled with peace.
The more detached your mind stays, the closer it stays
to the inner Self, the sharper your power of memory
will be. When your mind becomes one-pointed you
receive great inspiration from within. Poetry or some
other great writing may spring from within, or great
bliss may bubble up. Therefore, learn to keep your
mind focused on the inner Self. Or select any name of
God and repeat it constantly, without a break. There
is such power in the divine name that it will make your
mind strong, it will improve your memory. Not only
that, it will increase the vigour of your mind, it will fill
it with great inspiration. It was as a result of this inner
divine inspiration that the ancient seers could compose

such monumental works that it is not even possible for one person to read all the writings of even one of them.

The mind is the most important thing. Your happiness and sorrow depend entirely upon it. Your mind is the master of your future. You will find out from your own experience that during those moments when your mind is free from thought, when it is not disturbed by worry or anxiety, you experience a most wonderful kind of peace inside, you experience great freshness, great inspiration.

If you could understand the true nature of the mind, if you could win the grace of the mind, everything would come to you, because every power is inherent in the mind. It is only because you don't understand the nature of the mind, you don't have the grace of the mind, that you are what you are. If you have the grace of the mind, it is not difficult to rise to a divine state. It is only when you are without the grace of the mind that you are in the state of bondage. So if you want freedom, if you want perfection, win the grace of the mind. Make your mind your dearest beloved. Look after your mind like a miser takes care of each little penny that he has. Do not let your mind wander off among all kinds of thoughts. Keep your mind calm and serene. If you win the grace of the mind it will not take you long to rise to the highest state. If you win the grace of the mind, then there would be no question of your getting grace from somebody else, you would be worthy of giving your grace to others. Keep your mind focused on the inner Self. It is only because your mind keeps wandering among external objects, thinking all kinds of thoughts, that it has become inert, like that table lying against the wall. So purify your mind, love it, give it all your love and win its grace. If you are able to win the grace of your own mind, tremendous powers will be liberated inside you. Omniscience will come, and so many other miraculous powers will arise. All these miraculous powers belong to the mind. If you look after the mind and keep it pure, you will be the master of wonderful powers. If you want to become more calm, if you want to increase your memory or concentration, then you should love your mind absolutely and take utmost care of it.

Kalyani: *How can we determine whether the inspiration to perform a particular action is originating from desire or divine will?*

Baba: When divine will becomes active in you, it doesn't leave any scope for doubt. When the divine will wants you to accomplish a certain task, it will totally immerse you in that task. You wouldn't have the slightest doubt or hesitation about it. Divine will is extremely powerful. Divine will is so powerful that if it wants you to do something it will not let your mind wander to anything else. It will not even let you wonder whether the inspiration is divine or not. If something makes you wonder whether your inspiration is coming from a fantasy of your own mind, or from divine will, it means that you are still not in harmony with divine will.

I never thought that one day I would go around the world. If such a suggestion came up, I wondered what I would do if I went abroad because I don't know English. I was quite conscious of the many people who had gone abroad and come back without having achieved very much. But when the time came, I did go around the world and you know what has happened. All this was inspired by divine will, not motivated by a personal desire.

Take the case of this Ashram. It has been growing in the most phenomenal manner. If you wanted to build such an Ashram without divine power behind you, how much money would you need, how many engineers and how many architects and how many planners would you need? The fact is that here we don't have any engineers, we don't have any planners, we don't have any architects, and yet the Ashram has been built in the most effortless manner. That indicates that it is a product of divine will. You all know how many people live here, and how many people eat here every day and how our daily routine is carried on most punctually day after day. We do not come up against any serious obstacles. All this shows that divine will is with us. I am only an instrument; divine will is acting through me. Elsewhere there are famines, droughts, floods, and other hardships, yet here we never lack anything at all. Obviously it is the divine power that is behind us.

So, whatever the divine will wishes you to do will happen by itself, and you won't have to worry about it. You receive noble inspiration from within again and again, you find noble thoughts arising in your mind again and again and you find your mind becoming equipped with new power, with the powers that are necessary for the execution of the task at hand. That is an indication that divine will is working within you.

When I was a child I was extremely fond of seeing devotional plays, and I would become fascinated by the sight of a sage on the stage. Nothing else interested me, and I would dream of becoming a sage like the one on the stage. I could think of nothing else for months after. That's what my mind was like when I was a boy. And the thing about the sage which attracted me most was his power to make things happen just by his command. So in my fantasy I would see myself saying things and things changing right before my eyes. That was how my mind worked in those days. As time went by I renounced everything, and I didn't have to face any conflict. It all happened naturally. So when divine will wants you to do something, it will lead you to the right place at the right time so that what has to be accomplished will be accomplished. You don't have to worry about it. Everything happens very naturally.

August 22, 1972

Stan : *Often when I cover my eyes with my fingers, even inadvertently, various patterns and light shine forth and then merge into a bright oval-shaped white light, in the centre of which is a dark light. It somewhat resembles an eye and is very clear and pleasant to see. What causes this and is this practice of placing the hands over the eyes beneficial or not?*

Baba : The experience of lights is good, but it is not good to depend on placing one's fingers over one's eyes in order to see them. As you meditate from day to day you will pass in a natural manner from the gross plane to the subtle plane, and as you pass to the subtle plane, you will see lights, again in a natural manner. This passage from the gross plane to the subtle plane occurs in the eyes, as a result of which you are able to see different lights. But it is not proper to place your fingers over your eyes or to press your eyes with your fingers. For one thing, it may be injurious to the sensory nerves in the eyes, and for another, the experience that you may get that way may not be a genuine experience. Sometimes when people fight, if they happen to hit each other's eyes, they may be able to see various lights. Would you call that experience a spiritual experience? It has no value. You should try to get deeper into yourself in meditation and then these lights will arise naturally in the eyes.

In fact, these different lights dwell in everybody's eyes, but in the ordinary state one is not able to see them. In your ordinary state your attention is directed towards outer objects and you are not accustomed to drawing your attention inwards. In meditation the attention is drawn inwards, so when the meditator passes from the gross to the subtle planes, the lights appear automatically. These lights are not imaginary, they are real, authentic phenomena; they are the lights of God. You should be able to see them without any mechanical aid, such as placing your fingers over your eyes. You should be able to see them as you dive deeper into your own depths in meditation.

In our present condition we are not able to see these lights because we are not sufficiently pure. When our impurities are washed away, these lights will appear by themselves. In our present condition we are limited by ignorance. I don't like to use the word ignorance—in fact there is nothing that can obstruct the vision of the divine nature. Instead of ignorance I like to use the term, 'lack of understanding.' Somehow or other this deficiency of understanding is found in perfect knowledge. It is quite paradoxical. When the deficiencies are made good, when the impurities are washed away, all these lights will appear to you spontaneously. You won't have to seek any outer aid. These great lights should arise spontaneously. If you force them in any way, even though you may be able to have these visions, they will not give you the benefit which you should get from them. Also, if you manipulate your eyes in any way, the fine sensory nerves in the eyes may be affected adversely. By the help of these sensory nerves you see different lights and your eyes acquire the extraordinary power of seeing distant things.

When the *Gita* asks you to concentrate your attention between the eyebrows or on the sahasrar, it does so because these are the natural centres which the scriptures refer to. As I said before, these lights should arise naturally, and if you interfere, if you press them by placing your fingers over them, you will not get the full experience of these inner lights. You may be able to see some lights, but that light will not reach the real light which is all-pervasive.

The fact is that the entire universe is composed of light, and this you will see only when the veil of lack of understanding is lifted. When you have overcome your lack of understanding, you will see that your entire body, from crown to toe, is pervaded by one great light. It is for this reason that I insist that you do not torture the body. That doesn't mean that I belong to the sect of Virochana, that doesn't mean that I subscribe

to his doctrine according to which the body is the Self.
I say this only because I know that the body is nothing
but one uninterrupted, unbroken light from crown to
toe. My constant message to everyone is: meditate on
your Self, kneel to your own being, adore your own
spirit. Do the japa going on in you continuously because
the Lord dwells within you as you. Behind this message
is the realisation that God, who is pure light, dwells in
this body which is made of light. Just as the body is
enveloped by light from crown to toe, likewise the
entire universe is enveloped by light, regardless of what
view scientists may have. Man is accustomed to seeing
things from his own particular angle. He is accustomed
to seeing things through the glasses that he happens to
be wearing, whether those glasses are blue or yellow
or green. But the truth is that the entire universe is made
of light. It is swimming in light and so is the body.

Take the case of Tukaram Maharaj. He was a great
seeker of truth. He was a great investigator into the
realm of reality. Tukaram says, "When I obtained
divine vision by the Guru's grace, I saw the world not
as the world, but as chinmaya, pure consciousness."
Chinmaya is just a different name for the shimmering,
sparkling blue light. "This universe is nothing but shimmering, sparkling blue light, and this is what I beheld
with the divine eye." Tukaram goes on to say, "What
people refer to as the world is not really the world."

Only those who haven't had the direct experience of
reality, who are incapable of penetrating to the nature
of things, see the world as a mundane phenomenon. The
world is, in fact, pure consciousness, pure chinmaya.
The world is nothing but God. The world is nothing
but the Supreme Being. This is the experience of the
realised ones. It is for this reason that in our prayer
to the Sadguru we beseech him to kindle our inner light
with his light. This prayer is not mere ritual, it is full
of deep significance. Divine light not only dwells in the
eyes, it permeates even the toenails. Light is emanating
from them all the time. We are not able to see this
light because we don't have the right eyes. When we

enter into the depths of our being in meditation, we
will be able to see this all-pervading light spreading
throughout our body. We will be able to see the blood
circulating in this light, and rays of this light sparkling
through the blood corpuscles. Whatever is happening
inside the body is happening in the expansion of the
divine light.

Meditation is a great mysterious means of realisation,
because through meditation you get to know not only
your inner reality, but also the reality of the outer world.
Through meditation you are able to get at the truth of
things.

Stop placing your fingers on your eyes from tomorrow,
and instead of that, concentrate your attention behind
the eyes and try to see your own eyes within your eyes.
As you do that, lights will arise. As lights arise, keep
watching them and then be guided completely by the
lights. Go wherever they take you.

Cliff: *Nityananda and Ramana Maharshi both did
intense sadhana after they realised God. Would you
explain this lila?*

Baba: The secret of this lila should be sought in the
deficient brain of the one who put such a question, or
in the utter lack of intelligence of those who hold such
a view. One pursues sadhana only until one becomes
fully realised. One practises tapasya only as long
as he has not become realised. After full realisation,
the question of pursuing sadhana any further does
not arise, because it would be impossible to do any
sadhana after full realisation. It is a strange irony
that people who have no understanding of these matters
begin to write books about these things, and then people
who are incapable of understanding these matters read
these books, and as a result form all kinds of strange
opinions.

What is the meaning of sadhana after all? What
meaning could sadhana have after realisation? For
Ramana Maharshi the goal of sadhana was the inner
Self. For Nityananda the goal also was the inner

spiritual state. For a being who reaches the goal, who becomes established in the Self, his only sadhana is that his mind is united from moment to moment with the inner Self. There is no tapasya higher than this, there is no sadhana higher than this.

I have already narrated the story of Vasishtha and Vishvamitra to you many times. Vishvamitra was the absolute prince of ascetics, while Vasishtha was the prince of jnanis. Nityananda and Ramana Maharshi are referred to not as ascetics, but as jnanis, knowers of their inner nature. If you attain true knowledge even for a moment, that is equal to the tapsya of 1,000 years. Then the question of a jnani or an enlightened being doing tapasya does not arise. I wonder what these writers write about, and what these readers understand when they read their strange writings. Such a question or piece of writing shows a deficiency of understanding, nothing else.

However, I would say that both Nityananda and Ramana Maharshi, before attaining final realisation, practised meditation. They meditated all the time. Even in the waking state Nityananda would sit with his eyes closed and his mind focused on the inner Self. He was always drunk with spiritual bliss, which lies beyond the mind. Once you have had the experience of the inner state, there is no higher tapasya than constantly looking inwards. The scriptures describe this state as follows: In this state a seer looks as though he were looking outside because his eyes are open, but his gaze is fixed within. He is looking not at external things, but at his own inner Self. People outside may think that he is looking at them, but that is not the truth. His gaze is always directed towards his own inner Self. For such seers, for such beings, the question of any external tapasya would not arise.

Kalyani: *What is the nature of the subtle bodies? What are they composed of and what are their functions?*
Baba: The subtle body is made of exactly the same elements of which the gross body is made. The nature

and functions of the gross physical body are exactly the
same as those of the subtle body. The only difference
is that the subtle body functions in a subtle form. For
this you will have to study a work called *Panchikarana*.
It is a short work by Shankaracharya. It is available in
English in the library, and it is accompanied by a commentary on it by Sureshwaracharya, a disciple of
Shankaracharya. All of you should study it.

The five gross elements are divided into 25 equal parts.
Those 25 parts combine in different proportions and
result in the gross body. The subtle body is composed
in exactly the same manner. All the activities of the
waking state take place in the gross body and all the
activities of the dream state are carried on in the subtle
body. It is in the subtle body that one experiences sleep.
Just as the individual soul while dwelling in the eyes
in the waking state experiences gross pleasures, in the
dream state it dwells in the throat in the subtle body
and experiences subtle objects. Just as the gross body
is the basis of the waking state, the subtle body is the
basis of the dream state. In the waking state the
experience of pleasure is had through external activities
such as eating, drinking, talking and going around. It
isn't so with the subtle body. The subtle body is much
finer than the gross body, and for enjoyment the subtle
body does not turn to gross activities such as eating,
drinking and moving around. The subtle body experiences its pleasure by doing nothing, in the sleep state.

Visitor: *When I met you the first time and asked you
which commentary on the Gita I should read, you suggested Jnaneshwari. It was only after reading Jnaneshwari that I started coming to you. Now that I am
coming here again, I find that I will soon be joining your
trip to Alandi. Is there some mystery behind it? What
exactly is my place in it?*

Baba: Alandi is the place sacred to Jnaneshwar Maharaj,
the place where he lived, and every seeker has a place
there. The *Gita* is an immensely important work and
thousands of commentaries have been written on it.

Each commentator has tried to explain the *Gita* from his particular standpoint. That's why you find the commentary being coloured by religious politics. When I came to know about Jnaneshwar; when I looked at his age—he was very young, he finished the commentary when he was 16—I became convinced that there could be no religious politics behind his commentary. If he could write such a commentary at such a young age, that commentary must be divinely inspired. So I turned to Jnaneshwar. Jnaneshwar was so young, he wasn't at the age at which one would understand the *Gita* much less write a commentary on it. The *Gita* is such a fine work, such a significant work, that you wouldn't expect a young boy like Jnaneshwar to write a commentary on it. But the fact is that he did write a commentary on it, and the commentary must have arisen from his inner depths spontaneously.

When you read *Jnaneshwari* you do not feel that he is trying to defend any particular sect or expound any particular doctrine. Jnaneshwar is only describing the inner Self, and his commentary is full of nothing but the inner Self. When you read the commentary, you get closer and closer to your own inner Self. Those who are followers of the path of meditation, who are followers of Shaktipat, feel that *Jnaneshwari* is their very own.

During the period of my sadhana I was quite an avid reader. I had read so many works, and in none of them did I come across a satisfying description of the different stages of sadhana, the different spiritual experiences and visions that come to a seeker. It was only in the works of Jnaneshwar that I came across the perfect explanation of what had happened to me, a perfect description of all the different visions. That was why I was so fascinated by him.

It is true that in the sadhana of Shaktipat there comes a stage at which you can, if you like, retain your body in its living and conscious state for any length of time, and Jnaneshwar Maharaj took this kind of live samadhi, by entering a pit and having it sealed. And this has been fully vindicated by Eknath Maharaj. When

Eknath Maharaj opened the Samadhi of Jnaneshwar
after several hundred years, he found that his body was
still warm and alive.

Then there is a particular variety of tree called ajana
vriksha, which is growing on Jnaneshwar's Samadhi.
This tree is very important in the Nath tradition because
it grants desired powers. It has great alchemical powers.
This tree grows only where a great saint has taken
samadhi and left his physical form alive and conscious.

There is a back door leading to the Samadhi, and if
you go there you get powerfully affected. When I was
taken there I felt as though I was being drawn in, sucked
in. I was very powerfully affected.

All the saints of Maharashtra have referred to
Jnaneshwar as the king of yoga and knowledge, and
outstanding among the saints belonging to the Siddha
tradition, the tradition of Shaktipat. Therefore, Alandi
is a place where a seeker gets supremely blessed, as a
result of which he will be able to make progress in
sadhana. There is nothing like being around the
Samadhi for a few hours or spending the day there, in
the study of serious works, in tapasya, in meditation.
It would be well worth it. If you get into deep meditation there you will be able to have a vision of Jnaneshwar
sitting inside his Samadhi in his physical form.

August 25, 1972

Daga: *Sometimes I succeed in meditating a little, but
the meditation breaks quite soon and all kinds of ideas
attack my mind. Should I continue to try to meditate
at such a time, or should I give up?*

Baba: Even if you were to stop meditating at such a
time, what would you do if you were faced with the

same problem the next time? If thoughts begin to arise, you will have more and more thoughts flooding into the mind, and if they begin to subside, you will have more and more thoughts subsiding. Therefore, shoving the thoughts to one side, one should keep trying to meditate. Your mind will never stay free from thoughts. The mind is nothing but the organ which is thinking all the time. The moment it stops thinking it will no longer be the mind. Once thinking ends, that is the end of the mind also.

To get rid of all kinds of thoughts, the best thing to do is to start thinking about the goal, the object of meditaion. That is the meaning of sadhana: to subdue the various kinds of thoughts that keep arising in the mind, making it restless, and to make the mind calm and steady. There are two kinds of sadhana. The first kind of sadhana depends on perception, on understanding of things, on the sharpness of the intelligence of the seeker. The other kind of sadhana depends more on kriyas, on the mechanical process. If one were to practise sadhana with an understanding of the truth, then his sadhana would go very well, and he would also be able to achieve the highest state very soon. On many previous occasions also, I have described the nature of the mind.

There is a question which is quite often asked in the scriptures, "What should an intelligent person do?" Why should an unintelligent person do anything, because whatever he does doesn't mean very much. There is no need for one who fully understands the nature of the mind to suppress the mind, because the fact is that all the thoughts which arise in the mind are arising from that which is not-thought. No matter what thoughts arise in the mind, whether they are good or bad, noble or ignoble, auspicious or inauspicious, you shouldn't bother about their quality. Only try to see where they arise from, where they subside and where they stay for the brief period in which they last.

There are so many books on sadhana, and so many seekers are doing sadhana, and so many nice things have been said about sadhana, but I come back to the original

question, and that is, "Why should an intelligent person
do any sadhana?" Because an intelligent person understands the nature of things, and he knows that whatever
thoughts or fancies arise in his mind arise from that
which is not-thought. And what is the point of an
unintelligent person doing anything, because whatever
he may do, however hard he may practise, he will not
be able to overcome his lack of intelligence, and whatever he does will not make any difference.

According to the Shaiva school of philosophy, even
when thoughts and fancies are present in the mind, one
does not lose one's divinity, one does not lose one's
perfection, one does not lose one's Godhood. The mind
is not at all different from Chiti, and the thoughts that
arise in the mind are nothing but the outer expansion
of the power of Chiti. The thoughts, before they appeared in the mind, did not have any existence. They
originated as movements of Chiti, which is essentially
formless. So thoughts acquire form from Chiti which
is formless, and as long as they last in the mind they
are sporting in Chiti, and when they vanish, they vanish
into Chiti. Thoughts do not vanish into ears or into
eyes or into the stomach or some other part of the body.
Thoughts vanish into the same formless Chiti from which
they arose. Thoughts are nothing but Chiti. Anyone
who understands this truth, anyone who understands
this perception, what use does he have for sadhana?

The term used for thoughts in the scriptures is vikalpa.
If you understand the true nature of these vikalpas,
then it would not be difficult to realise your divinity.
In Pratyabhijnahridayam this matter is taken up. There
it is said that Chiti is the power of consciousness, the
power of light. So all the thoughts which arise in the
mind are things which are made of Chiti. To be more
precise, there are no things which are not made of Chiti.
According to Pratyabhijnahridayam the five-fold process
is going on all the time. I am not going to talk about
the five-fold process now, because it is quite elaborate
and complex. Here it would be enough to understand
that the three-fold play of Chiti, namely creation, sus-

tenance, and dissolution, is going on all the time. It is
Chiti which is creating the thoughts and images that
are constantly springing into the mind, and it is Chiti
which dissolves them into the nothingness from which
they arose. So one who perceives this truth, one who
perceives the true nature of Chiti, what use does he have
for sadhana? In other words, this is sadhana. To understand this perception is the sadhana of one who
understands.

Then there is the other kind of seeker who resorts to
different methods of sadhana such as pranayama and
mantra repetition, and by means of various devices and
techniques tries to suppress and overcome his mind.
For suppressing the thoughts which arise in his mind,
he starts learning so many external things. He changes
his clothes, he changes his appearance and he may even
shave his head, and he begins to learn all kinds of
different techniques. To overcome his mind, he resorts
to all kinds of practices. For instance, he may stop eating salt, he may stop moving in the western direction or
he may stop looking towards the east, or he may become
absolutely mute, or he may not look at anyone. Other
people, particularly those who are weak-hearted, become
scared and say, "If that is what Rama is, or if that is
what Krishna is, I would be much better off without
Rama or Krishna. My worldly life is quite O.K. I don't
have to change it." In spite of all this hard work, in
spite of all this toil, he finds that his mind has remained
the same as it was before.

You should also remember this: when you sit in
meditation, stay as a witness to your mind and watch
the play of thoughts and images inside. You should also
decide whether you are going to occupy yourself with
your mind or you are going to keep your attention focused
on your inner Self. There is absolutely no need for you
to run after the running mind with the stick of your
sadhana. Leave the mind alone. Switch your attention
to the inner Self who is the constant witness and who
is watching what is happening in the mind, and who
understands the nature of the mind. Identify with that

Self. That is how you should meditate. The mind will remain what it is because nothing in nature ever changes its nature. Take the case of prana. It is the nature of prana to keep moving in and out. Whether you are a yogi or an ordinary worldly person, your prana will keep on moving in and out. The only difference between you and a yogi is that in his case the breaths may be a little longer. But the prana will not stop moving. If the prana stops moving, then it means that you are either in a state of samadhi which will last for a while, or the state of mahasamadhi, permanent samadhi, the samadhi of death.

It is the nature of the mind to think, to entertain thoughts, fancies and emotions, and the mind will never shed its nature. Instead of chasing the mind, you should chase the witness of the mind. The inner Self, the inner light is the witness of the mind. That should hold your attention. If you leave the mind alone then the mind will start chasing you. It will give up its restlessness and become quiet by itself. I would like to draw your attention to your daily experience. Every night before going to sleep each one of you lets his mind alone. You do not worry about it, you do not start fighting with it. When you leave the mind alone, you glide into sleep effortlessly, and you enjoy sleep. During that period what inner happiness you dwell in, what inner peace you enjoy! But after you get up you become conscious of your ego, you become conscious of yourself and you begin to identify a certain hand as your hand, a leg as your leg, a nose as your nose. And if the nose happens to be running, you begin to worry, "O Lord, my nose is running." Your weeping starts, and there is no end to it. It lasts as long as the waking state lasts.

You should not think that sadhana is just a matter of studying a few scriptures such as Patanjali's *Yoga Aphorisms*, devotional scriptures, or scriptures dealing with the nature of reality. Your everyday life is in fact full of sadhana, and each one of you is a seeker. You have only to acquire correct understanding. If you acquire that, you will realise that every moment is a moment of

sadhana. At night when you sleep you stop fighting
with your mind, and that is how you are able to enjoy
peace and happiness. Meditation is very similar to that.
As you glide into sleep effortlessly, without any struggle
with the mind, likewise you should meditate without
getting involved with your mind or ego, without chasing
or trying to expel this thought or that. What is the point
of sitting with closed eyes when in your heart you are
fighting all the time?

When you meditate you should leave your ego, your
mind, your body, even your prana alone. Don't bother
how deep or long your breaths are. Leave all of that
aside. Try to see from where understanding arises and
stay identified with that. Then you will see that even
though your mind and ego are still there, you are in a
state of meditation.

You should not stop meditating. You should only stop
fighting with the various kinds of thoughts that arise in
the mind. Leave them alone and try to keep your attention focused on the inner Self, on the source from which
thoughts emerge. That is what meditation is. Do not
look upon thoughts and senses and concepts as inferior
things, things which must be discarded, as different from
Chiti. Meditate regularly and remember the Lord, repeating the mantra all the time. The deeper you enter
inside yourself, the greater you will become, because
within the heart of man there lies hidden tremendous
greatness. It is just waiting to be discovered.

Visitor: *After the awakening of Kundalini is it possible
for a seeker to get to know exactly which chakra the
kriyas are taking place in and which chakra he is experiencing, and is it possible for him to know how much
he has progressed?*

Baba: After Kundalini awakening, a seeker gets to know
everything. After the awakening of Kundalini, when
movements begin to take place in different chakras, the
seeker comes to understand the nature of those movements. He gets spontaneous insight into whatever is
happening inside him. He who begins to revere Kunda-

lini as the supreme reality, with unshakable firm faith, will get to understand everything, because Kundalini is a divine power, and all knowledge is inherent in it.

Why wouldn't a seeker get to know how much he has progressed? Aren't you conscious of how you were before you started doing sadhana? If you compare your pre-sadhana state with your present state, you will understand how much progress you have made. It is not at all difficult.

The yoga of meditation yields fruit immediately, and as a result of that understanding all things arise from within immediately. Just as when foul passions such as greed, jealousy, lust and wrath move within, you become conscious of the suffering they cause, likewise you become conscious of what is happening inside you after the Kundalini awakening. You begin to understand and know how much distance you have covered and how much more still remains, at what stage of sadhana you are, what you have done and what the goal is. All these matters reveal themselves to you. This Shakti has been described as the unobstructed Shakti. It is pure will power. By Her will power She can do anything in the space of the seeker's heart. She can show him any vision, convey any knowledge. There shouldn't be the least doubt about it.

Since such divine Shakti dwells in our heart, it is not at all surprising that we should understand ordinary things. By Her grace we begin to understand far greater secrets of the universe. A seeker begins to understand the nature of everything. But he should not make a show of it. If one were to get addicted to making a display of the things which are happening to him, of the inner miracles which are taking place, he would not be able to enjoy a joyful sleep. Those whose minds get fascinated by external miracles, lose their sleep. But those who are only interested in the inner miracles, for whom the external miracles have no use, enjoy most sound and joyful sleep. The science of Kundalini is the science of freedom. It frees you from slavery. Continue to meditate.

Mohini Amma : *What is the nature of the final realisation?*

Baba : This is not a matter for a question and answer session. This is something that you should find out from your own experience. One should continue to practise sadhana until the final realisation comes.

Once while I was in America I was talking to a couple of seekers and I happened to describe the nature of the final vision. The next day they started claiming that they had had the final vision. But I was too clever for them. I changed my tactics and the third day I changed my description of the final vision. Accordingly they also changed. Then I told them, "Whatever I told you yesterday has nothing to do with the final vision," and they had to admit that they had never had the final vision. In the course of meditation, when the Lord reveals Himself to you, that is what the final vision is. The beatific vision is nothing but the revelation of God.

Realisation may come in different forms to different seekers depending on their own wishes and inclinations, but reality does not change its nature. Reality remains the same though it is experienced differently by different people. I accept the great truth that the Supreme Being is without form, that the Supreme Being is not like a human who exists in a particular place at a particular time. The Supreme Being is all-pervasive, pure consciousness. But even though the Supreme Being is all pervasive, without form and without attribute, it has the power of becoming anything in a moment and can do anything it chooses to do. The Supreme Being becomes Rama when it is time for the incarnation of Rama. He becomes Krishna when it is time for Him to incarnate as Krishna. He becomes Durga, and also assumes various other forms. I don't have the least doubt about it, nor should you. When the Supreme Being can become such a vast and varied universe, full of manifold objects, why would it be difficult to assume the form of Krishna or Rama? When millions of children are being born in this world, why should it be difficult for the child Krishna to be formed? There was a time when I had doubts about it, but now

I don't have any doubt about it. The same pure consciousness will appear as Rama to a seeker like Tulsidas, and as Krishna to a seeker like Mira. The same Being appeared as a little protector of cows to Suryadas. There are many ancient saints who had visions of the Lord in particular forms, and all these visions are valid.

When even an ordinary meditator can see gods and goddesses after meditating a little, why should it be difficult for those who practise tapasya unflinchingly, with absolute firm faith for a long time, to have a vision of the Lord in a particular form? Consciousness can do anything. It can assume any form. There is nothing hard to understand if different seekers see the same consciousness in different forms.

The final vision is the final blessing of the Lord on a seeker. After the final vision the seeker is reborn and his new journey starts. That is the pilgrimage to Vaikuntha. Just as you see things outside, similarly you see things inside. If you see an image of the Lord outside, well that has value, but if you could see a form of the Lord inside, that would have far greater value. An outer Krishna or Ram may disappear after some time. But when you see Rama within, He doesn't vanish from there. And when you feel that now Rama or Krishna dwells within you. He will never leave you.

Susan : *Would you please tell us more about Jnaneshwar and also more about the special tree, and if there is ever extra time like last week, would you please sing to us?*

Baba : The time is already up. I will speak about Jnaneshwar tomorrow and the day after at Alandi. Jnaneshwar is a great Siddha in the tradition of Siddhas. Many seekers derive inspiration from Jnaneshwar's place. It is only in the local language that the tree growing at the Samadhi bears the name ajana vriksha. Its real name is yogavali, that is the yogic tree. Its leaves are eaten for yogic reasons, for accelerating certain yogic processes inside. Normally you are not even allowed to touch that tree and when you eat the leaves of that tree you are not supposed to touch anybody else. I was given the leaves of that tree to eat, and for four months

I did not touch anyone else. It is not just a matter of going to that tree and picking the leaves. The leaves are picked in a certain ritualistic manner, on a totally dark night, when there is no moon. Then they are left to dry in the shade. It is only after that that they are eaten; then they are to be eaten in different proportions. After you eat those leaves you acquire certain supernormal powers such as seeing distant things or hearing distant sounds. There is no book in which you find a description of the exact amount of these leaves which should be eaten. Those leaves grant great powers. Jnaneshwar and all those who belong to his line possessed enormous power. I ate those leaves for about four months in a solitary place in Yeola, and I got all the results. I still have those leaves and you never know when I may eat them again. That is a very great tree.

August 29, 1972

Roderick : *What is the value of one-pointedness?*

Baba : What have you gained without your mind being one-pointed? It's the normal condition of the mind to wander all over the place. Whatever you get in your life, from the best to the worst, whether it is the attainment of the divine state of God-realisation or falling into the worst kind of hell, you get by the mind. As long as your mind is not calm, steady and inward-turning, whatever you may have—you may be the ruler of not only one state but of the whole world—you cannot experience peace and happiness.

The Indian philosophical treatises have said truly that the only cause of one's joy and sorrow is the mind. We don't have to depend just on philosophy. We can see from our own daily experience that as long as our mind is not happy with us, as long as we do not enjoy its grace, as long as it is not calm and steady, we do not find any joy even in our friends, whether they are boy friends or girl friends, we are not able to sleep joyfully, we are not able to experience inner peace.

It is for the pleasure of the mind that one turns to external activities such as dancing, eating and various other things. It is just to satisfy the mind that one keeps roaming in the outside world. Yet the irony is that in spite of one's utmost seeking in the outer world, one doesn't get anywhere. One doesn't get peace because the mind is greater than all external pursuits or possessions, and that is why the mind cannot be satisfied by them. And the more we go outside ourselves, the more external we become, the more restless we become. Hoping to become more peaceful, we only end up becoming more restless.

The value of one-pointedness of mind lies in inner peace. The various illnesses which afflict the body arise basically from disturbances of the mind. It is these mental disturbances which create imbalances in the seven constituents of the body and hence the various sicknesses. Indian philosophy honours the mind very highly, because it is only by the grace of the mind that you can sleep joyfully, live joyfully, and deal with others joyfully.

In ancient times a great conference of seers was held. One of the seers there raised this question: "What is the nature of God, the God who grants us peace?"

Another seer stood up and said, "God is the witness of the mind."

The value of one-pointedness lies in the fact that the Divine Being, the God who lies hidden behind the mind, reveals Himself when the mind becomes one-pointed. The *Upanishads* say—and for us the *Upanishads* have the highest authority in spiritual matters—that the Supreme Being dwells in the mind but is superior to the mind; He is the One whose body the mind is, the One who moves the mind but who cannot be grasped by the mind. And He is immortal.

One-pointedness of mind has the greatest value. Its

value is much greater than the value of all your arts and
sciences and skills. If you could overcome the restlessness, helplessness and perturbability of the mind, your
inner eye of knowledge would open. Such is the value
of a mind which is at peace with itself. It is by the mind
that everything is: by the mind, man; by the mind,
everything else in the world. The ability to foresee the
future, the ability to understand inner phenomena, all
these are inherent in the mind. And they become
available to us when the mind is pleased. If the mind
becomes calm, it means that you have received the
highest grace of the Lord.

Martin : *What is to be done once this state of one-pointedness has been attained?*

Baba : These questions are very precise, very well phrased and very significant. Once the mind has become one-
pointed, nothing more remains to be done. One's spiritual endeavours have meaning only as long as the mind
is not one-pointed, as long as the mind is not united with
the Self. Once the mind becomes one-pointed, once it
becomes one with the Self, there is no further need of
any spiritual discipline such as japa, charity, tapasya or
any other method.

It is wrong to think that God is something man does not
possess. It is because of the impurity and restlessness
of the mind that it appears that man is without God. The
Lord, the one who provides the motive power to the
mind, who moves the mind, who watches over its con-
tents, all its ideas thoughts and fancies and who is
constantly noticing what is happening in the mind, is
already present. God appears to be absent from us
because our mind is troubling us all the time. It is
because of the presence of the inner Self, of God within
us, that we are alive, that we are human, that we are
able to function. God is always in us. It is by calming our
mind that we are able to have a direct experience of Him.

It is for this reason that I keep saying again and again
it doesn't matter whether you are able to understand it
or not—that the Lord dwells within you, and you should

meditate on your own Self, worship, remember and honour your own Self because God dwells within you as your own inner Self.

Man's plight is extremely strange. Though the highest Lord actually exists in his heart all the time, he does not pay any attention to Him. He makes images or statues of different gods and begins to worship them. He makes a statue of Ram or Krishna and identifies it as the Lord and begins to worship it. Or he begins to worship a cross. But he never cares to worship the God who is actually present within his own heart all the time. As a result of that, he continues to underrate himself, disregard himself, disregard the Lord who is dwelling within him. I wonder how to make man understand that the Lord dwells inside him, not outside.

Effort has meaning only as long as the mind is not one-pointed. As soon as the mind becomes one-pointed, effort has accomplished its task, and there is no further need for it. When the mind becomes united with the Self, it no longer remains the mind. In that case the question of doing anything doesn't arise, because it is only with the mind that one can do anything. When the mind itself has merged, the question of doing anything becomes irrelevant. This is the end of the spiritual journey, the consummation of all spiritual endeavour. After one achieves total inner contentment, after one becomes one with the inner Self, nothing more remains to be done. That is the end, the consummation of all actions.

After that, as long as such a being stays in his physical form, he will live happily. He will see the world as a place of happiness, and all his actions will be full of joy and delight. Such a one becomes completely blessed, and after achieving this state he will be able to attend to practical affairs also in the most effective manner. It is only then that one becomes worthy of being awarded a title such as jnani or bhakta or Guru. Until then he is not at all worthy of anything.

Susan : *I notice that many people have coral and pearls*

*on their malas in honour of Ganesha. Please explain
how one should carry on this worship when one is worshipping the Guru?*

Baba : Coral and pearl are two of the nine precious jewels
that stand for the nine planets, not for any deities. In
Indian culture a very high place is accorded to these nine
jewels, and it is for this reason that people wear them
on their malas. There are some people who make malas
of coral and pearls for japa.

Even if coral or pearl were symbols of Ganesha, you
shouldn't forget that the Guru encompasses all gods.
Ganesha is also referred to as the Guru, because it was
Ganesha who wrote down many scriptures. Vyas
dictated and Ganesh took down everything that was said.
Coral and pearl have value because they are two of the
nine jewels.

Larry : *How can a man reach the state of self-effacement
where he can serve his beloved without thoughts of self-
comfort or interest? How does he become content only
with the happiness of his Guru?*

Baba : A man can do this only when he makes a total surrender of his life to the Lord or to the Guru, holding
back nothing. It is only because of identification with
the body that man becomes slack in the performance of
his duty. The more you think of the body, the more
attached you become to your body, the weaker you
become and the further you get away from duty. Man is
weak, not because weakness is inherent in him, but
because of his attachment to the body. When his attachment to the body breaks, divine powers arise in him.

Man becomes petty and small because he continues to
be led by all kinds of thoughts which arise in his mind.
He continues to be guided by all sorts of decisions which
his mind arrives at from time to time. He continues to
pay attention to all kinds of fancies which his mind falls
prey to. You must have seen from your own experience
that sometimes when you forget yourself, when you
forget your body even for a few hours, you work with
great enthusiasm and joy, without feeling the least bit

tired. But the moment you become conscious of your body, you get tired very soon. You may get tired even after having a hearty meal. To put it briefly, the divine state can be achieved when one overcomes his attachment to himself and offers himself to the Guru. Man has great powers inherent in him and he is not able to realise them because of imperfect understanding. Man feels weak or strong, small or great according to the kind of thoughts and fancies that move in his mind.

Gauri : *How does one please the Guru?*

Baba : You don't have to please the Guru. If you become pleased with the Guru, the Guru is automatically pleased with you. The Guru is ever-fulfilled, the Guru is ever-contented and he is always swaying in joy, in ecstasy. So how does the question of pleasing him arise? All his desires have been gratified. So how can there be a question of pleasing him when he is all the time swaying in inner bliss? If the disciple finds that he has become fully pleased with the Guru, then he should feel that the Guru has also become perfectly pleased with him. What possible reason could the Guru have for being displeased with anyone? He has enough money, he has enough food, he has enough clothes, and the question of his being pleased with one or displeased with another cannot arise. In fact, this kind of disease cannot gain admittance to his mind. If the disciple becomes fully pleased with the Guru, with all his heart, he should think that the Guru has become fully pleased with him.

Everybody has his own nature, and so does the Guru. And the nature of the Guru is that he is ever-content, ever-fulfilled. He lacks nothing. The Guru is content whether a rich person or a poor person approaches him. If a beggar comes and takes two pieces of cloth from him, it does not affect his contentment. If on the other hand, a rich devotee comes and brings two large bundles of cloth as a gift for him, that too does not affect his contentment. His contentment is perfect every moment, regardless of outer things. If some devotee comes and gives two thousand rupees for holding an open feast, the

Guru is content. And if thousands of people come and partake of that feast the Guru is content. The Guru is content regardless of what one gives or what one takes.

The only way to please the Guru is to be pleased with the Guru yourself. Just a look at the Guru should over-whelm you with love. Just a look at the Guru should release great happiness within you. That would be an indication that the Guru is pleased with you. The Guru's pleasure does not depend on what somebody gives or takes from him. There are some who give generously. What they give is used by others, so the question of the Guru's being pleased or displeased, contented or dis-contented does not arise. In fact, the Guru is a sort of middle man who is doing his work for nothing. There-fore, the way to please the Guru is to be pleased with the Guru yourself. To surrender yourself to him, to be pleased with him every moment of your life, would indicate that the Guru has become pleased with you. You don't have to do anything else to please him.

It is the disciple's pleasure with the Guru which is of far greater significance than the Guru's pleasure with the disciple. Even if the Guru is pleased and the disciple is not pleased, if the disciple is bitter with the Guru, then the Guru's pleasure would not be able to help the disciple at all. There were so many with whom my Guru was pleased, but because of their own bitterness they have come to nothing. There were certain people who tried by fair or foul means to grab what was Baba's, but what-ever they grabbed has been grabbed away from them. If the disciple is fully pleased, then the Guru is fully satisfied with him.

When Arjuna was learning the art of archery from his Guru, Dronacharya, there was a tribal boy also living there who had as much ability as Arjuna. Dronacharya did not want to teach him along with his princely students. Eklavya prayed intensely to Dronacharya to teach him the art of archery. Dronacharya refused to teach him because he was a black tribal boy. The Guru was obviously displeased with him, and the boy was turned out.

But the disciple was not displeased with the Guru. The
Guru gave up the disciple, but the disciple did not give
up the Guru. We did not have cameras in those days,
but people did paint and sculpt, and Eklavya took a
good look at the Guru, and when he went home he made
an exact likeness of him. He installed his Guru's idol
in his hut in the forest and began to worship it with great
reverence. To him it was not a lifeless idol. To him it was
his living Guru himself. And as Eklavya continued to
worship his Guru with faith and reverence, his Guru
became fully active within him. As a result, all the skills
came to him. There are certain skills which Gurus do
not reveal even to their best disciples, but Eklavya got
even those secrets out of his Guru.

Arjuna and the other princes were practising on one
hill, and Eklavya was practising on another hill. A dog
wandered by and Eklavya released an arrow with such
skill that the arrow struck right between the dog's teeth
without hurting him at all. The dog began to bark with
the arrow hanging between his teeth, and in this condition he went running to Dronacharya.

The moment Dronacharya saw the dog he was amazed
because he had not imparted that secret of archery to
anyone, and he began to wonder. He commanded all his
students to go around and find the person with the bow
and arrow and bring him there.

Eklavya was roaming about with his bow and arrow.
The princes grabbed him and asked him who had shot at
the dog.

He said, "I did."

"Who taught you this?"

"My Guru, Dronacharya."

Then they said, "In that case, come along with us
because Dronacharya is calling you."

Eklavya was presented to Dronacharya. He asked
him, "Who taught you this skill?"

Eklavya said, "You."

He said, "How did you learn it from me?"

Eklavya narrated the entire story of how he had learned the skill from him. "I made a statue of you and

worshipped it with great faith. As a result, you entered into my being and revealed all the secrets of archery to me from within."

And this is exactly what Shaktipat is. In Shaktipat the Guru Himself enters the disciple in his fullness and becomes fully active within him. Most of you do not understand this, and it is because you do not fully understand the nature, the grandeur and the glory of Shakti, that you are not able to develop fully. It is the inner Shakti of the Self which the Guru transmits into his disciple. The Guru enters his disciple in seed form. It is for this reason that a disciple is referred to as one who is begotten of the mantra. A son is begotten of the semen of his father, and through the semen it is the father who is reborn as the son. Similarly, when a disciple is begotten of the mantra, it is the Guru who becomes active in his fullness within the disciple.

Therefore, before starting to please the Guru, you should start pleasing yourself. When the disciple becomes pleased with the Guru he is able to make the Guru fully active within him. He is able to get the full advantage of the Guru's Shakti within him, even if the Guru is displeased with him. One who does not have the faith that it is the Guru himself who is active within him in the form of Shakti does not deserve to be a disciple. He is a fake disciple. A disciple should not be like a plastic mannequin which you find in the showcases of different shops when you go window-shopping.

You may remember the story of what Krishna said to the Gopis. Once a controversy took place between Krishna and the Gopis, and Krishna pretended to be angry with them. That is what happens in the play of love. Krishna threatened, saying, "I am going to go away from here."

The Gopis: "Please do not go away."
Krishna: "No, I must."
The Gopis: "You must not."
Krishna: "No, I must."
The Gopis: "All right, if You want to go, go, but we want to see how You can depart from our hearts."

This made Krishna absolutely speechless, because even Krishna didn't have the power to go away from the hearts of the Gopis.

So it is the disciple who should be pleased with the Guru in his heart. If the disciple becomes fully pleased with the Guru with all his heart, it shows that he has done all that was necessary for him to do.

*　　　*　　　*

Our trip to Alandi was extremely good. Murlidhar Dhoot looked after all of us in a most generous and beautiful manner, with all his heart, and everything took place on schedule. I am saying this to bring your attention to the fact that there are some people here who, in spite of the fact that they get everything here on time, are late for every session. They come fifteen minutes late to *Guru Gita* and five minutes late for the Arati. Yet Murlidhar was not late for anything, in spite of the fact that he had so many people and so many details to look after. If the food was needed at 10 o'clock, it was ready by 10 o'clock; it wasn't late. And he provided hot water for such a large number, and quite early in the morning. The trip was extremely good. Nityananda Baba looked after us, and that was how he blessed all of us.

September 1, 1972

Visitor: *What is the importance or significance of rituals or mantras in pursuit of God or Self-realisation?*

Baba: Rituals and mantras have as much significance as the Self. Anyone who is engaged in the pursuit of Self-realisation needs rituals and mantras as much as he needs food, sleep and various possessions. No one can do without actions. There are many jnanis who hold that man doesn't need actions. By following what those jnanis say, a seeker may become indifferent to actions and may give up different modes of worship. But can he ever give up sleeping or eating, bathing or discarding his faeces?

In the *Gita* the Lord has emphasized the yoga of action very much. The Lord says that he who truly understands the secret of action knows that action arises from inaction and merges into inaction. So there is, in fact, no dispute between karma and jnana, action and understanding. If there appears to be a dispute, it is the creation of those people who are fond of disputes, and those people will raise disputes in any field.

There is no point in adopting an extreme position in this matter, because action arises from inaction and the true state of actionlessness can be achieved only through action. The very word realisation implies action. Action is something which is performed by the senses and the mind. Experience, too, is had by the mind. Therefore, action is not futile. The Lord tells Arjuna in the *Gita*, "Continue to perform actions with enthusiasm, with dedication, but without expecting their fruit."

This large Ashram is also the result of action. If I had given up action and confined myself only to jnana you would have found me sitting under a tree, not in an Ashram like this. As I did not confine myself to knowledge, as I did not despise action, the result is this splendid large Ashram, in which so many seekers live and attain the same knowledge which is emphasized so much by the jnanis. Shankaracharya says that the Lord Himself, the Absolute Being Himself, assumes various names and forms and actions. Where then is the question of separating karma or action from meditation or jnana, or from the Self? Action is conducive to meditation, a friend to knowledge, and a brother to bhakti, devotion.

There are, however, some people who seem to believe that a few words, which to them constitute knowledge, are enough. But this is the view of those who do not have

right understanding. Just as to a jnani, his own sense
organs are not different from his knowledge, likewise,
this entire universe is not different from his knowledge.
When such is the case, how can action be given up, how
can it be considered futile or irrelevant? Action, activity
and ways of performing action have been very well
discussed in the commentary by Jnaneshwar on the
eighteenth chapter of the *Gita*. He says there that action
can never be different from God.

Take the case of Tukaram Maharaj whose path was the
path of devotion, who himself was a supreme devotee,
and whose mode was the practice of the divine name.
Even he says in one of his verses, "The essence of Vedanta
is that the universe itself is the Lord of the universe."
The *Puranas* say that it is Narayana Himself who
pervades everywhere in the form of the universe. All
the saints have said that people themselves are Janardan,
the supreme Lord. In his everyday life Tukaram followed the example of the sun. Just as the sun illuminates
everything yet remains detached from everything, like
wise he lived in the world and yet remained in a state
of detachment from the world.

One should not partition the Lord like India was
partitioned into India and Pakistan. We should not take
away a part of the Lord and call it the universe, or take
another part of Him and call it action or activity. Do not
consider any mode of sadhana, any method to be different
from the Self, because everything arises from the Self
and merges in It. The entire universe and all its functions and activities are nothing but an outer expansion
of the Lord, who is light.

Man is already caught up in the consciousness of dif-
ferentiation. He is burning as a result of being
entrapped in his sense of distinction. Man seems to have
surrounded himself with all kinds of differences. The
moment he is born he begins to look upon himself as
separate from others. He looks upon one person as his
father, while another person is not his father. He
considers one building his house, while another building
is not his, and he also thinks that his house is not anybody

else's house. When he grows up he assumes a caste and thus differentiates himself from others even more. Then he begins to identify himself with a society, later with a village and still later with a country, and thus he becomes more and more plunged in differences. As a result he loses his vision of equality, of oneness, and what was the Lord Himself is reduced to a' bound creature. Therefore, do not consider anything to be different from God. Do not consider yourself to be different from God either. Whatever method appeals to you, follow that.

Badri Amma : *When a yogabrashta, one who leaves his physical form without completing his sadhana, is born again, what characteristics or signs does he exhibit?*

Baba : The only difference between him and others is that right from a very young age he devotes himself to sadhana. His mind turns spontaneously to yoga in his early childhood, the art and secrets of yoga spring up within him spontaneously, and he becomes a yogi, a perfect yogi very soon. Generally speaking it is true that those who die before attaining perfection are reborn as great yogis. Take the case of my own Guru. In his very early life, even before he was a youth, all the yogic powers had come to him, all the yogic secrets had revealed themselves to him, and instead of learning from others, even in his early life he was teaching others.. However, he was only teaching what he had learned himself, not what he had not learned himself. A yogabrashta has the wealth of many past lives with him. As a result of that you find extraordinary spiritual dynamism in him. You will find him extremely lovable, dear and fascinating.

Once your inner Shakti has been awakened, once you have received the divine touch, you will not be able to escape the inner Shakti any time, now or later. If you die before completing your sadhana, when you are reborn you will be reborn at the stage at which you left your body in your last life. Such yogis do not have to work hard to acquire knowledge from the scriptures. Even if they happen to hear a particular mantra from the

Upanishads just once, that mantra imprints itself in their hearts, because the knowledge that they had acquired in their past life becomes active within them again. Then in his present life he consummates his yogic sadhana and becomes a perfect yogi. He not only becomes a perfect yogi himself, but he is able to turn others into yogis. He is able to guide large numbers of other seekers.

Carol: *Please speak about the state of viraha. Can one regard all of one's pain as separation from the Lord?*

Baba: It would be marvellous if you could consider all your pain as pain of separation from the Lord. Then all the sick people in the world could use the same device. Pain itself would become elevated to a path of sadhana, a way to God-realisation. If you are experiencing pain which is the consequence of your having gone astray, that pain too would be quite dignified and valid; you could even recommend it to others. Everyone would begin to think that all the healthy people were useless and good for nothing, and that all the diseased ones were true devotees of the Lord because they were in pain.

It is wrong to consider all one's pain as pain of separation. The pain of separation from the Lord is due to not being united with Him, not attaining what you set out to attain. The pain of dysentery which follows irregular eating, the pain in the stomach or the pain in the head which results from irregular habits, cannot be considered as pain of separation from the Lord. That is only the pain of irregularity and indiscipline. The intense longing of the heart for union with God, because you have not yet become one with Him, is the pain of separation. In spite of one's great devotion, heroic renunciation and strict discipline, the experience of God does not arise in one's heart, and the pain resulting from this is the pain of separation.

According to the scriptures, the pain of separation is in fact the pain of union. Separation is not different from union, if the feeling of separation becomes extremely intense. Compared to the pain of separation, the disease of separation, all other disease or pains fade into insignificance. In Krishna's time, two great divine physicians came down to attend upon Radha, who was reported to be sick. When they asked her what they could do for her, Radha said, "There is only one sickness which I am suffering from, and that is separation from Krishna. If you can give me medicine to cure me of that pain I would be grateful. As far as things which appear to be illness to other people, such as dysentery or cough, I am not even conscious of them."

The pain of separation dominates all other troubles and ailments one may be suffering from; it even dominates one's consciousness of them. No disease can enter the being of one who is in the flames of renunciation, or in the flames of the pain of separation. I wandered such a great deal, and though many times I was without food, even without sufficient clothes, no disease could enter my body, because I was already afflicted with one supreme disease, and that was the disease of the pain of separation. All minor ailments are burnt up in the fire of separation. The same applies to the fire of renunciation. I am not referring to outward, showy renunciations, the renunciation which involves disease. When you are a wandering renunciant like I was, you have to eat whatever is given to you, you have to sleep in any shelter which comes along. Yet I did not contract any disease. That is how pure my body was. And that is how pure the body of a renunciant should be.

Therefore, if you are afflicted with the pain of separation, other disturbances or other troubles will not arise in you. If anything happens to go wrong with your body, you should consider it to be the result of irregularity.

Noni: *What is the effect of food on the mind and on meditation? How much should a meditator eat and how often? What food is best for him?*

Baba: You must already know from your own experience. My guess is that today you overate and because of that your mind is somewhat dull and indifferent. (Yes, I overate last night.) The scriptures say that food must be taken like medicine. Devotees bring me so many different kinds of food, but from looking at what they bring you cannot have an idea of what I eat. You should not treat your stomach like a general warehouse, like a rich businessman of Bombay who would dump all kinds of things into his warehouse. You should give great importance to your stomach, as much as you attach to meditation and even to life. In yoga there is only one exercise for meditation, while there are six purificatory exercises for the stomach. There is a popular saying which people attribute to Tukaram Maharaj, but they totally misinterpret it. The saying is, "Your stomach comes first." People take it to mean that first you must fill your stomach and then the Lord can take care of Himself. The meaning of the saying is that you must first take good care of your stomach, keep it in order. If your stomach is in good order the Lord will come and dwell there Himself. Therefore, food, your digestive system and meditation are very closely inter-related.

Good food is easily digestible, and has a lot of prana, a lot of vital force in it. It does not make the body dull or heavy. Our yogis were not mean, sadistic persons who were only interested in tormenting people with all kinds of prohibitions. If they asked people not to eat meat or eggs or other kinds of food, it was because those foods do not help anyone. If they forbade certain kinds of foods, the reason was because those foods go against meditation and against good actions. One who slaughters a goat and swallows it up, one who catches a few fish and swallows them, and puts on a lot of fat, should realise that one day, in the same manner, he too will be swallowed up by Yama, the god of death. What good will all the flesh of goats and fish do him then? Therefore, be very careful about what you eat.

You should always feel a little hungry. If you have a strong appetite all the time, it will produce digestive juices inside. If those juces are not released inside, you will not be able to enjoy your food at all. And what is the point of eating food that you cannot enjoy? If the digestive fire becomes even slightly slow, the prana

11

becomes dull, the mind becomes dull. And when the mind becomes dull, you are faced with a great obstacle in meditation, and the subtle inner kriyas which were taking place inside you stop for a while.

Food is your very prana, your very life. Eat with discipline. Eat with regularity. If you are not regular and disciplined in your food you cannot be regular and disciplined in any other field either. Your eating habits are of prime importance.

I shall narrate a short story from the *Mahabharata*. After the war ended, the great ones were sitting together, thinking about the fact that all the great seers were no more, the heroic and valiant kings and princes were no more, the righteous and principled men were dead and gone, the best time was already past and Kali Yuga was fast approaching, and what could they do to prevent the impending degradation? This conference was being held in the court of the great king Parikshit. When everybody was absorbed in deep thought on this question, all of a sudden there appeared on the scene a wierd figure who was completely naked. He was holding his tongue in one hand and his male organ in the other and doing a wierd dance. Everybody was shocked and wondered whether it was the latest fashion to appear like that in the court of a king. When this figure was questioned he said, "I am the Kali Yuga all of you are so anxious about. I will reveal a great secret to you. I will be able to exercise my power only through the tongue, the palate, and the sex organ. In no other way shall I be able to exercise my power over anyone."

Therefore, guard your tongue and do not become a victim of your palate. Your mind should be occupied with what is written in the scriptures about it. It is for this reason that regularity in life is essential. One poet says that one who follows vows and rules becomes a yogi easily, because yoga is nothing but discipline, regularity. That poet says, if you sleep regularly at night, if you eat regularly, and if you talk only as much as is absolutely essential you can congratulate yourself, because you are then entirely safe from the clutches of Kali Yuga, the clutches of death. He who pursues the gratification of his palate, who can exercise absolutely no control over his palate, has sold himself for his palate. One who has sold himself to be able to sleep endlessly, is bound to sink. There is no need of another to sink his boat, because it will sink itself.

Therefore, pure thoughts and regular habits, frugal eating and disciplined conduct, are very essential for a seeker. If one doesn't possess these qualities, one is not a seeker at all. What is the point of filling your stomach and then depending on drugs to digest your food?

September 8, 1972

Alka : *Some say that one should tell one's difficulties and problems to the Guru so that he may remove them, while others say that there is no need to tell him, because when the time comes he will remove them himself. What should one do?*

Baba : Both views are valid on their own levels. During the period of sadhana there is no harm in telling your problems and difficulties to the Guru, so that they may be resolved quickly, instead of waiting for the Guru to resolve them on his own, later. There are two kinds of seekers: one type gladly suffers the misfortunes that may befall him; he doesn't like to talk about them to the Guru. The problems that come up during the period of sadhana are not the type that will last forever, and they vanish even while you are explaining them to the Guru. One who doesn't want to talk about his problems to the Guru needs great strength. If you are the right sort of seeker, during the period of sadhana, by the force of the discipline that you are practising, you would be able to bear all misfortunes and hardships without difficulty. In fact, misfortunes will not appear to be misfortunes; misfortunes will be seen as positive advantages. Difficulties will not appear to be difficulties; difficulties will appear to be boons. It is only those people who are not really interested in sadhana, who are weak and raw, who feel the shock of misfortune too much, who feel driven to talk about it at great length.

A seeker sometimes comes up against this problem: even though his sadhana is going very well, it appears to him that things are going wrong and as a result he begins to feel miserable. At such a time he should talk about it to the Guru and have his problems resolved. Sadhana is not an easy affair; it is very hard. When the Self which is hidden inside has to be revealed, when an ordinary bound man has to attain the state of divinity, when from the human level one has to rise to the level of Narayana, you can imagine how difficult the journey would be. In fact, spiritual sadhana is far more important and even more difficult than your worldly sadhana, than all that you do for attaining worldly gains. It may appear to worldly people that a seeker is only sitting with closed eyes, which is something very easy, or child's play. But that is not the case. Even when a seeker is sitting with closed eyes, he is making a very strong effort, trying to concentrate on the inner Self, which isn't that easy.

Virendra : *By the use of intoxicants, and in the initial stages of Kundalini awakening, one experiences temporary upliftment, or momentary ecstasy. Does this intoxication, this rapture, this feeling of upliftment persist every moment after one has become fully realised?*

Baba : The intoxication produced by intoxicants cannot be compared to the intoxication produced by Kundalini awakening. If it were the same kind of intoxication, what would you need Kundalini for? The bottle would be preferable since it is far more convenient. If one who is practising Kundalini Yoga cannot forget the bottle, what is the point of practising Kundalini Yoga?

How can the two be combined? The important question is, why does the yogi of alcohol resort to alcohol? On the other hand, why does one practise Kundalini Yoga? One who is practising the yoga of alcohol finds it useful because he is unable to experience inner rapture or a sense of upliftment. So he turns to something external to give him a temporary lift. Why does a Kundalini yogi want to have Kundalini awakening? Obviously, before Kundalini awakening he doesn't experience the kind of intoxication that he experiences after the awakening takes place. Once he has attained the intoxication of Kundalini there would be absolutely no need for him to turn to the intoxication of the bottle. If he still does, there is nobody more stupid than he. Who would call the alcohol yogi a happy yogi? You find him lying in gutters. Even drug yogis cannot be called happy yogis. There are so many sadhus who consume ganja very liberally, and they are seen lying in a state of stupour all the time, in a state of stupidity. That is not what Kundalini Yoga is.

If the bliss of the final realisation were not to last, what would be the point of the final realisation? Is the final realisation the name of a state which comes and goes, waxes and wanes like the moon? The intoxication of Kundalini is not like that. The Kundalini yogi knows no waning. His intoxication only increases as time goes by. And when the final realisation is attained, that intoxication becomes permanent. That is the whole point of the final realisation, otherwise it would be meaningless.

In ordinary life you find many healthy people who do not resort to sleeping pills or other drugs to get joyful sleep. Sleep comes to them naturally, in a spontaneous manner, because their minds are healthy. When even ordinary healthy people can have the experience of the joy of sleep without any intoxicants or drugs or pills, what is there to prevent a Kundalini yogi from experiencing the joy of Kundalini without any external crutches? Sleep is a most natural kind of intoxication, but there is nothing artificial about the joy which you experience in sleep. That joy cannot be produced by any drugs or chemicals. Sleep is the great intoxication which has been provided by nature. Likewise, Kundalini Yoga gives you the most unique kind of intoxication. Those who get into deep meditation get into a state for a period of time in which they are unable to attend to their ordinary life, in which they even forget ordinary relations, and even the sense of self vanishes.

Kalyani: *I always feel torn between meditating on you with my senses, that is watching and listening to you in action, and meditating on you with my eyes closed. Is there a difference? Which should I do?*
Baba: It is always better to meditate on one's own Self, not on another. However, if you happen to develop a great love for another, you can make him entirely your own and you can become his. The Gopis were in this state. They used to meditate on Krishna, considering the entire universe to be Krishna. To them, even their children and households and the things around them were only different forms of Krishna.

In *Chitshakti Vilas,* while talking about meditation on the Guru, I have said that meditation on the Self is meditation on the Guru. The best kind of meditation on the Guru is to identify your own Self with the Guru, to feel the Guru within you. Why don't you worship the Guru within you instead of worshipping the Guru outside? Don't you think that is much better?

The poet Krishna Suta, in one of his poems answers such a question, "For one who worships an idol, the idol turns into God." That is quite true, the idol does turn into God. After all, God is everything. Everything is God. Stone is God, water is God, trees are God. There are some unintelligent, foolish people who hold that there is no God in stone or water or trees. Such a person will not be able to find God anywhere, if he doesn't see Him in stone, trees, and water as well. What is the entire animate and inanimate universe if not God? One who sees God everywhere, in everything, will be able to see God within himself also, but one who thinks that God's

presence is confined only to certain places or to certain
things, will not be able to see God even in those things.
He won't even be able to have the experience of the
impersonal, attributeless Being.

Everything depends on the intensity of your feeling,
attitude and devotion. Whatever object devotion becomes
attached to, becomes God to the devotee. The poet says
that those who worship stone images of God experience
God through their stone images; they are able to see God
in them.

In the case of a stone image, first the image has to be
made, then it has to be installed and infused with divinity. Or one has to imagine that God is in it. But that is
not the case with a living human being. God is already in
the heart of a human being. God is already within you,
and if you worship Him within you, there is no reason
why you shouldn't become God, why you shouldn't
experience Him, when you can experience Him even in
stone.

We find that since time immemorial people in the
world have been spending their entire lives loving each
other. Two people begin to love each other intensely,
but neither loves himself that way. When two people
are in love, what happens? The lover projects the love
of his own heart, the love which is inside him, onto his
beloved; and he experiences satisfaction and happiness
as a result. The beloved is doing the same: she is pro-
jecting her own love onto her lover and experiencing
satisfaction and happiness. But that is not what Vedanta
or yoga teach. Vedanta says that you should project
the love which you have in you onto your own Self, and
find your happiness, your joy right within your own
heart, not in somebody else. What happens is that one
projects the love which is in him onto another individual
and thinks that happiness and joy are coming from him,
which is not the case. This is not the teaching of Vedanta.
Vedanta says that you should become Nityananda
yourself. See what happens by yourself becoming
Muktananda. There is not much point in worshipping
another as Muktananda. Worship your own Self as

Muktananda.

The love that you receive from others is not going to last; it waxes and wanes; it depends on the other person. It is not a dependable support, it is feeble and temporary. You should experience the love that is in your own heart. Make an effort to have your own love arise from your inner depths. Then you will know what true love, true bliss is. The moment one becomes saturated with the flow of love that springs up within, that love will flow towards every object you see. Then you don't have to make an effort to love another person. You don't have to indulge in all the hysterics which you call love. You don't have to cry, you don't have to shout at the top of your voice, "I love you, I love you, and my love is true." That is nothing but a theatrical, melodramatic affair. That's not the real thing. It is only when you begin to love yourself that you will know what love is. These play-actors of love swear in the name of God, in the name of every other deity, that their love is true, which is utter falsehood. You know from your own experience that whenever anger arises within you, it pours out on whoever comes in contact with you, regardless of whether that person is dear to you or a stranger. When anger flows out of you towards others in a most natural manner, why won't love? If it has been released in your heart, why won't it flow out towards others? Then you won't have to make protestations of love, you won't have to swear, you won't have to make any other outer gestures to convince the other person that your love is true. Your love will flow out in a most natural way.

He is no Guru who himself becomes the Guru and makes everybody else his disciples, and leaves them in that condition even after leaving his physical form. Only he is a true Guru who, having himself become a Guru, makes everybody else a Guru also, takes discipleship away from all his disciples and turns them into beings like himself. All other Gurus are false. The view which insists that only one person can become the Guru and all others must remain as disciples is held only because somebody has a vested interest in it. The true message of Guruhood is that no one is a disciple. Everyone is the Guru. All are one. All are equal. All are divine. That is the only genuine message. Every other message is false.

Therefore, make your own eyes the Guru's eyes, make your own ears the Guru's ears, your own stomach the Guru's stomach, your own legs the Guru's legs, and keep repeating *Guru Om, Guru Om* to yourself. Feel that you yourself are the Guru. That is the one genuine state, that is the one authentic ideal or goal.

Uma: *Many gurus, both from India and abroad, come to the Ashram. But they soon depart, being unable to take the discipline. How do you explain that?*

Baba: The discipline is insisted upon here more than in other ashrams, and it is for this reason that in this Ashram only seekers live. There is no place here for jokers or pretenders. A true seeker is interested only in sadhana, only in spiritual progress. He does not come to an Ashram for comfort or pleasure. In an Ashram he does not seek the kind of gratification that people seek in hotels or clubs or theatres or other modes of recreation and entertainment. But one who is not a seeker, who has spent his life only in hotels and clubs and other frivolous places seeking pleasure and excitement, would find it very difficult to live here, because his primary interest is not sadhana. The so-called gurus who are interested only in comfort and luxury, pleasure and excitement find it difficult to survive here.

Take the case of one who has become addicted to what is called solitude: if such a person comes here, he doesn't like to stay in this part of the Ashram. He wants to stay in the other wing, because he is addicted to solitude and can't survive without it. Similarly, one who is addicted to pleasure-seeking, to a certain sort of company, would not be able to last here for a long time.

If a person has lived in this Ashram for some time and followed the discipline of the Ashram, he would not be afraid of discipline anywhere. He would feel quite at home no matter which Ashram he went to, because he

has already become accustomed to discipline. As far as
discipline is concerned, you can't go farther than we do
in this Ashram. We have discipline at its highest in this
Ashram. Take the case of one of our Ashram boys. In
the Ashram he was just one of the many boys. When
he went away from the Ashram for a short period, to
Haridwar, he was considered to be a great teacher, a
yogiraj, and he was looked up to with great admiration,
with great reverence. After he returned here, he became
a mere boy again, and nobody pays any attention to him.
That is what happens to many gurus.

In most of the ashrams, in India or abroad, people
generally get up after sunrise at the earliest, say about
8 a.m. This is perhaps the only Ashram in India and
maybe even in the world where everybody gets up at
3 a.m.

These gurus also begin to suffer from a complex. They
say to themselves, "If we stay here for a long period of
time, people will regard us as his disciples." Then they
will no longer be gurus. So in the interest of maintain-
ing their guruhood, they have to run away from here
very quickly.

There was a certain guru who was put up next to
Uma's room. After getting up, the first thing that she
would need was a cigarette. I could smell the tobacco
right here in my room. If that guru had not left, she
would have been turned out in a few days, so what could
the poor thing do? She found it much more dignified
to leave the Ashram on her own, rather than be turned
out. I wonder what you can ever learn from such gurus?
You can certainly learn the art of smoking in secret,
without anybody getting even the faintest smell of it.
Or do they have something else to teach?

Just as you find people deluded in worldly life, you
find people getting deluded in spiritual life, believing
that they are gurus when they have not attained true
Guruhood. Before attaining Guruhood I lived in so many
different ashrams, and I didn't have to leave even a single
one of them like that. Whichever ashram I was in, I would
follow the discipline diligently. I would do all the tasks

which were given to me.

You find many of these gurus teaching one thing in their own places, and while they are here, practising something else. If they were to spend a long time here, their fear is that their students might feel that they have abandoned what they were teaching previously. So they have to run away because they don't want to lose their students. If one is conscious that he is a guru in his own right, he has to be very particular about the length of time he stays here.

Everyone has some addiction or other, which becomes natural to him. Take the case of a poet: wherever he may be you find him scribbling verses. Or take the case of an engineer: wherever he may be, he would look at buildings with great attention, seeing how they were designed and built. Even if you don't ask his advice, he is most willing to offer it. That is because he has become addicted to that kind of thing. It is just like a person who is addicted to tea: the moment he enters a restaurant he asks for a cup of tea. You find everyone living his life this way. One gets addicted to the kind of thing he is doing, and everything else ceases to interest him.

Likewise, such a guru is addicted to teaching all the time, so he suffers from an inner compulsion to have students around him. After coming to this Ashram, that sort of thing is not possible for him. Even I don't like to teach. I like people to do their own work and meditate and remain absorbed in themselves. After coming here these gurus do not get any students, because the people here are not interested in learning all those tricks. And since they don't get any students, they begin to feel uneasy. Those gurus are addicted to teaching, and you are addicted to not learning, so there is no point of contact between the two. That is why they have to depart. It is your fault. You do nothing to keep them here. I see it happening again and again. Sometimes a musician comes here, and he wants to play for me, but I am not interested in his music, so he leaves this place with an injured heart, and he doesn't return. He may be addicted to playing, but I am not addicted to listening. This is exactly what happens in the case of these mini-gurus: they come here and you don't pay any attention to them. You don't sit at their feet in the posture of learning, even by way of a joke, and this hurts them very much.

A guru should not get addicted to gathering more and more students, to instructing others. A guru should, on the contrary, be addicted to remaining absorbed in his own Self. I am also aware of the fact that so many of these people come here and depart. Just the other day one of these gurus was here, and he left quite soon. It is only those who are disciplined who can survive here, because here you have to observe many restrictions. You are expected not to engage yourself in unnecessary talking. You are expected to wake up regularly at a certain hour, to go for meals at a certain time, to do all other things punctuality, to remain silent and self-absorbed. Those who do not like this kind of discipline find this place an oven of slavery. They begin to wonder what kind of place they have come to. It is not surprising that they should leave in a hurry.

It is wrong to think that if you are following discipline you are becoming a slave, or you are becoming dependent, or you are losing your freedom. To get up early and to retire early, to have healthy habits—how beautiful that is. This doesn't go against independence and freedom. What makes you think that freedom consists only in selling your life to tobacco or tea, or pawning it for a bottle of beer? Is that your idea of freedom—to sell your life for a bottle of alcohol? If you are really intelligent, you will realise that freedom consists in being free of all addictions, in living a healthy creative life. Being impressed by your mode of life here, there is one very high official, whose name I won't mention, who felt compelled to come here and see for himself what was so special in the Ashram routine, in your way of life here. Another person asked me, "If I put a question to any of the seekers here, will I get an answer?"

I said, "Certainly."

"What kind of answer will I receive?"

I told him, "This is the least which everyone here will vouch for: that this Ashram has liberated him at least from the slavery to smoking, the slavery to the bottle, the slavery to drugs. This Ashram has granted at least that much freedom, freedom from slavery."

September 12, 1972

Ved Amma : *If in a dream a seeker receives an asana along with the hint to sit for meditation from the Guru, what does it indicate?*

Baba : Dreams in which you have a vision of great saints or God are very significant. They are true and divinely inspired, and you can be sure that they are going to bear fruit in your life. Tukaram Maharaj received not only initiation but also the mantra, in a dream. In that dream his Guru also revealed his name and the line to which he belonged. The verses which Tukaram Maharaj has written, which are called abhangas in Marathi, are equal to Upanishad verses so far as profundity and perception of the ultimate truth are concerned; with the only difference that Tukaram writes in a very simple, spoken language which even a child can understand. On the path of meditation, a seeker has all the significant experiences either in the dream or the tandra state in meditation. It is in these two states that he receives instructions from above.

If you read the history of our country, you will find that many important persons had dream visions which came true later. In the *Ramayana* there is a portion called 'The Dream of Mandodri' which is very interesting and significant. That portion has been rendered into Marathi verse. The description of the events which

she sees again and again in her dreams is quite graphic.
She sees a vast army of monkeys invading her country
and destroying it. Then she sees an extraordinary, large
monkey entering her country and setting it on fire. Then
she sees her husband being killed. When she has such
a dream again and again, she even goes to her husband,
Ravana, and pleads with him to change his attitude.
But Ravana does not listen to her, because when your
bad time has come, your intelligence gets vitiated, as a
result of which you don't listen to good advice.

It is very good that you received a hint and also an
asana in a dream. That is quite significant for you. Do
not think that all that happens in a dream is mere fantasy
or just imaginary. The difference between the waking
and dream state is that while in the waking state we
experience gross sense objects with the gross senses of
the gross body, in the dream state we are in the subtle
body experiencing subtle sense objects with subtle senses.
In fact, there is no reason why every single dream that
one has should not be true. In most cases, dreams do
not come true because most of us are caught up in all
kinds of thoughts, entertaining all kinds of cravings and
ideas. Our minds get confused and we don't have true
dreams. But those whose minds become pure, free from
unnecessary thinking, are bound to have dreams which
are true.

Chandraprabha : *I met several saints and held satsang
with many of them. I also read their writings. I did
get some understanding and devotion, but what my inner
Self had been looking for, for years and years, it received
only after coming here. Was something wrong with my
effort before, or is there some other explanation?*
Baba : You would be a better judge of it. It was you
who hadn't attained anything, and again it is you who
has attained something. In spite of all your earnest
efforts, in spite of all your seeking, in spite of everything,
you did not receive anything. Now you say that after
coming here, in a short time you received a great deal.
So you would be a better judge of what has happened.

You can give a more satisfactory explanation than I can.

It happens quite often that in the course of one's seeking, one visits many places and meets many gurus. But you cannot receive from all gurus, you can only receive from one. That is what my experience has been also. There are, of course, differences between one guru and another, one seeker and another. A seeker goes to many different places and many different teachers in the hope of getting something, but how can one be certain that there is really something to be received from the one he has gone to? Therefore, it is not easy to say anything for certain in this matter.

There are gurus of all kinds, and one who in spite of all the defects and shortcomings in a disciple, can show him his own inner miracles, the miracles happening in his own soul, is extremely rare. The Masters who can enable you to experience your own inner miracles are very rare.

I am reminded of a dialogue between the two great yogis, Matsyendranath and Goraknath, which has been put in verse. The poet is talking about someone and he says, "He is uncooked, he is inexperienced. He is not only not the Guru, but he is not even the Guru's son. There is no harm if you are not the Guru, but you must be the Guru's disciple, you must be the Guru's child. One may renounce everything, retire into a forest, live there in a cave or on a mountain top and practise rigorous sadhana. As a result he may even attain extraordinary supernatural yogic powers. But without the Guru he is still unripe. One may acquire the yogic power of making oneself visible and invisible anywhere. One may even be able to fly in the air. That is not so difficult. If you have mastered the vital body, it is quite easy to fly in the air like a bird. But even then, without the Guru, one is uncooked, inexperienced, unworthy. But one whose inner Shakti has been awakened by the Guru, and as a result has risen from the muladhar to the sahasrar and become established there, experiencing complete identity with Shiva who dwells in the sahasrar, such a one is the true Guru's son, he is fully ripe, fully worthy."

If a yogi flies, what is so extraordinary about that? A crow also flies. What's the difference between the two? If a yogi can materialize something, well so can a magician. What's the difference between the two? The difference lies only in the eye of the beholder. It is the beholder who thinks that the yogi is performing his tricks as a result of divine grace, while the magician is showing his tricks as a result of the grace of magic. But the fact is that both are performing tricks of the same order. The only difference is that while one is called a yogi, the other is called a magician. There is really no difference between the two. Only gullible beholders think that one is superior to the other.

You may meet any number of saints or teachers, but that doesn't mean that you will receive something from them. You can receive something of value only from the Guru who can transmit Shakti into you, who can bless you with divine Shaktipat, who can pierce your chakras, who can raise you to the sahasrar and give you the experience of inner bliss, who can make you experience within yourself the bliss which is the nature of your own true Self. There are, of course, gurus and gurus. Your mother is a guru, your brother is a guru, your sister is a guru; you have gurus in your neighourhood, there are gurus all around. There is no dearth of them. If from that point of view I would count the number of gurus I learned things from, the number would be end-less. Somebody taught me *Jnaneshwari,* another taught me *Panchikarana,* another taught me the *Upanishads,* still another taught me something else.

Unfortunately, if someone happens to materialize something and give it to us, we begin to consider him a Guru. Or if someone gives us a present, talks to us sweetly, or communicates a mantra, he is mistaken for a Guru. In that case, the one from whom you buy fruits when you go to the market is a Guru too, because he is giving you fruits.

Only he is a true Guru who can make you experience

the bliss which is hidden in your own depths, who can
make you experience your own divinity. As Tukaram
Maharaj puts it, he can make you like him instantly.
Such is a true Guru. A true Guru is one who has awakened your inner Shakti, revealed the bliss hidden in your
own depths, and enabled you to overcome your own
bondage.

Chandraprabha : *For the past several years I have been
experiencing different kriyas and inner intoxication. Only
I did not understand what was happening to me until
you revealed the secret to me. Now if these kriyas stop,
or if they begin to occur only intermittently, would it
indicate an obstacle in spiritual unfoldment? Would it
blast my hopes of getting higher and higher experiences
in course of time?*

Baba : You must not forget that you have not one, but
three bodies. The gross, the visible kriyas which you
experience belong only to the gross body; you will
experience these gross kriyas only as long as you remain
in the gross body. As you pass from the gross into the
subtle body, physical kriyas will stop. After Kundalini
passes to the subtle body, having purified the gross body,
physical kriyas stop. Do not think that your sadhana
has come to an end, or that it has been interrupted. On
the contrary, you should feel that you are advancing.
Continue to meditate without the least worry or anxiety.
Once your inner Shakti has been awakened, it is the very
nature of the inner Shakti to make sure that your
sadhana is consummated, so you shouldn't have the least
doubt about it. These kriyas will take place only as
long as the Shakti is working on the physical level. As
you go deeper and deeper into yourself you will become
calmer.

For example, Muktananda Swami is sitting here in
this room. At this moment he is not in the inner room.
If you were to look for him there, you would be dis-
appointed. Your disappointment would not be rational,
because you are looking for someone in a place where
he is not. Similarly, when you go deeper and deeper

12

into yourself, the physical movements become calmer and calmer.

As you descend into your depths, you will pass from concrete, physical experiences to subtle and more subtle experiences, to the state of void; from there to the great void. After crossing the great void you will experience pure light. You will merge with your true nature, with Shiva, with your true Self. Your true Self is beyond the reach of all visible phenomena. As you pass from visions to the experience of the bliss of the Self, even visions will stop. Seeing visions is not the highest state. The highest state is the state in which you only experience pure bliss. You don't see anything. Nothing is happening on the physical level. The awareness of pure bliss within is the highest state, the final attainment.

When even a little disturbance in the bodily fluids affects all the parts of your body, there is no reason to believe that the divine Kundalini would not work in all parts of your body, purifying it completely, finally leading you to the sahasrar. When you get even an ordinary little fever, your entire body gets hot. Whichever part of the body you happen to touch you find it hot. Likewise, when you begin to experience true bliss, it begins to vibrate in all parts of the body, in every single cell. It is not confined to just one part of the body. Just as you experience physical sensations of heat and cold running through your entire body, likewise, after you have achieved the highest state, you will experience pure bliss coursing through every single cell of your being. That bliss is not confined to any one part of your body. Tukaram Maharaj says that the entire body becomes divine. What he means is that bliss begins to permeate every single cell of the body. The poet-saint Krishna Suta, says that in the state in which one transcends the waking state, the dream state, and deep sleep state, one even gets beyond meditation. In that state it is irrelevant whether you are meditating or not. In that state absolute bliss vibrates through the entire body. It vibrates not only in the sahasrar or in the heart, but in every single cell. Your ultimate experience will not be

physical kriyas, but subtler than the subtlest inner bliss
which I have described.

Daga : *If somebody begins to speak ill of our Guru, what
should we do? If we oppose him, it is possible that the
hostility between us would increase.*

Baba : The first place where I received spiritual instruction was Hubli, at the Ashram of Siddharudha Swami.
When I was there, an interesting thing happened which
was very significant for me. In Kannada there is a
term of abuse which, translated into Marathi or English
or Hindi, would sound very foul. But in Kannada it is
used commonly in speech. It is a term of abuse against
one's wife. A sadhu once came to meet Siddharudha
Swami. He asked for something from him, and when
he did not get it, he used that term of abuse against
Siddharudha Swami.

The fifteen or twenty devotees who were there got
furious. They caught hold of the sadhu and wanted to
teach him the lesson of his life. They wanted to beat
him black and blue. But Siddharudha Swami asked
them to stop. They were not willing to let him go but
Siddharudha Swami prevailed upon them to become
calm, and asked the sadhu to leave the place first. After
he had left, Siddharudha Swami said, "That sadhu was
certainly foolish, but you have been even more foolish.
I never married. I don't have a wife. So if he used a
certain term against a wife, how could that affect me?"

Likewise, if somebody says something against your
Guru, why should you fight with him? If what he says
really applies to your Guru, then accept it quietly. You
shouldn't behave like those other devotees who wanted
to beat the sadhu who had abused a non-existent wife.
Even in the time of Lord Rama there was a washerman
who said something foul against Sita. But he was just
one. I wonder how many such dhobis there are these
days. Even in the time of Lord Krishna there was
Kamsa. But in the present age, the age of Kali, one
wonders how many Kamsas there must be.

A Guru or saint who is not opposed or spoken against—

his line probably would not flourish. He probably would
not get the fame which should come to him. This has
been the way of the world. Mansur Mastana was
hanged and later considered to be a great saint. Jesus
was crucified and now he is worshipped as the son of
God. And there have been many other saints in our
country who were sent to heaven much before their time
by the people, and now their statements are considered
to be gospel.

You will always have these two classes: those who
praise, who glorify, and those who disparage or oppose.
The best thing is to listen without getting disturbed.
But if the situation demands it, there is also some point
in answering back. The number of intelligent people in
this world is not very large. It must be for this reason
that Tulsidas said, "O my mind, give up the company of
those who have turned away from the Lord. Give up
the company of those who interrupt your devotional
practices, your prayers and chanting".

Even the greatest saints, such as Jnaneshwar and
Tukaram, who were absolutely pure, were disparaged by
people. But that is only due to the times, and one
should not attach any importance to it. The advice given
by Siddharudha Swami is the best.

Neena : *Can there be real social revolution without inner
revolution? What should one say to people who think
it is egoistic to be working for one's salvation?*

Baba : To say that you can work for another's salvation
without having worked for your own, is nothing but
childish prattle. Then your seeking will be like a shop-
keeper who displays his goods, not for himself, but for
others. Take the case of the fruit seller here. He will
tell you that his fruits are the best and you must buy
fruits from him. Or take the case of the flower seller
across the road. He, too, will call you, saying, "My
flowers are very good. You must take a garland to Baba".
He himself has never come with a garland, and the
fruit seller doesn't come with an offering of fruit. It is
all for others. It is all for making money.

That is exactly what will happen to your sadhana also.
If you haven't brought about a revolution within yourself, how can you work for or talk about an inner
revolution in others? Those who say that it is selfish to
work for your own salvation—aren't they being selfish
if they expect you to work for their salvation? Generally
people are victims of delusion, and they use very nice
words, beautiful language to express their delusions,
and thus cheat people. Those who worry about others'
salvation are really secret businessmen. Social welfare,
too, has become a trade.

September 19, 1972

Indrara Anand : *When I begin to meditate, I repeat
So'ham combining it with the incoming and outgoing
breaths. After some time, my breath gets so adjusted
that I am no longer aware whether I am inhaling or
exhaling. Incoming and outgoing breaths seem to merge
into each other and make a circle. Then it is difficult
for me to split So'ham into its component elements. I
find it difficult to hold onto 'aham'. Only 'So' remains.
At times even 'So' is lost. What should I do in such a
situation? Is it good or bad to lose the mantra in
meditation?*

Baba : Repetition of *So'ham* is only relevant to sadhana;
it is meant for the period of practice. *So'ham* is not an
indication of the final attainment. The concepts embodied
in the syllables *So* and *aham* are relative. It is because
of the existence of *So* that *aham* arose. As long as *aham*
is there, *So* will also be there, and vice versa. The
existence of *So* depends on that of *aham,* and the existence of *aham* depends on that of *So*. When both are
lost, when both merge, what remains is God.

One lover of Krishna describes her state of remembrance of Krishna: she says that as she remembers
Krishna, she is no longer aware of who she is, where
she is, or whether her mind is working or not. That is
true remembrance. If in your state of remembrance you
are still aware of yourself, you are only practising
remembering the Lord. You haven't yet risen to the
state of true remembrance. Tukaram says, "The best
remembrance of the Lord is the one in which one completely forgets oneself".

A poet-saint of the Punjab says, "When the sense of
self is overcome, one becomes God Himself. By meditating on the One who is void, I also melted into the void.'

If by meeting the Lord you still remain you, if you do
not lose your self-consciousness, what is the point of
meeting the Lord? If after meeting the Guru you do
not become the Guru, what is the point of meeting the
Guru? If after remembering the Lord you do not forget
yourself, then what is the use of remembering Him?
Therefore, in true remembrance of the Lord there is no
self-consciousness. True remembrance of the Lord is
total self-forgetfulness. In true remembrance of the
Lord, you are no longer conscious that you are remembering the Lord or doing the mantra with perfect
attention. If a seeker is even slightly conscious of himself, the hand of the Lord, which had been raised to
embrace him, drops again.

Just as a person who is very particular about his looks
likes to have a shave first thing in the morning, likewise,
one who is remembering the Lord should be able to shave
off his sense of self, transcend it completely. Only then
will true union with God be attained. It is because of
ego or self-sense that one develops into something which
one hadn't even imagined. Then he begins to blame the
food, the Ashram or someone else. Unfortunately, he
does not know that he himself is responsible for what
has happened to him. It is his own self-sense which has
kept him back.

Thus in the course of the recitation of *So'ham*, when
the recitation stops, when *So'ham* is lost, one comes face

to face with truth. The repetition of *So'ham* is most
effective. *So'ham* is usually repeated by those seekers
who have already attained a very high state. Jnaneshwar
Maharaj says, "When I am in the grip of *So'ham* awareness, that is, when I sleep, I lose self-consciousness completely. Because if I were to remain awake it would
mean that I hadn't risen to *So'ham* awareness, I would
only be repeating *So'ham.*"

Man takes so much pride in his petty name, he
subjects himself to so much suffering, he fights and he
gets caught up in so much unpleasantness, in spite of
the fact that by repeating *So'ham*, the true name, the
divine name, he could attain the divine state. *So'ham*
is not a sectarian mantra. There is nothing artificial or
imaginary about it. It is self-begotten. It has arisen
itself. It is the mantra for all renunciants, for all sadhus,
for all holy beings. *So'ham* is vibrating within by itself. It
doesn't have to be artificially created. This mantra is going
on in every one, but as long as we are outward turned we
do not become aware of it. It is only during meditation,
when we plunge into our own depths, that we become
aware of *So'ham*, which has always been going on
within us. Therefore, a poet-saint says, "*So'ham* is ajapa-
japa. Do japa of it. Then you will get beyond both sin
and virtue."

So'ham is enormously helpful for attaining perfection
in Siddha Yoga, because when this mantra is repeated,
Kundalini is awakened much more quickly than it would
be in any other way. Kundalini begins to work with
much greater force and experiences come far more easily.
So'ham is a great mantra and it is good to lose self-
consciousness while repeating it. You get into a higher,
transcendental state of meditation only when you forget
yourself for some time. You should forget yourself to
such an extent that you have to look for yourself after a
while. Unless that happens, you are not really meditating,
your meditation is not very deep. It is good to have your
mind one-pointed on the mantra, but as long as you are
conscious of doing it, you have not yet attained the true
state of meditation. He who becomes *So'ham* while

repeating *So'ham*, becomes the Lord. Even the Lord
begins to worship him. So the question of what you
attain as a result of *So'ham* becomes a very petty question. The highest state is gained.

To a true seeker the world does not appear as the
world. The world appears to be the play of the Supreme
Being. It is unfortunate that some scriptural writers have
misled people by creating artificial concepts which
produce a sense of duality. The world is nothing but
God, the Supreme Being. Only the seeker who experiences this truth, who looks upon the world not as the
world, but as God, as divine play, as an outer expansion
of the Lord, attains the true divine state. In the course
of his meditation he gets beyond the distinction of seer
and seen, knower and known, perceiver and perceived,
and experiences only the one true Lord. Krishna Suta
says, "There is no being higher than one who after having
become Brahman plays in this world which is also
Brahman. I would like to fall at his feet".

So'ham is a symbol of the highest attainment. *So'ham*
is the final goal of man. Every being should grow into
So'ham awareness.

Amrita : *In the scriptures only So'ham is mentioned as
ajapa-japa, the unrecited mantra. Can mantras such as
Om Namah Shivaya and Guru Om also rise to the state
of ajapa-japa after one attains perfection in repeating
them? What exactly happens at that stage? Are these
mantras experienced as Om Namah Shivaya and Guru
Om, or as So'ham?*

Baba : *Guru Om* and *Om Namah Shivaya* become transformed into *So'ham* in the final stage, merging into it.
Om Namah Shivaya has, in fact, arisen from *Om*. Its
final form is *Om*. As one keeps repeating it, all the
letters of this mantra dissolve into *Om*, and what remains
is only *Om*. Anyone who repeats *Om Namah Shivaya*
with intense concentration would become more and more
aware of *Om*. It is *Om* which would hold his attention.
Namah Shivaya would gradually merge into *Om*. In
fact, I ask every seeker to repeat *Namah Shivaya* by

enclosing it with *Om* on each side, *Om Namah Shivaya Om, Om Namah Shivaya Om*. *Om* is the basic syllable, the basic sound. All other sounds have arisen from it, and all other sounds merge back into it.

This is also what happens with *Guru Om*. As you keep repeating *Guru Om, Guru Om, Guru* also dissolves into *Om*. *So'ham*, too, has arisen from *Om*, and in the course of repeating *So'ham* the first and last syllables are lost and what remains is *Om*. So *So'ham* too merges into *Om* in the final stage. Finally it is only *Om* which is the supreme truth.

Therefore, instead of feeling, "I am a human being," feel, "I am God". And with this feeling repeat your mantra.

There are seekers who, in the course of repeating *Om Namah Shivaya* or any other mantra, get into that state in which it is impossible for them to continue repeating their mantra, because they begin to hear *So'ham* going on within. I tell them to go ahead with *So'ham*. Others get into a state of inner emptiness in meditation and are no longer able to repeat their mantra and I tell them to let go of the mantra. When they let go, they get into the state in which *So'ham* arises itself. All mantras finally dissolve into ajapa-japa or into *So'ham*. Any mantra practised with incoming or outgoing breaths turns into ajapa-japa. Ajapa-japa is nothing but reciting your mantra once while the breath goes out and once while it comes in.

The mantra is an effective vehicle for soaring in the inner regions, but for the attainment of supreme bliss, the true inner state, one has to transcend the mantra.

This is true not only for *Om Namah Shivaya* and *Guru Om*, but also for *So'ham*.

Neena : *Is it one's duty to teach what one has learnt?*
Baba : Whatever promotes the health, happiness, joy and tranquillity of mankind, whatever is honoured by wise persons, is worth learning, is worth teaching.

But then there are some who have learnt to take drugs, thinking that it will induce meditation, and this is what they begin to teach others. That teaching does no good. That teaching only causes more harm. Only that teaching is worthwhile which makes one supremely free.

Kedarnath : *Why does one feel so sleepy during the period of sadhana? What special purpose of Kundalini is achieved by Her causing this kriya of excessive sleepiness in a seeker? And how should a seeker tackle this problem?*

Baba : If a seeker feels excessively sleepy, if his senses begin to torment him, and he begins to be pulled by all sorts of cravings and appetites, that is a sure sign that he is no longer a seeker; he has fallen away from sadhana, he is heading towards degradation fast. One who is truly brave and courageous in a spiritual sense, a true seeker, will find it impossible to sleep for even a minute longer than it is absolutely necessary, he will not be a victim of sloth or laziness, nor will he be tormented by his senses. A true seeker, whose goal of life is sadhana, who lives only for sadhana and nothing else, will not be overcome by sleep. In fact, he will wake up earlier than the time for which he has set his alarm, because he becomes so wakeful inside, his yearning for sadhana becomes so intense, that it does not allow him to waste even one moment in sleep. Only those who are not really interested in meditating, who only make a pretence of meditation, fall asleep, like a heron pretending to bathe while he is really interested only in catching fish. So a fake meditator meditates only to fall into sleep.

One who is overcome by laziness and sleep, what sadhana can he possibly do in this world? You may not be a seeker, a yogi, a jnani, or a devotee but even if you are conscientious about performing your duty, sleep will not be able to overcome you. Take the case of the young boy, Ramdas. Since he started working with me in here, he has been getting up as early as 3 a.m., and he is here at 3.15 sharp every day. He has not been five minutes late even once, because he knows that if he were to get here late he would be questioned by me. So he comes on time

every morning. He is no yogi, no jnani, no bhakta.
Nor is he making any kind of pretence. When even
consciousness of duty can make you so alert, so wakeful,
if you are a true seeker how can sleep overwhelm you?

Take the case of the night watchman. He has been
here for such a long time, and so far no complaint has
come to me, even once, that he was five minutes late or
neglecting his duty during the night. It is because he
is so conscious of his duty.

Only that seeker is overwhelmed by sleep who is not
a genuine seeker, who is interested in personal comfort
and living a life of ease, a life of no challenge. Sleep is
certainly not the goal of nirvikalpa samadhi. Sleep is
not the destination of sadhana by any stretch of the
imagination. Sleep is only the culmination of sheer laziness. Sleep overwhelms those who have no fear of the
Guru, who don't feel any sense of responsibility. No
purpose of Goddess Kundalini is served by sleep. On
the contrary, Goddess Kundalini Herself feels sleepy
towards sleep.

During the period of sadhana, instead of sleeping, one
should meditate and get the rest one needs through
meditation. The joy, the rest you get in tandra or
meditation, yogic sleep, is a million times more than
what you get from ordinary sleep. It is only when one
transcends sleep and fixes one's mind in the state of
tandra that one will be able to advance further. Otherwise one will remain caught up in sleep and that is where
his sadhana will get stuck. It is right there that a seeker
should exert himself fully. He should resist sleep with
all his might and keep himself awake so that he may be
able to get into the further realms of the inner territory.
If one becomes addicted to sleep, his sadhana gets stuck
there. You should resist sleep. You should overcome
it by inner wakefulness, and get beyond it into the state
of tandra.

Vicki: *Sometimes when I look at you I feel negative
emotions, like fear, hatred, doubt, suspicion, and repul-
sion. Other times when I look at you I feel love. Most*

of the time when I look at you, whether I am feeling
anger or love, there is a strong undercurrent of fear. I
am so scared of you. Would you please talk about this?
Baba : You will meet many sister disciples here, so you
shouldn't feel uneasy. You are not the only one. There
are many right in front of you and behind you. This is
nothing but a phase of the mind.

I have studied the writings of saints and there are
many passages which describe such a state. You find
poet-saints sometimes feeling terribly angry with the
Lord, even turning away from Him and feeling hate for
Him, yet they cannot leave Him. They fight with Him,
they even abuse Him, yet they cannot find a substitute.
It is nothing extraordinary to feel cross with the Lord,
or to get angry with Him, or to doubt Him. One poem
has just struck me. A devotee stood before the Lord at
Pandharpur and began to speak his heart. "O Lord,
I marvel how people can call You kind and compas-
sionate and tender-hearted. You are so cruel, so
insensitive, so stone-hearted. Can you show me even
one person you helped quickly? Whoever turned to You
out of devotion, You sank his boat completely. You
made him completely unfit for anything else. You deprived him of all his precious passions such as anger, greed
and other lusts, and You made him unfit for his life in
the world. Such is Your glory. Take the case of Janabai.
You made the poor woman spend her entire life at the
grinding wheel. Of course, You sat in front of her, but
You did not give her respite for even a moment. She
was grinding away all the time. Not for a single day
did You let her lie comfortably in a bed with soft
cushions. You did not serve her. You did not let her
enjoy any delicacies. Such is the glory of Your compassion".

This way he also describes the condition of all the
other saints. He talks about the potter saint, Gora who
lost his son, and he also says, ". . . You tormented
Tukaram so much that the poor fellow could not get even
two square meals a day".

And after having described the miserable plight of all

the devotees, in the end, this poet says, "Lord, You have done enough. Out of Your compassion, now relent and do something really good for me".

September 15, 1972

Ram Biharwallah : *You say that we should make our life regular, and at the same time you say that we should continue our professions. I have to work on a shifting schedule, sometimes in the morning, sometimes in the evening, and sometimes at night. How can I make my life regular? I can't give up work. What should I do?*

Baba : One who has no work, who is without a profession, who is not doing anything worthwhile, what need is there for him to be regular if he is just spending his life in sheer laziness? Wherever you work, in an office or factory, there must be some discipline attached to your work. Can any business be run without the discipline of regularity?

Just as you have day schools, you also have night schools. If you are attending night school it doesn't mean that your life has become irregular. If you attend night school regularly you are as regular as you would be if you were attending day school regularly. One who has to work in the evening can do his practice in the morning. One who has to work in the morning can do his practice regularly in the evening.

To get up regularly, to sleep regularly, to eat regularly, to be punctual for everything—you can do all this wherever you may be, whether in India or abroad, in heaven, the world of the moon or in hell. What is day here is night in America, and what is night in India is day in America. So when you are in America follow what is suitable there, and when you are in India follow what is suitable here.

If you are transferred from one shift to another, you can also change your routine of meditation. Regularity pertains to the senses, the mind. For this we are not concerned with the factory or the particular shift system which may be followed there. Wherever you work, whatever your work, your life can be regular. There is nothing to prevent you from eating regularly and frugally, from sleeping only as much as you need, from refraining from unnecessary conversation and from contemplating God constantly. Whether you work at night or during the day should not make any difference. If you work at night you will sleep during the day, and if you work during the day you will sleep at night. And that, too, can follow a regular pattern.

Chandraprabha : *If those who live far away from you continue to remember you with devotion, will that be considered sufficient surrender? If a disciple remembers you with a true heart, will he be able to receive guidance from you on different occasions? And if he receives guidance directly or indirectly, will he be aware of it?*

Baba : No matter how far you may live from the Guru, it is an illusion to think that you are far from him, because the Guru is your very inner Self, and how can you be far from the inner Self, from the inner Guru? As long as a disciple thinks that his Guru is confined to one particular place, there is no use in his having a Guru, or in his being a disciple; nothing would come out of such a Guru-disciple relationship.

When we accept a Guru, we should do so with full consciousness, full awareness. That is what Kabir says in a verse of his, "My dear friend, drink your water after filtering it, and make somebody your Guru with full consciousness, full awareness." What is the use of having a Guru who is as imperfect as you, who just like you is confined to one particular place or temple, or ashram? Unfortunately, the whole world is gripped by illusions concerning Guruhood. So many who claim to be Gurus teach what no scriptures teach, claim absurd attainments and profess what they themselves do not practise. You should turn to a Guru with full awareness. There is no need to rush. It is not like going to a market and buying something on sale that will be sold out if you don't get there first. That kind of thinking does not prevail here. It is necessary to be extremely careful when choosing a Guru. There is absolutely no hurry. Before accepting a Guru you should get to know him very well. The most important thing to remember is that whatever your sect, creed, religion, ritual or country, if you accept somebody as your Guru who is without true Guruhood, who has not attained perfection, it is of no use. If your Guru is not all-pervasive, if your Guru does not exist in all places at one and the same time, if your Guru is confined to a particular physical form, then there is no use in having a Guru. Then having a Guru would be no more meaningful than having a wife.

The Guru has fully merged in Parabrahman. He has become one with the highest reality, with God. He has obliterated his separate ego completely. When a pot breaks, the space inside merges in the space surrounding it. Then the space inside is no longer a separate identity. The Ganges, after entering the ocean, becomes one with the ocean; it no longer retains its separate existence as the Ganges. Likewise, one who has become one with the supreme God does not exist as a particular individual, as a separate identity any longer. Such is a true Guru. Only such a being is worthy of Guruhood. The rest are mere human beings, and are unworthy of being called Gurus. If they pretend to become Gurus they are committing the great crime of usurping what they do not deserve.

You turn to the Guru only to fulfil your spiritual quest, to realise God. If you turn to the Guru with some ulterior motive, desiring some trivial end or material benefit, there is no point in the Guru-disciple relationship. The Guru-disciple relationship is valid only if your goal is spiritual. If your goal is worldly prosperity, monetary gain, then it is a business like any other worldly business, and there is nothing sacred about it. The reason you find disciples leaving their Gurus, or Gurus leaving their disciples, or disciples changing their Gurus, or Gurus changing their disciples, is that neither the Guru nor the disciples are perfect.

According to Vasuguptacharya, the Guru is the divine power of grace. He is one who transmits divine power into a seeker and awakens his inner Shakti. Only such a being is a Guru, nobody else. Only he is a Guru who has saturated his own being with divine power, and as a result is able to transmit the same power into his disciples. By transmitting the divine power into a disciple he causes an inner awakening. Through that inner awakening he pierces all the chakras and leads the disciple to the final state. Only such a being is a true Guru.

You must not forget that it is the Guru himself who enters his disciple in the form of grace, in the form of Shakti, through Shaktipat. It follows logically that if the Guru himself has entered the disciple, wherever the disciple goes, the Guru goes with him, regardless of where the Guru happens to live. Such a disciple cannot be far from the Guru. He may be far from the ashram, but he can never be far from the Guru, because the Guru is right within him. When I went to America my Guru was with me. He was within me in the form of Shakti, in the form of grace, in the form of inner inspiration.

As long as the Guru does not become your own Self, as long as the Guru remains apart, as long as the Guru is considered as dwelling far from you, in a particular picture or a particular ashram, you have not understood the true nature of the Guru, and hence you cannot attain anything from him. If you think that Muktananda Swami is present only in Ganeshpuri, then you haven't understood what the true Guru is. You can't gain anything from Muktananda Swami if you confine him only to Ganeshpuri. It is only when the Guru becomes your inner Self, when you begin to experience him within, that you begin to grow. The closer you feel to the Guru, the greater, the faster will be your progress. If the Guru becomes your very Self, you are no longer a disciple. You become one with the Guru. If you consider the

Guru to be far away, to be other than you, you raise
a barrier to your own progress, depriving yourself of
inner unfoldment, becoming your own enemy.

The Guru is a mass of pure light. When you remember
the Guru, the Guru is with you. If you keep remembering him, he is with you all the time. It does not matter
if you have not studied religious scriptures and are without dry scholarship. It does not even matter if you do
not understand the nature of the truth. But you must
have true knowledge of the Guru, of Shakti, and of your
inner Self.

When a farmer plants a tiny seed in the soil, in course
of time that seed grows into a huge banyan tree. That
means that the huge, vast banyan tree is already contained in that tiny seed. The right understanding of
the Guru is that the Guru, through Shaktipat, is not
only awakening your inner Shakti and effecting inner
yogic processes, but through Shaktipat the Guru is entering you in all his perfection, in all his fullness. This is
the true understanding of the Guru. If you have this
understanding you will make quick progress. If you
are without this understanding, your sadhana will be
obstructed and instead of storing Shakti you will only
lose Shakti.

The Sadguru is not like other teachers. The Sadguru
is not one who merely gives you a mantra and points to
a picture of Rama, a tantric design, or a picture of Durga.
The Sadguru transmits his own Shakti into you and
causes an inner awakening, as a result of which, in course
of time, you yourself become the Sadguru. He alone is
the true Guru, the perfect Guru who awakens your inner
Shakti, who takes away your bondage and grants full
divinity to you, You should be aware that the Guru is
perfect, the Guru is all-pervasive, the Guru is the inner
Shakti Herself. The Guru in the form of mantra, in
the form of Shaktipat, in the form of grace, is right within you. And it is with such awareness that you should
practise your sadhana.

Uma : *Recently I came across a book which said that*
13

*you told the author that his kundalini was awakened.
Now he says that he is a living Siddha. Is Kundalini
awakening equivalent to attaining Siddhahood?*

Baba : If I tell somebody that his Kundalini is awakened,
or if one's Kundalini has been awakened, it means that
he is a very good seeker. If your Kundalini becomes
awake, you will be able to rise to very high levels of
sadhana. And after your sadhana has been consummated, after you have merged your individuality, after you
have dissolved your ego completely, then what remains
behind can be given any name. Don't think that the
status of Siddhahood is cheap. Don't think that Siddhahood can be gained easily. Nobody needs a testimonial
from me to testify that he is a Siddha. My testimony is
valid if it says that somebody is a seeker. If I give him
that testimonial it has some meaning.

That person's Kundalini might have been awakened.
That way, the Kundalini of so many people here is
awakened. Almost all the people here are awakened.
Then all the people here must be Siddhas, and many of
them must be more advanced than the author himself.

Just as the true child of a poet becomes a poet himself,
likewise, the true children of a Siddha will themselves
become Siddhas in course of time. And they will attain
Siddhahood easily, in a most natural manner. For this,
no certificate is needed. Siddhahood is not a matter of
a certificate, of making a claim in a book, or of running
an ashram. Siddhahood, true Siddhahood, means the
state of being centred in the inner Self. Lord Shiva,
the author of the Shivasutras, defines a Siddha: "A Siddha
is supremely independent." He doesn't depend on anything outside himself—for anything. So a Siddha is a
being of total freedom. A Siddha is not a slave to a
certificate. A Siddha is not a slave to an advertisement.
A Siddha is not a slave to a book. A Siddha is not a
slave to anybody else. He is totally free, supremely free.
Another aphorism on the state of a Siddha is: "As here,
so elsewhere." A Siddha will be present in equal fullness
everywhere. A Siddha will exist in every other place in
as much perfection, as much glory as he exists here. The

supremely free being who belongs to the line of Siddhas, has received grace and power from the Siddhas, has perfected his sadhana and attained Siddhahood, has mastered Siddhavidya, the science of the Siddhas. Those who follow the path of Shaktipat, the path of Siddhas, are known as Siddha students. Not Siddhas, but Siddha students.

A Siddha is he who through the practice of the yoga of freedom rises to the state of supreme freedom and becomes established in it forever. Such a Siddha meditates only on his Self, worships only his Self. He doesn't worship anyone else, he doesn't worship anything else. It is for this reason that I keep asking you to meditate on your Self, worship your Self, honour your Self, do the mantra going on within you. Become your own Lord. A Siddha is his own Lord. A Siddha is his own God. A Siddha cannot see anything else in the world but his Self. A Siddha does not regard anything else to be greater than his Self, and he sees his Self pervading everywhere, filling the whole universe. For him there is nothing but the Self.

A Siddha is a supremely free being. He has perfect self-control. He has acquired perfect mastery of his senses and his mind. Not a single movement or gesture will be made by his body or his senses without his command. His mind will not think unless he wants it to think. His intellect will not function unless he wants it to function. His senses will not work unless he wants them to work. Such is the perfect self-mastery attained by a Siddha.

A Siddha is not a slave to his senses, being driven about by his appetites. There are millions of 'siddhas' like that, and their siddhahood can be bought and sold in dollars. Sundardas says in one of his poems, "I have attained full Siddhahood, I have attained the highest state. Being fully aware of the nature and glory of my attainment, I am free from all rules, all restraints, all rituals, all religious and moral commands, all demands of action, and I am resting in my own Self. He is a fake, certainly not a Siddha, who has not attained the absolute

state but has given up his duties, who has not risen to
the highest state but has given up action. He has fallen
from a high state into a miserable, low state." And
Sundar says, "Such a siddha should be treated as commanded by Vasishtha: you should not touch such a
siddha even with a barge pole. Just as you keep away
from a person with leprosy, likewise you should keep
away from such a siddha."

First become a Siddha. There is no need to strive to
have yourself worshipped as a Siddha. Siddhahood,
perfection, dwells in everyone. The inner Shakti is
present within you in all its fullness. Selfhood is present
in you in all its glory. Siddhahood is present within you
in all its power. You should only attain awareness of
your inner perfection, your spiritual glory, your perfect
Self. And you should stay in that awareness all the time.
You should become fully aware of what your true worth
is.

Just as all the coins of a particular denomination
coming from a mint are the same size, made of the same
metal, whether there are millions or trillions, it would
make no difference. And it doesn't matter whose face
appears on the coin. Whether it is the image of Lakshmi
or the image of King Edward or George, the value of
the coin remains the same, and its size also remains the
same. Likewise, all beings, animate and inanimate,
come from the one divine mint, the same divine Lord,
and all of them are equal. The Self is present in everyone in its full perfection. All beings have the same
value, the same worth, the same perfection, the same
glory.

Therefore, it is of utmost importance that you do not
belittle yourself or consider yourself small in any way.
Nor should you continue to consider somebody else to
be higher than you. Instead of worshipping somebody
else, learn to worship your own Self. The inner Self is
never affected by the body, whether the body is pure or
impure, healthy or diseased. The inner Self remains
the same in all conditions. The inner Self remains ever
pure. The inner Self is affected neither by virtue nor

sin. Remain aware of your unchanging perfection, of your own Self. This awareness is the best japa, the best mantra repetition. We consider our body, senses and minds to be real, and we must not forget that far more real than these is the inner Self, far more real is the Lord who dwells within us as pure light. That is what true religion is. That is the essence of all religions. And there can be no religion higher than this.

Rana : *In Guru Gita there is a reference to the divine vision of the Guru in the 60th verse. What exactly is this divine vision, and why did Lord Krishna take back the divine vision He had granted to Arjuna?*

Baba : When did the Lord take it back? The Lord never took back the divine vision which He granted to Arjuna. The Lord only gives, he doesn't know how to take back. Even an ordinary decent person would not take back something he had given you, so the question of the Lord's having taken the divine vision back would not arise. In fact, it is absurd to talk that way. Once the Lord grants something, He wants it to stay with you. And if you are so unfortunate as to let go of what He has given, it doesn't go back to the Lord, it goes to some other person who is deserving.

Are you aware of the verse in the last chapter of the *Gita* in which Arjuna says to Krishna, "O Supreme Lord, by Thy grace my delusion is totally destroyed forever and I have regained Self-awareness. I now understand what's what, I have attained right knowledge." After that Arjuna goes on to say, "Now I shall do Thy bidding. I am established in a state which is beyond doubt, which transcends doubt and now I am ready to do Thy bidding."

It is quite obvious that at least up to this point the Lord had not taken the divine vision back. After this the *Gita* ends. So when did the Lord take the divine vision back? However, after the Lord accomplishes the purpose for which He took an incarnation, He sheds the individuality He had assumed for that work. After His divine mission had been accomplished, Krishna forsook the separate individuality which He had assumed. He

was no longer Krishna. He merged back into pure Being
from which he had emerged as Krishna, the particular
avatar. Arjuna, too, after his work was accomplished,
merged back into the Divine. It is only after a certain
mission is accomplished that something may be taken
back, or that something which has been given may be
lost. As long as the work is going on the question of
the Lord's taking back anything He gives does not arise.

Jnaneshwar Maharaj also says in his commentary on
the Gita that Lord Krishna granted the divine eye to
Arjuna and after having granted the divine eye to him,
He made him fight the war. That is, He made him perform his most essential duty.

The divine vision which the Guru grants is the state.
which the disciple attains, the state for which he has
come to the Guru. There are two ways of seeing: one
is the ordinary worldly viewpoint and the other is the
divine viewpoint, which is upheld by all great saints.
All of you are familiar with the worldly eye, mundane
life which consists of birth, distinctions of caste, sect, and
race, seeking to gratify the senses, and death. Contrary
to the worldly viewpoint is the divine viewpoint, which
a true seeker acquires from the Guru. By the Guru's
grace his inner Shakti is awakened and he rises to higher
spiritual levels. He gains the Guru's eye or the divine
eye, by which he sees the world not as the world, but
as the play of divine consciousness, the joyful sport of
the Lord. After acquiring this viewpoint he merges his
own limited vision in the Guru's vision. He merges his
own limited knowledge in the Guru's limitless knowledge.

Neil: *How does one distinguish between tandra and
dreaming?*

Baba: The dream state is the state which follows the
waking state, and all of you have experiences of the
dream state. The dream state is a good state even though
there is no activity as you understand it in the ordinary
sense. Yet this state is more restful than the waking
state. No matter how much you acquire in the waking
state—you may conquer the world, gain honour and fame,

get titles and degrees, earn as much wealth as you like—
you begin to get weary, and all that you have acquired,
all your wealth and titles, all your honour and fame, only
make you weary. The achievements of the waking
state do not fill you with enthusiasm or give you any rest.
On the contrary, théy only produce fatigue and weari-
ness. When you get weary, when you get tired, you
begin to long for sleep and rest. Sleep takes away all
the fatigue which the achievements of the waking state
have caused. In spite of the fact that during sleep you
neither eat nor drink, nor indulge in merry-making nor
converse with friends nor do any of the things which are
supposed to make you happy during the waking state,
when you wake up you are completely refreshed, you
wake up a new person. That shows how important the
sleep state is. The fact is that if you do not sleep well, you
will not be able to remain happy during the waking state
either; you will remain disturbed and restless and will
not be able to attend to any of the things that need
attention. From that point of view sleep is supremely
important. Without sleep, waking will not have much
use.

The Lord and all the great saints have spoken of the
three states of waking, dream and deep sleep. However,
it is the deep sleep state, the state in which you are not
conscious of anything, in which you achieve complete
forgetfulness, which provides the greatest rest. All of
you experience the deep sleep state every night. You
must have said to yourself on many occasions, "I slept so
soundly last night I wasn't aware of anything, and I am
feeling completely refreshed now." Then there is the
fourth state which is beyond the deep sleep state. The
fourth state is God's abode, the state of divine restfulness.
Its name is turiya. Tandra lies half-way between deep
sleep and turiya.

The two states, tandra and dream, are entirely different
from each other. The things that we see in our dreams
are mostly fancies and imaginations while the tandra
state is very close to turiya, the transcendental state, in
which we directly perceive the true nature of reality.

All that we see in tandra, all the visions that come to us,
are true visions, authentic visions. And the understanding that we acquire in tandra is correct understanding.
There is nothing imaginary or fanciful about it. Tandra
is gained through meditation. A yogi is able to see the
entire world in the tandra state. If on any occasion a
yogi has to see something directly, he gets into the tandra
state and sees it. The tandra state is the state of bliss,
the state of deep peace. There is nothing unreal about
it. Dreams may or may not be real, but the visions of
tandra are not unreal; they are true, authentic visions.
It is in the tandra state that a yogi is able to perceive the
past and the future, and all the different worlds of the
cosmos. These worlds are seen as clearly as you would
see any object during the waking state. In the course
of meditation, a yogi gets into a sort of sleep, which is
not like ordinary sleep. It can be called wakeful sleep.
This sleep is full of tremendous bliss, tremendous peace,
and it is a most healthful state.

Tandra is entirely different from the dream state.
Tandra is the state of higher consciousness. The tandra
state is so dependable, so real and so true that in it a
meditator who has full faith in his Guru or his deity
will be able to communicate with him, he will be able
to talk to him directly and receive guidance about the
course of his sadhana.

The reason I am against falling asleep during meditation is because then you cannot experience the state of
tandra; if you did not fall asleep you would get into the
tandra state. Just as an ordinary meditator learns to
plunge deeper and deeper within, without any difficulty,
likewise an advanced meditator gets the knack of entering tandra. He learns how to avoid sleep and get into
tandra instead.

In tandra the seeker has all his difficulties, even
practical difficulties, resolved. Wherever he may be,
no matter how far from the Guru, he can receive direct
guidance from him in the tandra state; he can converse
with him. Even if such a seeker is in a distant country,
he can see the Ashram while sitting right there. He can

actually see what is happening in the Ashram. Not only
that, he can see in which particular corner of the Ashram
a person is sitting. A meditating yogi handles all his
affairs through the extraordinary knowledge obtained
through the tandra state. You should learn how to avoid
sleep during meditation. If sleep seizes you again and
again, you should know the knack of resisting it. If you
are able to resist it successfully, you will be able to get
into tandra.

As you get into tandra, you will find yourself being
enveloped by an extremely beautiful, soft blue light. It
is so beautiful to look at. It is very different from ordinary light. Just as in ordinary light you are able to see
what other people are doing—for instance, during a
swadhyaya session you may find one person reading with
utmost concentration, another dozing off, and yet another
engaged in kriyas—likewise, in the beautiful blue light
of tandra all these things can be seen very clearly. Being
in the tandra state is like watching television. But all
the events and objects that you see in the tandra state
are real, and all the information is absolutely reliable.

The supreme state, the divine state, lies way beyond
the tandra state, however. In the supreme state the world
ceases to exist entirely. Yet the tandra state is much
superior to the ordinary state that we are in most of
the time. Try to attain the tandra state.

Girija : *What is sadhana?*

Baba : Sadhana is sadhana. Sadhana is nothing but a
technique, a way, a path. Sadhana is sadhana, nothing
else.

Larry : *Would you please speak about marriage and its
relationship to sadhana?*

Baba : Sadhana makes you completely independent. If
you are doing sadhana rightly, you won't feel a need for
anything else. You won't have to depend on trees or
other things for pleasure or happiness. You won't have
to depend on the pleasure of eating and drinking if your
sadhana is proceeding correctly. A boy wouldn't have

to run after a girl, and a girl wouldn't have to seek the friendship of a boy. You will be perfectly content within yourself.

First a seeker must understand very clearly whether sadhana is something relative, depending on other factors, or something absolutely independent. A seeker can find out from his own experience. When he gets into deep meditation, does he need a woman? If the seeker is female, in deep meditation does she need a man? Is she even conscious of such things?

Marriage is valid for two reasons. First, if you are interested in extending your worldly activities, marriage is all right. Marriage is, of course, necessary for the perpetuation of the race. If you are oppressed by the sexual appetite, you can find an accepted outlet through marriage. Otherwise marriage is of no use. Even when you are engaged in worldly pursuits, on certain significant occasions having a wife or husband becomes irrelevant. The astronauts who went to the moon had to leave their wives behind; they couldn't take them with them. When you are engaged in scientific research, you sit alone in your laboratory or study. When you are engaged in philosophical study, you do not want a companion with you at that time. So even for worldly pursuits, marriage doesn't seem to have much use. As far as sadhana is concerned, it has nothing to do with marriage, and marriage has nothing to do with it. However, it is quite valid if you want to live an ordinary worldly life, if you want to satisfy certain instincts. For these reasons marriage has been sanctioned by the scriptures. Also, the more highly developed the parents are, the more highly developed the children are likely to be. But for sadhana, marriage is entirely irrelevant.

Forget about marriage for the moment. During sadhana you reach a stage where even your own body becomes irrelevant. It cannot help you plunge deeper into yourself in any way. During the higher stages of sadhana, even if you happen to move your two fingers, you think it is an obstruction. During the higher stages of sadhana you can't bear the slightest noise, even of coughing, because you get beyond everything which is physical or gross. So another person is obviously an obstruction in that stage. He who wishes to get married is welcome to, but he should understand that it will not help him to advance in sadhana in any way. It may help him to regress.

Once Indra, the lord of heaven, went to Atharvan Rishi and asked him about sadhana. And the rishi obliged him. After Indra had practised the prescribed disciplines, he went back to Atharvan Rishi and reported all that he had done. He complained, "Though I have practised this discipline, I have not yet got its reward."

The sage said, "If you haven't got the reward as yet, give up your home, give up your country and sit in that forest for at least a year."

Indra practised sadhana for twelve months, and as a result he obtained six-sevenths of the fruit of sadhana. Indra said, "I have attained six-sevenths of it, one-seventh is still not attained. I have crossed the first six stages, but I haven't been able to get to the final stage."

Atharvan Rishi said, "Now for three months become a sannyasi. Renounce even your status of Indra."

He did that, and in three months, he attained the goal. Then Atharvan Rishi said, "Indra, now you can go back to your kingdom and resume all the affairs you had renounced."

During the period of sadhana, nothing is relevant. You don't need a companion. After the consummation of sadhana you can return to the world, because true spirituality is not against the world. During the period of sadhana, however, worldly life is of no use. Even during the day, if I find anybody talking aloud I get angry, because I don't want somebody who is meditating in the meditation room to be disturbed by somebody else's lack of consideration. Sadhana is, in fact, a jealous mistress. She cannot bear any rival. Sadhana is perfect in itself; through sadhana you get all the pleasure you are seeking otherwise. Through sadhana you get the pleasure a wife seeks in a husband, or a husband seeks in a wife. You get the pleasure you seek in food, in music, and other sense objects. All the pleasures, all these delights, are contained in sadhana.

I shall tell you the story of a high seeker who happened to be very wealthy. There was a rich young lad and he had lived the life of eating, drinking, and merry-making. One day he got fed up with it all. It is quite natural to get fed up with whatever you may be doing. For instance, at the last feast, we prepared a most delicious delicacy called oondhiya which you all ate. It was also served the next day, and you all got fed up. By the second evening you didn't even want to look at it. This is what happens with all sense enjoyments. You like particular sense enjoyments only if you haven't had them for a long time, but you get fed up soon. You might enjoy things for a day or two, but later you can't even bear to look at them. It is, of course, true that after a few days, when you have completely forgotten what was served, you may enjoy those dishes if they were served again. Such is the condition of everyone.

When we are bored with something, we readily listen to a lecture against it. If you are fed up with food and you happen to hear a lecture which says that food is nothing but disease unless you control your palate, you find yourself willing to give up sweet and rich items, and eat only fruit.

Now this young hero who was fond of luxury and all kinds of pleasure-seeking got fed up one day. He happened to hear a discourse by a swami who was a rigorous ascetic, in which he spoke vehemently against pleasure-seeking, against all worldly things. After hearing the lecture, that young man was convinced that all the dancing and eating and drinking and visits to night clubs had got him nowhere. He was absolutely convinced of the truth of what the swami had said. Since he was already bored with his way of life, he was attacked by a fit of renunciation, and in the heat of that fit he gave up everything. He discarded all his suits, all his luxuries and all his wealth. He went to a distant spot in the hills and sat under a tree. This young man was suffering from acute dysentery, contracted as a result of habitual overeating, and not only was his stomach protesting, all his other senses were also protesting. He was sick of the vulgar things he had seen in night clubs, and he was sick of everything else, too. His mind was now in the grip of dispassion, and he was sitting calmly under a tree.

When the neighbouring villagers saw him sitting calmly under the tree, they were particularly impressed by the fact that he didn't have any clothes, not even a loincloth. They thought that a great saint had come, so they rushed to meet him. Unfortunately people all the world over lack discrimination. They accept things blindly, and their blindness extends to their search for a Guru also. The fact was that this young man was sick of his sensual life and it was as a result of sheer boredom and nothing else that he had given up his comforts, his clothes and his wealth, and not because he was a true renunciant. But the people thought that he was a great Guru because he had given up everything, and devotees from all directions began to seek him. People came by cars and carts and even flew to have his darshan. None of them knew the reality. Only he knew that he was no Guru, but everybody else thought that he was a great Guru. He was already sick of everything, so now when he found such great crowds around him, he got even more sick and he lost interest in food. He would only eat if somebody put something in his mouth, not otherwise. Then he would sleep only when he was put to sleep and he would relieve himself only when he was led into a corner to answer the call of nature.

You know, there are blind guides who make blind even those who see. Shouldn't people have enough discrimination to realise that a true Guru would be an intelligent being? A true Guru would not be so helpless and pathetic as that young lad was. A true Guru would not depend on others to feed him. He would not depend on others to wake him up. He would wake up himself, he would eat his food himself. He would not put people to unnecessary hardship. Shouldn't people realise this?

But the young man kept sitting with closed eyes and the people kept waiting around in the hope that one day he would open his eyes and take notice of them. But people who lead a worldly life cannot last too long. They may wait for two or three days, then they are confronted again by the memories of their houses, children, families, offices, and factories, and they turn their cars around and go home. When the Guru did not open his eyes, people began to leave. Some people began to think, "What shall we do about him? We have to leave. What arrangements can we make for him? He doesn't eat."

They had a meeting and arrived at two decisions: first, that they would post a man there who would give him food and look after his other needs, and second, that since so many people were coming to have his darshan, it didn't look nice to have him naked, so they tied a loincloth around him. On the fourth day the loincloth was tied around him and a man was posted there to look after him. Every day the attendant brought him food and washed his loincloth.

Now a new problem arose. When the loincloth was put to dry, a rat would come and nibble at it. It was changed, and a new one put out, and that began to be nibbled at also. People began to wonder what to do next. (He was in a forest which was infested with rats.)

Then the weekend visitors, the clever visitors, decided to bring two cats there which would drive the rats away. The cats were brought there, and after that the loincloth was of course safe from rats.

But another problem arose. Where to get milk for the cats. The cats began to run around looking for milk. One devotee offered a cow. The cow came, but who would look after the cow? Who would remove her dung? Who would feed her? Who would milk her? So another two boys were kept there.

Now the problem was, who was going to cook for him? It was inconvenient to bring his food every day from the village. Three women offered to cook for him, and they started to take turns cooking.

This way new things kept happening, and things around the young sadhu were becoming more complicated and his condition was changing. One day an educated young girl happened to come, and she was carrying a book by a certain guru, and the book was about samadhi through the sex act. The girl said, "Babaji, look you shouldn't be that obsolete. If you want to attain samadhi, I will show you the shortest route. Come with me."

By this time the young man had also overcome his dysentery, and he began to desire good food once again. He was not a true sannyasi. He had not renounced the world from true dispassion. He had renounced the world because he was bored with it. He began to long for all sorts of things. Finally, the young swami left his hut, put his arm around the girl and walked away with her. This is what happened. What started out as one thing turned into something else.

A woman is all right if you are interested in worldly life. But in spiritual life you get away from worldliness and a woman is entirely irrelevant. Otherwise, your sadhana will be like that of the young lad who had given up clothes and gone into a forest, but who returned to the city with a loincloth on. That is not what should happen to you. I am not against living in the world, I am not against marriage. But as far as sadhana is concerned, it is entirely independent. For sadhana you don't need any company. You don't need anything else. Just as for deep, restful and joy-giving sleep, your wife, your children, your family, your friends and everything else are completely irrelevant—what is relevant is the state of your mind—likewise, for sadhana the only thing which is relevant is the mass of pure blue light rays in the sahasrar. For sadhana nothing else is needed. For meditation or any other spiritual discipline, you don't need a man or woman or some other companion. Keep everything in its proper place and continue with your meditation.

September 26, 1972

Shaun: *Please explain how to overcome body-conscious-ness.*

Baba: Body-consciousness can be overcome by making friends with meditation or meditative consciousness.

Helen: *How can I stop worrying over small passing states in the present, memories, and thoughts of the future, and just remember you constantly?*

Baba: This question is relevant only as long as discrimination has not arisen in a seeker. When true discrimination or knowledge arises, this question loses all meaning. In all ages, all countries, all races, it is the nature of Nature to manifest herself in negative as well as positive forms. We feel something strongly if we are not accustomed to it. If we are accustomed to a certain way of life, and something alien to that happens, we feel shocked. For instance, Indians are used to living peacefully. If a war breaks out on the border, they get so upset, it is nothing short of a calamity. But in Viet Nam, war has been going on for so long that for the Vietnamese, it is nothing shocking or new. They have accepted it as something almost natural, and they live their normal life and also fight.

One should have courage, steadfastness and discrimination. One should always be aware of the fact that whatever is happening in God's creation will happen, so what's the point of worrying? And what's the point of applying your mind to all these things? If you must apply your mind to something, apply it to the inner Self. Times keep changing, things keep changing. I have studied history and I have seen that mankind has passed through periods worse than the present—worse wars and worse famines. The fact is that things never stay the same, and those who think that they can arrest change are mistaken, no matter what label they employ for their ideology, whether communism or some other ism. It is for this reason that those who attain true knowledge say that this is how things in the world go on. Misfortunes, catastrophies, accidents, all these things are a part of life, so why worry about them? Remain absorbed in the inner Self. Do not be anxious about anything that happens outside. So many things have happened in your life and in what way have they affected you? So many things will happen in the future. You shouldn't worry about what happens. Just ensure that your mind stays constantly engrossed in the inner Self.

Rick: *What is tapasya and how is it experienced?*

Baba: The routine you follow regularly in this Ashram is tapasya. Tapasya does not mean retiring to a far away mountain and sitting there with closed eyes, eating very little, not speaking, not seeing, not sleeping, or tormenting your body. True tapasya implies that you live on the fruits of your own labour, do your own work, and withdraw your senses from the outside world and focus them on the inner Self. It is the nature of the senses to keep wandering in the outside world. Take the eyes; they want to see one form after another, and they never get tired. That is what happens to the tongue; it is always seeking some fresh stimulation, one thing after another. The sense of touch seeks gratification constantly. So the truest tapasya is to withdraw these senses from their objects and absorb them in the mind, focus the mind on the inner Self and remain in that state.

Tapasya does not mean that if you feel hot inside you go and sit outside where there is a cool breeze. Tapasya does not mean that if it is cool inside you go seek the sun outside. Tapasya means developing the power of endurance, the power of fortitude and the performance of your duty most faithfully, bearing all the hardships that it may involve. Tapasya means the capacity to bear all the rigours of climate and changing weather cheerfully. There are many renunciants and ascetics living in the Himalayas, who rush down to Bombay during the winter and rush to the Himalayas during the summer. Do you call that tapasya? What kind of tapasya is that?

14

When I go to Delhi many such persons come to see me
and they tell me that they come to Delhi because it is too
cold in the Himalayas. This is not tapasya, this is only a
mockery. It is pursuit of comfort. Tapasya means the
capacity to bear the rigours of the climate where you
live, without letting it affect your inner state in any way.
There are some people who are sitting out right now,
at this very moment, because they find it a little too
warm in this room. That is not tapasya; it is only
feebleness. It is nothing but comfort-seeking, a comfort-
loving mentality. Why should you get so affected by
heat or cold or rain? In this respect animals are superior,
because they can bear all these changes and yet survive.

Shall I tell you what highest tapasya is? The highest
tapasya is to have the inner Shakti awakened by the
grace of Sri Guru, to purify your body completely in the
fire of inner yoga and to saturate it with the divine.
There are so many varieties of tapasya; fasting on certain
days or going on pilgrimages to holy places or sacred
rivers to have a dip. But that is not the real tapasya.

Amrita : *There is an aphorism in the Shivasutras that the
Self is a dancer. In other words, the Self or Chiti Shakti
is proficient or has mastered the art of dancing and
drama. So what is the relation of Kundalini Shakti and
dramatics and the art of acting?*

Baba: Kundalini Shakti is a great lover of sport, and
the universe outside is nothing but Her sport. And
Kundalini devours everything, She is the great devourer.
Acting and dancing are manifestations of Kundalini.
When Kundalini merges or brings about the state of
highest knowledge, She manifests Herself through acting
and dancing. The Nataraj, dancing Shiva, performed His
cosmic dance under the divine inspiration of Kundalini.
In ancient times, the great saints and seekers acted and
danced under the same divine inspiration, not like these
days when you have to learn the art of acting or dancing
from someone else. There is no inspiration of Kundalini
behind that kind of dancing. Even yogis, when Kundalini
enters the sahasrar, give up their sitting postures and

begin to dance rapturously. It is true that Kundalini is the greatest dancer, the world is nothing but the dance of Kundalini.

If dancers could have their Kundalini awakened through meditation, they would be able to perform much better. Their dances would acquire an extraordinary, divine quality.

The word dancing occurs in our scriptures quite frequently, including the *Upanishads*. The scriptural writers say that the goal of Vedanta, the Supreme Being, is a dancer. There is a verse in the *Srimad Bhagavat Purana* which describes the state of the Gopis. It is said that the goal of Vedanta, the supreme Lord Himself, used to dance in their courtyards.

Gods dance, goddesses dance, human beings dance. Dance is, in fact, a means of giving expression to inner ecstasy, inner joy. In our ordinary life also, we find people dancing all over. Under divine intoxication even Ramakrishna Paramahansa once assumed the dancing pose and began to dance in rapture. Bhagawan Nityananda also danced under divine intoxication, and other yogis also dance when they are possessed by the intoxication of Kundalini. In that state they forget about everything else. The difference between a divine dancer and an ordinary dancer is that while the former is seized by bliss and is compelled to dance under the intoxication of divine bliss, the latter compels himself to dance because he is without inner inspiration. He has to learn it and it is only an acquired skill which he displays. It is said that all our fine arts are pursued by all gods and goddesses. In fact, they are the divine patrons of the arts. But these divine patrons never turn their divine arts into businesses. Nor do they turn them into a mode of pleasure-seeking. They did not turn them into hopeless addictions either.

Bill: *How do we protect ourselves from negativity and grossness which our living and working conditions may expose us to, and at the same time see and love you behind it all?*

Baba: The seer Shuka once put a similar question to
King Janaka when he was in his court. The king's court
was absolutely magnificent. It was full of all kinds of
performing artists, actors and dancers. Shuka Muni was
standing in a corner watching it all, fascinated, amazed.
In the midst of all of them King Janaka was sitting.

The king welcomed the young seer. Shuka was held
in high esteem in Janaka's time, so the king called him
to the throne and asked, "What brings you here, Sir?"

That is what etiquette demands. Here also, when
people come I ask them what brings them here. That
doesn't mean that I don't want them here. Some people
misinterpret this question and think that I don't want
them here. But if I don't ask them what brings them
here, they may complain that they went all the way to
Ganeshpuri and Baba didn't have the courtesy to ask
them why they came. Anybody who is cultured would
ask a visitor or a guest what the purpose of his visit
is, and that is exactly what King Janaka did.

Shuka said, "Your Majesty, this world is full of inequality and disharmony, and when I see it my heart is
full of pain. In one place a new child is born, somewhere else somebody dies. One person is dancing with
joy, and another is weeping sorrowfully. Some people are
merry-making and others are depressed. I have heard
that you have attained equality-consciousness and that
you are established in that bodiless state. What is the
secret? How can you remain unaffected even while
looking at all this inequality and hearing all these dis-
cordant notes? Please explain this to me very clearly,
so that it may sink into me."

The king said, "I will explain it to you tomorrow in
a very concrete way. You will realise the truth of what
I tell you through direct experience."

The king gave orders that all the festivities which were
usually held in the court, should be held the next day
in the main street of his capital. When Shuka came to
the court the next day, the king ordered that a dish
full of water be placed on Shuka's head. Though Shuka
had a shaved head already, he was given a fresh shave

and that dish was put on his head. Then the king ordered four armed sentries to serve as his escorts. He said, "As he goes through the capital, if even a single drop of water falls from the dish, cut off his head. Don't show the least pity. Just cut off his head on the spot and don't bring his body back here."

When Shuka heard these orders, he regretted asking the king such a question. Shuka wondered whether he had acted intelligently in putting such a question to such a man. But nothing could be done. Shuka was quite intelligent and discreet. He accepted the situation and went through the main street with that dish of water on his head. He made sure that not a single drop fell from it. Then he returned to the palace. He put the dish of water down. Not a single drop had fallen, he was still alive and the king honoured him. "Holy Sir, did you watch all the festivities that were going on in the main street—the acting of the actors, the dancing of the dancers and the other things?"

Shuka said, "No, not at all. My mind was fastened on the dish of water on my head the whole time, because I knew that if even a single drop fell, I would be no more. So that was where my attention was focused. No festivity could distract me."

This is exactly how we should carry ourselves in the world. Let's leave the world alone. All kinds of things keep happening in the outside world. We should keep watching them with witness-consciousness, without being affected. All the time our minds should be fastened on the sahasrar.

The world is full of change and inequality. Everywhere you find that if there is progress in one direction, there is decline in another. Increase in one field is always balanced by decrease in another field. If you find people enjoying more individual freedom, you also find them losing their health. If you find wealth increasing in one nation, you also find morality declining. This is what goes on, and this will always go on. There is really nothing in this world by which one should feel amused or become sad. The world is nothing but a

play, a sport. It would become monotonous if it stayed
the same. Sport is constantly changing. A wise person
realises this truth and remains unaffected. If we are
without discrimination and do not think rightly about
things, we do not realise that for the play of this world,
for the drama of this world, we need opposing forces. A
single force could not sustain the drama. It was only because Rama was opposed by Ravana that we had the play
of the *Ramayana*. It was because Kamsa existed along
with Krishna that we had the play of the *Mahabharata*.

There will always be inequality in the universe. There
will always be opposing forces. Realising this truth, a
wise man remains unaffected. The world will always remain as it is. Sometimes it seems to progress and other
times it seems to decline. You should keep your mind
fixed on the sahasrar.

Kedarnath: *The routine in our Ashram is full of variety.
From morning until evening we have swadhyaya of different texts and bhajana and arati and japa. What is
the scientific basis of this routine? How can one derive
the utmost benefit from it?*

Baba: There is no point in just asking about it. You
should participate in the routine fully and find out for
yourself where its validity lies. If you don't participate
and only ask a seemingly clever question, what's the
use? To doze off during swadhyaya or to absent oneself, or to sit there without interest and then ask about
it when it is not time for swadhyaya, shows that there
is something basically wrong with one's mentality. A
wise man knows that swadhyaya is the best means of
achieving one-pointedness and purifying the mind. If
you are not interested in swadhyaya, what is the point
of renouncing your home and joining the Ashram? If
in the Ashram also you are only interested in eating
and drinking and sleeping and excreting, what's the
point of it all? If your attention is always caught up
in what other people are doing, by the holes in a person's
dhoti, or by the hairstyle of a particular girl, and things
like that, what purpose will be served by your being

in the Ashram? There are many visitors from Bombay who, even after coming here, like to dwell in the hell to which they have become accustomed. Even after coming to this heaven they keep eating offal, they keep eating hell. Sometimes, on my rounds, I see these people relaxing in the dormitories and cutting the swadhyaya sessions. What's the point of coming here? I have absolutely no hesitation in saying that there are some old devotees in this category who cannot get out of their miserable hell even after coming to this heaven. My Guru would quite frequently speak about devotees with the mentality of a crow. When he was asked what he meant, he would say that a crow, even when he goes to heaven, would insist on eating shit, because that is what he has been accustomed to. And this is exactly how these devotees behave. If Lord Indra, the lord of heaven, were to invite a crow to heaven out of sheer compassion, he would also have to invite at least two persons from India to produce enough shit for him. If there wasn't enough shit there, the crow would be without the delicacy which he has been feeding himself on.

Swadhyaya saves you from the habit of fault-finding, from the habit of imagining sins in places where they do not exist, from the habit of indulging in silly gossip, from the habit of wasting time. Man should make an earnest effort to improve himself day by day. Particularly for people who come here from Bombay, covered with the dirt and filth of all that they do in Bombay, swadhyaya is the means to wash all that dirt and filth away. Swadhyaya must be done regularly. If you are not interested in swadhyaya while living in the Ashram, what else will you do? You will only fall into more tamas. And tamas does not like to stay alone. If tamas comes, it will also invite its other companions. Swadhyaya purifies you from within and without. It prepares the mind for the state of samadhi. It is the magnet which draws the Guru's grace. Swadhyaya is an aid to meditation.

September 29, 1972

Davina Saraswati: *How can we deal with the instinct to compete?*

Baba: While doing sadhana we shouldn't indulge in competition. Sadhana is not like horse racing where you have stakes on a particular horse. There is no point in competing with somebody else. In this horse race there should only be one horse. It is not at all good for a seeker to have his mind occupied with others; it is an obstacle. The moment you find your mind bother-- ing about others, you should be aware that you have come up against an obstacle. Sadhana is not like an Olympic competition where for a particular event you have only one gold medal, and if one person gets it, another can not get it.

In sadhana, God's peace is boundless, God's bliss is boundless, and any number of people can get this bliss in full measure. Even if all of you attain God's bliss, there will be so much still left. It is not limited in quantity.

In sadhana one should only be concerned with the divine light in one's own sahasrar, with the bliss throbbing in one's own heart. That is what attainment means —experience of the heart's bliss and the light in the sahasrar. So whatever others do, don't worry about them. Keep your mind focused only on your own bliss, your own inner light. The sahasrar is a fort which is fully fortified against others, against foreign attacks. In your sahasrar, only you can enter, others cannot. You shouldn't take notice of others. While you are engaged in sadhana, you should feel that you are absolutely alone.

Unfortunately you are not aware of the importance of purity and loyalty or single-minded devotion in a seeker. Jnaneshwar says that the light of the Self, the light of the soul is ever new. The inner bliss, the inner love, the inner light is most high; it is much greater than the happiness which gods or even the lord of heaven enjoys. It never becomes old. It is constantly manifesting itself in ever new ways. It never diminishes and it never changes. It always remains the same. So the experience of this bliss will be the same for a yogi who is just a young lad about 16 years old, as it will for a yogi who is a centenarian, and has been practising sadhana for many years.

Jnaneshwar says, "This inner light can be seen only by the light of the Self. The Self alone is the means to its own attainment. The Self alone is the lamp which illuminates itself."

And to relish the food of inner bliss, you must hide it away even from your own senses, your mind, your intellect, your eyes, your nose, your ears, your tongue, your sense of touch. None of your senses should get the slightest suspicion of the bliss which you are drinking secretly within yourself. How then can the question of competing with somebody else arise? Another person is quite far away, compared with your own senses. When even your own senses are not to be taken into confidence, where does the question of competition with others arise? For drinking the inner nectar, only you are needed, and you should forget all others.

Virendra : *Can one overcome the obstacle caused by opposition from one's family by taking refuge in Sri Guru's grace?*

Baba : Opposition from the family can certainly be overcome. But even if this opposition persists, by Sri Guru's grace, a sadhaka can get into a state in which he will remain unaffected by outer opposition and will be able to persist in his sadhana steadfastly. In the present age one should be extremely fortunate indeed if he has friends and relatives who agree with his sadhana. What we usually find is that one is surrounded by people who oppose his sadhana. You rarely meet a family in which other members are happy if the mother goes to a temple, a son practises bhajan, or the father goes to Kashi. In this world you usually run up against opposition. If a new movie, particularly from Hollywood, is released at one of the local cinemas, all the members of the family

will be eager to go and see it. But if they come to learn
that a particular group who does devotional singing has
come to town, one of the family would be laid up with
headache, another would have a stomach ache, a third
would be suffering from dysentery, a fourth from excessive urination. There would be hardly one or two who
would attend kirtan. Such is the way of the world.

Not only this. You even find old people opposing young
people if they happen to read spiritual literature or
engage in spiritual disciplines. Such is the pathetic
condition, such is the poverty of man's heart.

Moreover, not only does he suffer from it himself, but
he inflicts it on others also. There is a devotee who
retired as a high official. He used to come here for meditation and immediately after meditation he would leave.
One day as he was leaving, he came across a friend of
his. He was going out the gate and the friend was coming
inside. The friend was surprised to see the former official
coming out of the Ashram, and said, "How come you are
here?"

The official whispered in his ear, "I have come here to
see Swami Muktananda, but please don't tell my family
about it."

I overheard what he said to his friend, and it set me
wondering. Here was a man who held such a high position and pronounced verdicts in such important cases,
yet he was afraid of his family, afraid of coming to a
holy place. I said to him, "My case seems to be so bad
in your eyes that if you come to see me, you don't want
anyone else in the family to know about it? Am I such
a disreputable character?"

He said, "No, that's not it. The fact is that it is my
case that is bad. Some of my people are interested in
dancing, and if I stay home I have to go with them. They
also have other addictions, and if I stay home I have
to join them in all their frivolous pursuits. That is why
I come here. And if I come here my case becomes bad
in their eyes. That is why I don't want them to know
about it."

The character of a man's mind is determined by his

previous karma. What he is interested in depends on the character of his mind. And his sadhana depends on his interests. Whether he is going to do sadhana depends on whether he is interested in Rama or sex, spiritual life or pleasure-seeking, inner bliss or outer frivolities. God, meditation, purity, nobility—these things are not dear to everyone. They are dear only to a few. It is as a result of the meritorious deeds of many past births, of the tapasya of many past lives, that one becomes inclined towards the Self, yearns for a vision of God. A genuine interest in sadhana, in having an experience of inner bliss, in achieving awareness of the inner Self, happens as a result of the sattvic glow which results from the merit of past deeds. Such people are very few. Everyone is not worthy of sadhana. It is only a very few fortunate individuals who are surrounded by friends and relations who are favourable to their sadhana. Generally most people are antagonistic to it.

If other people in your family have no respect for what you are doing, why should you have respect for what they are doing? If they have no respect for your love of God, why should you have respect for their love of pleasure-seeking, movies and dancing? In fact, there is no need to depend on other people. In such cases you should let them alone and be concerned only with your quest for truth, your spiritual sadhana.

Everybody can chant a divine name, everybody can talk about God, everybody can occasionally think of Him. But it is a rare one who becomes passionately devoted to God, who is able to embrace Him in his inner heart. According to our scriptures, the *Bhagavad Gita*, the *Mahabharata*, and other sacred books, it is only at the end of countless lives of meritorious deeds that one is able to take a genuine interest in God, engage himself in the spiritual quest and derive happiness from meditation. Otherwise, most people keep rushing around in the world. They are no better off than the musk deer who keeps running around in search of the musk which is right in his own navel; while running he crashes into

a rock or a tree and drops dead. That is how his life
ends.

Amrita : *There are some people who even in a divine
Ashram like ours behave with cunning and hypocrisy.
They occupy themselves in either flattering or belittling
others all the time, and their talk is also promiscuous.
This is how they spend their days in the Ashram. What
kind of sadhana, what kind of yoga are these people
practising?*

Baba : The kind of yoga these people are practising is
not Siddha Yoga or Maha Yoga or the eight-fold yoga.
It is the yoga of complete, utter depravity, low yoga.
A yogi may meet other yogis. There is nothing wrong
with that. But he must not meet a depraved yogi. Contact with depraved people brings about one's downfall
very fast. There were a few people who used to complain to my Baba, "There are people who behave like
that even in such a sacred place."

Baba would always retort, "A crow will always be a
crow even in heaven. Even in heaven he will always
be looking for shit, because he cannot stand the smell
of nectar."

You can be certain that the spiritual vibrations of the
Ashram atmosphere, the Chiti Shakti here, is very bad
for such people. Seekers experience bliss and love, their
minds turn inwards and they experience peace in this
Ashram. But those people have to drink the poison which
is generated by the same vibrations that generate bliss
for others. Though surrounded by nectar, they get only
hell, only poison as their share. We should seriously
think about whether they are really worthy or not, about
what kind of worth they have.

The other day, somebody asked me privately, "Swamiji,
even in certain well-known great ashrams, people behave
badly. Is that possible? Can people live in a pure ashram
in a disreputable manner?"

I said, "There is nothing surprising about it, because
one who is impure, who is depraved, will remain impure
and depraved anywhere."

Even an elephant, after coming to this Ashram, has improved compared to other elephants. Even tiny little puppies, having been born in this Ashram, are better than other puppies. Isn't it a pity that certain people, even after living in the Ashram for such a long time, should continue to wallow in the same filth they were in before they came here? The only reason, the only explanation is that the sinful deeds of their past lives are driving them around, making sure that they do not improve but only degenerate.

I once read an instructive story about a king. One day the king called his barber to give him a shave. While he was shaving him, the king dozed off. The barber shaved him so gently that the king was not disturbed even in the least. When he got up he was so pleased with the barber that he said, "You have done a wonderful job. Ask any boon and I promise to fulfil your wish."

At that time the learned brahmins were respected highly in court. The king used to give them liberal gifts, honour them and treat them with great respect and reverence. This barber was a person of meagre intelligence, and he thought that the highest thing in life was to be a brahmin. So he said to the king, "Please make me a brahmin. That is what I want."

The king said, "Very good. That's easy. There are so many brahmins who at my command would make you a brahmin immediately."

Next morning the king sent for a few learned men of his court. He asked them to take the barber with them and commanded them to make him a scholar and bring him back in three or four days.

The learned men were perplexed because they could not turn a fool into a scholar in three or four days. They finally decided to hold a yajna on the bank of the Ganges. They made a beautiful altar and started performing the yajna, reciting the mantras. That barber was made to sit there because he was going to be made a brahmin. As all this was going on, Kalidas happened to come there. Kalidas was the most intelligent person in the kingdom, and the learned men put their problem to him. They said, "We're in hot water. Please help us out."

Kalidas said, "Don't worry. Hold the finale of the yajna on the third day, and invite the king to witness it."

The third day came and the finale was about to begin when the king appeared on the scene. In the meantime, Kalidas also arrived with an old, feeble donkey. He tied the donkey to a post, picked up a rock and began to scrub the donkey's body. He scrubbed very hard, and as it hurt, the donkey began to bray. He was being scrubbed so hard that his skin almost came off. This raised quite a hue and cry and the king started wondering what was happening. On one side of the river this sacred ceremony was being held, and the barber was being turned into a brahmin, and on the other side a donkey was braying at the top of his voice.

As the donkey screamed louder and louder, the brahmins found it impossible to continue with their recitations. They had to stop. The king asked them, "What's the matter?"

The brahmins said, "We can't go on if that donkey does not shut up."

The king asked what was happening and was told that Kalidas was scrubbing a donkey and the donkey was braying because of that. When the king heard the name Kalidas, he became quite alert. If it had been an ordinary man scrubbing a donkey, the king would have had him punished at once. But since it was Kalidas, he knew that there must be some great significance, some meaning to it. So he himself rushed to the spot.

Kalidas did not even look in his direction. He was pretending to be completely absorbed in scrubbing his donkey. The braying of the donkey was interfering with the recitations and the brahmins were adamant that the donkey be shut up, or they could not continue their recitations. The king said to Kalidas, "Please stop for a while. Let the brahmins finish their recitations."

But Kalidas did not listen. He went on scrubbing the donkey harder and harder, and the donkey kept on screaming louder and louder. The king stood in front of Kalidas and said, "Kalidas, what are you doing?"

Kalidas said, "Wait, I have no time to answer your question."

The king repeated his question. Kalidas looked up and saw that it was the king himself. He said, "Your Majesty, I have to turn this donkey into a horse by this evening."

The king said, "Kalidas, what has happened to you? Have you gone out of your mind? Can a donkey ever be turned into a horse, regardless of what you do to it?"

Kalidas said, "Your Majesty, what is it that you are doing? You are trying to turn a barber into a learned man in three days. If a barber can be turned into a brahmin in three days, surely a donkey can be turned into a horse in a day."

How can a person who has been accustomed to eating hell all the time be interested in drinking the heavenly nectar available here? The man whose intelligence is noble, who values his human birth, who lives only to find God, who is sincerely interested in pursuing sadhana, will be afraid of committing such a sin.

Even the slightest contact with bad company can destroy in a moment all the merit gained in the past. Narada says in his *Bhakti Sutras,* "Even if you have an ocean of pure milk, it will be turned into curd by just a few grams of sour curd."

It is for this reason that I lose my temper when I find people gossiping or mixing with unworthy fellows, or trying to collect all the news of the Ashram when it is none of their concern, trying to serve as some kind of press reporters, forming their own groups. It is not my nature to become angry. My nature is to laugh all the time. It is only when I find people indulging in misdeeds that I am compelled to lose my temper, because those people do not listen to any other kind of language.

A true seeker is interested only in sadhana. Sadhana is his father, his mother and his greatest friend. He finds it impossible to take interest in anything but sadhana. Nothing else is relevant to him. One whose mind is distracted by others and by all these things is like a person who tries to make a boat from rocks in order to go across the ocean of worldliness. Such a person will never get across. He is only making his own grave.

A seeker should only be interested in his sadhana, in realising God, in realising his inner bliss. That should be his greatest friend. I find it hard to understand how a seeker can look for a friend other than God, other than his sadhana. I am not looking at it from a worldly point of view. In ordinary life, relationships may be all right. I am looking at it from the viewpoint of a seeker. A seeker should not be interested in contacts and relationships. He should be interested only in sadhana. Who can be a greater friend than your own Self? This question has given me great pleasure. I am reminded of a verse of Sundardas. "O my mind, give up the company of those who are going to interrupt your sadhana, who will vitiate your purity. Give up the company of those who have turned away from God, whose contact will interfere with your spiritual practices." The injunction to give up bad company is being given because a wicked person is not going to give up his wickedness, no matter what you do. A serpent will never get rid of its poison, no matter what you do. A crow will never enjoy the fragrance of camphor and a dog will not become pure however much it may be washed in the water of the Ganges. Likewise, if you mix with a wicked person, it is not going to help. No matter how much you try, he is not going to improve. The poet is talking to his own mind. He says, "What's the point of washing an elephant in a river? He is just going to cover himself with dust again. What's the point of adorning a monkey with ornaments? He will only play with them until they break. What's the point of smearing a python with sacred sandalwood paste? He does not value it." The poet says, "Give up the company of those who have turned away from God. If the company of certain people interrupts your meditation, if it agitates your mind and makes it difficult for you to remain in a state of continued recollectedness, then you should have nothing to do with them."

Man does not realise what he should do in certain places. One renounces his home and joins an ashram, but he doesn't know how to behave in an ashram. What's the point of changing your residence if you don't over-come anger, lust, and the habit of fault-finding? If we have not been able to give up our wickedness, purify ourselves, change our attitudes, what is the point of merely changing from one place to another? In that case can we be called seekers? Are we even human? If a man is singularly unfortunate, even if he happens to be in a place which is blazing with Shakti, he will not be able to benefit from being there, because he is not worthy of attaining higher states. He is not worthy of sadhana. He is not worthy of anything, in fact.

You should preserve Shakti with great care. If you lose Shakti and gain only weakness and evil habits, what is the point of tapasya? Even after coming to the Ash-ram, if you spend your time only sleeping and bathing and eating and gossiping, and then complain that you are not able to meditate, that you are not able to see any visions, that you are not able to penetrate to any of the subtle bodies, who is responsible for that? Who says that you haven't seen anything? You are seeing the results of your own actions.

October 3, 1972

Girija : *My mother has received a mantra from you and now she is worried about whether you would approve of her saying your mantra and continuing her other religious practices which are daily Bible study and twice-weekly communion services.*

Baba : All the religions of the world, particularly the sectarian ones, have been created by man, not God. Of course their founders were noble, but they were still men. The different religious scriptures that we have were

composed by religious teachers who believed that their
way was the only way. An important question arises
now, and I am not talking about any particular religion,
I am talking about religion in general. Who sanctifies a
particular religion—its founder or God? Who says that
a particular religion is the only way, higher than all
other religions, the only valid path—its founder or God?
You find this happening in the case of every religion.
The founder of every religion seems to think that his
way is the highest way and all other ways are inferior,
that if you follow some other way you commit sin. The
view of a religious founder that his particular creed is
the only valid one and all others are trash, or that if
you follow some other creed then you will be roasted in
hell, cannot be the view of God. If this were the view
of God, would God be any better than a partisan politician, a clever, cunning politician who sometimes sides
with this group or sect and sometimes with another?
Would that show any wisdom on the part of God? God
is not any religious teacher's advocate.

The founding of different religions does not seem to
have been very beneficial to mankind. If you read the
scriptures of any one particular creed you will not get confused, but if you read the scriptures of different creeds,
your mind will be a welter of confusion and perplexity.

God is supremely free—that is the highest truth. And
God can never become the exclusive property of any one
creed or sect, or its founder, because God remains
established all the time in His own nature. No matter
how we repeat God's name, we are not going to please
a particular sectarian deity. It is the Supreme Being
who is going to be pleased by the japa that we do with
love and devotion.

I have studied the scriptures of different sects, particularly of India, and have found that they all said
different things. After studying them I have often
wondered whether those writers really understood the
truth. After that doubt came into my mind, I also
wondered whether I was competent to make such a state-

ment, I being so small as compared to the founder of
a religion.

People seem to believe, foolishly of course, that if you
follow a particular sect, you please its deity, and if you
discard that path and take to another, your previous
deity will be displeased or angry with you. What makes
them think that God is a jealous creature of limited
vision, full of wrath, lacking understanding of how things
are, and a victim of a sense of differences? No one has
ever been able to please God, no one can and no one
will ever be able to please Him by language, observing
caste distinctions, or being faithful to a particular creed.
God can be pleased only by love, devotion and depth of
feeling.

I studied the works of different sects, particularly the
Indian Vedantic philosophies, and then I asked my
teacher a question. "I wonder whether any of the
authors of these works had a grasp of the truth. How
can it be, if they all had grasped the truth, that they
expressed it in such divergent ways?"

He told me a humorous story. Six blind men were
sitting outside and were having a hot discussion. Then
the sound of the bell of an elephant was heard and
someone told them that an elephant was going to pass
that way. They became eager to see it. The mahout
took pity on the blind men and stopped the elephant
near them. They rushed towards the elephant and
grabbed different parts of its body. One grabbed a leg,
another a tail, a third the ear, a fourth the tusks and
so on. They were in ecstasy, each one of them thinking
that he was holding the whole elephant. Each one
exclaimed, "What a wonderful elephant," though he was
just holding a part of the elephant. Then the elephant
went away. Each of them was carrying a strong impression of the elephant in his mind.

They started telling each other about the elephant,
describing what the elephant was like with the passion
and zeal of a philosopher describing a new system of
philosophy. The one who had held the ear said, "An
elephant is just like a winnowing basket."

The one who had held the tail said, "That's a lie. The elephant is not like a winnowing basket. The elephant is like a broom."

The third, who had held his leg said, "I don't know what you are talking about. The elephant is just like a stout club."

The fourth one, who had grabbed the elephant's tusk, said, "None of these fellows has the least idea of what an elephant is like. If you want to know the truth, listen to me. An elephant is the size of a human arm, slightly curved and quite hard."

The fifth said the elephant was like a hose and the sixth argued that it was like the bottom of his washtub.

So six blind men, none of whom had seen the elephant, were each defending their particular viewpoint and attacking the others. Those six fellows had not seen the elephant in his entirety; they were only describing the different parts of his body. But a man with eyes, who saw the elephant, knew that those descriptions were just partial. Those blind men are like those who haven't seen God, who are incapable of seeing things in perspective, who haven't been able to grasp the truth.

God is beyond language, God only recognises inner feeling, inner devotion, inner love, even though your inner devotion may not be recognised by priests or the clergy or founders of different sects. Man thinks that he belongs only to one path, but God accepts and embraces all paths. A particular founder· may think that his way is the only valid way, but to God all ways are valid. God will not be displeased if you repeat a particular mantra or say a particular prayer. What matters in the eyes of God is your devotion, your love.

Kalyani : *Would you please speak about the process of evolution and involution—how that which was supremely free became bound and limited, and how we then came to take a human body in order to return to where we started?*

Baba : This is an illusion of one who is seeing things this way. It is only a spectator who feels that the Supreme

Being becomes bound and limited and then tries to achieve His original freedom. As far as the Supreme Being is concerned, He is not aware of becoming bound or trying to regain His original freedom. This is what Vedanta says. Kalyani, if in the course of your spiritual journey you happen to meet God and put this question to Him, I can assure you that He will claim complete ignorance of what you are talking about. He will say, "I never become anything else, I never do anything. I don't know how to change, and I am incapable of being anything else." He will tell you, "I am always ecstatically absorbed in My own being and I am not at all aware of the difference between evolution and involution, birth and death, worldliness and spirituality." He may even ask you to explain what you mean by all these terms.

Vedanta does not recognise the process of becoming, and after you have had a direct vision of truth you will also realise that there is no such thing as becoming. Becoming is an illusion. It is a mere appearance. Whatever the Supreme Being may seem to become, He doesn't really become anything. He remains what He always has been. His nature seems to be most surprising. If a press correspondent were to interview God and ask Him, "Why did you become so many?" He would say, "I don't understand what you are talking about. I never became many. I am absolutely alone." And that is the truth.

It is only your understanding which makes things appear different. He, while living in the body, is bodiless. You have studied the *Gita* and the Lord says in the 13th chapter, "Though I live in the body, I am separate from it, I have nothing to do with it. I don't depend on the body. In fact, I have no relation with the body at all."

God appears to become something else only to one with wrong understanding. Vedanta is very subtle and to be able to understand it we have to have an extremely refined intellect. The pure Supreme Being, whom we call God, is free from evolution and also from involution. He is free, completely free from becoming. He always remains what He is. This question seems to be relevant only as long as you have not realised the final truth. When you realise the final truth you don't see any process of becoming, of evolution or involution. You only see the one Supreme Being expanding in all directions. So wonderful is the Supreme Being, such is His power, so miraculous is His way of manifesting Himself, so marvellous is His Shakti, that though He appears to assume countless life forms, He does not become any of them. Though He appears to suffer so many torments, He is beyond suffering. Suffering does not even touch Him. Though He appears to undergo so many changes, He is far from change, being immutable.

Even when you are caught up in your worldly life and you lament and wail, take birth and die, even in that condition none of these can reach your pure inner nature, because your innermost Self, the core of your being is beyond all these. Only as long as you keep looking outside does the world process appear to be a process of evolution and involution. If you look within, you will see something quite different. What you see within is the truth, not what you see outside.

Ram : *Some people say that brahmacharya has nothing to do with the waste of semen, that it is a matter of consciousness, and that knowledge, devotion, yoga and eligibility for Guru's grace and genius have nothing to do with the conservation or waste of semen, because they are inner wealth. Is this true?*

Baba : My question to these people is, what is consciousness? Is the Self consciousness, or is semen consciousness? If the pure Self is consciousness, that is quite acceptable to me. But then the question arises, "What is brahmacharya and what does it pertain to? Does it pertain to the inner Self or does it pertain to the body?"

The question of celibacy will not arise in the case of consciousness because it is without sex organs. It is only the body which has a sex organ. So celibacy can pertain only to that which has a sex organ.

Another question arises here, "What is the basis of the inner state and how exactly is that achieved?"

Take the case of all geniuses, except saints of course

—actors, dancers, musicians, all other men of genius—
you find that one day they all get weary and when they
finally get weary, what is it that gets weary? Consciousness or something else? When a genius retires from his
field, is it his consciousness that is retiring?

Take the case of my Baba. He retained the power of
grace to the very last moment of his life, and he retains
it still. This is because he was an urdhvareta: his seminal
fluid flowed upward, never downward. Some of you have
experienced in meditation the upward flow of the seminal
fluid above the navel. Others will experience it also.
Knowledge, true knowledge can be gained only in that
state when the seminal fluid begins to flow upwards.
Devotion implies single-minded loyalty. Perfection in
yoga requires vigorous self-control. The bliss which a
jnani experiences after his sadhana has been consummated is a thousand times greater than the bliss which
ordinary people experience from all the various sense
objects and activities of their everyday life. The bliss
of devotion also is infinitely greater than the bliss of the
various senses, of eating, drinking, dancing and sex. It
is as boundless as an ocean. The same holds true of yoga.
Yoga does not depend on any other pleasure or pursuit.
Yoga is complete in itself. It finds all its bliss within, not
outside. Yoga will never disown self-control.

When this is the truth—that the bliss of knowledge,
devotion and yoga come entirely from within, having
nothing to do with anything outside—why should a jnani
or a bhakta or a yogi or a genius feel driven to waste his
semen? For what? Why should he be hostile to semen?
And if yoga, devotion and knowledge had nothing to do
with semen, what purpose would be served by losing it?

I would like to raise another question, "If your body
were saturated with this precious fluid, would you lose
something. Would your knowledge be affected? Would
your practise of devotion be affected? Would your genius
grow weaker?" Even if for the moment one were to agree
that semen has nothing to do with these things, another
question arises, "Why does one waste semen?"

The Self is supremely free. The Self is beyond what

is and what is not. The Self does not depend on the
body at all. If people say that knowledge and devotion
have nothing to do with loss or conservation of semen,
then why should one lose his semen? I also hold that
the Self has nothing to do with semen. The Self is beyond
semen. But what purpose of the Self is served by losing
or wasting your semen? Seminal fluid is full of radiance,
vigour and nobility.

To say that yoga, devotion or knowledge have nothing
to do with semen is not sanctioned by any of the Indian
scriptures on yoga, devotion or knowledge, or by any
Indian theory. Therefore, one should think very deeply
about this question of semen.

The thrill that one experiences in the moment of
orgasm cannot be compared to the thrill a meditator
experiences in every single cell of his body during
meditation, while fully retaining his semen. Even in
ordinary life, if one doesn't have the virility provided
by semen, one is either considered a child or a useless
old man. Radiance and beauty and attractiveness, all
these things dwell in semen. Therefore you should conserve semen. It is only as long as we conserve semen that
we feel true affection for one another. If semen is wasted
indiscriminately, in course of time even that mutual
affection will disappear. I am not against pleasure. I am
not against worldly life. I am not against perpetuating
the race. I am only against the waste of semen. If you
waste your semen, you are nothing but a pathetic
creature. What can one without semen do in this world?

In this connection there are descriptions of elephants
who remain celibate, and just as in the case of a celibate
yogi, the elephant's seminal fluid begins to flow upward.
It finally moves into the sahasrar, where it turns into a
most precious jewel, and that jewel is supposed to be
worth millions. There are celibates even among cobras. As
the seminal fluid of a cobra travels up into its head it gets
concentrated into a jewel which is said to cost billions.
These jewels are called nagamani. When a cobra goes
into a thick forest, if it is dark all around, by the light
of its jewel it can see everything and find its food. You

should watch the large hill carefully, particularly during the rainy season. On a rainy night, if it gets completely dark, you may see a flash of light in the middle of the forest. That is the light of the jewel of a celibate cobra.

Such is the glory of the seminal fluid. What's the point of giving big lectures about it? Semen is infinitely precious and one should expend it with great care, and only after deep thought as to how much of it is to be expended. While discarding semen you experience such pleasure, such thrill. What makes you think that you won't experience a thrill if the semen were to be retained inside the body? In meditation it begins to flow upwards, and just as you experience a thrill while losing semen, when the upward flowing semen reaches the heart, you experience an enormous thrill, far superior to the thrill occasioned by the downward flow of semen. The delicious pleasure which one may sometimes experience in the heart, that fascinating experience of the heart's bliss which fills one with peace, is only possible when the semen begins to travel upwards in meditation.

This kind of question cannot concern a true yogi, jnani or bhakta. A true jnani, bhakta or yogi will never be interested in losing semen. His semen has already taken an upward direction and he is not at all interested in giving it a downward flow again. He is not fascinated by its downward flow. In fact, he is so established in his celibacy that not even a mechanical device could force his semen to flow downward. I haven't known a single yogi, bhakta or jnani—I am only talking about renunciants, not householders—I haven't known a single worthwhile Guru, who was ever fascinated by the so-called pleasure of losing his semen, or who ever found this question even interesting.

October 10, 1972

Sumitra: *How does a disciple surrender his will to the Guru?*

Baba: Will is the most important power. The divine will is the divine power of creation. God creates the universe by the power of His will. The power of will is nothing but Kundalini. The scriptures say that Kundalini is the maiden Uma, Chiti, and by that power God creates this universe as He likes it. Man's will compared to God's will is ordinary and much weaker. When this divine will functions through an individual it indulges in ordinary desires and cravings. When you direct your will to the adored Lord you worship, when you withdraw it from the senses and direct it towards the Guru, that is what is meant by surrendering to him. The divine will is not different from God, it is the very Self of God. Divine will is Shakti, Shakti is Shiva, and They live in undifferentiated unity always. So the qustion of the surrender of will in that context would not arise, because it is already surrendered. The divine will never functions separately from the wishes of the divine.

But the question of how to surrender the power which gives rise to various cravings and desires in us is a relevant question. This question is not phrased properly. It would have been much better if you had asked, "How can I surrender the various cravings and desires that arise within me to the Guru?" Did you mean to ask that? (*Yes.*) The various cravings which agitate the human mind can be classified into five or six categories: the various cravings for form, smell, taste, touch and sound. How are these cravings fulfilled? All the different cravings for sense pleasures find perfect gratification in the inner Self, which is our deity. To experience the Self we meditate. It is in the inner Self that the craving for beautiful forms finds its highest satisfaction, because there is nothing more beautiful than the inner Self; the inner Self is the limit of beauty. The craving for soft touch can find satisfaction only in the inner Self, because

there is nothing softer than the inner Self. The moment
one is touched by the inner Self, one begins to tremble
with gladness. The craving for musical sounds can be
gratified only by the inner Self, because it is from the
inner Self that the sweetest melodies arise. If you experience the inner Self, all your sense cravings will be
automatically gratified, and this is how your will will become surrendered to the inner Self. Therefore, you should
understand that all cravings merge into the Self. Then
you will be able to surrender your will to the inner Self.

S. M. Kavi: *Now I am able to meditate well, but I keep
getting sick. For instance, I feel terrible pressure in my
brain, as a result of which it is difficult for me to decide
what to do. My eyesight, too, seems to have been adversely affected. When I asked the doctor about it, the
doctor said that all this was perhaps due to meditation.*

Baba: Your eyesight was already very bad. Meditation
cannot make it worse. It is not your eyesight which has
been affected, it is your understanding. Pressure in the
brain is certainly a sign of meditation, but that is not
sickness. When the downward-flowing prana begins to
flow upward by the power of Kundalini, a seeker feels
pressure in the brain. This pressure should not be confused with disease. If you could understand it rightly,
you would see that it is not a disease, but a yogic process.
It is your understanding which is defective. Instead of
considering this pressure in the brain as a yogic process,
you have mistaken it for a disease.

This pressure is highly significant, because it is caused
when Kundalini begins to dance in the sahasrar. If you
could focus your constantly wandering mind, if you focus
all its fugitive thoughts on this sensation of pressure in
your head, you would get into a very high state, the state
of samadhi. Though you feel this as pressure, it is not
really pressure. It is the spiritual ecstasy of sadhana.
That ecstasy will become more and more intense and
that is very good.

Your eyes were already weak before coming here, and

you can feel certain that they won't become weaker. My eyesight has remained the same since 1940. In 1940, when I got eyeglasses, my eyesight was just slightly weak. Since then it has improved; it hasn't become weaker. You can be certain that your eyesight will not get weaker; you will not need stronger glasses.

Your mind should dwell on right thoughts. You should do your sadhana regularly and also be very careful about your food. A seeker should not be attached to the body. However, he must honour it. But he should honour it without being attached to it. When you become too attached to your body, you lose your self-control. Then you begin to eat all sorts of things at all hours and you find it impossible to observe any discipline. Even when you go to sleep you like to have some snack in your palm. Even though you may not need it at night, so great is your attachment to your body that you like to have some food in your palm, you like the feel of it.

This is nothing short of suicide. Whether you are a house-holder, a person living a worldly life, or a renunciant, if you do not exercise self-control in the matter of food, you will have to suffer bad consequences. Your attainment, too, will be quite different. You will only fall lower and lower. Just as I am fond of reading about yoga, I am fond of reading poetry, I also sometimes like to read about machines. According to technology, it is necessary to give complete rest to an engine for a short while. They suggest that if you give it complete rest for a while, it regains its efficiency. When even a machine needs rest, you can imagine how much more rest the organs of your body need. It is necessary for a seeker to give rest to his inner organs by keeping the stomach empty. The digestive organs should be given rest for at least four to five hours. It is only then that they maintain their vigour, or regain it if it has been lost. If you keep on feeding yourself all the time, your visceral organs will be constantly at work and they will lose their tone, they will lose their power. If you overwork a machine you shouldn't be surprised if it meets with an accident one day, some of the nuts and bolts may give

way or the boiler may burst. It is not good to eat too
little, either. One should be able to digest fully what
one has eaten, and the stomach should be left empty
for a while. Everyone should take great care of his
health, because health is great wealth. Your eyes will not
get worse and the pressure that you feel is quite all right.

Davina Saraswati : *How should we approach our work?*

Baba : You should get completely immersed in whatever
kind of work you are engaged in.

First we must examine our motives, our attitudes. We
must decide what our objective is, the purpose of doing
the kind of work we have decided to do. Reflecting on
these questions leads to more basic questions: Who am
I? What is the purpose of my existence? What is my
relationship with the Creator?

And this inquiry will lead to the discovery that you
are His, that you belong to the Creator and that you
should work entirely for His satisfaction. You work
because it is His law that everyone work. Work should
be offered as a sacrifice to Him, and Him alone. It should
be done with reverence.

Work is its own reward. Doing work skillfully is an
end in itself. While doing work we should become completely one with it. If we work from a selfish motive,
we become liable to self-deception. Work must be done
without selfish motive, whether it is worldly work or
spiritual work. In fact there is no difference between
worldly and spiritual, and this becomes clear when you
gain right understanding. Before that, worldly and
spiritual appear to be antagonistic. The world which
appears to be so diverse, which is perceived by us in
various ways—full of agreeable and disagreeable things,
sometimes favourable, sometimes unfavourable—this
world is nothing but the expansion of the one Lord. This
is the understanding we should arrive at. The world is
not an illusion, it is not maya, nor is it a brief episode.
The world is as real as God. This is the true knowledge
of the nature of the world. If we are full of this awareness, we can work in the right spirit: all work is a way

of serving the Lord. It is nothing but a divine yajna. If we are full of such awareness, and if we have this attitude towards our work, we will always be able to do it in the right manner and we will always be free from selfish motive.

Take the case of water: how long have we been using it? We use water to wash our bodies, we drink it, and we use it in so many other ways. Water has never complained. Water has allowed itself to be used by us without expecting anything from us, without making any demand on us. Take the case of air; how long have we been using it? Our very life depends on it. We take air in all the time. We can't live without it. Yet air does not ask anything from us. Air serves us in the most selfless manner. Take the case of fire or earth; they sustain us all with no selfish motive. And the same is true for space. So when air, earth, fire, water and space do not expect anything of us, make no demands on us, why should we have any selfish desires? Why can't we work without selfish desires like these elements?

This is also the essential message of the *Gita*: we have right to action, but not to its fruits. So while doing work you should not seek any reward for yourself, you should not seek any fruits for yourself. Work should be done with skill, with intelligence, with understanding, with efficiency, but without expecting any reward, without seeking any selfish gratification.

Kedarnath : *It has been seen that in the presence of some Siddhas or yogis, a seeker experiences spontaneous meditation. He experiences great love, knowledge comes to him, but he doesn't experience any physical kriyas. Some of these Siddhas are even against physical kriyas. On the other hand, there are some Gurus in whose presence a seeker has violent kriyas and also some subtle experiences, but he doesn't undergo any extraordinary inner change. Those Siddha purushas are rare in whose presence one experiences physical movements, knowledge, love and devotion, and a total inner transformation. How do you explain this? What is the place of physical kriyas* *in sadhana? Are these an essential phase?*

Baba : You use the term Siddha indiscriminately. Which university is awarding degrees in Siddhahood to yogis? What is your criterion for calling someone a Siddha? This question shows that Siddhas can be put in several categories: the Siddhas in whose presence you have one kind of experience, the Siddhas in whose presence you have other kinds of experiences. That means that there is not just one kind of Siddha, but several kinds of Siddhas. From which university have you acquired this most extraordinary knowledge?

If you can get into a meditative state in the presence of a yogi, that is no proof of his Siddhahood. That can happen in the presence of even an ordinary seeker. When a new seeker comes I ask him to sit with an old meditator who is still an ordinary seeker. If you have been meditating successfully, Shakti will pass from you to others automatically. The new seekers' Shakti is also activated when they sit with the old meditators. Can we call them Siddhas? There are many boys and girls here who meditate very well, in whom spontaneous kriyas also take place, and in whose company others' Shakti is also awakened and activated. Now, are we going to call these boys and girls Siddhas?

If you have been able to store some Shakti, if you are able to meditate a little, if your Shakti has been activated, it doesn't mean that you have become a Siddha. This is a very ordinary state, and there are lots of people who achieve this state. These people can not be called Siddhas by even the greatest stretch of the imagination. If you call such persons Siddhas, then all the people living in the Ashram which is saturated and strongly charged with Shakti, would be Siddhas.

The meaning of the term Siddha is very profound. A Siddha is not one-sided. A Siddha is perfect in every sense of the term. He is certainly not one who is stuck in the middle of his sadhana, unable to go any further, or one who falls from a state after having experienced it. If you experience involuntary meditation in someone's company, it does not mean that he is a Siddha. All that you can say is that he is a helpful friend, who can perhaps take you some distance on the path. People use the term Siddha loosely. If you have been able to rise to a certain level in your sadhana, if you have had some experiences of the heart centre, it doesn't mean that you have become a Siddha.

A Siddha is he who has perfected Maha Yoga. A Siddha has brought his sadhana to its highest consummation. A true Siddha has attained all that can be attained through yoga. All the different yogic powers begin to manifest themselves fully in him. A few inner experiences do not make one a Siddha. Only the other day I came across a newspaper full of glowing accounts of various Siddhas and it set me wondering. Who has decided that all of them are Siddhas? Obviously those who are themselves bound, and the editor of the newspaper, of course. One who is a Siddha is most strange, and so are his ways. The path of a Siddha is most unusual. Can the judgment of those who are bound be trusted in this matter? If you are bound, how can you have any knowledge of what a Siddha is? One should think deeply about this matter. Who exactly is a Siddha? You do not become a Siddha if you have crossed some stages of sadhana, or mastered a few aspects of yoga. You become a Siddha only if you have achieved total mastery of all the different aspects of yoga. If you have perfected what is called Maha Yoga.

I also hear of so-called Siddhas who go on stage and give profound spiritual discourses, and then they have to go back to an ordinary school for a high school degree. Then there are others who wander from one place to another and make a show of their silence. These persons are still caught up in certain processes. They are not Siddhas, they are still in the stages of sadhana.

A true Siddha is he who receives the grace of a Siddha, who belongs to a line of Siddhas. As a result of that grace, he crosses all the stages of sadhana, mastering all the aspects of yoga which are described in the scriptures. He acquires full power. He has seen all that a yogi must see on the way to the highest perfection. He has experienced all that a yogi should experience during his spiritual journey. Such a Siddha has achieved the highest perfection. That implies that he is completely content within himself. He doesn't look upon anything as being different from him. He recognises no other knowledge than the knowledge of his Self. There is no other place of pilgrimage than his Self. To him nothing is separate from his Self. He becomes everything to himself. He becomes one with the Self. He delights in the Self all the time. And the knowledge that he receives is absolute. It is entirely beyond the reach of doubt. So a Siddha is one who has achieved total freedom in every sense. He constantly sees the goal of all the different schools of philosophy, the supreme Beloved of all devotees, all worshippers, standing before his eyes. He doesn't lose sight of the supreme Lord even for a moment. Such is a Siddha. If one could be a Siddha just by being called a Siddha, then there would be thousands of them. In my home state many people are called Siddhas.

To a Siddha the distinction between worldly and spiritual is invalid. Both are one to him. He sees only the Self everywhere. A Siddha is so firmly established in the Self that nothing can shake him. So absolute is his inner conviction, so unwavering is his absorption in his own inner Self, that no talk can distract him, no reasoning, no argument, no philosophy can shake him from his own inner state. A Siddha lives all the time in a state of oneness with himself.

If you could become a Siddha just by crossing a few stages in sadhana, there would be no lack of Siddhas, especially in this Ashram. There are people here who can awaken Shakti and activate kriyas. It is only that I haven't yet permitted them. If I asked them to go out and spread meditation, they would be able to go out and pass Shakti to many. But it would be foolish to call them Siddhas. A Siddha has constant vision of the final truth within himself.

16

October 13, 1972

Baba : In a few days I shall be leaving on my tour of Delhi and this will be the last question-answer session before I go. I will be staying in Delhi just a few days. I am aware that many of you want to accompany me to Delhi. But I am not at all interested in putting you to the hardship of travel that could be avoided. I won't stay more than three days at each of the places I will visit and I will be back in a few weeks. This is perhaps going to be my last tour because I don't like to go out very much.

When it begins to get cool, it is a very good time for meditation, and until I return you should all meditate more and more. Achieve deeper meditation by the time I get back. It is much better to look within, to see the beauty of the inner world, than to go around looking at the beauty of the external world, becoming weary in the bargain. Though on the outside I may seem to go from one place to another, those who are able to go deep in meditation will meet me within themselves, and it is that meeting which is truly worthwhile. Outer meetings don't have much use, much love, much significance. It is the meeting within which has true meaning, true significance. Try to attain that.

Once I read about two bhaktas of Rama. One was His true bhakta and the other was obviously suffering from the pangs of separation from Him. One was enlightened, and he said to the suffering one, "Why are you suffering so much? Rama dwells in every single cell of your body. Why confuse Rama with a particular physical form and suffer as a result of separation from it, when Rama is present in every single cell of your being? Why are you weeping if one Rama has gone away? There are countless Ramas in your body. There is one Rama in each and every cell. The scriptures say that the Lord is without beginning, He is infinite, and He is sitting in the heart of everyone. When this is the truth, why don't you look for Him within yourself, instead of in a particular

physical form?" Tika the poet says, "The perfect Lord
is seated in the heart. Look for Him there."

And this is the way of the saints. Saints do not weep
for one particular Rama when they can find countless
Ramas within themselves. Fill your heart and mind with
the Lord, and do not worry about the external world.
The external world is constantly in flux. People try to
improve things, but those improvements never last. Old
things are destroyed and new things are made. There is
no real joy in the external world. What really matters
is the inner world, and there alone you can find true
rasa, true sweetness.

Dassera is approaching fast and it is very good that
on that auspicious day a road in Bombay is going to be
named after our Baba Nityananda. It is a matter of great
happiness for all of us.

I will soon be leaving for my tour, and while I am
away you should tour within. The mind is extremely
restless and unsteady. It can promote your welfare to
any extent and at the same time it can cause your downfall, so you must keep it focused on your mantra. Such
is the power of the mind that it can take you to the
glorious gardens of heaven or to the stinking mire of
hell. Keep your mind on your mantra, in contemplation,
in awareness of the inner Self. Nobody can guarantee
how long you are going to live, so there is a great need
for you to be vigilant, to be extremely careful. Learn
to value your time. It is no great achievement to spend
your life weeping and grumbling, crying and groaning
all the time. You should be ashamed of such a life. Spend
your life in joy, in meditation, in awareness of the inner
Self, in bliss.

Time is very powerful. It has spread a most intricate
net around us. The power of time is amazing. Time tries
to deceive us. Our days are spent just looking at our
watches, finding that fifteen minutes or a half hour have
passed since we last looked at it. Minutes add up to
hours and hours add up to days and days add up to years
and this is how we spend 20 or 30 or 40 years of our
lives. If we look back and try to see what we have

done, we don't find anything to be proud of. Most of
us have spent our lives worthlessly, without reaching
anywhere, without achieving anything. So we have to
be extremely careful, we have to be alert all the time.
I thank everyone and I hope you will remember what
you have heard here.

George : *My work here is finished and now I am leaving. Have you any last words for me?*

Baba : George has done very good work. He has undergone great tapasya to render *Mukteshwari* into English.
A poet is honoured by all people, but he is worthy of
true honour only when he is able to see the inner light
which blazes brightly in everyone. My message to you
is that the one who is the goal of the poetry of poets,
the goal of the artistic creations of artists, is the only
one worth seeking, and you can become worthy of true
honour only by finding Him. If you have found Him in
your heart, you can dwell in heaven wherever you may
be. You should go away from here with your heart full
of love, full of reverence, full of respect. And we shall
certainly meet again.

Steve : *Please explain how one receives inner guidance
from the Guru in making necessary decisions when one
is living outside the Ashram, in the world. Is it true that
the all-knowing Shakti will make even worldly decisions
for us if we are receptive?*

Baba : Even if a seeker has been able to rise to a high
stage in sadhana, has attained some experiences and
meditates well, he remains incomplete as long as he is
not aware of the true nature of the Guru. I have said
this on many occasions before also, and if you understand what I am going to tell you, you won't have to work
very hard, you won't even have to meditate very much.
If you understand this, you will be able to receive
messages from within without any difficulty, you will
see the truth again and again. The Guru is not a physical
form. The Guru is not an impressive figure peering at
you from a picture. The Guru is not a person with long

hair or a beard, who wears all sorts of adornments. The
Guru is the divine power of grace. The Guru is not a
physical form. The Guru is Shakti Herself. If you
consider Shakti to be the Guru, this kind of question
will not arise.

The divine power of grace has two aspects: bestowal
and control. The Guru is the embodiment of the power
of grace. Even if you receive Shakti from the Guru, it
is not his personal possession. The Shakti comes from
the divine source, from the supreme Lord, and this you
must never forget. It is just like someone who gives me
some dollar bills, thinking that those notes belong to
him. But that isn't true, because those bills have not
been made by him; they were made in the treasury, they
really belong to the treasury. He is only passing them on.

The Shakti the Guru transmits is the same Shakti by
which God creates this universe, by which God controls
this universe and by which He holds His five-fold sport
of universal creation, maintenance, dissolution, retention
in seed form, and grace. If you do not have this knowledge, no matter how much you meditate, it will not lead
you anywhere. If you are ignorant of the nature of the
Shakti, you can't achieve much. If you are ignorant of
the nature of Shakti, no matter how much wealth you
have, you are poor. You may be a great artist, but you
are a barbarian if you don't have the knowledge of the
true nature of Shakti. You may be a virtuous person,
but you are without true virtue. Just as the seed of
a banyan tree, in spite of being so tiny contains the vast
sprawling tree in its being, likewise in the heart-seed, in
Shakti, there dwells the power of creating an entire
cosmos, the power of sustaining it and dissolving it. In
the heart-seed is contained the entire animate and
inanimate universe. If you are not aware of the true
nature of Shakti, what can you do? All that you need,
wherever you are, is this constant awareness of the true
nature of the Shakti, firm faith in it, true devotion to
the Guru. Believe that the Shakti is real, that the Shakti
actually exists. If you have such firm faith, Shakti will
guide you wherever you may be, Shakti will take the

form of the Guru, or Shakti will give you messages from within. You will have absolutely no difficulty. Shakti will, in fact, take complete charge wherever you may be.

I always worship Shakti with great reverence within my being, and as a result of that I receive messages from Her from time to time. If you have just a few possessions in the world you become so delighted, you begin to dance and feel very proud. If you have been able to acquire a little wealth, that seems to fill you with great happiness. If you are able to make a little name in the world, that brings you tremendous satisfaction. If you are able to gather a few friends around you, that too expands your chest. When that is so, I wonder why you don't begin to dance and leap knowing that the all-knowing, the all-powerful Shakti that has created the universe dwells within you. Why doesn't this awareness keep you intoxicated, full of bliss all the time? The only explanation which I can give is that you are not aware of the true nature of the Shakti which actually resides in your heart.

If you continue to look upon Shakti as an ordinary force, Shakti will not unfold Herself within you. It is Her unfolding that you should be able to achieve. That should be your goal. The world is a creation of Shakti, and a spiritual seeker, a meditator, should not look down upon the world or regard it as something other than Shakti. If he does, he only shows ignorance of the nature of Shakti. Shakti does not only manifest Herself as Kundalini within the body, Shakti is, in fact, Chiti, grace, the Divine Mother. It is Shakti who projects the cosmos in the pure void. It is Shakti who makes this world while staying different from this world. It is Shakti who becomes good as well as bad. It is Shakti who manifests Herself in our worldly pursuits and also in our spiritual pursuits. So we should not regard our mundane life as different from Shakti. That is an aspect of the same Shakti we are trying to attain through meditation. The Shakti creates this sentient and insentient universe and dwells in the human being in the form of Kundalini. A yogi worships Her and awakens Her. So nothing is really different or apart from the Shakti.

The right understanding of Shakti is most necessary. The scriptural authors say that there are many who listen to discourses about Shakti, but one who becomes aware of Her true nature is rare. Shakti manifests Herself in the outer world; the outer world is the external sport of Shakti. Yoga is the inner sport of Shakti. The two should not be looked upon as different from one another. Ordinary knowledge differentiates between worldly and spiritual, external and internal, but one who has true knowledge knows that both are, in fact, one.

Wherever you are you will receive guidance from Shakti, because Shakti Herself manifests in your worldly life. The Guru enters you in the form of Shakti, and pervades your entire being. It is not at all difficult for him to assume a particular form and manifest himself in your heart and give you a message. It is a very ordinary phenomenon.

Kedarnath : *What is the place of physical kriyas in sadhana? In the presence of certain Gurus, physical kriyas do not take place at all, and some Gurus are even against them. Why should it be so?*

Baba : If in the presence of a certain Guru you do not experience kriyas, outer or inner, physical or subtle, it obviously shows the quality of the Guru, because it is the Guru himself who manifests in your meditation. If there are certain Gurus who oppose kriyas or who disregard them or ridicule them, it shows that they have absolutely no understanding of what kriyas are. They are being led only by certain books; they haven't found out from their own personal experience. They are complete strangers to the state in which kriyas take place. And if one of those Gurus finds the disciple of some other Guru getting involuntary physical kriyas, it is quite humiliating to him, because his own students don't get them. So he has to condemn them. Otherwise his students will begin to think that their Guru is deficient, that their Guru is not powerful enough.

There is nothing imaginary about kriyas. Kriyas are
not a product of the mind. Kriyas are activated by the
divine Shakti. If a Guru disregards kriyas, ridicules
kriyas, it shows that he doesn't understand what inner
Shakti is, and how She manifests Herself. There are all
sorts of Gurus in this world and he is only one of them.

The body consists of 72,000 nadis or subtle nerves which
are full of impurities. All kinds of impurities or dis-
crders caused by imbalance of the three body fluids—
wind, bile and phlegm—are present in the nadis, and
these impurities are removed through kriyas. Don't you
think that is a most significant process? Through Hatha
Yoga it can take a seeker as long as twelve or even fifteen
years to purify his body completely, yet this purification
can be achieved through spontaneous kriyas very quickly.
If there is a Guru who ridicules these kriyas, who makes
light of these kriyas, then he is not a Guru. In Marathi
guru also means cowherd, so he belongs to that category.

Everyone who claims to be a Guru should at least be
aware of what kriyas are, even if he hasn't attained them.
Kriyas belong to Maha Yoga, Kundalini Yoga, Siddha
Yoga, the yoga of Guru's grace. If one who calls himself
a Guru hasn't attained Siddha Yoga, he should at least
know what this yoga is. Otherwise he is not worthy of
Guruhood. A Guru may speak against kriyas, he may
even deride them. But if he sees a seeker doing spontaneous pranayama, bhastrika or other kriyas that are
actually occurring, what would he say to him? Would
he say, "You are a fake, you are only feigning these
movements. These are not spontaneous movements. You
are performing them deliberately"? What is he going
to say to the seeker? A seeker in search of liberation
should be very careful about the Guru. He should beware
of false ones.

Davina Saraswati: *How can I stop myself from going
out for food?*

Baba: Another person here was exactly like you when
he was teaching in a college. On the way there and
back he would go to a sweet shop, buy a package and

put it in his pocket before he knew if he had enough money to pay for it. But in the course of his sadhana he has come to realise that sweets are not good for him at all and by constantly talking to himself, by reasoning it out with himself, he has been able to give them up entirely.

Eat a little if it is absolutely necessary. I am not saying that you should not go out for food at all. You can eat out a little if you feel it is absolutely necessary for you. Yet one should follow some discipline in the matter of food. Firm control must be exercised in this matter. One should not get bloated as a result of overeating or emaciated as a result of undereating. The divine power of Kundalini should not be compelled to digest all sorts of things. Her entire energy should not be spent on motivating kriyas just to get rid of the filth that you put in your system by eating all sorts of fried things from the neighbouring canteen or by filling your stomach with endless sweets either inside the Ashram or outside. You should be careful that your prana does not become encumbered with excessive food. Eat only as much as will keep you light. If while walking or standing up you feel the weight of food in your stomach, it is not good. It becomes a great burden for the body to carry and the body loses its agility. Kundalini also becomes dull. She no longer works as actively as She did before.

If you get very hungry, if you find the gastric fire getting agitated, there is no harm in going out and eating a little. But one should not get addicted to it. Addiction to eating outside is bad. It is much better for a seeker to eat fruit than nuts such as almonds, cashews, pistachios or peanuts. Fruit is preferable. Chocolate is not good because it is too fattening and very hard to digest. It is much better to eat bananas instead of chocolate.

November 24, 1972

Dr. Wallben : *What advice would you give to someone wishing to combine the contemplative life with life in the world, away from the support and regular discipline of an ashram?*

Baba : Regular discipline is not peculiar to this Ashram. It is necessary for life in the world also. And what is necessary for life in the world is followed here too. The Ashram does not have its own special code of discipline. The Ashram is only following the example of those great men who have risen high in the world, who while living in the world made sure that the world did not come in the way of their development and unfoldment.

Take, for instance, the simple rule: go to bed early and get up early. This is a principle taken from the science of medicine, the science of health, the science of Ayurveda, and it is necessary for happiness in the world. That is why we are following it in the Ashram.

Then take another aspect of the Ashram discipline, namely regular work. In the Ashram nobody is allowed to waste time on unnecessary gossip, conversation or impure thoughts. This again is something taken from worldly life. In the world everyone works for at least eight hours a day, and after working in his office he also has to spend some time doing his personal chores at home. In this way people work for about ten hours a day. In the Ashram also people are asked not to be lazy, not to be careless, but to work regularly and hard. Those people who live an admirable life in the world do not like to gossip, and whatever they say is conducive to the welfare of others. They speak the truth. This is something that we have taken from worldly life and followed in the Ashram as well. And it is also true that from the Ashram these things spread to the world outside.

It is wrong, it goes against the scriptural spirit, it is even a sin to consider the Ashram and the world to be different, to be separate. The Ashram is a part of the world. To consider the Ashram as a corner which has nothing to do with the world outside is a very wrong approach to the Ashram. Most people in the world feel small by thinking they are worldly, insignificant. When man sees God, when he understands the fundamental truth, when he has the final vision, he realises that what he has so far regarded as the world is not really the world. It is nothing but an outer expansion, a glorious unfoldment of the beauty of the Lord, a temple where the Lord is holding His play. The world appears to be worldly or mundane only as long as you do not understand its true nature. Once you understand its true nature, it no longer remains the world.

What exactly does the word 'world' imply to you? Does it imply your office, your house, your factory? Does it imply your wife, your children, your husband, your servants? Does it imply your possessions, your cars, your dogs? It is only because you don't have right understanding that you regard the world as worldly. Vasuguptacharya says that the wise man knows that this entire universe is nothing but a glorious play of consciousness, a playful drama of the Goddess Chiti, the great Goddess Kundalini. It is because of a wrong understanding that we experience pleasure and pain in this world. It is because we do not regard the world as a play of consciousness that we get trapped.

We should determine the origin of the world. Take, for instance, the body. We identify a certain part of it as hand, another part as foot, another part as mouth. But we forget that all these various parts have the same origin, they are all made from the same essence of food. And food emerges from the earth. So the body springs from the earth, is maintained by the earth, and finally it merges into the earth. That is what the body is; it is not different from the earth. Likewise, the entire universe has sprung from the blissful Lord, is maintained by that bliss and finally merges back into it. So it is not different from Him. If we look at the world like this, we will be filled with bliss.

To go to bed early, to get up early, to meditate, to chant, to understand one's own nature, and if one gets

time, to read books which deal with inner life—this is
what constitutes Ashram life, and this is not different
from a good life in the world. A person can easily combine meditation with an active life in the world.
Wherever you live, consider that place an ashram. The
house that you live in should be considered as an ashram
of meditation. Through this outlook you will be able to
have your own ashram in the world.

Davina Saraswati : *I have been feeling a reluctance to*
meditate recently. What should I do?
Baba : It happens sometimes in the course of one's
sadhana that the mind becomes lazy, or infected with
some impurity. Therefore, it is essential for you to do
inner japa intensely and to continually pray to the inner
Shakti, Kundalini, without considering Her different or
separate from you. Then you will again be able to take
interest in meditation.

It is the nature, the way of the mind, to take interest
in something or other. The mind cannot live without
some interest. It must engage itself either with eating
or drinking, sleeping or reading, or gossiping at least. If
the mind gave up all its interests and focused its entire
attention on the inner Self, it would be most beneficial.
That would yield samadhi.

Pray again and again to the Lord within and the Lord
without, and then you will be able to meditate again.

Barry : *How do I find the Self?*
Baba: You can find the Self through meditation, through
right understanding and through sadhana. It is right
understanding or knowledge which is most important.
The Self is not like some worldly acquisition. To find
the Self you need a very subtle, highly developed, ideal
kind of understanding.

The common failing of almost all the people in the
world is that they do not focus their understanding on
the things they should; they focus it on things they should
not. And that is responsible for almost all their misery.
One man is curious about the bank balance of his

neighbour. A teacher wants to know how many students there are in another teacher's class. If man's mind keeps roaming outside, and remains concerned with petty things such as who steals a banana or a puri and eats it where, and who had a secret conversation with somebody under a certain tree, he will be constantly on the lookout to find out how a particular person is sinking into hell. He will only be interested in detecting others' faults and defects. When this can happen to a person living in an ashram, what must be happening with people who live outside?

There are some people in our Ashram who eat hell all the time. It is because before they came to the Ashram they were addicted to eating hell. Before coming to the Ashram they used to wander around the Hanging Gardens or Chowpatti Beach or the streets of Bombay, obsessed with what other people were doing. They would notice only other people's sins but would remain happily oblivious of their own. This is how they spent their life in Bombay. Even after coming to the Ashram this tendency doesn't leave them, and because of this they begin to see impurities even in people who are pure. Even after coming to the Ashram they do not give up their awful attitude, and here also they project their own failings onto others and see impurities where there are none.

If one thinks of sin all the time, if one's mind is obsessed with it, then even after coming to the Ashram, what can such a person do? He is a victim of his own past habits. I wonder why people don't feel ashamed of themselves, ashamed of their tendency to see only hell even after coming to a pure ashram. Why can't they concern themselves with themselves? In the company of such people, even good people become spoiled. It is for this reason that I do not encourage the Ashramites to have any connection or even talk to certain people. I am afraid that they will be affected with their contagious disease and receive the 'Shaktipat' of their wickedness very soon.

You can find the inner Self by turning the attention of the mind within, by continually thinking about the

Self, by trying to understand its nature. It is essential to know the Self. The Self is pure consciousness. The Self is knowledge. The Self is the illuminator of everything. Try to understand its nature. The Self revels in the outer world when your senses are active. And the Self does not lose its awareness of the outer world even when the senses become inactive. For instance, when you close your eyes, and even during the dark of night, it illuminates all the worlds which appear to a dreamer in his dreams. The scriptures say that knowledge is light, and the source of this light is the Self. Just like the sun: the sun illuminates the entire world by its rays, as a result of which you can perceive everything distinctly. Not only this, but by the same light it reveals itself also. See the Self by the light of the Self. The first thing is right understanding. Then comes meditation. And if you combine the two, you will be able to find the Self.

Kalyani: *How is the Guru able to fulfil the desires of all his devotees at the same time? Doesn't this keep him very busy? Would he have more peace if we had fewer desires?*

Baba: The Guru is established in the state which is beyond peace or peacelessness, beyond happiness or sorrow. The true Guru lives in a place beyond the reach of anyone else. In that state the Guru is not even conscious of being a Guru. In that state he merges his identity completely in the Supreme, just as ice merges its identity in water when it melts.

You haven't yet travelled to the sahasrar. Staying far away from your own sahasrar you make all kinds of guesses about the Guru. But I am conscious that your curiosity is the product of love, and I welcome your love for the Guru very much. The desires of a devotee are fulfilled automatically from within him, and I don't have to do much work.

The inner Guru dwells quite close to the sahasrar. Your inner Guru is close to your sahasrar and somebody else's inner Guru lives quite close to his sahasrar. And

this applies to everyone. So everyone has his own Guru
within him. The Guru who is different from all these
individual Gurus is perfectly content within himself. On
behalf of the Guru, the Gurus within different individuals
do whatever is necessary. It is for this reason that I
am always insisting that you be true to your own Self. You
may be able to cheat others but you can't cheat yourself,
because the one who awards the fruits of your thoughts
and actions lives within you, and he is always watching
your thoughts and actions. The Guru's grace bears fruit
through the inner Guru. You experience happiness or
sorrow again through the inner Guru. That is why I always say that you should be true to the Guru within you.

It is a great mystery. The Raslila, the play of Krishna,
is an example of such a mystery. Krishna was only one
and the Gopis were 16,000 in number. One day the Lord
declared that He would meet all 16,000 Gopis in a certain
forest at a certain time. At the appointed time, every
Gopi there found that she had Krishna all to herself.
16,000 devotees had 16,000 Krishnas. If somebody looked
from afar, he could see that there were 16,000 Krishnas,
because the first Krishna was standing in the kadamba
tree. Every Gopi felt that Krishna was with her exclu-
sively, but when she looked around she saw Krishna with
the others also, and she saw Him standing in the same
posture under the same tree. Therefore, I am always
repeating that man is not man, woman is not woman—
the apparent differences between man and woman are
merely physical. Both are embodiments of the blue
jewel which is present within them. The secret was that
each Gopi saw the Krishna who dwelt within her own
blue pearl. The inner Krishna embodied Himself in a
visible form and emerged. So it was no surprise that
there should be as many Krishnas as there were Gopis.

Only today we received a few letters from foreign
devotees saying that they had wonderful experiences in
meditation, they received knowledge from within themselves, and they saw me there, and were blessed by me.
Now all of you know that I didn't leave India. Doesn't
that show that I am present there also? Amma read a

letter this afternoon, written by a woman who has three children, two boys and one girl, all of them under fourteen. She wrote that those three children began to worship my picture. Then they meditated. In their meditation they saw me enter their worship room, heard me talk to them, and they received a message from me. The mother described these experiences in her letter.

When somebody reports such a matter to me I keep silent, without saying yes or no. If I say yes—I know that I am here, I haven't left this place—that would be a lie. And if I say no, that too would be a lie, because those seekers have seen me. So I keep silent. But all these experiences are quite authentic.

If one were to travel in the physical world it would take a long time to go from one place to another. But from within one can reach anywhere in an instant. If a reporter wanted to report on a certain event in New York personally, it would take him a long time to get there, even if he went by plane. It would take at least 26 hours or so to reach New York. But by turning the dial of the radio just half an inch, he can hear the same news from New York while sitting here.

Most people think that they are surrounded by the universe and they are insignificant creatures, that they are tiny drops in this vast universe. The truth is that the universe is a tiny drop in our heart. Vasugupta-charya says that just as the vast banyan tree exists in a tiny seed—not just one tree, but countless trees exist within one seed—likewise, in the heart-seed countless universes dwell. And this truth you will be able to experience directly only when you have a vision of your heart-seed. At present you feel that you are tiny drops in the universe, but then you will realise that the universe is a tiny drop within you.

The Guru doesn't remain busy. On the contrary, he sleeps peacefully, and eats and walks around merrily.

Usha : *It has been seen that whatever demand a devotee makes, whether it be for worldly pleasure or spiritual bliss, knowledge or devotion, it takes him a long time*

*to have it fulfilled. Or it may not be fulfilled at all.
Others, who are not even conscious of such demands, have
them fulfilled without any effort. How do you explain
this?*

Baba : Things don't happen this way. You feel this way
because your understanding is defective. One wonders
for how long those who receive things easily have been
secret devotees. Whether the desires of a devotee are
fulfilled or not depends on his faith, his actions, and the
convictions that he has had from previous lives to the
present.

In Delhi a top political leader came to see me. While
we were talking about inner peace, I happened to touch
him, as a result of which he went into meditation. He
got so deeply absorbed that he did not respond even when
he was called several times, and he had to miss two very
important meetings. He was in a deep state of samadhi.
He got up after about two and a half hours. He was not
sitting in a proper meditation room, nor was there a cave
which had been properly inaugurated for this purpose.
He was sitting in an ordinary room. People might begin to
wonder how such a thing had happened to him and not
to them, but the fact is that there were many who I tap-
ped on the head not one time or two but ten times, and
they could not go into meditation for even fifteen minutes.

Therefore, it all depends on a person's worth. It
depends on how sincere a devotee is. If a devotee is a
hypocrite, if he calls himself a servant of Rama but worships money and wanders from house to house like a dog
begging for things, what can a saint do for such a person?

True devotion does not bother about what has been
given by the Guru or what has been received by somebody else. True devotion does not depend on any of
these external factors. The kind of devotion which is
concerned with buying and selling is just business.
Genuine devotion has nothing to do with buying or selling, and does not make demands.

The fact is that the Lord Himself is standing within
you all the time, just waiting to give to you. You should

17

put this question to the Lord within and ask Him why
He is causing such a delay.

Everyone has the same Self within him. That leader
had an experience of his inner Self in no time. Others
find it difficult even after doing long sadhana. Why it
should be so is not for me to explain. Those who receive
easily must have devotion. But the other devotee who
is making complaints will also receive everything when
the time comes.

All of you should be devoted without making any
demands. You should increase intense japa and reduce
gossip. There are certain people from Bombay who are
half mental. They do not find anything worthwhile in
Bombay so they feel frustrated and come here. In certain
countries during my world tour, I found that when our
plane landed, the officials insisted on Flitting our air-
plane. When we asked why, they said that they did
not want people to carry germs with them into their
country. Now I want to give you a warning: some people come here with hellish germs from Bombay, and you
should stay away from them. Otherwise you will also
become infected with their germs and you will be completely finished. Talk less and do more japa, and stay
away from the germs. Certain visitors want to make
others like themselves, they want to spread their own
hellish state everywhere. The discipline of the Ashram
is not a punishment. It is, in fact, a device to save you
from the dangerous germs of certain visitors.

Therefore you should all be very careful. You should
not lose awareness of the fact that life is passing by.
When people go to a dance hall they spend their time
there dancing. When they go to a restaurant they spend
their time there eating. When they go to a mountain
path, they spend their time walking. If you go to an
ashram, spend your time there doing what should be done
in an ashram. If you continue to indulge in frivolous
pursuits, how much better it would be if you had not
come to the Ashram at all. I can assure you that this
time I have many cylinders of DDT, and I am going to
Flit all the visitors coming here to make sure that they

do not import any germs into the Ashram.

Live a pure life here. Be clean inwardly. Stay to yourself. I welcome everyone and I am happy that everyone has listened with such love. Without health one cannot enjoy peace and happiness. So unless certain germs are killed in the Ashram also, there cannot be much peace or happiness.

November 28, 1972

Gauri : *The Gopis had such great love for Krishna, why did He leave them?*

Baba : What makes you think that the Gopis were like ordinary worldly wives who are so possessive that they wouldn't like their husbands to go anywhere or talk to anybody else? Could Krishna be possessed like that? The love of the Gopis for Krishna was free from craving or desires. It was pure, motiveless love, and they did not mind where Krishna went, whether He left them or stayed with them.

Love becomes true only when it is without motive. The moment any motive enters into love, it becomes business. Love is not like an exchange of commodities in the market, like trading salt for chillies. It is not demanding, "Since I love you, you must love me."

The Gopis' only interest was motiveless, pure love for Krishna. Whether Krishna went away or stayed with them was not their concern. The Gopis were not fools. They were quite wise. They knew that Krishna was within them, and they were not the type who would weep simply because one Krishna left them, because they had countless Krishnas within them. The Gopis knew

that Krishna could never go away, because each Gopi
had her own Krishna within her.

When Lord Krishna wanted Uddhava to know the
nature of true love, He sent him to the Gopis on some
pretext. Uddhava was supposed to talk to them, reason
with them, but Krishna's idea was that while Uddhava
talked to the Gopis, he would come to realise what true
love was. When Uddhava reached the bank of the
Jamuna and stood in the midst of the Gopis, he saw the
play of their love. They were in a most wonderful
condition. One Gopi was holding a tree and exclaiming,
"O Krishna." Another was hugging a child calling, "O
dear Krishna." A third was looking at the water of the
Jamuna and seeing Krishna there, and a fourth was looking at the sands and seeing Krishna there. This was the
sight that made Uddhava aware of the state the Gopis
were in.

But the pity is that even when man is confronted with
truth, his vision is obstructed by his previous notions.
Take the case of someone who is walking into a forest.
He meets somebody on the way, and that person frightens
him by saying, "Be careful. There's a ghost without a
head right at the edge of the forest, and he swallows
humans alive."

The fact is that it is only a log standing there. As
that man reaches the forest and sees the log, because he
has in his mind the sort of vision that was presented to
him by the man on the road, he mistakes the log for a
ghost and gets frightened. Only if he gives it thought
and looks at it carefully will he be able to see that it
is not a ghost, it is only a log.

When Uddhava saw the Gopis in that condition, because
of his previous notions, he thought that the Gopis were
deluded, that they had gone insane, because they were
calling stones Krishna, trees Krishna, children Krishna.
They were calling everything Krishna. So they must have
gone stark mad. And Uddhava was just like that person
who became scared of the log, mistaking it for a ghost.

When the Gopis recognised Uddhava they greeted him
and welcomed him warmly, and they inquired about the

health of Krishna. They asked him about all the news that he had brought and in the process they came down from their high state of intoxication. In the course of conversation the Gopis said, "If Krishna could come to us it would be very good, but if He can't, it doesn't matter. What we have is our love for Him, and that's enough. Anyway, Uddhava, tell us about Krishna."

Uddhava decided that he had to help these poor Gopis, so he began to talk to them about the yoga of meditation. He discussed asanas and pranayama and other yogic practices. Uddhava said, "In the heart there dwells the most beautiful form of Krishna, wearing the vijayanti garland, holding a discus in one hand. If you meditate on the heart, you will see Him there." Uddhava said, "This is what I have learned directly from Krishna and I am communicating to you His direct teaching."

The Gopis exclaimed, "O Uddhava. How can we meditate on our heart? We had only one heart and that is with Krishna. We had only one mind and that is with Krishna. With what are we going to worship the Lord. With what are we going to meditate? Uddhava, what you have learned from Krishna is fine for you, but we see Him everywhere. To us the bowers are full of Krishna, Vrindavan is full of Krishna, the banks of the Jamuna are nothing but a form of Krishna. We see Krishna in the sky, we see Krishna in the clouds, we hear Krishna in the blowing wind, in the songs of birds, and we see Him floating in the water. We see Him all around us. So why should we try to find one tiny form of Krishna in the heart, when we see the living Krishna all around us? What's the point of leaving the living Krishna who is present all around us to meditate on an imaginary form of Krishna?"

When Uddhava heard the Gopis, he realised that it was he who was deluded, not the Gopis, and that the Gopis had arrived at true understanding, true knowledge. They didn't really need any of his teaching. They didn't need any of his yogic practices or knowledge, or anything else.

The Krishna of the Gopis was not confined to a tiny

physical form. Their Krishna pervaded everything around them. And who says that Krishna left the Gopis? Their Krishna was not the Krishna who would come and go. Their Krishna was the Krishna who was always with them. It is only because of wrong understanding that some people think that Krishna left the Gopis. They don't understand who Krishna is.

Uma : *You have said that true love is so hidden in the heart that even the senses don't know about it. Would you please talk about this?*

Baba : True love can be experienced only in silence. It cannot be expressed through speech. True love is so hidden in the heart that it cannot be perceived by any of the senses. One lover-poet says, "The only language through which love communicates is silence. If love begins to talk it is not genuine love, it is phony."

There was a temple of love whose master was the Lord Himself. The Lord said that anyone who had true love could come there; he would be able to enter the temple and perform worship there. So all the lovers who were true were allowed to come in. One day a strange person came there and began to knock loudly on the door. The voice inside said, "Who is that?"

The stranger said, "I am a great lover. I am a wandering teacher. I have come here with my heart full of the greatest love."

The voice within said, "You are not worthy of love. Get out of here."

Then another came. He also knocked on the door, shouting at the top of his voice. The voice asked, "Who are you?"

And he said, "A great lover."

The voice said, "What sort of lover are you? You also get away from here. You are not worthy of coming in."

A third one came and knocked softly. The voice from within asked, "Who is that?"

He made this sound, "Hmmm."

Then the question was repeated from inside, and again the voice only said, "Hmmm." And the door was opened and that person entered the temple and the door was locked after him. In the temple of love, even one word is not allowed to enter. How can a long string of words find entrance there?

One lover says, "If you want me to communicate the secret of true love, the madness of divine love, I can communicate it only in silence. Trying to describe the experience of true love is like a mute person trying to describe the taste of the sweets he is eating."

Love is not a matter of exhibition or display. Love is not a piece of play-acting. Love is the secret inner light, and nobody outside can see it. Only the lover remains absorbed in this secret light, fully contained by the love which dwells within him secretly. He is absolutely without craving, without desires. He doesn't want anything in return. He doesn't want to see anything or do anything else. Love is the highest attainment. To find love, to kindle it within yourself, to experience its fullness, is the height of inner attainment. The poet says, "True love is beyond all outer things. A true lover becomes so absorbed in his love that he is no longer conscious of what time it is, what day it is, where he is or what is happening to him. He is enraptured by his love at all times of the day."

Kedarnath : *They say that our Ashram is making great progress and that it is constantly developing. What exactly do progress and development of an ashram mean?*

Baba : Many people keep saying that the Ashram is making great progress. I also keep hearing this. This question reminds me of a lecture by Samartha Swami Ramdas. In the lecture a question is asked, "Who does this house belong to?"

The father says, "The house belongs to me."
The mother says, "No, it belongs to me."
The son says, "No, it belongs to me."
The servant says, "No, it belongs to me."
The accountant says, "No, it is mine."
Everyone claims that the house belongs to him. There was a crow sitting on the roof of the house, and he said,

"This house is mine."

There was a rat inside and he said, "No, this house is mine."

There was a sparrow on the windowsill and he said, "No, this house is mine."

All those creatures were inside the house. So Ramdas began to wonder, "Who does the house really belong to? Is it the exclusive property of the owner, or is it the joint property of all these claimants?"

That applies to the Ashram also. The workers here may say that the Ashram is progressing because they are working so hard. The cook may say that more and more people are coming here because he is making such delicious food. The fruit seller outside could say that more and more people are being attracted to the Ashram because he serves them sweet fruit juices. And the photographer may say that he is responsible for the progress of the Ashram, because he supplies such fascinating photos. The canteen proprietor may say that people come here because they are able to have light refreshment at his place. So each one may claim it for himself. The pujari may think that the Ashram is progressing because he performs worship in such a faithful manner, and the manager may think that the Ashram is progressing because he manages it so well. The writers may think that the Ashram is progressing because they write such wonderful articles. I keep looking at them all and wonder what is happening.

When the war of the *Mahabharata* began, the field was consecrated and a post was fixed in the centre and a sacrifice was made to it. One person's head was cut off and fixed on the post. Then the war began. It was a most devastating war. We can imagine what must have happened then by looking at the destructive power of modern weapons. When we look at modern weapons, we are compelled to believe that the weapons described in that book must have existed at that time. The war ended, and the Pandavas won. Bhima began to twirl his moustache and exclaimed, "The war was won because of my mace, because I displayed such heroism."

Arjuna said, "No, it was because of my skill in archery that the war was won."

Thus, every fighter began to claim the credit for himself. Unfortunately after the war ended, egotistical feelings took possession of everyone.

That same post with the head on it was supposed to be worshipped at the end of the war also. A large bell that had been tied around an elephant's neck was lying beside the post. Lord Krishna was also there, and He began to praise the various heroes there. Addressing Bhima He said, "Bhima, the war was won because of your prowess." Then He turned to Arjuna and said, "Arjuna, the war was won because of your skill in archery."

Suddenly the head on the post began to speak and said, "No, that is not true. Pick up the bell and see what's underneath."

As they picked up the bell, they found a tiny young sparrow there. Then the head asked, "Who has saved this tiny sparrow? Was it saved by Bhima or by Arjuna or by one of the other Pandavas?" Then the head said, "The One who saved this tiny sparrow really won the war. It was He who defeated all the foes. No matter what these heroes here may claim, none of them could have won the war. They have not even been able to achieve victory over themselves, they are their own slaves. So how could they have won this great war? The One who saved the sparrow really won the war."

The head on the post is not here, but the head of Muktananda is here, and Muktananda can say that no matter what tall claims people around here may make, the only one running this Ashram is the one who told Muktananda to stay here and not to go elsewhere. It is only by his power, by his glory, that this Ashram is making such great progress.

Dr. Prakash : *There are some people who only find fault with everyone else yet regard themselves as quite great meditators and enlightened, noble souls. They claim to be experts in the yoga of meditation, yet all they do is criticise, find fault and see sin. What happens to such* *people?*

Baba : People who claim to be experts in meditation must be speaking the truth, and I also accept their claim. There are two kinds of objects of meditation. One object is virtue, and those who see good, see good everywhere, even in evil, because their minds are always focused on that which is good. In the *Gita* the Lord says, "The truly wise person regards the learned, the wicked, the cow and the dog as equal. To him all of them are embodiments of the same divine glory."

This applies exactly to the seer of evil also. His mind is always focused on evil, so he sees only evil even when he is confronted with good.

My interpretation of those people who claim to be great meditators but see only faults in others is that they are experts in the contemplation of evil. They have mastered the art so fully that they see evil even where it does not exist. If a visitor from Bombay, who had mastered the art of seeing only evil in good, saw only evil here, I would not be surprised, because his mind has been obsessed with evil from his early life. His mind is full of evil all the time. Their claim that they have become experts in meditation must be quite genuine. They have become adept in the art of meditating on evil, and their eyes have become so subtle that they can perceive evil even where it does not exist.

They have become just like the chataka bird, they have achieved the very height of single-mindedness. The only water that bird will drink comes from certain drops of rain. Such is the single-minded devotion of the chataka, that even though the weather be completely dry, drops of rain will fall for the chataka, it will receive drops and quench its thirst. Likewise, these meditators on evil have acquired such power that even in a place which is absolutely pure they are able to see impurity. They are justified if they take pride in the fact that while others are not able to see impurities, they are able to. Their eyes are so sharp; they have become masters in that great art.

A high meditator focuses his mind on the sahasrar and is able to see the thousand rays of the sun blazing there.

When he sees this dazzling light he begins to sip the inner nectar and taste the purest bliss. After that, even when he comes out of meditation, the delight still persists, and when he talks he talks about this experience, saying, "I have really found something."

Exactly the same thing happens to these adepts. They take such delight in their art that like the other meditators they feel compelled to talk about the result of their meditation. They go around talking about the imagined faults of people who have no faults. Otherwise they would not be able to sleep. They would not be able to digest their food. They would not feel secure. They would not feel they have done something worthwhile. The germs of this kind of yoga of meditation are most dangerous, and if you receive this kind of 'Shaktipat' the germs of the previous Shaktipat will be killed, because these germs are far more powerful. So you have to be extremely careful.

I have been asked what consequences they would suffer. To explain that I will narrate a story that illuminates the consequences of one's way of seeing things. Once, a royal courtesan lived in a tall house, and on the other side of the street, right opposite her, lived the royal Guru, who was supposed to be a great yogi. There are all sorts of people in the world. Some only worshipped the royal Guru. Others only worshipped the royal courtesan. But there were others who treated both equally. They would visit both, one after another. The courtesan and the yogi could see each other's ashram. After visiting the yogi, some would go straight to the courtesan's place. The yogi would watch them carefully, and the moment he saw them begin to climb the opposite stairs he would begin to tremble with anger and abuse them, "They are wicked, they are beasts, they are absolutely corrupt, they have no sense of shame."

When the courtesan saw some of her clients go to the yogi she would be filled with a sense of shame about what she was doing, and she would feel great respect for those clients, saying, "They are finally doing something good. This act of theirs will be rewarded with a long stay in heaven. These are very pure, very good beings. How noble the yogi is, how great he is, how much he is doing for the people."

So the yogi spent his time watching the courtesan, keeping an exact account of who visited her. He was obsessed by her wickedness and he kept abusing her, "She is such a wicked creature, she will rot in hell after her death."

Likewise the courtesan kept an exact account of what was happening on the other side, and the moment she looked in the yogi's direction she would be filled with great remorse and addressing him, she would say, "O noble souled one, O great Guru, forgive me. What evil karma has made me such a wicked creature in this life? What will happen to me? Who will save me? I don't know what I will suffer as a result of my wicked deeds."

Days went by like this, and both of them became old. Eventually both of them passed away. The mahatma was held in high esteem in that city, so his body was treated with utmost reverence. Precious perfumes were applied to it. It was bathed in the holy water of the Ganges. A magnificent funeral procession was taken out and the body was cremated according to scriptural rights: a pyre was made of sandalwood, pure ghee was poured on the fire, and all the other sacred things which are prescribed by the scriptures were put into the fire. The body was cremated with great honour.

That courtesan also died, but she had no heir. The municipal van came and her corpse was dumped and burnt in a most irreverent manner, and everyone forgot about her. All her wealth was given to the royal treasury, because nobody would touch any part of the wealth belonging to a prostitute.

After their death both of them were taken to the final court of justice, the court of Yama. They were made to sit in front of Yama and the files were taken out and they were very carefully examined. Yama said to the mahatma, "You did not perform a single good deed in your life and you will be sent to hell. You will, of course, be treated as a first class hellish creature."

Then the turn of the prostitute came and Yama said to her, "Though some of your deeds were not good, your mind was dwelling on pure, noble, good thoughts all the time, as a result of which your bad deeds have been nullified, so you will be sent to heaven. However, you will be treated as a third class heavenly creature."

The yogi began to dispute the verdict, saying, "I did such good deeds. I lived such a pure, good, austere, ascetic life. Is this the reward of the tapasya I did?"

Yama said, "That was all done by your body and your body was treated with utmost respect and honour. But your heart was foul, and as a consequence of that you are being sent to hell. You should thank yourself that you are going to be treated as a first class hellish creature."

Then the courtesan was told, "You did evil deeds with your body and so your body was treated in a most unceremonious fashion. But your heart was good. As a reward of that you are being sent to heaven and there is no appeal against this verdict."

What happened to that yogi is exactly what is going to happen to those meditation adepts. You suffer the consequences of your attitudes. You must not see evil in good. In fact, you should learn to see good in evil, because the way you see things will bring rewards for you. The way that noble yogi looked at things brought fruit for him in the form of hell.

December 1, 1972

Virendra : *What is the difference between the happiness that flows from Guru's grace and the happiness that comes from good fortune, and how can one recognise the difference?*

Baba : You have seen both. Haven't you been able to recognise the difference? The only fortune that can be considered good is that which brings you to the Guru. The fortune that does not bring you to the Guru, no matter how much prosperity it may bring, is not good fortune; that kind of fortune can be snatched away by bad luck or by the income-tax collector, so how can you consider it good? And if some money is left after the income-tax people have visited you, it can be plundered by thieves at night, and they may also take your life along with the money. Would you consider that good fortune? That is really bad fortune.

Before India attained independence, I used to be acquainted with a number of Indian princes, and people considered them to be very fortunate at that time. After independence, when their kingdoms had been taken away, they were considered very unfortunate. What they had had was not really a gift of good fortune, because a gift of good fortune would last.

It is only those people who do not understand what good fortune is, who are blind, unintelligent and undiscriminating, who consider outer prosperity to be a gift of good fortune. Truly, good fortune is that which completely removes evil and misfortune from your life. If gifts of good fortune do not put an end to your weeping, keep you in bondage and do not bring the highest good within your reach, then what is the use of those gifts?

There is so much material wealth around me, and it doesn't evoke even the slightest reaction in me. It doesn't cause the least ripple of delight within me. I am not even aware of it. It is only when my mind plunges deeper into my heart and I am able to explore more of the inner world that I feel delight. Then I feel that truly good fortune is arising.

You find ordinary people feeling elated when they get wealth. Then when they lose it, they begin to cry, thinking that fortune has turned an evil eye on them. You cannot consider that which comes and goes to be really good fortune. Really, good fortune is that which brings you to the Guru and enables you to have your inner Shakti awakened. That inner awakening is the true gift which will not go. What people consider to be happiness coming from good fortune is really great sorrow, but the happiness that flows from Guru's grace is an ocean of peace.

Those people who are generally considered to be fortunate, who have enormous wealth, are in a miserable plight today; their condition is worse than that of factory workers even. Factory workers are able to have an anxiety-free sleep at least, but those wealthy people are anxious all the time about what is going to come next. How can you consider wealth or property to be gifts of good fortune—things which cause so much anxiety, so much tension, so much grief?

In fact, our fortune is much greater than the fortune of so-called fortunate people, because here we are living in peace and happiness. We are free from anxiety. We get such sound sleep that we don't even want to get up early in the morning. So-called fortunate people have to consume sleeping pills in order to sleep, but here some measures have to be adopted to wake you up. So the people who are living here are really fortunate. You have no anxiety, you have no worries, you have no fear, and the days appear to be short and so do the nights. Here you don't feel the day go by. If you happen to work an hour longer, you don't get any spare time—it's time for the arati. And if you happen to sleep a little longer at night, it's time for morning arati. Both day and night are short, and fortune is much longer, if one may put it that way. So-called fortunate people find it difficult to pass their days and nights; days and nights are too long for them. Where days and nights are too long and difficult to pass, you are a victim of bad fortune. But where days and nights pass quickly, where you feel that they are becoming shorter and shorter, you are enjoying good fortune.

Therefore, the really worthwhile gifts of great fortune are inner awakening, contemplation of the Self and constant absorption in one's own being. These are the gifts which will never leave you once you have them, and these are the gifts which will never cause tears, suffering or agony. What are generally considered to be gifts of fortune cause so much suffering when they go, and everybody knows that they do not last forever. That is not good fortune.

Janaki : *What is justice? Is there any meaning in our ordinary ideas of right and wrong, fairness and justice? When something appears unjust and wrong to us, should we act on that feeling, or should we passively accept everything that happens as being God's lila?*

Baba : How can you be sure that what you consider to be justice is justice? What is your criterion? What is the authority for deciding what justice is or is not? Take, for example, the Ashram discipline. It is the Ashram rule that you must get up at three. If you don't get up at three, you are being unjust to the Ashram. If you get up at three, then you are being just. Justice is a relative concept, and it depends on what field you are talking about. In different contexts, in different fields, justice would have different connotations. Justice does not imply that you may act any way you feel like. My attendant, Ramdas, follows certain rules here, which are different from the rules followed in the office. If the trustees go to the office they are allowed to enter. If the secretary wants a certain file, they permit him to take that. But no trustee can enter this room. If a trustee were to come here, Ramdas would not allow him to enter. So the justice that prevails here is different from the justice that prevails in the office. If a trustee told Ramdas, "Look, I am a trustee of the Ashram, let me in," Ramdas would tell him, "You may be a trustee for the Ashram but as far as I am concerned, the only trustee is Baba."

There are certain rich devotees who have donated millions to the Ashram. If one were to walk into the kitchen and demand a chapati from the cook, saying, "I have donated so much to the Ashram," the cook would tell him, "Go and tell this to him you have made the donation to. You haven't made the donation to me. My instructions are quite different, and I am following the instructions of the one to whom you made the donation. So go talk to him."

What may be considered just in the office will not be considered just in the hall. And what would be considered just in the hall would not be just in the kitchen. What may be considered just in the kitchen would not be considered to be just here. And what would be just here would not be just in the meditation room. Therefore the discipline that prevails in a certain field is justice in relation to that field.

Everyone should fight for justice of course, but then first you must be sure that what you are fighting for is really just and your mind is not playing a trick on you, duping you into thinking that what is justice is really injustice.

There was a cook here who was slightly deaf. One day his brother turned up and wanted to meet him. Thinking that his brother was working here, he tried to come in without permission, and he was stopped. Then the matter came to me. I said that the boys in the hall did the right thing by stopping him. It is true that his brother is working here. But it is his brother, not he who works here. What does he have to do in the kitchen? If he wishes to talk to his brother he should tell the one on duty and that person would send for the cook.

We must be quite clear in our minds about whether what we consider to be justice is really justice or injustice. Justice will never cause suffering; justice will always bring happiness.

Anandi: *Does faith in a great person come only by seeing him, or does it come from some experience?*

Baba: The things that create faith in a great saint are what you hear about his greatness, what you know about his life, or what happens when you meet some fortunate people who have received his grace. You can't have faith in a great saint without reason. There has to be some basis for it. How can you decide whether a person is a great saint or not?

The scriptures say that the first factor which creates faith is what you hear about a saint's greatness, his glory, particularly from persons who are sincere and noble. If

18

you move in the company of those who have faith, your faith also becomes stronger. Then you yourself may begin to have experiences which further strengthen your faith. Your faith will take you further and further until you have the final realisation. Then your faith will also become absolute.

To have faith in a great saint just on seeing him, you have to be a highly evolved, highly developed soul. Don't think that a great saint wants more and more people to have faith in him. In fact, truly great saints behave in ways that are very strange. If you were to see them do certain things, you would lose even the little faith that you had before you came to them. Take the case of Zipruanna. He was a very great saint. Absolutely extraordinary. He was not a lecturer, not an ordinary teacher who would pray for you most willingly, or bless you readily. He spent his time sitting on a heap of garbage, yet his body was not at all affected by what he was sitting on. In spite of sitting on dirt for so many hours, his body used to emit fragrance. That's how pure it had become as a result of being purified in the fire of yoga.

Then there was a great yogi in Aurangabad, whose name was Balkrishna. He, too, had strange ways. Whenever he passed by a school, all the children would leave their classes and begin to follow him. He would share their mirthful spirit and would begin to run with them. Then he would take them through the market and ask them to eat anything they wanted at a sweet seller's shop, and they would do that. Then he would disappear. Then, of course, the shopkeepers knew that whatever he did was a blessing, so they didn't mind. For bathing he would descend into a pit of filth into which all the gutters of the town flowed. He would stand half-submerged in it and smear his body with the filth, saying, "Hara Hara Hara Mahadev." If somebody happened to stand nearby, he would pick up some of the filth and throw it in their face. But the filth that was thrown by him would smell like a most expensive perfume and the fragrance would not leave the person's nostrils for days.

Take the case of Hari Giri Baba. If he saw anyone

wearing a nice coat, he would ask him for it and put
it on. If somebody was wearing a gold ring, Hari Giri
Baba would ask for it, wear it himself and never return it.

How could you have faith in any of these saints just
by seeing them? Baba Nityananda appeared to be quite
calm, quite saintly, while he was lying down, but the
moment he got angry he would get completely transformed. Instead of a saint he would start looking like
something else. He would pick up anything within his
reach, whether a stone or a brick or anything else and
hurl it at the person who happened to disturb him. Then
he would shout the foulest terms of abuse. You can't
believe—unless of course, you heard him use those terms
—that a great saint could ever use such filthy terms of
abuse. Therefore, it is very difficult to recognise a true
saint.

Still, you have to recognise him, and that is possible
through discrimination. Anyone who has attained a
worthwhile state will be living in a strange way, acting
and behaving in ways we are not accustomed to.

There was a certain poet in Benaras, he was a Siddha.
In one of his poems he says, "He whose heart always
dwells on the Lord of his heart will behave in ways
contrary to our expectations. Their ways are so strange,
so contrary. If it is cold, they take cold drinks which
freeze their systems, and then they visit colder places.
If it is hot, they use a substance which heats up the
system terribly. During the heat of summer they go to
the South where it is really hot, to spend the summer
there. Such are the ways of these ecstatic saints that
in the rain you find them dry and in the sun you find
them wet. You may find one sleeping the whole day
and awake the whole night. You may find them fighting
with heroes and running away from cowards. If somebody is not willing to give them something they ask
for it again and again, but if somebody is really willing
to give them something they don't accept it. These are
the true emperors, and even kings go and beg from them.
Such are the ways of these saints, they will teach the
learned and learn from fools. Benarsi says, all that I

have told you is not my own invention. I have spoken the truth."

Therefore, it is difficult to recognise a truly great one. Very few great saints behave according to society's injunctions. Therefore, how would you get faith in them just by seeing them? Sometimes they behave like inert logs, sometimes like little kids, at other times like madmen or demons. Another poet, Devi, says, "One thing is true, however: what ordinary people consider most precious has no value for them. And what is considered most difficult comes quite easily by their grace."

There were so many persons who received my Guru's grace, and though outwardly he behaved in a puzzling manner, inwardly he was in such a state that people could get extraordinary experiences in a moment just by being in his presence. It would be quite natural if you had faith after having certain experiences by their grace. Or you can also get faith by listening to the words of noble and sincere people.

Usha : *We do not wish to disobey the Guru's commands, but sometimes, in spite of ourselves, we disobey them. How do you explain this?*

Baba : This shows that you haven't yet attained control or mastery of your senses, your mind, or your body. Once Baba Nityananda said to me, "Don't eat mangoes." I gave them up, I didn't even touch a mango. After twelve years, Baba one day gave me two mangoes and then I started eating mangoes again. I completed my tapasya under a mango tree. I spent twelve years under a mango tree, and whatever there was to see in the world was seen by me under that tree. It is for this reason that we have mango trees here in the courtyard where I sit, because under a mango tree I did so much tapasya, I had so many experiences, I saw so many visions. People say that one should go to a cave for tapasya, or one should go to a solitary corner, but I did all my tapasya under a mango tree. I did not go to the Himalayas nor retire to a cave. And that's why I have planted so many mango trees here.

Realisation comes only through complete obedience to

the Guru. Many disciples live with a Guru and though the Guru is the same, some of them receive more than others. It is not due to the fact that the Guru is partial. No one who is worthy of being a Guru can be partial. Shankaracharya says, "A son may turn bad, but a mother will never turn bad. You may have many bad sons, but you will never have a bad mother."

You can have degraded disciples, but you will never have degraded Gurus, because the true Guru is established in such a high state. The fact that some disciples receive more and some less, and some do not receive anything cannot be attributed to partiality on the part of the Guru, because the Guru will never be partial.

It is, of course, true that the Guru may treat different persons differently. He may adopt different methods. He may sometimes treat a person very gently, sometimes he may be very harsh and rude. At other times he may even go out of his way to help him. But as far as the question of transmitting spiritual wealth to disciples is concerned, the Guru will never be partial.

Therefore, we should achieve true freedom by attaining complete mastery over ourselves. My Guru never liked to beg. He was so against begging that he would not even ask for water when he was thirsty. He would sit quietly and keep scratching his head, and if an attendant happened to come and ask, "Can I fetch water for you?" he would say, "Yes." But he would never ask anyone to fetch water for him. This is what he taught me, never to beg, and though such a large Ashram has come up here, I haven't begged anyone for anything. I never begged anyone even for food, or even for a small piece of cloth. And it is as a result of total obedience to the Guru that today there is so much in the Ashram, and when people offer to give more, I tell them to wait. I tell them, "I have enough here. Better give it some other time."

My Guru was not in favour of going from house to house, and though I spent twelve years in Yeola, I did not see the whole of Yeola, I did not visit more than ten houses. And I still don't know more than ten families in Yeola. Even now when Baba is no longer in his physical form, I follow his commands most faithfully. When I go to Bombay I receive at least one thousand invitations from different places, but I stick to one place, and meet all the visitors and devotees there. Therefore, we should have the strength to obey the Guru's will fully, and that would be our greatest tapasya.

The Guru's word must be obeyed because there is great mystery behind the Guru's command. Powers or realisations are not things which descend from the blue sky and enter us. Powers and realisations are achieved through obedience to the Guru's command. All realisations dwell in the Guru's word. Therefore, you should obey the Guru's command most faithfully. You should strive again and again to be faithful to his word.

Uma : *The Gita says that what is day to an ordinary man is night to a yogi and what is night to an ordinary man is day to a yogi. What exactly does that mean? Does it mean that a yogi should sleep during the day and stay awake and meditate at night?*

Baba : What it means is that a yogi sleeps to the world of ordinary people. What is day to ordinary people? Their day consists of the notion of I and mine, identity with the body, a sense-ridden life. The day of an ordinary person consists of eating and drinking, indulging in so many different pursuits and pleasures. The yogi sleeps through this world, because this world of outer activity, outer pursuits, is tasteless to him.

Dhyan, dharana and samadhi, going to bed early, rising early, discipline, renunciation, contemplation of the inner Self, spiritual pilgrimages, dwelling on the inner Self— these things constitute day to a yogi. And it is precisely these things which have no interest for the ordinary person; he remains asleep to them. Here day and night are used as metaphors, and you shouldn't take them literally. Dwelling on the inner Self is what is day to a yogi, and dwelling in the external world constitutes day for the ordinary person. Therefore, what is day or wakefulness to an ordinary person is night or sleep to a yogi, and vice versa. An ordinary man's paradise is void of all delights for a yogi and a yogi's paradise is void of all delights for an ordinary person.

I have met people who interpret this verse of the *Gita* literally. They come and tell me that they are sleeping during the day because they are following the command of the *Gita*. They obviously haven't understood what the *Gita* says. The day of an ordinary person is constituted by his interest in his wife and children and various activities of business. And it is to this world that the yogi is asleep.

You should go further and further ahead on the spiritual path every day. You should acquire complete mastery over your body. I can assure you that if you have mastered your body you can do anything in it. Don't be afraid that if you master your body it will become useless for the world. It doesn't take even a minute for a renunciant to turn to the other life, and live it most effectively.

Your mind should dwell on the noblest and purest thoughts, and you should be concerned with yourself, not with others. Do your work faithfully and after you have finished, concentrate all your thoughts, all your energies on your own Self. Reform yourself more and more every day. Think higher and nobler thoughts. Some ancient philosophers or religious men, I don't know for what reason, have written certain things which make a man who is already miserable, already suffering from feelings of inferiority and insecurity, feel even more miserable. You should not follow that kind of stuff. That kind of book will instill very unhealthy ideas into us, the kind of notions which we have become accustomed to through countless lives, namely, that we are sinners, inferior, helpless, wicked, depraved and so on. I don't know why some writers are so obsessed with failure and weakness. They don't write about their triumphs, about their conquests. If they did, people would be inspired and they would also be able to develop themselves.

Do not compare yourself with others and try to feel secure that way. You should raise yourself to a very

high level and stay there. Only today I read the story
of a great avadhoot and I was very moved by it. I read
it three times, and have been pondering it since then.
The writer says that people try to imitate great men
without understanding what state they are in. So one
should not lose one's discrimination.

December 5, 1972

Prof. Chowdhary : *What is the relationship between japa
and nada? What should one do to increase one's interest
in nada? After nada has arisen, should one concentrate
only on nada in meditation, or should he do japa and
also try to keep the mind focused on the ajna chakra or
the sahasrar?*

Baba : It is japa which begins to vibrate later as nada.
As a yogi keeps practising japa, when he becomes one
with it, it turns into nada. It is for this reason that great
yogis like Patanjali have commented that one should do
japa being fully aware of the meaning of the mantra.
Japa is a great, a pure means and it can take you to the
highest state by itself. If meditation is combined with
japa, then meditation becomes many times more effective.
Lord Shiva also says about japa, "O Parvati, all realisations come from japa." And He repeats it three times.
You must have read in the *Gita* many times that the
Lord says, "Among yajnas I am the yajna of japa." That
means that japa is the Lord Himself.

You can understand the power of japa from a very
simple example. Even in ordinary life you are so
affected by words. I don't know how to abuse in English,
but if I were to call somebody a foul name, say a bastard
—the word doesn't consist of more than a few letters—
it would have a powerful effect on the listener. A term

of abuse bears fruit inside you at once. You did not receive that term from a great saint, you did not repeat it for a long time, nor did you meditate on it for years and years. When a term of abuse can bear fruit instantly, there is no reason to think that japa cannot be effective.

Japa is the repetition of the name of the Lord, and the name of the Lord is the Lord Himself. In course of time, when japa begins to bear fruit, it turns into nada. When that happens it means that the Lord Himself has begun to speak in the divine spaces. Nada is, in fact, the highest japa, the great japa which occurs in the space of consciousness. Once nada has arisen, there is no point in persisting in the earlier japa. Just listen to the nada. Listening to nada is the essence of yoga, and meditation, too. Nada comes straight from the lips of God. Nada vibrates in the space of consciousness and through it Chitishakti sports directly. It is said that there is no mantra higher than nada. After nada has arisen, the only duty of a yogi is to keep listening to it. In course of time, he will begin to move in the space of consciousness.

All the objects of the universe are products of the sound vibration which God set in motion. It is from nada that the entire universe has arisen, and as one listens to nada, nectars arise within and one begins to see distant objects and to experience the divine touch.

After nada has arisen, one does not have to focus one's mind on the chakras, because nada is beyond the chakras. One should only become fully absorbed in nada itself. Nada has enormous importance. Listen to it in meditation and become one with it. Jnaneshwar Maharaj says that the state called turiya is quite close to nada. Once nada has arisen, a yogi should become completely absorbed in it. He should only listen to nada, think about it all the time. He should eat nada, as it were, he should drink nada. Once nada has arisen, there is nothing else of any importance for a yogi to do than to keep listening most attentively to the nada itself. Whatever form nada may take—whether you hear it as *Om Namah Shivaya*, or *Shivo'ham* or some other sound—that doesn't matter. What matters is nada, not the form it may take.

Amrita : *You transmit Shakti to different seekers in dif-*
ferent ways. You touch some, you look at others, and
transmit Shakti by your thought and word to others. Is
there any special reason why you use different methods?
Baba : The different methods are only instruments for
transmitting Shakti, and they have no more importance
than that. Seekers are different, and even the same
seeker does not remain the same all the time. Different
seekers have different karmas, different impressions of
past lives which they carry within their central nerve.
The inner feelings of different seekers are not the same
either, and inner feeling has great importance. There
are some seekers who even before coming to this Ashram,
even before receiving my touch or seeing me, have some
experiences of the divine Shakti. They even receive
Shaktipat while on the way to the Ashram. They receive
Shaktipat first and then they see me. There are others
who have to work quite hard after coming to the Ashram.
They work for a time and then they receive Shaktipat.
What is of importance here is the inner feeling which
a seeker has for the Guru. It is this feeling which will
determine what is going to happen, which is of vital
importance here. Whether the Guru transmits Shakti
by look, touch, thought or some other means is of
secondary importance.

There were four boys who were living with Kalidas
and in course of time they turned into great poets without even studying poetry. Then there were two girls
with a great musician of this country, and those girls,
without even studying music, became great musicians
themselves. Such is the power of the presence of a Guru.

Your Shakti should get awakened by itself, without
any effort on your part or the Guru's part. That inner
awakening should take place in a most natural, spontaneous manner. If it doesn't take place in spite of your
living with the Guru, it means that something is wrong
in your inner heart. Your feeling for him is not the
right sort of feeling.

Everyone here should be aware that he is living in an
Ashram where the Shakti is alive. The Shakti is so

alive here that there are seekers who receive Shaktipat just by listening to letters in which experiences of Shaktipat are described. There are others who receive Shaktipat just by looking at pictures. If there are seekers whose Shakti has not been awakened, in spite of their long stay here, it shows that their feeling for the Guru is not the ideal feeling. Instead of starting to blame others, they should start examining themselves seriously, and make a serious effort to purify their own hearts.

We should not have any interest in petty things, petty concerns, petty gossip. Instead we should keep our minds focused on the inner Self all the time. Isn't it unfortunate that in spite of the fact that the divine light is alive within him, man allows his attention to be diverted, misdirected by external things, and instead of surrendering to the inner light he surrenders to these meaningless, trivial, worldly things?

We should treat the Shakti with utmost reverence. We should worship Her with reverence. We should do Her japa with reverence. We should be seeing Her as She is, in Her live form within us.

The different methods are employed because different seekers move in different mental atmospheres. What is important is not the method employed, but the inner awakening.

Veena: *Can one who has become a disciple of a Guru be tormented by evil spirits, and if so, should he still live fearlessly?*

Baba: It is most natural for a disciple to be completely fearless, because the disciple has been put on the path by the Guru, and in fact, he lives surrounded by the Guru's Shakti all the time. He lives in a fortress of Shakti which nothing can penetrate. Ghosts and evil spirits cannot touch such a person. They cannot touch even those who are courageous and intelligent, even if they are without a Guru.

There was a time when I used to wander from place to place. I went through the whole country, and I spent days and nights in funeral grounds; I passed through places which were supposed to be inhabited by ghosts and evil spirits. Yet no ghost or evil spirit ever dared to approach me.

A ghost or evil spirit does not retain its form for a very long time; it is much more short-lived than the human form. Evil spirits are much weaker than men, and it is a pity that men become scared of them. What happens most of the time is that man projects an image from his own mind and begins to live in fear of that image. In other words, he lives in fear of himself.

The human form is equipped with four bodies: gross, subtle, causal and supra-causal. If man happens to commit an evil deed, he may pass into the form of an evil spirit after death. In that form he does not possess a physical body. He only possesses subtle and causal bodies. Isn't it surprising that one who is in a human form, who possesses such an effective physical body, should feel scared by creatures who have no physical body, who possess only subtle or causal bodies which are much smaller than the gross body? Isn't it strange that those without a gross body should try to scare those who have a gross body and that those who have a gross body should get scared by those who are without one? The ghost form is entirely dependent on the human form. It is only men who become ghosts. Yet men feel scared of ghosts. That surprises me. Besides, ghosts cannot do you any harm, because they cannot touch you. You can only see them, you can only see the gestures that they make. But they cannot attack you, or do any harm to you.

Veena : *What is the nature of karma and bhoga, and what is their relationship?*

Baba : Karmas are the actions performed in the gross body with the help of the five organs of perception, the five organs of action and the four-fold inner psychic instrument. The good or bad consequences, the pleasure or pain, joy or sorrow that we experience, is known as bhoga. Some karmas bring fruit instantly and others bear fruit in course of time. Some past karmas are already in force, others will mature later on.

If you perform a good deed, that will have a good effect on your body through your mind. In fact, every action is bound to bring its consequences. When you meditate calmly, if your mind gets immersed in your heart, you experience great bliss. That experience of bliss is the consequence of your good karma, of your meditation. If, on the contrary, you sit with an impure heart and your mind dwells only on the imagined failings or impurities of others, you end up by becoming miserable, with your heart completely dry and dessicated.

We should be very careful about our actions. We should act only after careful thought, being fully aware of what great saints have said about the desirability or undesirability of various actions, especially those which appear to be fascinating at the moment but may not be good for us in the long run.

There was a king who wanted first-hand knowledge of the condition of his subjects, so he decided to go walking through the gardens of the kingdom at night, incognito. In the Hanging Gardens of Bombay he saw four girls sitting and talking, so he casually stood where he could hear them.

The first girl said, "I have wandered around a great deal and I have come to the conclusion that the best thing in life is to eat meat. But I have never tasted meat because my family are Vaishnavites."

The second one said, "Well, promiscuity is far more preferable, because if you are promiscuous you will be eating meat, of course, and besides, you are not tied to one man and trapped to all sorts of duties, restraints and disciplines. Isn't it far more enjoyable to have any number of lovers and have a nice life with them?"

The third one said, "Drinking is the best thing in life. If you drink, promiscuity and meat-eating follow automatically. In my street there are so many drunkards. When they come home drunk, they are beaten severely by their neighbours, yet they do not give up drinking. So there must be great happiness in drinking."

And the fourth one said, "All of you are ignorant fools. You don't know what the best thing in life is. The noblest thing, the most praiseworthy thing in life is learning the art of telling lies. Eating meat, promiscuity and drinking will come to you naturally, but you can indulge in them without any sense of embarrassment or guilt if you can tell lies. Such is the power of lies that people become great leaders, great businessmen. Leaders have triumphed by the power of lies. So telling lies gives the greatest happiness in the world."

The king was listening to them very carefully. The girls seemed to belong to respectable families. The king told his constable to approach those girls and get their addresses. The next day he sent for them. When they arrived at court the king said, "Were all four of you talking to each other in the Hanging Gardens last night?" They admitted it. He addressed the first one and asked her, "You said that meat-eating gives the most happiness in life, in spite of the fact that nobody in your family has ever eaten meat. You find it so fascinating that you don't mind going against your family tradition. Why?"

She said, "Quite a few of my neighbours eat meat. On the days they cook meat, their children, full of enthusiasm, yell at the top of their voices how wonderful the mutton is. I have seen donkeys dying in the streets, and in spite of the fact that their flesh is rotten, vultures and dogs seem to like it very much. So this forces me to the conclusion that there must be something in it, that meat must have some special relish."

He said to the second girl, "You said that promiscuity was the best thing. How did you get interested in that?"

She replied, "Your Majesty, there was a widow living in our street. One day people found her pregnant. People were shocked and she was summoned to a meeting of the heads of the community and they decided to excommunicate her. So she moved away. In course of time her child was born and grew up and went to college. After some time she became pregnant again. In spite of the fact that she had been punished so much, her head had been clean shaven, she bore a second child. After some time she became pregnant again, and bore a third child. So this forces me to conclude that there must be some special fascination in promiscuity because she could not give it up in spite of torture and hardship."

The third one said, "Your Majesty, there are quite a few drunkards in our street and a few of them are hopeless alcoholics. When they return home at night, their condition has to be seen to be believed. They fall into gutters. People treat them in the most foul manner, they are abused and beaten, and their wives lock them out until they sober up. In the morning they take a solemn pledge not to drink again, but in the evening you see them drunk again. So when they suffer so much and yet cannot give up drinking, it makes me conclude that there must be some special charm in drinking."

The fourth one was asked, "Why do you think that the highest happiness is found in telling lies?"

She said, "Your Majesty, allow me six months and I will give you my answer."

That girl moved away from the city and joined a monastery. After some time she got initiated into sannyasa. She left the monastery and went into a forest and built a temple. She installed the image of Lakshmi-Narayan, and also learned a few magic tricks. By moving her right hand in a certain manner she could materialise sacred ash, and by moving her left hand she could materialise chocolate. By some other gesture she could materialise a picture and by yet another gesture she could materialise an image of the Lord. She got hold of ten or twenty disciples and asked them to go around telling people that Lord Narayan had incarnated Himself in the form of a great sannyasini with miraculous powers, and if you were allowed in her holy presence, she would materialise anything you wished for. And not only that, if you were really interested, that sannyasini, that Guru, would even call the Lord Himself down from His heaven and you would be able to see the Lord face to face. The Lord is at her beck and call. He will do whatever He is commanded to do by that great Guru.

The girl's fame spread, and thousands of devotees began to go to pay their respects. Even courtiers began to be drawn, and some of the most important people who were holding positions of authority in the kingdom started going there. Before entering the temple, they would be told by her disciples, "If you are honest, if you have never cheated the king, you will be able to have a vision of the Lord Himself. So before going inside you better be careful."

There are all kinds of people. There are people who have become so blinded by their faith that they see anything they want to see, and there are others who claim to see what they have never seen, for ulterior motives.

So a courtier would be taken inside and be told, "Now you are going to have a vision of the Lord." And that sannyasini would pretend to pray very fervently to the image. In spite of her fervent and prolonged prayers, the Lord would not reveal Himself there. Now this courtier would start saying to himself, "If I go out and speak the truth and tell the people that I didn't have a vision of the Lord, I will be taken for a dishonest person, I will be branded as a cheat and the king will expel me from the kingdom. So the best course to take under the present circumstances is to claim, "Yes, I had a most wonderful vision of the Lord. He came to me and blessed me and smiled at me."

The great Guru's fame spread throughout the kingdom, and it reached the ears of the prime minister also. The prime minister asked one of his subordinates if the stories were true, and the subordinate said, "Yes, I myself went there and had a vision of the Lord."

The prime minister was tempted. He said, "If these lesser people can have such remarkable experiences, why can't I?" So he also went to the great Guru. He was brought into her presence. First she moved her hand and materialised some sacred ash and asked him to put it on his forehead. Then she said, "Our Lord becomes lifeless, inert like a stone if He is confronted with a person who is ignoble, who is a liar. If he is confronted with a person who is noble and virtuous, He becomes alive again and He will even give a message." So, after these words, the prime minister was asked to go into the inner part of the temple where the image was.

He began to pray before the statue with folded hands. He prayed quite fervently, but in spite of his prayer the statue did not move at all; it did not speak a single word and remained as stoney as it was before. He began to wonder if the statue would ever speak to him. Now he said, "If I speak the truth, people will know that I have had to resort to dishonest deeds from time to time to run the affairs of the kingdom. If I tell them that the Lord did not speak to me, I will be exposed." So he came out and pretended to be in ecstasy. He threw his arms up and declared, "I have had a most inspiring vision of the Lord." Then he fell flat at the feet of the great Guru by whose grace, by whose benediction he had been able to talk to the Lord.

The prime minister was sent for by the queen, and she asked him whether what was being said about the Guru was true. The prime minister said, "It is absolutely true. I have experienced it myself. The Lord appeared to me and gave me holy water to drink through His sacred conch."

The queen decided to meet the great Guru. She reached the temple and was brought into the presence of the Guru. She saluted the Guru most reverently and prayed with folded hands, "Please grant me the vision of the Lord inside."

The Guru said to the queen, "You will certainly have a vision of the Lord. However, I must tell you that there is one condition. If you have been loyal to your husband, the king, then the Lord will appear to you instantly, but if you haven't been loyal to him the statue will remain a statue and will not speak to you." With these instructions the queen was sent inside and the curtain was drawn after her. The queen prayed, yet the Lord would not appear in the statue. After some time the queen started saying to herself, "Now if I go out and tell people that the Lord was not pleased with me, I will be branded as a disloyal wife. The king may even get rid of me." So she came out obviously enraptured. She was dancing around, saying she had a most wonderful vision of the Lord. There was a large crowd outside, and there were some press correspondents waiting to get a statement from the queen. They asked her what happened, and the queen said, "The Lord came down from His statue and blessed me. Not only that, He said, 'There is no other woman as loyal as you.' I could have such an experience only by the grace of such a great Guru, and my prayer is, 'Let such Gurus flourish in the kingdom'."

When the queen returned to the palace she told everything to the king and the king became impatient to go. He couldn't even sleep that night, waiting anxiously for the morning to visit the Guru.

Next day the king went to the temple with all his royal paraphernalia and regal grandeur. There was a large procession with elephants, and so many sentries, and most precious gifts of clothes and food. When he arrived, the Guru first materialised some sacred ash and applied it to the different parts of the king's body. She said, "I have purified you with sacred ash, but I don't know whether God will recognise it or not. Generally speaking, kings are considered to be sinners. But if you happen to be an exception, if you have been absolutely pure and spotless in your life, you will be able to see the Lord inside."

The king was sent inside and the curtain was drawn after him. He sat down before the statue and began to pray. He began to call upon the Lord most fervently. But the Lord remained a mere piece of stone. After some time, the king realised that the Lord would not appear to him, and he said to himself, "If I go out and speak the truth to the vast crowd outside—they already believe that a king is a sinner—that will be confirmed and people will revolt against me, and I may even lose my kingdom. So I must now adjust my words according to the demand of the occasion. There would be absolutely no harm in telling such a lie."

He went around the statue dancing and declaring, "I had a most radiant vision of the Lord. The Lord appeared and touched my crown, and He declared, 'It is after a very long time that the kingdom is blessed with such a noble, virtuous king, and I am going to stay in your kingdom for a long, long time'."

Then everybody left. During the night the girl dis-carded the robes of the sannyasini, left everything and returned to the city. Next day she appeared at the court and said to the king, "Your Majesty, when I said that the greatest happiness comes from lies, I requested six months to show you how. Now I have completed the six months, and I have come to prove that today."

The king said, "Let me hear what you have to say."

The girl approached him and whispered in his ear, "Your Majesty, I was the sannyasini in the temple, and you know very well that you told a most flagrant lie. Now you know from your own experience what happi-ness comes from telling lies."

This story was written by a very great saint. Even though you may actually see people do certain things and you may feel that there must be some special happiness underlying those things, in fact there is no happiness; these persons are only miserable victims, they are not their own masters. The drunkard cannot give up his drinking in spite of the fact that night after night he has to fall into the gutter and have his sacred bath there. It is no wonder Shankaracharya said, "We do not enjoy pleasures, pleasures enjoy us." The promiscuous woman cannot give up her promiscuity because she is a help-less victim of that. The liar cannot give up his lies and the meat-eater cannot give up his meat eating. So when we see people do certain things, we should not be fooled. We should take the trouble of making ourselves conscious of their true condition.

I thank you all and I wish all of you the greatest good. Meditate intensely and have a true vision of the Lord living in your heart. Then live your life according to the message that you receive from Him.

December 8, 1972

Rana: *During chanting some sadhakas see dancing girls who dance to the rhythm of the chant. Who are they and where do they come from?*

Baba: Anyone who becomes absorbed in chanting would be able to see the Gopis living in Golok, their divine world, from time to time. When you have this vision again, try to know exactly who they are. There is nothing surprising or improper about having certain visions which correspond to the chants you are chanting at a given moment. It would be quite all right to have visions of Vrindavan or Mathura and other places or other worlds if you are chanting with absorption.

According to the *Shivasutras* this world is a creation of mantra, so by the power of mantra you can have any vision. But no matter what vision you have, you should not become oblivious of your goal. Whatever you see, look upon it as an embodiment of the same Divine Mother. According to the scriptures, God originally manifested Himself as sound, and all the various objects cf this universe arose as sound vibrations. God's name is also a sound, and this sound can give rise to visions of any form. Whatever forms you see in a vision, you should not forget the One whose name you are chanting.

Ramesh: *What is the importance of the Guru's lineage? Is it necessary for a Guru to belong to a line? And isn't the Guru's name the highest mantra?*

Baba: A Guru who has no lineage, no tradition behind him, doesn't deserve the name Guru. At best he can be called a teacher, someone who can impart a skill of some kind. The ancient saints, each one of them came from a line and each one had the power of his line behind him. Whenever one saint met another, he was interested in knowing what line he came from. If you do not come from a line, from where will you get power?

If one belongs to a line, however small he may be, he will have some worth, he will carry some weight, and he will command some respect. Take a simple example of an ordinary constable. You show respect and obey him because he has the power of the entire government behind him. On the other hand, if a man much more important than him, such as a big businessman, tried to order you around here, you would just laugh at him, you would refuse to pay attention to him.

Your lineage has great importance. If one comes from a line, he carries the weight of the entire line behind him. Jnaneshwar Maharaj says that Adinath, Lord Shiva, the primal Lord, is at the head of the line of all the Siddhas. Jnaneshwar traces his own line. His line originated from Lord Shiva. Lord Shiva's direct disciple was Matsyendranath, Matsyendranath's disciple was Goraknath, Goraknath's disciple was Nivrittinath and Nivrittinath's disciple was Jnandeva. This indicates that the flow of Shakti, divine power, is coming from the primal Lord in an unbroken line. That is also the secret of the power of an ordinary constable; if the authority of the government were not behind him, you would not take him seriously. Such is the importance of lineage that if you suffer from diabetes or blood pressure, a doctor will ask you, "Did your father have it? Your father's father? Did your father's father's father have it?" One of your ancestors might have had it, and if the doctors come to know about it, they will say, "Yes, you got it from him."

So you can see how important spiritual lineage is, particularly a line through which the Shakti of the primal Lord has been flowing without any break. This is the importance of the Guru's lineage that the power of the primal Lord and the whole line he belongs to is behind him. Anyone who has the power of a line behind him will not find it at all difficult to go across the ocean of change.

Take the case of Tukaram. Tukaram was entirely on his own, yet he describes in one of his poems that on a particular day he was visited in a dream by a Siddha from Siddhaloka and initiated by him. And he mentions his name, Baba Chaitanya. In this way he shows his

path, demonstrating that he belongs to the line of the
Siddhas. Siddhaloka is full of Siddhas who live there in
perfect bliss. A Siddha is an embodiment of pure consciousness, and his world is the world of consciousness.

It is not the Guru's name which is the best mantra,
it is the mantra received from the Guru which is the
best mantra. The name which the physical body has
been given will have importance only as long as the body
lasts, and when the body falls the name, too, will fall.
We should understand the true nature of the Guru. The
scriptures say that the Guru is Shiva and Shiva is the
Guru. That means that unless one has attained perfection, he does not deserve to be a Guru. He is still a
disciple. And if he begins to function as a Guru he
is committing a great sin, he is behaving worse than
wives who commit sins against their husbands or vice
versa. When you assume Guruhood for ulterior motives,
for fame, for wealth, for many disciples or glory—all
these motives are ignoble. Even though you claim to
be a Guru, there is no worse sinner than you. It is only
when a Guru is without true Guruhood that he falls
victim to attachment and begins to care for worldly
things. And when he begins to care for worldly things,
he falls from his high position into misery.

Only he is worthy of being called a Guru who, in the
course of his sadhana, has totally annihilated his individuality, having merged it into the Guru or into Shiva,
and thus become Shiva Himself. There is absolutely no
difference between the Guru and Shiva. Only the words
are different. A true Guru who has become Shiva by
having merged with Shiva cannot have a name different
from the name Shiva, so Shiva or *Om Namah Shivaya*
embodies his name. A particular name such as Nityananda
or Muktananda has only ephemeral significance, while the
name Shiva is an eternal name, a true name. It has
remained unchanged, and it is divine. If Muktananda has
remained Muktananda, if he has not merged his individuality in Shiva, become Shiva Himself, then what is
the point of being a Guru? If a Guru has become Shiva
by merging into Shiva then his name is Shiva, and if

we still repeat the name of the Guru, it is something very ordinary, it doesn't have much significance.

Even though a Guru may participate in the world of action, he is not guided by worldly considerations, even though he may appear to be so, because his inner heart is elsewhere. He looks upon himself, not as an embodied being, not as a limited individual, but as Shiva Himself. He looks upon his own Self as Shiva, Hara, the supreme Lord. If you are really interested in attaining perfection —wherever you may be, with me or somebody else, even with God—you will not be able to attain perfection unless you look upon yourself as Shiva, at least while meditating. If while meditating you continue to regard yourself as a particular individual who ate ice cream yesterday, or who went to see a movie the day before, or who did this or that, you will not be able to attain perfection, because in meditation you should be able to discard identification with the body and get free from all worldly thoughts. It is only then that you will be able to identify yourself with Shiva. It is only then that you will be able to attain perfection. Lord Shiva Himself, while describing the glory of the divine state, the state of Shiva, to Parvati says, "He who constantly lives in the state of Shiva, who has realised his own divinity, comes to have all deities, all mantras, all cosmic powers at his command. Such is the glory of the state of divine perfection."

I remember some of the statements of my Guru very vividly and I even jotted them down; they keep springing to mind again and again. Once a person came to him and said, "Babaji, I have committed a great sin." Baba said, "What happened?"

The man said, "Last year I ate mutton once."

Baba said, "You ate that last year? Well didn't you get rid of it by excreting it the next morning? When it is no longer in your system, why do you keep the memory alive?"

Therefore, while meditating you should not remember worldly things, you should not identify yourself with them. Only identify yourself with Shiva, regarding yourself as the highest Lord. *Om Namah Shivaya* is the Guru's name and *Shivo'ham* is also the Guru's name.

Bill: *What is the way of karma and what exactly is the nature of prarabdha?*

Baba: While speaking on the subject of karma, even the Lord would not say more than, "Mysterious are the ways of karma." What exactly destiny has in store for you, what is going to happen to you the very next moment, is very difficult to know. This morning the white bird which we had here in the cage, was sitting on my palm and I was playing with it; I have been playing with it for a long time. The bird was full of great love, and it was pecking affectionately at my cheeks again and again. Some girls, including Marie, were standing around. They thought that the bird was kissing me and they were delighted watching the play. Then all of a sudden the bird flew across the wall and landed right in the jaws of death. A dog was sitting there with his mouth open, and it did not lose any time in swallowing it. Such is the effect of prarabdha or destiny or karma.

There is an important dialogue between Yajnavalkya and King Janaka. King Janaka wanted to know about his past life. This story is narrated in full detail in a book called *Chandrakantha*, but it hasn't been translated into English. He asked Yajnavalkya many times, "What was I in my past birth, and can you explain the mystery of karma?"

Yajnavalkya said, "Your Majesty, you shouldn't bother about these things. Just meditate and try to realise the Self, because if you start trying to understand the nature of karma, you will spend your whole life at it, because the chain of karma is endless, and you will get nowhere."

The king said, "I can't find peace without knowing that."

In spite of his best efforts, Yajnavalkya could not bring the king around. Yajnavalkya said, "This is not a matter for me to discuss. I suggest that you go to a certain village. Set out on your trip tomorrow. As you approach the village you will see a girl carrying a pot of water on her head. The moment she sees you she will call you by name, and the moment she does that, ask her, "Can you tell me what I was in my past life and explain the mystery of karma?"

What Yajnavalkya predicted happened. The king was amazed that the girl recognised him, and he asked, "How did you recognise me? Please tell me what I was in my past birth and explain to me the mystery of karma."

The girl said, "I can't do that. Go to another village and ask the wife of so-and-so about it."

The king went there and that woman said, "I am sorry I don't have time to explain that to you, because I am going to die within three minutes."

The king said, "How can that be possible?" He took just a few steps, and when he looked back he found the woman dead. The king sank into even greater amazement. He began to ponder this matter deeply. Even though that woman knew she was going to die, she did not make any effort to save her life. (It is a very long story, so I will shorten it a little.)

Then the king went to another place where he saw a millionaire. The millionaire invited him, calling him by name, and the king was amazed. How could he know his name? The millionaire took him into his room, welcomed him with great respect and asked him, "What brings you here, Your Majesty?"

The king told him all that had happened. The millionaire's wife fed the king with most delicious food and he was enjoying his stay very much. Then a very strange thing began to happen. The king began to remember that he had eaten that same sort of food some other time, but he couldn't remember exactly where or when, and he asked the woman, 'Did you ever serve this kind of food to me before, and where?"

The woman said, "Please don't stop eating." And she did not answer the question.

When Janaka put the question again and again, she said, "I can't answer that question. Go to Kashi. The king of Kashi is without a son and his wife is pregnant. The day you arrive, she will deliver a son and the event will be celebrated with great pomp. But the same evening the child will die and the royal family will be sunk in grief and they will bury the child in the funeral ground. Follow the funeral procession and when everybody has left and nobody is around, dig up the grave and take out the corpse. Wash it in the Ganges, utter some mantras and call the child. The child will immediately arise. Then put the question to him and he will give you all of the answer. After receiving your answer you should immediately go back to Yajnavalkya. There is no greater teacher than Yajnavalkya. He alone can expound these mysteries."

The king arrived in Kashi and found a celebration taking place with a grand procession of elephants. Generous gifts were being given to the brahmins and food was being distributed liberally, because the king had been blessed with an heir after a long time. In the evening, as had been predicted, the child died. He was taken to the funeral ground and buried. Janaka was watching the whole thing from a distance. As he had been instructed, when everybody left, he opened the grave, took out the corpse, washed it and performed certain rites, chanted certain mantras, and as he held the child, the child spoke all of a sudden, saying, "My dear father, how are you?"

The king was stunned. He thought, "The child was born this morning and died this evening, so how could I be his father?"

The child said, "You shouldn't feel amazed. I will tell you all. I will answer the question that has been bothering you. I was your son in your past birth. The first woman you met with the water on her head was my wife. You have been a king in so many lives because of your good karma. Since I did not always do such good acts, I fell from my high position in the next birth. Sometimes I have been born in royal families and in other births elsewhere. This morning, because of my good karma, I was born into a royal family. But because of my bad karma, I died this evening. The woman who said that she was going to die in three minutes was one of your wives in a past birth, and the woman who fed you so lovingly was also your wife in another birth. That is why she fed you with such love and devotion, and that was why you seemed to recollect the taste of the food that you had enjoyed in your past birth from her hands. Now put me back. I can tell you only this much. In my next birth I am going to be born in such-and-such a place in such-and-such a family. Now you can return to Yajnavalkya."

So mysterious are ways of karma, that a bird that was sitting on my palm this morning, caressing my cheek, delighting everyone who was watching, flew out and landed right in the jaws of a dog. The bird could have died inside also, but he seemed to insist on dying outside. It was that incident that reminded me of this story. It is really true that mysterious are the ways of karma.

The conversation between the infant and the king is of great significance. I shortened it considerably, but one of the questions that the king asked was, "Why have I remained a king through so many births?"

"It is because you have always been in a divine state. You have always looked upon yourself and all that you did and the entire universe as God.

You never fell from this contemplation, so you never fell from your royal status. The rest of us who were related to you, your wives in different births, did not always contemplate our divine nature and that is why we were born in different places and in different families, some of which were much lower, and that is why we had to suffer so much."

The king put the dead child back and returned to Yajnavalkya. And that is the end of the story.

You may live in any country, you may pursue any course of action, you may speak any language, but you must not forget that God dwells within you, that your Self is the Supreme Being Itself. If you live in such contemplation continually, you will be able to go across the ocean of wordliness.

December 12, 1972

Chandra: *Around the Ashram remarks are heard quite frequently like 'I didn't want to lose my temper and get angry, but Baba made me do it'. 'I know Baba is making me suffer to test me'. 'It isn't up to me whether I leave or stay at the Ashram. If I go, I know that is what is supposed to happen and what Baba wants'. People seem to be able to sanction any action or feeling by putting the responsibility on the Guru. To what extent is a sadhak responsible for his own actions or feelings?*

Baba: It is very good to feel that you didn't want to lose your temper and it is Baba who made you angry, but then if you lose your temper with a certain person and that person beats you with his shoes, would you see Baba's play in that also? If even then you feel that it is Baba who is beating you, or the person who is thrashing you is doing it on behalf of Baba, then you would be justified in saying that it was Baba who made you angry. But what happens most of the time is that you lose your temper because you have no self-control and you have to suffer the consequences of it. Then you begin to blame the person concerned. This is just a delusion. Why should Baba make you angry? Baba would, on the contrary, like to fill you with the bliss of Brahman. You may be interested in getting angry, but Baba is not at all interested in making you angry after entering your heart. Those persons who feel that it is Baba who is making them suffer are obviously deluded. There are so many people in the Ashram and all of them do not suffer. If you are abiding by the Ashram rules and discipline, the question of suffering should not arise. Why should you suffer? If a person were suffering from a hopeless disease, I could accept his statement that he was suffering, but what could possibly make you suffer here? Take the case of Desai, the old man who keeps watch outside the meditation room. He contracted throat cancer and was operated on for it. He hasn't yet recovered his voice. Yet he gets up at 2:30 a.m. and is on duty right up to

9 p.m. Have you ever seen him miss his duty? He has never said that he is suffering here. On the contrary, he is quite happy. Yet there are some people who get exhausted after working just two hours. Not only that—there are people here who feel exhausted by seeing other people work.

What do you take the Guru for? Do you think that he is a messenger of the god of death, that he should punish you with suffering? Whether or not you stay long in the Ashram depends on whether you are worthy of living in this Ashram. This is not an ordinary Ashram, it is not a place of mere brick and mortar. It is alive with Chiti, and it depends on Chiti how long She wants to keep you here. If you are unworthy of staying in the Ashram, She will kick you out very quickly. And if She decides to kick you out, however hard you may try to stay here, you can't; it is beyond your power. It is quite obvious that if you wish to stay here for a long time without wavering, you should be worthy of it. Otherwise you would be continually seeing faults and impurities even in purity, and you would become so obsessed by this consciousness of faults and impurities that the Ashram would start feeling like hell and you would have to leave one day with the unbearable burden of an evil eye, or impure attitudes.

The Ashram will appear to you as you see it. If you see the place as a mere structure made of inert brick and mortar it will be just like dead matter. And if you see it as full of consciousness then it will work on you actively as consciousness. If you see it full of Chiti then you will see the play of Chiti everywhere in the Ashram. The fact is that it is Chiti who is sporting through all the leaves and flowers and trees here. But to be able to perceive that you have to be very worthy, you have to rise to a certain level.

Why should the Guru make you suffer instead of enabling you to remain in a calm, tranquil, meditative state, sipping the inner nectar constantly? Is it just clever tactics on your part to hide your own flaws and attribute everything to the Guru? I am not the sort of person who

would ever want anyone to suffer. Chiti, who is manifest
in me, would not be able to bear any evil thoughts, any
evil desires, even if they were to arise in me, because
Chiti is absolutely pure. My wanting anyone to suffer
is absurd. If you suffer here you suffer because of your
impure attitudes and perverse understanding. Otherwise
there is no reason to suffer here.

This reminds me of a disciple of Swami Ramdas. He
had a number of disciples and one of them was a most
strange person called Kalyan. Kalyan had the wonderful knack of remembering the statements that his Guru
had said, out of context. He would always forget what
the Guru had said first and only remember what the
Guru had said at the end. One day the ashram elephant—
there was an elephant in that ashram also like we have
here—lost his temper. It is not at all surprising that
an elephant should lose its temper when you find human
beings losing their tempers every moment. The elephant
ran amuck and started destroying things all around him.
The elephant was running madly, and Kalyan was coming from the opposite direction. People shouted at him
to get out of the way. But Kalyan said, 'The elephant
won't harm me. My Guru has said that Ram is in all
beings, so Ram is in that elephant also, and He will take
care of me."

But Ram in the elephant didn't seem to bother about
Kalyan, and the elephant crushed him under his feet and
that was the end of this great devotee. So that is what
happens when you remember the Guru's statement and
forget the context. A great hue and cry was raised and
the Guru was informed. He came, and Shivaji, the king
at that time, also came. Ramdas was a saint of divine
power and by virtue of his power he treated Kalyan and
brought him back to life. Ramdas asked him what had
happened. He said, "This is the result of following your
teaching."

Ramdas said, "What did I teach you?"

Kalyan told him what he had heard. Ramdas said,
"What you say is quite correct, I said Ram is in all beings.
But why didn't you hear the voice of Ram in the warn-

ing which was given to you by all those people? Why did you forget to see Ram in them?"

Why should I be interested in making you suffer? You don't come to the Ashram to suffer, you come here to be delivered from suffering through meditation. Those who get up regularly, who sleep regularly, who eat regularly, who meditate regularly, who work regularly, have no problem here. They receive all respect and love from the Ashram. But those who violate the Ashram discipline, who wish to follow their own ways—it is their own ways which make them suffer, it is not I who am responsible for their suffering. This reminds me of a verse from the *Mahabharata*. Duryodhana says, "It is wrong to hold others responsible for your pleasure or pain or joy or sorrow. You suffer the consequences of your own actions. It is stupid to hold anybody else or any external factor responsible for your suffering. You bear the consequences of your own actions, of your own attitudes."

You have come here to stay, obviously not permanently. You have a short time at your disposal, so you shouldn't waste even a single moment in gossip. You shouldn't make a nuisance of yourself with others. Make the best use of your time as long as you are here. Your mind should take interest only in those things which enable you to rise steadily higher and higher in your sadhana.

Carol : *Sometimes when Ashramites are told to behave in a certain way because Baba likes it so, they reply, 'But Baba really doesn't care what we do, he loves us no matter what we do or say'. Even though the Guru is beyond likes and dislikes, does it mean that he is always pleased with us?*

Baba : The Guru may be beyond likes or dislikes, that doesn't matter. What matters is where you stand, what state you are in. Are you quite happy about doing whatever you feel like, saying whatever you feel like ? Leave aside whether the Guru will be pleased or not, what is it that makes you so contented about all that you do or all that you omit doing? And what would make the Guru

so wonderfully pleased with you? Is the river of absolute
bliss flowing through all your actions and omissions? Is
the current of the bliss of Brahman streaming through
your actions so much that the Guru should be dancing
all the time in ecstasy, "O what a wonderful disciple I
have"?

Rana : *Please tell us something about visions of the
future, and is there any way to repeat the same vision
again and again?*

Baba : Suppose you have a vision about your future that
you are going to attain realisation after twelve years.
Once you have had this realisation, what is the use of
having it repeated over and over? All visions come from
the divine source, they come from Parashakti or other
deities. Would Parashakti or the other deities be so idle
that they should be obliging you by fulfilling your desire
to have the same vision again and again? What is the
point of having a certain vision repeated? Once you have
had it, that should be enough.

There should be some meaning in your question. If you
describe a particular vision and ask me to comment on
it, there will be some meaning to your question. Just to
use vague expressions like visions of the future would
not call forth any worthwhile answer. Whoever puts a
question should first be sure about what he is asking.

Jon : *What exactly causes illness? Is it the purificatory
kriyas of Shakti, or our own negligence and slavery to
our senses?*

Baba : It is sense slavery, lack of self-control which is
responsible for illness. I know that people go from here
to Bombay and eat at different restaurants. They like
to visit all the restaurants that they pass on their way.
So it shouldn't be surprising if they are laid up with
dysentery. What are you going to ascribe that to? It is
obviously not divine dispensation. It is irregularity, lack
of control. It is our own lack of self-control which holds
us back from final realisation, from the most beautiful
discovery of the inner world. Otherwise it shouldn't take

you long to achieve your goal once the Shakti has been activated within you. It is your craving for sense pleasure which is the main obstacle in the path.

Take the palate for instance. It is unfortunate that the palate doesn't get satisfied even though you have been eating through countless lifetimes, overloading your stomach and intestines without mercy. Even when you fall sick, you vomit day in and day out, you keep on eating. It shouldn't be surprising if you do not progress quickly enough. The most important set of exercises in yoga, namely the six purificatory exercises, are meant only to keep the digestive system in good shape. If your digestive system is not in order, what sadhana can you possibly do?

Tukaram Maharaj has said in this connection, "The stomach god comes first, and then comes the supreme Lord." Some people misconstrue this statement to mean that first you must fill the stomach to more than capacity and then worship God, which is obviously absurd. What Tukaram means is that first you must keep your digestive system clean and pure, and it is only then that you will be able to worship the Lord. The Lord, in fact, will come to you Himself.

I am not suggesting that you shouldn't eat as much as you need. You must. But you must take care that what you eat does not upset your digestive system. It is irregularity which is responsible for illness. A poet has said, "If you wish to practise yoga, if you wish to live happily, then you must follow discipline in your life. You must live a life of regularity and work. Then you will see how peace comes into your life."

Uma : *How important is meditation for one who is doing Guruseva?*

Baba : Meditation for such a one, namely one who is doing Guruseva, has hardly any significance. But one should be really serving the Guru. Jnaneshwar Maharaj says, "If you have acquired the worth by means of which you can serve the Guru, you should consider yourself to to be extremely fortunate, to be extremely blessed. You

20

don't get that desire to serve the Guru without God's grace."

Meditation fades into insignificance compared to Guruseva. One who is truly serving the Guru does not want anything. He does not want meditation, he does not want peace, he does not want liberation, he does not want anything else in life. If there is still a craving, then it is not service that he is doing, he is just involved in some business with the Guru.

There was a saintly person in Yeola, Pandit Shatho Singh. It was he who taught me *Jnaneshwari*. He narrated a story concerning Eknath.

Once all the saints of Maharashtra decided to go on a pilgrimage to Hardwar and take a bath in the Ganges. On the way they thought to invite Eknath also. They went to Eknath and requested him to join them. Eknath said, "It would be great to go on a pilgrimage with you, but my Guru is very old and needs someone to take care of him."

His Guru's name was Janardan Swami. Janardan Swami was a great yogi and also a great fighter. In fact he was a general in command of the forces stationed at the Daulatabad fort. I lived in that fort for a long time during my sadhana. Eknath said, "How can I come with you, leaving my Guru here?" He thanked them for the invitation and saw them off. While they were leaving Eknath handed them one little piece of betel nut and one paisa, saying, "Put it in the Ganges on my behalf."

This is a custom in our country. Coins are thrown into the Ganges and it is considered very sacred. The saints left for Hardwar. They all went into the river, had their bath and worshipped the Ganges. One of them put in the betel nut and the one paisa given by Eknath. He said to the Ganges, "Mother, this is the offering of Eknath."

It is said that immediately two hands appeared from the river to accept the offering. They were all astonished. The coins of all those people who had actually taken a bath and worshipped the Ganges had sunk into its water, while the offering made on behalf of Eknath, who wasn't there, was accepted by the Ganges Herself. They started discussing this among themselves and the conclusion they arrived at was that it was the reward of Eknath's ideal service to his Guru. It is said that because the Lord was pleased with Eknath's devotion to his Guru, the Lord Himself used to serve Eknath, disguised as a man called Srikhand. He used to fetch water for Eknath. Such is the glory of service to the Guru. There are two large water tanks in the place where Eknath lived. It is said that Srikhand would fetch water only once, pour one pail of water into one tank and another pail into the other tank, and that was enough to fill both the tanks. He did not have to carry water from morning to evening. When people discovered that Srikhand could fill the tank by just two pails of water, they were astonished and they began to wonder about the identity of Srikhand. It was much later that Tukaram Maharaj found out that the Lord Himself, being pleased with Eknath's service to his Guru, was serving Eknath in the guise of Srikhand.

Those tanks still exist, and every year a great fair is held there which is attended by thousands of people from all parts of the country. Every year they celebrate the day on which the Lord was caught red-handed carrying water for Eknath. On that day thousands of people fetch water from the river in their tiny pots and pour them into the tanks and the tanks get only three-quarters full. All of a sudden the remaining quarter is filled. The crowd there is so vast that it would be difficult to find out which person's pot filled the remaining quarter. After the tanks get filled, people get ecstatic and they dance and sing. I lived there for nine months, on the bank of a sacred river where they carry water. Thousands of people come with their pots and everyone tries to identify the character in whose guise the Lord must have come, whose pot filled the remaining quarter, but nobody can spot Him.

Meditation is something very ordinary for such a person. Through meditation you can only attain a certain state, whereas through service to the Guru you can even command the Lord. Where there are devoted servants of the Guru, Hari Himself carries water.

This Ashram owes its existence to love for the Guru,
to devotion for the Guru, to service to the Guru. Whatever vibrations, whatever beauty you have around you,
whatever peace you experience here, all come from love
for the Guru. Therefore, service to the Guru is far
superior to meditation, to austerities, to yoga and other
holy rituals.

December 15, 1972

Mr. Witter: *Is it possible that a seeker has a Guru but
doesn't know it?*

Baba: Yes, it is possible. There are many kinds of
Gurus. There are some who exist in a physical form in
this world, while there are others who exist without a
physical form in Siddhaloka. As far as a Guru in a
physical form existing in this world is concerned, if he
becomes your Guru then you will get to know of it
because such a Guru bestows grace according to certain
laws. But if you were to receive grace from a Guru
without a physical form, who is in Siddhaloka, then you
may not know about it at all. Gurus from Siddhaloka
descend and initiate seekers either in meditation or in
dreams, and it is quite possible that a certain seeker may
not know about it. However, as he advances more and
more on the path of sadhana, he will come to know by the
force of his sadhana who exactly he received his initiation
from and to whom he owes his spiritual progress.

How Guru's grace works is beyond the power of human
reasoning to grasp. We had a seeker here from Switzer-
land some time ago and she stayed for about a week.
During that period she didn't feel anything. She left
the Ashram and spent some time visiting the country.
Then she went back home and started meditating. It

was only there that she received grace and kriyas began to take place. She had wonderful experiences which made her aware of the fact that she had found her Guru at Ganeshpuri Shree Gurudev Ashram. This compelled her to return to the Ashram.

Narada, while talking about the power of grace of the Siddhas or divine beings, says in his *Bhakti Sutras*, "Grace is beyond the grasp of reason; it is difficult to attain and it is unfailing in its effect."

It is possible that one can have a Guru without even knowing about it. It is only later, after you have undergone inner transformation, that you come to realise that some being's grace has been working inside you. Some times you receive grace secretly, as it were, even without your knowledge. This was a very good question.

Ken: *Most people seem to have some type of spiritual experience while they are here. I don't feel that I have had this experience. Why?*

Baba: Many people have been living here for a long time and that is why they have had some spiritual experience. You have been here just a short while. And who knows what may happen tomorrow? You may get the experience while leaving the place.

The company of a saint will exert a powerful influence even on birds, animals and plants, so the question of a human being remaining unaffected cannot arise.

Twenty-five years ago I read a book called *Jnana Sindhu* in which I read a story. One day in Vaikuntha, many people had gathered and they were asking Vishnu different questions. Narada was also there and he asked, "Lord, please tell me, what is the effect of seeing a saint, of living with him?"

The Lord said, "Narada, it is not for me to answer this question. Only a person who has first-hand experience can answer it. However, I can give you the address of one who will answer your question. If you go to a certain lake you will find a swan sitting on the shore, and if you put this question to him, he will give you the answer."

Narada went to the lake, saw the swan there, bowed to him and said, "I have been sent here by the Lord because I had put a question to Him. The question was, 'What is the effect of seeing a saint just for a short while, what is the effect of living with him?' Can you answer this question?"

The moment the bird heard the question he began to flap his wings violently and he fell over and died. Narada began to wonder what had caused his death. Narada rushed back to the Lord and told Him what happened.

The Lord said, "Even now I can't answer the question. You will have to go to someone else to get the answer. Go to the capital of a certain king who was blessed with a son just three days ago, and ask that baby. He will answer your question."

I just remembered the earlier part of the story. Before being sent to the swan, Narada was sent to an insect living in a cake of dung. It was a black beetle. As Narada put the question to that beetle, he too died on the spot. It was after that that Narada was sent to the swan.

Narada reached the capital, met the king and said, "Your Majesty, I have been commanded by the Lord to come here. I have been told that a son has been born to you and I have to ask him a question."

All the people there were amused that a tiny baby would be able to understand the question and give an answer, but the king said, "You are such a great saint, so you must know what you are talking about. I shall certainly take you to the baby."

Narada paid his respects to the baby and put the question to him. Immediately the baby stood up and began to emit light. He acquired the power of speech. He was transformed and began to look like a most fascinating god. The child said to Narada, "You are most welcome here. I have been able to attain my present state by the blessing of your grace. I am so grateful to you. As a result of my past bad karma I was born a beetle living in dung, and the moment I saw you I was released from my suffering. I was again born in the form of a swan. I had the good fortune of your darshan and I was relieved from that form also. Then I was born as a prince and again I had your darshan. Your darshan has transformed me into a divine being."

So isn't that a sufficient answer to your question? What more can I say? Just by looking at a saint you can gain such a great benefit. Tulsidas says that if you spend just twenty minutes with a saint, if not twenty, ten, and if not ten, just five, the sins of your countless births will be washed away. Such is the divine power of a saint. If you spend even a short while with a saint you experience its beneficial effect. And if you are with him for a long time, how great the benefit would be is quite obvious.

I can assure you that your stay here will not go to waste. You will certainly go back richer and nobler. The time that you have spent here will bear fruit in course of time. When time spent even in bad company brings its fruit sooner or later, why won't the time you spent here bring fruit?

Swami Kriyananda: *What should one do when, while practising So'ham japa, the breath reaches a state where it keeps stopping?*

Baba: If you practise japa and it does not stop of its own accord after some time, then it means that your japa has not borne fruit. If you try to meditate and you keep on trying hard and you don't reach the state where effort becomes unnecessary and you become lost in meditation spontaneously, then there is no point in your effort, however hard it may be. If you are chanting and you do not reach the stage where you get beyond chanting, then it means that chanting hasn't borne its fruit.

Whenever involuntary kumbhak takes place, whenever the breath is held automatically, that means that the particular practice which you are doing is bearing fruit. This spontaneous inner kumbhak is of enormous value. If you do not experience this spontaneously while doing japa, then you haven't been doing japa properly. This spontaneous kumbhak is the state in which the japa stops and along with that the mind also stops. For a while

the mind gets completely emptied of all objects. This
state has very great significance. The I-consciousness
which is absolutely pure, the consciousness which existed
before the thought, 'Let me become many', emerged in the
mind of the Lord, should not be confused with ordinary
ego. That pure I-consciousness of the Lord is a divine
state. If, in the course of japa, one gets into this state
of pure I-awareness and his mind gets suspended, that is
the state of spontaneous kumbhak according to the yoga
shastras. This kumbhak is even more significant than
samadhi. It is this kumbhak which equalises prana and
apana and which activates Kundalini. And after Kundalini has been activated, it helps Kundalini do Her work
more intensely and effectively.

Swami Ramanand : *Though I see different lights in
meditation, I haven't yet experienced the kriyas which
follow Kundalini awakening. What is the reason?*
Baba : Why are you so attached to kriyas? Attachment
to physical kriyas is just like an addiction to bhajias
or pakoras, coffee or tea, or something else. Light is
beyond kriyas. If you are seeing lights, you shouldn't
bother about kriyas. Kriyas are a means to purify the
nerves and that is all that there is to them. You should
not attach too much importance to them. If Kundalini
is not able to find any impurities in your body, why
should She effect any kriyas? If you have been able to
see inner lights, that experience is far more significant
than kriyas, because lights are beyond kriyas. These
lights are the lights of the Self. If you see these divine
lights with reverence you will be able to swim across
samsara easily, such is the glory of these inner lights.
The scriptures say that the inner lights are not imaginary,
not hallucinations, they are actual divine phenomena.
They are self-existent. If you are able to behold those
lights you are most blessed. When the inner lights arise,
that signifies a very high stage in sadhana, because it
means that you are experiencing the inner Self. These
lights arise only after the eyes have been purified of all

impurities, and this shows how highly evolved you already are.

Continue to see these lights considering them to be divine and you will experience great bliss and get closer to the Lord. Jnaneshwar says, "He alone is a true saint who has been able to see the light dwelling within his eyes." As you see those lights you should try to become completely absorbed in them. When you are seeing such significant divine lights, what is the point of shaking your limbs?

Uma : *Will one who is not meditating but just doing Guruseva have spiritual experiences?*

Baba : One who is absorbed in service to the Guru and who does not consider anything higher than service to the Guru, what does he need spiritual experiences for? The various spiritual experiences will wait on such a one hand and foot.

There was a boy with Eknath Maharaj who had a weakness for puranpolis, a sweet delicacy. He could not enjoy his meal unless he had puranpolis. That was why he was named Puranpoliya. Sometimes we have them here and you must have eaten them. He was the son of poor parents, and the mother could not afford to feed him puranpolis every day. Finally she got sick of him. If parents get sick of their children then the best way of getting rid of them is to offer them to saints. The mother one day brought the child to Eknath Maharaj and said, "This boy is excessively fond of puranpolis and I cannot afford it. You have such a large number of devotees. Some of them are very rich and I am sure that you can afford to cater to his weakness, so I am going to leave him with you."

Eknath accepted him and Puranpoliya used to sweep the floors and wash clothes and render personal service to Eknath Maharaj. He would eat only puranpolis, so he was always floating in bliss. Eknath was a divinely inspired poet and he compiled a very important work called the *Eknathi Bhagavat*. That work is of such great importance that even the greatest scholars in Maha-

rashtra feel the need of studying it closely. It was only
the other day, in the last lecture that I told you about
the glory of service to the Guru. Eknath Maharaj was
an ideal servant of his Guru. In the last part of the
book Eknath began to translate the *Ramayana* into Marathi. When he had finished just half of the work he left
his body. Everyone said, "Sir, you are departing and your
work is not yet complete. Who is going to complete it?"

Eknath said, "Don't worry, somebody who has been
with me, who has partaken of my food, who has served
me, will be able to complete it. My inspiration is bound
to flow into someone who has been around me."

Puranpoliya was present and all of a sudden he
exclaimed, "I am going to complete this work."

This made people laugh and they said, "All that you
will write about will be puranpolis."

Eknath departed and Puranpoliya completed the work,
and he did it with such remarkable skill that nobody,
even today, is able to tell which part of it was composed
by Eknath and which part by Puranpoliya. It is very
difficult to write the kind of poetry that such a great
Master as Eknath wrote. Yet, Puranpoliya finished the remaining half. Service to the Guru is superior to meditation, it is superior to yoga, it is superior to samadhi.

There was a disciple of a saint called Bharadwaja, who
was a most dedicated disciple of his Guru. He was an
ideal Gurubhakta, that is, a devotee of his Guru. He
was completely absorbed in serving him. He would do
whatever his Guru told him to do. The result was that
even Lord Rama was so pleased with his service to his
Guru that He Himself came to meet the disciple whose
name was Sutikshan. After finishing the task given to him
by his Guru, he was sitting in his hut absorbed in meditation. Lord Rama came there. He met Bharadwaja and
He said, "Now I want to meet your disciple, Sutikshan."

The hut was locked inside, so both Lord Rama and
Bharadwaja stood outside and knocked at the door.
Bharadwaja called him and got him out of his meditative
state. The moment he heard his Guru's voice, Sutikshan
got up from meditation and came out. He saw both

Lord Rama and his Guru standing in front of him. Both should be greeted with reverence. In our country we are very particular about protocol. You have to be careful to greet people in the proper order, the greater ones first. As he saw both Rama and his Guru standing before him, he was in a dilemma. Whose feet should he touch first? On one hand was his Guru, and on the other the Lord Himself. He said to himself, "It is by the grace of the Guru that I have been able to have darshan of the Lord." He decided to touch his Guru's feet first.

All spiritual experiences will come to one who is absorbed in service to the Guru. Take the case of Jabali. Jabali's Guru told him to go into the woods with a few cows and not return until they multiplied to 1,000. He took very good care of the cows. About fourteen or fifteen years passed and then the number rose to 1,000. It was then time to return to the Guru. On his way back he was greeted by all the great elements, and they all revealed their innermost secrets to him. Fire appeared to him, the god of water appeared to him and the god of wind appeared to him, before he returned to the Guru's place. Such is the glory of service to the Guru. Jnaneshwar says that one who begins to enjoy serving the Guru is truly blessed, because everyone cannot enjoy serving the Guru. Such a one will be able to attain God easily. Not only that, all the riddhis and siddhis and all divine knowledge will come and serve him.

December 19, 1972

Kersee: *Will you please explain how a Guru is always with his disciple?*

Baba: The Guru lives with his disciple as his own inner Self. Just as a mother is always with her child from

the time it is born till it is about six years old, the
Guru is always with his disciple. Just as a mother wants
her child to achieve greatness in the world, to develop
fully, to be free from all addictions, to realise his full
potential, so is the Guru intensely concerned about the
growth of his disciple. The Guru may use different
methods at different times—from persuasion and love to
fierceness and punishment—but behind all these methods
his only motive is to make sure that his disciple
achieves true growth, that the best in the disciple is unfolded. A Guru who is not a businessman, a real Guru,
will consider his disciple's failings to be his own, and his
primary concern will be to rid his disciple of all failings.

There is no shortage of those teachers who in order
to have more and more disciples let them do whatever
they feel like. Those teachers don't have the confidence
to go against the wishes and inclinations of their
disciples. They are afraid that they would not be able
to retain their students' esteem. Those teachers have
secret selfish interests behind their actions, while a
genuine Guru is only concerned about insuring the full
development of his disciple, always seeing how he can
get rid of the various defects of his disciple and make
him fully worthy. Unfortunately, those so-called gurus
themselves are not free from selfish motives, and that is
why they soon fall from their dignified status. And when
the Guru falls, what can you say about his students?

A true Guru is without any ulterior motive. My own
Guru did not relent even in the least as far as a disciple's
weakness or his sadhana was concerned. If you relent,
if you compromise with the failings of a disciple, then
you are making sure that the disciple will only get worse
instead of better. My Guru's deity was discipline, and
as far as discipline was concerned he would not compromise with anyone, whether he was a great artist, an
aristocrat, or a business tycoon. To him discipline was
the most precious thing. He was completely free from
care. If nobody went to him, he was completely contented, and if he received a large number of devotees, he was
equally contented. Such was the state that he was in.

If a person roams around the world, going from one country to another buying absolutely useless, rotten things and resorting to all kinds of foul practices such as black marketeering, smuggling, cheating and what not, wearing a sophisticated suit during the day and saffron clothes at night, I wonder what kind of guru he is, and if he isn't just playacting. To put on saffron clothes and shake your body and thus pretend that you are an expert master, what's the use? If you meet a girlfriend or boyfriend, you don't take even a minute in getting rid of your saffrons. You put on your fancy clothes and rush off to a nightclub. I wonder what kind of guru such a person is?

A true Guru would not like to have such fake teachers even as his students, because they bring discredit to him. Already people are being cheated by all kinds of tactics in their worldly life, and on top of that you have so-called spiritual preceptors who resort to the same sort of sordid devices to cheat you. A Guru is constantly concerned with the true welfare of his disciple. He wants his disciple to follow exactly what he has followed in his life, to be as disciplined and self-controlled as he has been himself, so the disciple can realise the highest he has in him. A true Guru would feel ashamed of even being called a Guru without becoming worthy of it, without having risen to the state of true Guruhood. And if he arrogated to himself such a worthy function he would be committing a crime against God. A true Guru would not become a Guru unless he received a specific command from his own Guru. Without receiving a command from his own Guru he would not usurp the seat of a Guru, because he knows what responsibility is involved.

To be a Guru is not to be in a very comfortable, profitable position. However, those people who only know how to cheat and who have been cheating people in various other fields of life may find becoming a guru quite profitable. Guruhood seems to be the latest device through which they can exploit or cheat more and more people. Recently, while I was talking to a teacher privately, he told me that he had been doing sadhana for 25 years, yet he was without any worthwhile realisation, but he had a large number of students. That only made me laugh. What could I say to him? I said to myself, "It doesn't matter if you didn't find God, you have found so many students, and you have received far more from them than you could have received from God, so that is enough."

A Guru would always feel ashamed if he found that his disciples were wanting or suffering from certain lacks. If one is really worthy of being a Guru then he would not want anything from the outside world, and the question of his wanting disciples would not arise. Though people may find the prospect quite attractive— having so many disciples around you, adoring you, wor- shipping you—to the Guru all that is an obstruction, there is nothing pleasant about it. A Guru is like a parent bird who is taking constant care of his young ones. The bird does not rest until he has taught his young one to fly on its own, and he would be constantly watching him to make sure that no harm comes to him, that he grows properly, that he is able to fly on his own, that he is saved from all harmful creatures. So a Guru is also constantly thinking about how he can raise his disciples to higher levels and how he can make them progress faster. A Guru would not rest until he has brought his disciples to the same state of perfection which he himself is in. He would be at peace only when he finds that his disciples have become as worthy as him.

Kersee: *I am amazed that everyone who comes to you receives blessings that can be consciously known, whereas the same thing is not true with other teachers, even though their disciples have done sadhana for 20 or 30 years. Would you please explain this?*

Baba: You have put me in a dilemma. I don't know whether to blame the Gurus or the disciples. If I blame the disciples I would not be justified, because if a certain person has been following a Guru for 20 or 30 years, he must at least be sincere and earnest. To explain why a disciple has not received Guru's grace by saying that the Guru himself is not perfect, well, that too, would not be proper. But I can say this: in other fields you can have any number of people achieving proficiency. You can have many singers, many dancers, many artists, many painters, many musicians, many actors, many actresses. But the field of Guruhood is the only field where only really rare ones flourish.

The Guru must be perfect, and to be perfect, a Guru himself must have had a Guru. If a Guru hasn't himself had a Guru and claims to be a Guru, and pretends to function as a Guru, then he is a mere teacher. That is the law. You must first become a disciple to become a Guru, a perfect disciple. And you should serve as a disciple according to the scriptural injunctions, otherwise you would only be making a mockery of Guruhood. To be a Guru, first you must be a perfect disciple of a perfect Guru. Second, you must grow fully into his image. You must become completely like him. And even that isn't enough. Your own Guru must tell you to serve as a Guru. Unless you have received the command to become a Guru directly from your own Guru, there is no point in becoming a Guru. It is only when a Guru raises a disciple to his own level and tells him to go out and serve as a Guru, that a disciple becomes a Guru. If a disciple becomes a Guru on his own, just for his own worldly motives, or worldly satisfaction, just for name, comfort or personal glory, he would never be acceptable to God. If a person becomes a Guru without having received the command from his Guru, without himself having served as a disciple to his Guru, he will only be running a business concern. He can't carry out the responsibility of a true Guru. He would only be running a factory—in his case, a spiritual factory.

Then a true Guru must have lineage. I have already said that a true Guru is first and foremost a true disciple. By doing sadhana under the direct guidance of his Guru he rises to the highest level. Then he receives a direct command from his Guru to serve the function of Guru. If in the presence of such a Guru, a disciple should flourish spontaneously, that shouldn't be surprising at

all, because the power of lineage, the power of his Guru
is working behind him. A disciple who has been raised
to the level of his Guru, to the level of a true Guru,
and who is commanded by him to go out and serve as
a Guru, his Guru having transmitted his own power into
him—such a one alone can be considered to be a true
Guru. If people's Shakti is aroused in his presence with
the utmost ease, that is nothing surprising or unusual,
because behind such a Guru is the infinite power of God.

A Guru, a true Guru, does not rest on his laurels, he
does not allow his Shakti to diminish. There are many
people who raise this question, "What need does Muktananda Swami have of meditating even at this stage?"
"Why does he chant the *Guru Gita* himself? Why does
he enforce discipline on his disciples?" These people
forget that no millionaire would like to live on his past
earnings. Take the case of wealthy businessmen. What
makes you think that after attaining a certain degree
of affluence they would sit idly and live on their past
earnings? On the contrary, they continue to work as
hard as before and they expand their concerns and they
give employment to more and more people, and this is
exactly what happens with a Guru. He does not allow
the store of his Shakti to diminish in any way. He would
like more and more people to benefit from him. So what
you say is quite true. It is not at all surprising if people
receive blessings here, because behind me there is the
power of my whole line. What happens here is possible
only with a true Guru, if you have your Guru's power
and authority with you.

Rani : *What is the Lord's opinion of a yogi and what
exactly is his worth?*

Baba : If one is a true yogi, the Lord will have the
highest opinion of him. In the *Gita* the Lord commands
Arjuna to be a yogi. He says, "Become a yogi, Arjuna."
The Lord says a yogi is greater than an ascetic, a yogi is
greater than one who does great deeds. Yoga is in fact
far superior to all other spiritual practices and disciplines.
So therefore, 'Arjuna, become a yogi'. While commenting

on this verse, Jnaneshwar Maharaj says, "A yogi is God's
God. Just as everybody needs a deity, and everyone looks
upon God as a deity, likewise God Himself needs a deity
to worship and it is a yogi who serves as God's deity.
Everyone in the world is seeking happiness, and God too
needs an object of happiness for His enjoyment. It is a
yogi who is God's object of happiness." The Lord goes
on to say, "A yogi is my very Self, a yogi is the greatest
bliss to Me."

There is a verse in Arabic about the glory of prophet
Mohammed. The poet says, "Nobody should stop the
prophet from going anywhere, because He is the very
Self of God."

Tukaram Maharaj sings of the glory of a yogi in his
poetry, "A yogi who is completely without desires rises
to such a status that even God begins to follow him with
a certain craving. It is amazing to hear that God, too,
has a craving. The desire of God is to have His body
covered with the dust which is flying from a yogi's feet."

Such is the glory of a yogi. It is for this reason that
Shiva is referred to as a yogi. A yogi becomes the very
Atman, the very Self of God. He achieves complete unity
with the Godhead. In other words, he realises the very
highest within himself. Through knowledge and contemplation he sheds all chains, all bondage, and attains the
highest divinity. Lord Shiva says while talking about a
yogi, "When through meditation he has rid himself of
bondage, of separate existence, he has become one with
God and realised his own divinity, all the cosmic powers,
all the mantras, all the great elements are willing to
serve him. He acquires dominion over the entire cosmos,
and all its powers, even over God."

He alone can be called a yogi who meditates on his
own Self as the highest Lord. Until then he is only a
seeker, he is not a yogi.

Hanumandas : *How do faith and devotion for the Guru
increase in a disciple's heart?*

Baba : If you achieve the knowledge of the Guru's state,
your faith and devotion for him will increase. If you

21

want to have faith and devotion for anything or anyone,
first you must fully understand that thing or that person.
What Sundardas says about the glory of a Guru is worth
reflecting upon over and over. Sundardas says, "The
creatures created by God sink into hell again and again.
They are born, they die and they are reborn. They keep
on transmigrating from one form to another and suffering,
while the creatures reshaped, refinished by the Guru, rise
to the state of divinity, attaining bliss."

He who is aware of this, who knows that such is the
exalted, sublime role of the Guru, will find faith and
devotion for him increasing in his heart spontaneously.
In the world there is nothing, however precious it may
be considered by people, which has any lasting importance. Take the case of excellent food. You may be eating
the best food in the world, yet as a result of your constant
eating you do not become stronger. One day you find
yourself passing into old age and nothing can prevent
that. You don't find your sense organs becoming stronger.
On the contrary, you find them becoming more and more
feeble. And you don't find your mind becoming enthused
more and more with inner delight. On the contrary you
find it getting more and more weary. And that applies
to all other blessings or advantages of the world. Whatever you can acquire in the outer world will ultimately
leave you weak and feeble. There is only one thing
which will make you stronger day by day, which will
release more and more enthusiasm within you, and that
is the Guru's grace. As you pass into meditation through
Guru's grace, you find your life becoming sweeter and
happier. Shall I put it into just one sentence? When a
disciple becomes an ideal disciple then faith and devotion
for the Guru abound in his heart.

Douglas : *In meditation an orange light shaped like a*
small rainbow with black light in the background appears
and pulses on and off corresponding to my heart beat. I
also sometimes hear a high-pitched, electronic-like sound.
Could you please tell me what this means?

Baba : This is a very good experience and a prelude to

much higher things. This light is not an arch like a
rainbow, it is a radiant orange sphere. You have only
seen a part of it. This orange light is always surrounded
by sweet blue light. As your heart is filled with contentment, it throbs with delight, and as a result of that you
see the light pulsing off and on. The light is still all
the time, it only appears to you to be quivering. There
are lights within lights, there are divine sounds within
sounds and sounds within lights. If you see a light then
you will hear a divine sound and vice versa.

The divine sound you hear in meditation is a direct
word of God. It is a mantra more powerful than the
mantra which you have repeated. Keep listening to that.
That sound is the primal sound from which every other
sound originates. Nada is the mahamantra which throbs
in the space of pure consciousness, the space where Chiti
revels, the space where Chiti operates. This mantra is the
unstruck, unuttered sound. It is God who makes this
sound without a tongue. Nada is the most powerful, the
most effective mantra. As you continue to listen to it
you pass into a divine state. When you begin to hear
nada you should consider yourself to be extremely fortunate, very blessed. I am delighted to know about these
experiences of yours.

December 22, 1972

Savita: *Is it possible to fall from a high state in
sadhana due to carelessness or negligence, or some other
reason? If this happens, what causes it?*

Baba: If you have received sadhana through Guru's
grace, and as a result of that you have risen to a high
state, it is very difficult to fall from that. You may remain stuck there for a time. The only thing that could

bring about your fall would be turning away from the
Guru and turning against him. Otherwise, you cannot
possibly fall. After one has been accepted by Guru's
grace, after sadhana has been activated within him by
the Guru's Shakti, it means that he is already worthy,
otherwise. Shakti could not have chosen to bless him.
Such a person is worthy of rising higher and higher, and
the question of falling would not arise.

It is due to wrong understanding that one sometimes
thinks that one has fallen when no fall has taken place.
And it is correct understanding which helps one to rise
higher and higher. Wrong understanding could make one
decline. That is why the Lord says in the *Gita*, "One is
one's own enemy and one's own friend." There is no
outer power, no destiny or hostile person or hostile
environment which could cause your fall. It is only you
yourself who could serve as your own worst enemy, and
cause your own fall. There is no outer Shakti, no outer
power, no outer agency strong enough to do any harm
to a seeker. What happens is that he himself becomes his
own worst enemy and he causes his own fall from heaven.

Take the case of Prahlad. Prahlad was tormented so
much by his own father and all kinds of obstacles were
placed in his way. He was thrown into fire, he was
thrown into the midst of wild, violent beasts. Armed
sentries were set upon him to cut off his head, and so
many methods were tried to take Prahlad away from his
path, but none of these methods could deflect him from
the path on which he was walking firmly. Prahlad could
not be defeated because he himself remained firm, because he did not become his own enemy, because he did
not turn against himself. If you do not turn against yourself, then even if the whole world turns against you, it
cannot do anything. If a seeker has risen to a certain
state, no outer agency can cause his fall. Only he himself
can cause his fall.

B. M. Doven: *How does one know that one has found
his Guru and that the Guru has also accepted him?*

Baba: You already know that you haven't found your

Guru, don't you? So if you know that you haven't found your Guru, then when you find your Guru you will also know that you have found him. Whether the Guru has accepted you or not doesn't matter. What matters is whether you have accepted the Guru or not.

Eklavya was a tribal boy, an 'untouchable.' When he approached Dronacharya to be accepted as a disciple, Dronacharya rejected him outright because he didn't want to have anything to do with untouchables. Dronacharya was only interested in conveying his knowledge to boys coming from royal families. Eklavya was not only rejected but he wasn't even allowed to come to the place where the royal princes studied with Dronacharya. Dronacharya turned him out saying, "You are low-born and you can never be worthy of being my student."

But Eklavya did not reject Dronacharya. Eklavya looked at Dronacharya's form carefully from head to foot and then went back into the forest and made a statue of him. He enlivened the statue by the force of his own feeling. He got wild flowers and leaves and offered them to the statue, walked around it thrice and bowed to it, and sitting in front of it he was lost in meditation.

Far more important than the priest or even the object of worship is the worshipper's faith. The *Vedas* say that by means of faith it is possible to kindle fire. There is a Vedic verse which says that if you say to fire, "Kindle", tongues of fire would leap up immediately. But you must have the necessary faith. There was a time when priests could kindle fire just by reciting certain verses, by the force of their faith. It is faith which compels the Lord to manifest Himself even in a stone idol. Prahlad was asked by his father whether his Lord lived inside the pillar standing in front of him and Prahlad said, "Yes." Then the pillar was smashed and the Lord revealed His form. It was not the pillar which manifested the Lord, it was Prahlad's firm faith which manifested Him.

Eklavya began to repeat, *"Guru Om, Guru Om"* with utmost faith. As a result, he was able to manifest Dronacharya in the clay image which he had made. Through the intensity of his faith Eklavya absorbed the Guru in his fullness into himself. He got not only his knowledge, not only the secrets of archery from him, but he got the Guru himself within him. This is what happens in meditation. The power of meditation is such that through it one can absorb the whole of the Guru into himself. Meditation is the magnet which draws the Guru's Shakti into oneself. As a result of his faith Eklavya could learn even those secrets of archery which Dronacharya had not imparted to the princes, such as Arjuna and others, and which he had kept concealed within himself. If the Guru were to teach us verbally then we would know just a part of what he knows, but if we were to absorb the Guru into ourselves, then we would get all the knowledge of the Guru.

You don't need to be accepted by the Guru. What you need is to accept the Guru. You don't even have to know whether you have been accepted by the Guru or not. You get to know whether you have found the Guru by looking at your own Self. If you find any change in you when you compare your present state with your past state then you will know that you have found the Guru. As far as the Guru's acceptance is concerned, that is not of any importance. What is important is your acceptance of the Guru. So many devotees used to come to my Guru and so many of them were his disciples. Nityananda Baba never said that he had this or that disciple. Whatever those disciples got from Nityananda depended on the intensity of their faith, the intensity of their devotion, the intensity of their identification with him. So the more intensely devotees identify themselves with him, the more of him they absorb into themselves. It is the bhakta's concern to be a bhakta of God; it is not God's concern to be the deity of a bhakta. It is not the Guru who has to accept the disciple; it is the disciple who has to accept the Guru.

Swami Vimalananda : *After completing his sadhana, or after attaining perfection as a result of his sadhana, does a yogi automatically acquire psychic powers such as the*

*ability to see distant objects, hear distant sounds, enter
somebody else's body, multiply his own form and fly in
the skies? Or does a yogi have to practise specially for
the attainment of these powers, even after completing his
sadhana?*

Baba : There are two kinds of yogis: one kind does
sadhana according to the eight-fold yoga of Patanjali.
Through the practice of the eight-fold yoga they enter
deeper within themselves, and before the attainment of
perfection all the powers that you mentioned come to
them. None of these powers is a mark of perfection.
Clairvoyance, clairaudience, flying in the sky, or creating
miracles—none of these has anything to do with perfection, because perfection is without any outer marks. For
the attainment of these powers one doesn't have to be a
very great yogi either, because these powers belong to
a certain stage of yoga which is described in the *Yoga
Sutras* as the three-fold samyama in which dhyan, dharana and samadhi coalesce into unity. The three-fold
samyama of dhyan, dharana and samadhi is the coming
together into a perfect unity of the known, the instruments of knowledge and the knower. One who has
attained this state can acquire all these powers. These
powers are nothing but interesting creations of the mind
and are quite ordinary. There are some powers, such as
flying in the sky, travelling in the astral body from one
place to another, or vanishing from a certain place, for
acquiring which one has to do intense sadhana of a
different sort. The elements of earth and water have to
be conquered because it is these two elements which cause
resistance to flying and to other things. But even these
powers have nothing to do with perfection.

There is another kind of yogi, one who does sadhana
through Guru's grace, the yogi whose sadhana has been
started and is being maintained by Shaktipat. That yogi
also comes to acquire these powers during the course of
his sadhana. But he doesn't have to practise particular
methods to acquire these powers, because the Guru's
Shakti works within him. His Guru's Shakti enters him
in the form of grace, and brings him all his potency. The

Guru's Shakti is Chiti, and Chiti is the divine power of creation, the power from which the entire cosmos arises, the power which maintains and dissolves it in the end. This Shakti, this Chiti, is most amazing. She has eyes everywhere, She has ears everywhere, She has feet and hands everywhere. So astonishing is Her potency that when She is asleep or sitting in one place She is able to travel throughout the entire world. She sees all the different worlds in a moment. She hears all the sounds that fill the cosmos. Such is the marvellous power of Chiti. And it is Chiti which becomes active in a yogi who has received Guru's grace.

Such a yogi is a yogi of meditation, and he sometimes enters into the state of tandra, the state of higher consciousness, whose centre is situated in the heart. In that state he is able to travel from one place to another while sitting in one place. He is able to see distant objects from the spot where his physical body is sitting. He is able to move from one world to another. And all these powers come to him most naturally. He doesn't have to make any effort or undergo any hardship to acquire these powers; they are all gifts of grace for him. Such a yogi, in course of meditation, acquires the inner eye. He gets into a state in which he is able to see the entire universe while sitting in one place. This happens by Guru's grace.

So these powers come to a yogi in two different ways. It is difficult to acquire these through the practice of the eight-fold yoga. Only rare persons are able to do that. One who is practising the eight-fold path, even in spite of having acquired all these siddhis or miraculous powers, may not necessarily arrive at perfection. There was a yogi in Maharashtra called Changdev. He had mastered yoga to such an extent that while he was completely lost in samadhi, people would bring dead bodies, carcasses of animals, and leave them around him; and when he came out of samadhi and cast a glance at the carcasses they would come to life again. He was a contemporary of Jnaneshwar. In spite of having attained such great power, he could not win liberation by himself. It was Jnaneshwar's sister, Muktabai, who brought him liberation. But this does not happen with a yogi who is working by Guru's grace, because the Guru's grace would not let him get stuck in siddhis.

There are two kinds of yogis. One kind acquires these extraordinary powers in the course of sadhana in a natural manner and goes beyond them and achieves liberation; the other kind gets these powers by hard effort and generally falls after getting them.

Ian: *What influence does the moon have on the development of consciousness? What is the relationship of the moon with Shiva?*

Baba: The moon is the deity of coolness, the god of the mind. Each sense organ has its own presiding deity and it functions under the influence of that deity. If the position of the moon in your horoscope is favourable to your sadhana, only then will you be able to have undisturbed sadhana, sadhana with a calm and steady mind. If the moon is in an unfavourable position, your mind will be full of trouble and uncertainty. The sun is the god of the intellect, while the moon is the god of the mind. In our country the moon is worshipped so that by his grace the mind may become stable and free of agitation. Some people check their horoscopes to see which house the moon falls in and which house Jupiter falls in, because the moon and Jupiter have a lot to do with sadhana.

You will read the reports which will be brought out by Russia and America in course of time, that the men who went to the moon and stayed there for some time underwent mental transformation just by being there for a while. They have returned with their minds free of certain addictions, with their minds revitalized. One has come back with his poetic power awakened and others with some other power activated. One of them has now turned entirely to the pursuit of knowledge and cannot take interest in anything else. The men who will return from the moon will make great poets, great writers, great researchers. Such is the effect of the moon on the mind. But they went to the outer moon through scientific gadgets. If you get to the moon within your sahasrar, you will get into an entirely different state, a unique state.

Part of the soil brought from the moon has been given to the Government of India also, and in Delhi I met one of the persons who is doing research on that soil. He says that the moment he handles the soil his mind is powerfully affected and he is not able to think what he should do. It will be marvellous if Russia and America make arrangements for travel to the moon for all people and build up a few houses on the moon and enable people to live there for a short while, because it is enough to live on the moon to have your mind steady and calm. The moon is the deity which imparts peace to the mind. Shiva has the moon on his forehead, and that shows that Shiva is supremely tranquil.

Swami Vimalananda : *After the Kundalini has become fully awake, how much time does it take for Her to reach the sahasrar after piercing the six chakras and the three knots? And while going upwards from muladhar does the seeker envision an inner moon and sun and other deities dwelling there?*

Baba : After Kundalini has become fully awake, if one is a first-rate seeker, it will take him not less than three years to be established in the sahasrar. If one is not a first-rate seeker, just second-rate, third-rate or fourth-rate, it will take proportionally longer; it may range from 3 to 27 years, it may take 6, 9, 12, 15, 18, 21, 24 years. One may be able to pierce his chakras quite soon, one may even be able to touch the sahasrar, but that doesn't mean that he would attain supreme peace, because even after you have touched the sahasrar, a lot of work has to be accomplished. It is only after that work has been finished that one will get into the state of supreme peace.

If you go to a foreign country, you do not get to know the country fully just by entering, or if a tent is erected for a wedding and the bridegroom enters, it doesn't mean

that he married just by entering the tent. A lot more
has to happen before he can be said to be married. It
doesn't matter if it takes time to get established in the
sahasrar. Once the Kundalini has been awakened, your
sadhana is bound to go on by itself. In fact sadhana will
be chasing you, you don't have to chase sadhana.

Swami : *What happens if a sadhak dies at this point?*
Baba : That is very good because in his next life he will
be much better off than in this life. If one dies as a
sadhak before the completion of his sadhana, then one
is called a yogabhrashta. He is born with certain powers.
Right from the moment of his birth he is already at a
high stage, and he will have unusual intelligence and
other powers. If I had not reached the goal I would not
mind dying right now in order to be born again with
certain powers right from the moment of birth. Then I
would be spared so much of the travail I had to undergo
in this life.

While the Kundalini is rising from the muladhar to
the sahasrar, the yogi will be able to see all the worlds
on the way. Such a yogi is able to move through the
nether worlds and all the higher worlds—Siddhaloka,
Chandraloka, and Indraloka. I said a short while ago
that Chiti is the universe, and when a yogi becomes
established in the sahasrar he becomes one with Chiti.
That means that he becomes one with the whole universe.
He can see all the worlds in the cosmos. It is only to
the physical eye that the worlds such as the world of
Indra, the world of the Siddhas and other worlds appear
to be distant. If one gets established in the sahasrar,
those worlds come quite close; so close in fact, that just
as you are sitting right here and I am able to see you
quite easily, a yogi can see all these worlds with the
greatest ease. You can understand this from the ana-
logy of a simple radio. It doesn't matter how small the
radio is, if you move the dial a short distance, even less
than half an inch, you can get to America from India.
Likewise, when you are established in the sahasrar, all
the different worlds come very close to you. That is why

Tukaram Maharaj says, "I am always in Vaikuntha. The question of my going there and returning doesn't arise because the higher worlds such as Kailas, Goloka and Vaikuntha are quite near the sahasrar."

Such a yogi can see not only the inner world, the inner sun, the inner moon, and other inner planets and stars, he can also see the outer worlds, stars and planets quite distinctly. However, one should meditate with great reverence for the inner Shakti and with full faith in Her. It is only then that one can go deep. One shouldn't consider meditation to be something commonplace, something dead or dull. This is why I keep repeating that by belittling oneself one does great harm to oneself. It is essential for everyone to worship his own Self with full faith and reverence being fully aware of the nature of the Shakti that dwells within him. Parashiva says to Parvati, "O Beauteous One, he who worships, meditates on and adores his own Self as the supreme Lord becomes ever united with Him, and to him all siddhis, all realisations, all powers come of their own accord."

I thank everyone for having listened so quietly and I urge all of you once again to worship with full faith and reverence the Shakti who is blazing within you all the time.

Christmas Day, December 25, 1972

Baba : This afternoon we aren't going to have a question and answer session. For one thing, we don't have any questions, and secondly it is Christmas Day and the entire world is celebrating this day. We too will celebrate it in our way. Though not many people saw Christ personally, not many people were with him, yet countless people in the world today remember him, follow his

teaching and consider his birthday a day of great blessing for them.   The great sage Narada says in his *Bhakti
Sutras* that when someone who is dear to the Lord appears
on the surface of the earth, the earth also finds a Lord
and becomes ecstatic. She begins to dance in rapture on
having found a Lord. That obviously implies that all
the other people who are born cannot rid the earth of
her barrenness. In our country, when a mother gets very
angry with her child she tells him, "I don't know what
has happened to you. You are not following the family
tradition, you are not a good son, and it would have been
better if I had been barren and you had not been born
from my womb." Likewise, the earth also feels the same
way when she gives birth to countless people. It is only
when a great sage appears that she feels that her existence is justified.

One who is a slave to his senses cannot even enjoy sense
pleasures. People are under the illusion that they enjoy
sense pleasures, but the fact is that pleasures enjoy them.
Only he who has conquered his senses can enjoy sense
objects. He who spends his life only enjoying sense
objects wastes his life on this earth. There is no dearth
of people in this world who are born just to inflict suffering on others and who do things which will cause suffering to generations to come. These people come only as
some kind of punishment for mankind. It is only some
rare ones, who after appearing on the surface of this
earth, give a new life to thousands of others, who turn
them to God, filling their hearts with divine love and
devotion. It is only after getting such a child that the
earth feels that her motherhood is justified.

A devotee of the Lord is a great personage. In fact,
he serves as a symbol of the Lord. Tukaram Maharaj
says, "He alone is pure, only his body is a sacred place of
pilgrimage, only his senses are clean, whose heart is full
of devotion to the Lord, who remembers Him ceaselessly."

Those people who have filled themselves with worldly
concerns, with hellish thoughts, who have filled their
lives with all kinds of misery, achieve nothing. They are
no better than animals. A devotee of the Lord has a

special power by means of which he can show people the path of peace and happiness with the greatest ease. If you read the works of different schools of philosophy about God, you will find them so abstruse that you may even lose your interest in God. But great saints such as Jesus, Jnaneshwar, Tukaram Maharaj, Mirabai, Sundardas, Kabir, Janabai and others, have all shown the easy path to God-realisation. They talk about God in such simple terms that everybody can understand. Nobody gets frightened. It is the glory of the saints that they have rid people of the hardship of yajnas and ascetic practices. They have been able to bring God within easy reach. A true bhakta of the Lord, one whose heart throbs with true love for Him, would be able to illumine the world without the light of the sun. Bhaktas have such great power that by the force of their devotion they are able to make even the impure pure. Others who lack devotion, whose lives are full of the devil, make even the pure impure.

Great saints are called Siddhas, and there is a world of Siddhas which is full of such devotees. From time to time these Siddhas take birth in this world for the welfare and spiritual growth of mankind. They have risen completely above the distinctions of sect, caste, race or religion, and they do not indulge in any politics, even religious politics. Those who involve people in religious politics are not saints. Those who take sides, who show a partisan spirit do not belong to this category. Jesus was completely above politics. He belonged to everyone. These Siddhas appear only to expound the pure divine state and for no other purpose. The best description of them would be that they are dear to the Lord. It would be ridiculous to talk about them in terms of good or bad. A bhakta is he who sees the world as full of God, who sees the Lord everywhere, and who is completely beyond the reach of time and space, person or personality, or individuality. The Lord does not belong to any caste or sect, and if you were to impute any sect or caste to Him, He would not like it at all. Krishna did not belong to any particular sect or religion. Shiva—you can't talk in terms

of the caste of Shiva; no one knows when Shiva was
born or how He was born. Shiva, Krishna, all the divine
incarnations are above consideration of caste and personality and that is the case with a true bhakta of the Lord
also. If a bhakta of the Lord gets involved with caste
or sectarian distinctions he is a politician, not a bhakta.
A bhakta's sole concern is with love, and all that we can
say about him is that he loves the Lord and is dear to
Him. If you say anything else about him, it will be religious politics.

Those who are dear to the Lord, namely his bhaktas,
operate on two planes simultaneously. On one plane they
are filled with compassion for suffering people and they
give the message which will deliver them from their
suffering. On the other plane they see the world as
nothing but God, and when they see God all around them
they are filled with delight and they begin to dance in
ecstasy. To concentrate one's attention on poverty, suffering and sorrow in this world is something very ordinary.
These are ordinary phenomena. And besides, they are
ephemeral. The true concern of a bhakta, of a devotee
of the Lord, is with seeing God everywhere, with knowing the nature of the Lord, with knowing His ways, with
knowing the experiences of His bliss and His love. As
far as mundane problems such as hunger, clothing, housing and affliction are concerned, they will always be
there. They have been there right from the beginning
of the world, and a great saint's concern is not with
them. It doesn't mean that he has no compassion. It only
means that a great saint is aware of things which really
matter, with things that are really permanent.

It was only today that I read in a paper that a certain
part of America was rocked with an earthquake and a
large number of people were killed, and a few towns
were destroyed. The ordinary reformers concern themselves with reform in the mundane sphere, they like to
have more factories, more bridges and more dams. They
like to get rid of poverty and hunger and so on. But in
spite of all their endeavors, not really very much can
be done because these problems can never be really over-

come. They may seem to be overcome for a while, but they will appear again. But a great saint is not so concerned with these things. He is concerned with the human heart, with turning the human heart towards the Lord, with filling it with divine love.

The law is that in the world, in every place, there will be a shortage of something or other. God's creation is such. If not water, it will be the shortage of cloth. If not cloth, then copper. If not copper, then shoes. If you have an abundance of shoes then you will have a shortage of hats. Something or other will always be in short supply wherever you may be. There are many clever modern people who raise this question in connection with the great saints such as Jesus and Tukaram and Kabir and others, "Did they build any bridges, did they build any dams?" These people forget that so many bridges and dams were built before them and after them, and they have disappeared, and so many will be built and they will disappear too. But the bridges built by great saints still exist and are still growing. They build bridges to the Lord, they make it possible for ordinary human beings to experience heavenly bliss, divine love. That is the significance of their work. These saints disclose the abode of God which lies in our hearts, which is so close to us. If you leave God out, there is not much meaning in developing the world. No matter how much you develop it, you cannot be happy here; you will only be subject to birth and death over and over. And how many times are you going to be born and re-born and die and re-die? Deliverance from birth and death can come only if we become aware of God, only if we fill our hearts and minds with divine love, if our minds think of Him constantly. The path which has been built by the great saints can never be destroyed. It will always lead people to their final destination. It will always lead them to God, and no matter how much time may pass, that path will continue to exist. It will in fact grow. Hundreds and thousands of people have travelled along this path, and hundreds and thousands will travel it in the future. This is the true path because it leads you to the final truth.

However, I never underrate the world. I do not reject it. At the same time I do not exalt it as something eternal, as something everlasting. Man's greatest duty is to follow the path laid down by these great saints and by that path reach his innermost Self. Everyone should feel close to the Lord. You should feel as close to Him, in fact closer than you feel to your parents, your friends, your body, senses, or even your mind.

Therefore, the birth of a saint is full of great significance. The sages say that a great saint who has seen the Lord in his heart, who has worshipped Him on the altar of his heart, sanctifies his family, sanctifies the earth, sanctifies the religion or creed that he upholds, sanctifies the entire earth. The thing which was dearest to the heart of Jesus was prayer, inward prayer, or interior prayer—prayer which is more inside than the innermost prayer. And this is what is known as meditation. This inner prayer is nothing but deep meditation. Jesus turned people's attention to the Supreme Being who is all-pervading and who dwells in the hearts of all. Jesus said that the kingdom of God lies within you, and that is exactly what you are focusing your attention on here; that is what you meditate on, that is where you delight in meditation.

Now I am going to close my discourse this evening. I would like all of you to meditate and move in that inner kingdom for ten or fifteen minutes and thus you will be actually dynamically following the path, the command of Jesus. Every day we shout *Sadgurunath Maharaj ki Jai!* But today I would like all of you to say, *Jesusnath Maharaj ki Jai!*

All of you should sit calmly and follow the command of Jesus. Jesus says that the kingdom of God lies within you and this is exactly what I also say. Move in that kingdom for a while at least. Close your eyes for the love of Jesus.

22

December 26, 1972

Ian: *It seems that what you are giving us should be reaching more people. Have you any plans for the future, or will that depend on us?*

Baba: I am very happy that there are so many people who feel that they are getting something from me, and I am thankful to you for that. That means that what I have to give is not going to waste. Such is the law of God that if one star shoots from the sky another appears in its place. If one tree falls you will see two trees growing in its place. If one river dries up quite a few will spring up around it. God's work goes on without any interruption, so there is no cause for worry.

God does not depend on any external agency. He doesn't have to seek the aid of any other source. His work is bound to go on in the way it has been going on. If one Muktananda goes, there will be thousands of Muktanandas in his place. The world has been in existence since time without beginning. God has made plans for the future of everyone. In fact the divine planning committee is there in the upper spaces and it has most talented people on its staff: it has engineers, architects, and other people. Don't think that your future is without any plans. God's glory, God's power, is so great that when He opens His eyes a cosmos comes into being, and when He closes them that cosmos goes out of existence. When His power is so boundless, there is no point in our worrying about what is going to happen. His work is bound to go on and nothing can stop it. If we worry about it, it isn't good for us. My Guru only used a few words, telling me, "Stay here." At that time nobody knew what the implications of those few words were. Those few words included this magnificent Ashram, this kitchen and large numbers of devotees from here and abroad, and so many other things. At that time even I didn't anticipate that all of this would happen, so simple were those words uttered by him. So there is absolutely no point in worrying about things or in anticipating.

Since I rely absolutely on my Guru, on God, there is no need on my part to worry about the future or to make advance plans, because whatever has to happen will happen and the persons who are going to execute that will arrive at the right time, and everything will happen automatically.

Yet, I am certain that all the seekers who are here will do enormous work in time to come. More will be coming here and they, too, will spread the word, and you will see this movement sweep the whole world. When God's will is behind a certain work it is accomplished with the utmost ease, and all the people concerned get together and cooperate to accomplish that task. Take the case of our country: we won our freedom by means of non-violence and truth. Obviously God's will was behind it. When God's will is not behind something, it cannot be accomplished regardless of how strong your effort or what resources you command. When God's will is there, things are accomplished most smoothly.

You see for yourselves that those people who come here and stay for a while do excellent work after returning to their countries. They run meditation centres in America, England and other countries, the Shakti is passing from them into others, and more and more people are being drawn into it, more and more people are meditating. To answer your question, all that I can say at present is that enormous work is going to be done, and all the people here will be doing it. There will come a time when there will be meditation centres everywhere. Large numbers of people will be meditating, Shakti will be flowing from one to another and people will be having direct experiences of the inner Self.

Uma : *The other day when I was angry you told me to throw my anger away. How exactly does one do this?*

Baba : You can expel anger from your heart through understanding, through making yourself aware of its possible consequences, through making yourself aware of the fact that anger will burn up all your tapasya. I told Uma to throw her anger away, but if somebody were to tell me that, I would not accept it, because I find that since my anger has lessened, people are losing a lot. But as far as you are concerned, Uma, it is not good for you. Anger burns up the Shakti you acquire through meditation. Anger destroys the state of alertness, the state of wakefulness which you attain in meditation. Anger is not good for a meditator. The moment you get angry, the best thing is to get rid of it at once. You did a good thing because the moment you felt angry you came rushing to me and thus got it dissolved. If you had not come rushing to me, that anger would have consumed so much inside you.

Suddenly I recollect a verse that I read some thirty years ago. In this verse the sage says, "It is quite natural for anyone to get angry. The best people also get angry. But their anger does not last for more than a moment. The anger of the medium type lasts at the most for twenty minutes. The anger of the low lasts for a night, but those who are degraded sinners, their anger would last a whole lifetime."

The best thing is not to feel angry at all. If you do get angry, the next best thing is to get over it immediately. There is nothing healthy or wholesome about anger. Once you are seized by anger, your mind gets dissatisfied, your blood is also affected, and as a result, so many illnesses are produced.

One of the names of God means, free from anger. As far as possible, avoid anger. There are foolish people who think that one who doesn't anger is a weak person, but the truth is that one who doesn't get angry doesn't have his equal in the world, he is so powerful. Keep yourself aware of the evil consequences of anger, consequences that are bad for the mind, for the heart, for the body, for sadhana, for meditation. You should not let anger arise in your heart at all.

Kedarnath : *Some people start their sadhana very well and with great devotion, but after a while they become somewhat dull, and some even fall. What is the cause?*

Baba : There are two things which prepare a seeker for

hell. The first is his sense of self-importance and the second is his craving for the good opinion of others. These two weaknesses are sure to plunge him into the foulest hell, and a seeker should keep away from them. Nor should others encourage these weaknesses by indulging them. In the beginning one starts with great experiences, one begins to meditate very well, experiences come, kriyas take place and meditation keeps him absorbed. Then it is easy to be solitary. As long as he is solitary he continues to make progress. But as his progress is seen by others, people get drawn towards him. They begin to praise him. This person comes to have a companion. The companion tries to please him with sweet and nice words, or tries to put foul words about the failings of others in his ears. These things will cause a person's downfall, and obstruct his meditation. Once one becomes two, you have sadhana obstructed. During the period of sadhana you don't really need any friends. If you have a friend, then one of two things is bound to happen. Either you will influence him by your qualities or he will influence you by his qualities. It all depends on who is stronger. If a friendship or association is allowed to continue, in a short while the feelings get involved in attachment and aversion, virtues and vices. If such a person stays in the Ashram, it is not good for the Ashram either; it would be better for him and the Ashram if he stayed outside.

In one's central nerve, sushumna, impressions of countless lives are embedded, including the negative impressions of bad company through various births. It doesn't take long for those impressions or samskaras to become active, given a certain kind of influence or atmosphere. A person may appear to be very pure and imperturbable, yet he may have the foulest samskaras buried deep in his sushumna. A person's purity is tested only when he falls into bad company. If even in bad company he remains unaffected, then it is certain that he is really pure. But if he is easily influenced by bad people, it means that so far he was only pretending, he wasn't really pure.

What Narada says in this context is of great significance.
He says that a certain weakness appears in seed form
in the beginning. It appears to be quite harmless, but
through bad company this tiny wave, which seemed innocent, swells up into the most dreadful ocean and becomes
unmanageable.

It is for this reason that I insist when you are in the
Ashram that you don't waste your time chatting endlessly with each other, because it is through gossip that
you are influenced in a wrong way by each other. Don't
think that I am a jailor or a kill-joy or your enemy,
or that I am going by a magistrate's bad report about
your conduct when I am being so strict. I am being
strict only to make sure that you are not affected by or
exposed to undesirable influences and thus retain your
purity. What we usually see is that people living in
the world are not interested in the *Ramayana*, the *Gita*,
the Lord, or spirituality. What interests them is what
other people are doing, who is going where, whose wife
is going with whose husband, who ate what and who was
seen doing what, and so on. They become so accustomed
to that, that even after coming to the Ashram they cannot give up this weakness. For some time, out of fear,
they may refrain from it, but the moment they get a
chance, the moment they meet somebody who is of their
sort, this failing comes to the surface again. What they
were enjoying before coming to the Ashram, silly conversation and malicious gossip, they begin to indulge in that
once again. They are repelled by the *Gita*, by the
Ramayana, by devotional practices. They become so
affected that even in such a pure place they begin to
see impurities. This Ashram is so great, so glorious that
even before stepping into it true seekers receive the
Shakti which permeates this Ashram. If somebody living in the Ashram for a long time starts finding fault
with this pure innocent place, then he is not fit to live
in the Ashram. The Ashram would start burning like a
blazing furnace for him. He would not be able to endure
the heat of this place. Man is his own worst enemy.
You project your own failings outside and you begin to

see vices even where they don't exist because your heart
has become so contaminated.

I am reminded of a story of a girl who lived in the
time of Jesus. She was a young girl who had an illicit
contact with someone and became pregnant. She was
in the flush of youth and intoxicated with vigour. When
people came to know about it everybody tried to per-
secute her.

Unfortunately, people's attention is drawn immediately
towards others' failings. I wonder why. Is it because
they want to justify their own wickedness, soothe their
own hearts which are tormented by sins or guilt? Is
that why they see only wickedness in others and pat
themselves saying, "Everybody is wicked around me, so
there is no harm if I am wicked"?

People wanted to punish that girl. She was dragged
into the presence of Jesus, and everybody was shouting
that she should not be left alive, otherwise she would be
setting a horrible example.

Jesus said, "What you are saying is quite true, she must
be punished."

The moment he said that, all the people who were trying to take the law into their hands became calm. When
they became calm Jesus said, "I agree that she must be
punished, but she must be punished by a person who is
absolutely pure, who is a total celibate. Is there anyone
in this vast crowd who is worthy enough to punish her?"
Everyone stood with his head hanging down in shame
and Jesus said, "You scoundrels. You see her impurity
but you are blind to your own impurity."

Pure people do not notice anybody else's impurity.
They see only purity everywhere.

If you spend even a little time in bad company it will
exert its dreadful influence on you. Take the case of
Kaikeyi, one of the queens of King Dasharatha, Rama's
father. Kaikeyi was really noble, modest and virtuous.
It was only under the evil influence of Manthura, her
maid-servant, that she acted the way she did. She sub-
mitted to her evil advice just once, and the result was
that she insisted that Rama be exiled from the kingdom

for fourteen years. It was because of that that the King Dasharatha died. He could not bear the grief of separation from his son. So she became the cause of the death of her husband. A pure, noble, virtuous person did so much harm under the influence of evil company.

Take the case of Shakuni in the *Mahabharata*. He was Duryodhana's maternal uncle. He was wicked and it was his advice which ultimately led to the war of the *Mahabharata*. Thousands of people were killed, thousands of women became widows, children became orphans. So foul, so powerful is the influence of bad company.

Even after I moved into this place on Baba's instructions, for years I refused to meet anyone. I lived by myself. People thought that I was conceited. They did not know that I was quite conscious that I had nothing to be proud of, I had nothing to be conceited about. I stayed by myself because I did not want to get contaminated by the infectious diseases of other people. Sundardas says, "O my mind, give up the company of those who have turned away from the Lord, give up the company of those who interrupt your sadhana, who interrupt your devotional practices."

That is why I insist that you should not listen to certain words, not read certain works, not join any faction or group. However, I am not suggesting that you should turn away from your life in the world. All that I am saying is that you should not allow yourself to be affected by evil company. I mix with all kinds of people, but I don't listen to anyone, in spite of what people may think. I only listen to what I have heard from my Guru. That is why it is essential for a seeker to take the utmost care of himself during the period of sadhana. Almost everyone here complains that he is tormented by past memories, that in spite of hard effort he cannot get rid of them. You have to work very hard to get rid of past memories. So I say, what is the point of creating new memories which will torment you in the future? At least your present life should be such that it doesn't create the memories which will affect you in the future. You have already spent a lifetime trying to get rid of past evil memories. Therefore you should remain calm and steady, and as far as possible stay by yourself. Then you will find your mind being more and more immersed in meditation and devotion. Don't think that there is no point in keeping the mind empty. The more empty the mind remains, the stronger it becomes, the greater the power it acquires. The kind of thoughts that arise in your mind leave a very strong effect on the seven constituents of the body. If bad thoughts arise they will have a bad effect, and good thoughts will have a good effect. So you have to be very careful about the sort of thoughts you entertain. I was very fond of Zipruanna. I used to visit him frequently. He would talk in the most succinct language and utter the profoundest truths. Once he even came quite some distance to see me and I was very moved. While we were walking together, all of a sudden he said to me, "You must not say sweet or nice words to anyone. You must not say the sort of things which will draw anybody towards you, or make friends."

I thought about it and realised the wisdom of those words. During the period of sadhana it is very necessary to remain solitary. If you have to talk, if you have to move in company, make sure that you speak of things, move in the company which will help you to get rid of the unpleasant and painful past memories. You are sick of reading what is already written in your minds, so if you spend time in bad company you are only adding fresh evil to what is already written there, and you will have to suffer from it in the future.

Therefore, respect yourself, make sure that your heart is full of clean and good thoughts, that your mind remains immersed in meditation, in high thinking, in sublime contemplation. It is only when you respect yourself like that, only when you honour the divinity in you, that you can be called a worthy seeker, that there can be some justification in your living as a seeker. I repeat once again, allow only good thoughts, good intentions to fill your minds. You should be constantly striving to keep yourself aware of the divinity within you, and realise it. Live and act in such a way that you move closer and closer to God. It is only then that life will be worthwhile. If you do things which make you smaller, which make you pettier, they will certainly be effective, but they will only bring suffering and pain.

December 29, 1972

Chandraprabha : *Is there a distinction between devotion with desire and devotion without desire in the sadhana of following the path and teaching of the Guru and trying to please Goddess Kundalini through meditation? If a seeker strives to please the great Shakti and to receive the Guru's grace, should we call his worship with desire or without desire?*

Baba : Devotion with desire is that where you wish to have some ordinary desire fulfilled through your devotion. The desire for liberation is not in that category, even though it happens to be a desire. Desire for devotion is not considered to be a desire. If you have received your sadhana from the Guru, then it is implied that the Guru himself will make sure that it is completed and take you to the final goal. If he leaves you half-way, he is not a Guru, he is a cheat. Desire for God-realisation is not a reprehensible desire. It could be called a desireless desire.

However, there is another class of devotees, who are a different type all together. Those are the great bhaktas of the Lord and they are completely free from desire. They don't even have the desire for mukti or salvation, because they feel so completely contented, so completely absorbed in the bliss of devotion that no desire is left in their hearts. But such bhaktas are very rare. Such a one enjoys the bliss of absorption in the Self through

meditation so much that mukti or salvation doesn't mean
anything to him. Such a one alone is completely free
from desire. And though he may be completely free from
the desire for liberation, it is quite obvious that liberation
is bound to come to him. Whatever you are doing, even
if you don't desire the fruits of it, the fruit is bound to
come. If you are sitting on the branch of a tree and
cutting it, you are bound to fall down, even if you don't
want to. You can't remain suspended in mid-air. Likewise, if you are doing sadhana, mukti is bound to come
to you. Whether you desire it or not, the reward of
sadhana, which is mukti, is bound to come to you.

However, it is very good to be without desire. A
person who has become completely free from all desires
attains liberation in that very moment, and if such a
person turns to devotion, then his devotion is called para-
bhakti, transcendental devotion or supreme devotion. In
the case of sadhana or worship with a desire for God,
it doesn't matter whether you call that sadhana with
or without desire, because the desire is so lofty that even
if it is present, it doesn't matter.

Jon: *How can one overcome putting off duties until
tomorrow?*

Baba: The tendency to put things off until tomorrow
is sure to bring about defeat. The only way of overcoming it is not to give it the slightest encouragement
and to nip it right at this moment. There is a saying:
if you have to do something tomorrow, do it today; if
you have to do something today, do it right now. Right
now means this moment, this very instant. It is because
of this tendency of procrastination that one has already
wasted so much time, so many years. One must not
leave things to be done the next day. One must do whatever is to be done right now.

Kersee: *During meditation the breath is sometimes
forcibly drawn out and it stays out for a long time. What
is happening?*

Baba: If during meditation your breath is suspended

either inside or outside you shouldn't worry and get scared. There are some seekers who get scared that they are going to die. I can assure you, death comes only at its time, it can't come before that. It is only fear which keeps you separate from the Lord. Once you discard fear, you find that God is the closest thing to you. When in the course of meditation you become deeply immersed in the inner Self, inner love begins to well up into the heart, into the mind and into all the senses. When the mind is bathed in inner love, it doesn't like to think any thoughts; it doesn't even like to repeat the mantra. At that time you should not repeat the mantra. When this inner love reaches the heart, the heart refuses to imagine anything, to entertain any fancies, so you should not force the heart to indulge in fancies. When inner love touches the prana, the prana also becomes steady; it doesn't like to keep moving in and out. You shouldn't force the prana to resume its movement.

This suspension of prana is called kumbhak. This involuntary kumbhak is of much greater significance than the voluntary kumbhak which you force on yourself through pranayama. It is through this involuntary kumbhak that most important things happen. There is an intimate relationship between prana and the mind. They cannot act independently of each other. When the mind becomes steady the prana will automatically become steady. As you get more deeply absorbed in meditation, the mind becomes calm, giving up its usual mentation and feverish activity. As the mind becomes calm, the prana too gives up its restlessness. It doesn't like to keep moving. It is the steadiness of calming down of prana which is called prolonged kumbhak or suspension of breath. This prolonged involuntary kumbhak is of high significance. It completely purifies the abdominal organs, it pierces the chakras, it raises the Kundalini to the sahasrar. Not only that, it prolongs life and it strengthens and re-invigorates the entire body. This involuntary long kumbhak is a most significant event, it is the reward of deep meditation, and it has been given high place in the yogic scriptures.

Carol : *Why is self-control sometimes very easy and at other times very difficult, even in identical situations? Why are feelings of devotion and faith also subject to the same ups and downs?*

Baba : The only cause is the mind, the innate fickle nature of the mind. I have read a lot of poetry on this theme. It is the mind which changes according to the guna that predominates at the moment. It is the mind which makes you interested in something at one time and lose interest in that thing another time. The mind keeps on indulging in all kinds of thoughts, countless thoughts. This moment it will make you feel that you are a king and the next moment it will make you feel that you are a beggar. One moment it will make you feel that you are a very great yogi, a yogi raj, and the next moment it will make you feel absolutely abject; you will feel that there is no one worse than you. You should not attach any importance to this fickleness of the mind. Sometimes the mind is filled with pride, at other times it is very humble. Sometimes it works in a straight manner and at other times it behaves in the most crooked fashion. Sometimes it is filled with lust, at other times it is filled with intense renunciation. Sometimes it becomes pure, at other times it is contaminated with filth. This is the nature of the mind.

Therefore, acquire understanding of the mind through right discrimination. Once you have understood the nature of the mind, leave it alone. Do not judge yourself by what your mind happens to be doing at a given moment. You must not be led by passing thoughts of the mind. If the mind says that you are a king, don't start feeling sort of grand and regal. In course of time the mind merges into the Self. Then it stops becoming other things; it can become only one thing and that is the Lord. You should not get depressed by these mental ups and downs.

Are you aware of the existence of the witness who is watching the mind changing all the time? Have you ever found the witness changing as the mind changes? Therefore, do not pay attention to the mind. Pay attention to

the inner witness of the mind. You should not identify
yourself with the mind; instead you should identify yourself with the inner witness who keeps watching all the
movements of the mind from a distance. Then no matter
what movements arise in the mind, they will not disturb
you.

You fall into misery only because you remain ignorant
of your own nature. One doesn't have to hunt a big
cause for misery. I could feel miserable just by seeing
the difference between two patches of hair in my beard.
On one side the hair may be straight and on the other
side it may be crooked. But what is the point of feeling
miserable about it? The moment the barber comes you
get rid of the straight as well as the crooked hair. Likewise, all the fancies which appear in the mind vanish
after some time, whether you entertain delusions of
royal granduer or of beggary. Both will disappear. So
what is the point of identifying yourself with them?

Swami Vimalananda : *In the Vedanta system, that which
brings knowledge is the grand proclamations of the
Vedas, such as 'Thou art that.' It is presumed that if a
worthy seeker were to hear one of these proclamations
from the Guru's lips, he would immediately attain awareness of his true nature, feeling, "I am Brahman." So
without hearing the grand proclamation knowledge will
not come. What exactly in yoga brings about direct
knowledge? There is a Vedic mantra which says that
liberation cannot be attained without knowledge, so how
does yoga bring knowledge?*

Baba : The supreme state can be attained only through
knowledge. Knowledge is important not only in yoga,
not only in Vedantic philosophy, but also even in one's
daily life, because if you don't have knowledge then you
won't be able to run your life smoothly and efficiently.
We always use salt in our vegetables. If the same salt
is put into tea, what will it taste like? One must know
that salt is meant to be used for vegetables, not for tea.
Knowledge is important in every field. So yoga, too, or
one who is practicing yoga, must also have knowledge,

including those who are practising the eight-fold yoga or Ashtanga Yoga. One who is practising Siddha Yoga already has knowledge.

If one wishes to attain liberation in the Vedic way one has to be very highly evolved already, one has to be a very worthy seeker, already perfect. Then the moment he hears a statement such as, 'Thou art That' he becomes aware of the changeless inner Self. To a Vedantin it is the changeless which is bliss. A yogi, too, arrives at this knowledge through samadhi, particularly through nirvikalpa samadhi, or samadhi which is completely free from thought. But one who has received Guru's grace and who is meditating by the Guru's power will find that in the course of his sadhana this knowledge will arise spontaneously from within him. In Siddha Yoga this awareness comes itself, while in Vedanta the awareness has to be driven into you, as it were.

There are many seekers who have reported that true knowledge has arisen within them automatically. A disciple of Mansur Mastana said, "Such knowledge arose within me which made me feel that I am not the body. If I am not the body, who am I? I am the same being whose manifestation this entire universe is."

The inner Self has such power that it reveals itself to you by its own light. It is like the sun that illuminates both itself and everything else. The sages say that the Self is self-luminous and reveals not only itself, but also all other objects. It illuminates the mind, the senses and the vast outer universe. There is no difference whatsoever between the sun and its light, the two are one. Likewise, there is no difference between the Self and its luminosity. Jnaneshwar Maharaj describes it beautifully, saying, "The light of the soul is ever-new, but the soul can be seen only by itself."

One who is following Vedanta will come to the awareness of his divinity through the Vedantic proclamations, and one who is meditating will attain this awareness through meditation. In every spiritual discipline there is one thing which is of major importance and other things are secondary. Take for instance the path of devotion where the most important thing is love. The question arises, "Whom shall you love?" That is where knowledge comes in. So knowledge has importance even on the path of devotion. Therefore, the path of knowledge, the path of yoga are included in the path of the Vedas. The advantage of this path is that it is quite easy and also all-comprehensive. If you follow this path you will automatically attain the knowledge of Vedanta, the realisations of yoga and the love of bhaktas. Pushpadanta puts it beautifully in his *Shiva Mahimna Stotra* that you chant every night. He says that the goal of all three paths, Sankhya, or the path of knowledge, the path of yoga, and the Shaiva path, are the same, namely the changeless Supreme Being. The paths may be different but the ultimate attainment is the same. It is very essential for a seeker to get free of scriptural controversies because there is a danger of remaining caught there. If you can rightly understand the scriptures, the different creeds and the caste system, that knowledge will take you across, but if you do not understand their true importance, then all these things will only drown you. Therefore, one should redeem oneself by true discrimination, by the right knowledge of the scriptures.

Swami Vimalananda: *You said the other day that even if a Guru doesn't want to impart all his power and all his knowledge to his disciple, the disciple would be able to get all that the Guru has even by force, if he had faith and love for him. The best example is that of Eklavya. But if a disciple unfortunately does not have that same intense unwavering faith and devotion, will the Guru be impelled by sheer compassion to impart all his power and knowledge and Shakti and thus bless him?*

Baba: It can happen, but it is very rare. Eklavya was the only example. There is nobody else. And we don't have any other Puranpoliyas either. Eknath Maharaj had a boy called Puranpoliya whose whole life was Eknath Maharaj, and he didn't seem to be interested in anything else. He was not very educated. He was just like our Ramdas here, but our Ramdas is a little more intelligent. Now when Eknath had completed half of his great work on the *Bhagavatam*, time for his final departure came, and his learned disciples began to worry how that great work would be completed. Eknath said that Puranpoliya would complete it, and he transmitted all his power into Puranpoliya and Puranpoliya did complete it.

If you cannot be an Eklavya, you must at least live with the Guru as a Puranpoliya. If you cannot be even a Puranpoliya, then why should the Guru have any disciples at all? Why should he be partial to disciples? Why shouldn't he bestow his grace on everyone? Jnaneshwar's commentary on that verse of the *Gita* where the Lord says, "All beings are equal to Me. I am not attached to those who are good and I am not adverse to those who are evil. Those who have the noblest character, who perform the noblest deeds do not particularly please Me. On the other hand, those who are fallen creatures, who are wicked and sinful do not particularly displease Me," is worthy of serious study.

However, the Lord goes on to say, "I manifest Myself to a seeker according to the nature of his devotion for Me."

Swami Vimalananda : *That means that the Lord is partial.*

Baba : The Lord is not partial, the Lord is only granting the fruits of an action according to the desires of a particular seeker. I, too, have read in the *Bhagavat Purana*, "I am a slave to My bhaktas. I do not have any freedom." But that is the glory of the devotees, not of God. That is the reward of the intense devotion of the devotee.

There was a king who had no children. He had no children from his first wife, so he married again. He did not have any children from his second wife, and married again. He did not have any children from his third wife and married a fourth time. He did not succeed even then. A king can marry several times if he is without an heir. The king was greatly devoted to Narada and put his predicament to him saying, "I am still without an heir.

Who is going to look after the kingdom? You have divine power, please grant me a child."

Narada said, "That is quite easy. Do these particular rituals and you will certainly be blessed with a son."

The king did accordingly, yet with no success. Narada went to the Lord and requested Him to give that king a child. The Lord said, "That is not My work. I first have to check the past record of the king with the secretary who has all the files."

When the king's file was brought to Him, the Lord saw that the king was not meant to be blessed with a child, not only in this life, but even in the next ten lives.

Narada came back from the secretary dejected and said to the Lord, "He is not destined to get a child even in the next ten births."

The Lord said, "I can't do anything about it. The actions of a person must bring their consequences and if he has no child in his destiny, I can't grant him one." Narada left the place despondent.

Some time elapsed. In the kingdom of the same king, there lived a great devotee of the Lord. He had completely risen above any consciousness of the world; he was totally immersed in the divine name and he was entirely free from any kind of desire or craving. He was the sort of saint to whom even the Lord becomes a slave. One day he was walking through the streets of the capital and was shouting, "One child for one chapati, if you want one child, give me one chapati, if you want two give me two chapatis, if you want three, give me three."

While shouting that, he happened to pass the palace. The queen heard his voice and came rushing down with four chapatis, fell at his feet and said, "I would like to be blessed with four children."

He said, "You will get four children," and went away.

As the years passed, the prediction of the devotee came true and the king was blessed with four children. He had one by one queen, another by the second queen and two by the third queen. Since the king was an old devotee of Narada, Narada went to visit him one day. When he went to the palace he was amazed to see four children romping and screaming all over the place. He asked the sentry whose children they were. He said, "The king's."

Narada was amazed and said, "I personally went to the Lord's secretary, saw the king's file with these very eyes and there was no mention of any children in that file. How could the king get four children?"

Narada went to the king and said, "Could you tell me truthfully how all this happened?"

The king said, "There is a great saint living in that forest who is immersed in remembrance of the Lord 24 hours a day. He happened to pass the palace one day, shouting 'one child for one chapati, two for two and three for three, and four for four.' One of my queens happened to hear the shout and she gave him four chapatis, and that is how I have been blessed with four children."

Narada immediately picked up his veena and rushed straight to the Lord to get an explanation from Him. "I could not grant him a child, while the other saint granted him four."

When the Lord saw Narada coming from a distance He knew what he was coming for, so He laid down and pretended that He was suffering from a horrible stomach pain, and holding His stomach He began to groan.

When Narada reached the Lord, he saw Him groaning with pain. A large number of people had collected around Him and they were all worried. When Narada saw the Lord writhing with pain his anger vanished. There were a lot of physicians who were attending the Lord and they said that the ailment was beyond cure. The Lord can put on any act that He wishes to. They all prayed to the Lord, "Please tell us how You can be cured because none of us knows how to cure You. You alone know how to cure Yourself."

He said, "There is only one way out and that is if somebody could get me the liver of an absolutely pure person and tie it around my stomach, then the pain would vanish."

Narada said, "I'll get You a liver immediately Not

one, but many. Who will not want to part with his liver for the Lord?"

The jet in which Narada travelled went quite fast; it was much faster even than the supersonic jets, and Narada could reach any corner of the universe in no time. Narada went to different devotees, but nobody was prepared to part with his liver. Who would? Most so-called devotees are only caught up in their devotional rituals and are not willing to make any sacrifice to the Lord, not to speak of parting with their liver; they wouldn't part with even some material possession which they hold very dear. Those devotees feel very grand and proud just by offering a few dry leaves and water and useless things to the Lord, and they think that they have surrendered themselves to Him. Narada felt crestfallen. He went back to the Lord and said, "I am shocked. This world is full of devotees and yet none of them is willing to give his liver even for Your sake."

The Lord said, "There is one devotee living in that forest. Go and try him."

Narada immediately rushed to the spot and he found the devotee completely immersed in meditation on the Lord, chanting *Guru Om, Guru Om* ecstatically. Narada stood and waited because he didn't wish to disturb the saint who was so totally absorbed in meditation. After some time the saint opened his eyes and saw to his surprise that Narada was standing there. Immediately he asked him respectfully, "What brings you here, sir?"

Narada said, "The Lord is suffering from incurable stomach pain and the only remedy is the liver of a pure devotee."

The moment the saint heard this he was furious. He said, "Narada, why did you wait so long, why didn't you open my abdomen and take my liver to the Lord?" He immediately tore open his abdomen and gave his liver to Narada.

Narada gave it to the Lord. The Lord massaged his abdomen and He was immediately cured of the pain. In fact that was all a scene He had put on. The devotee, too, didn't die. The Lord can do anything, even what is considered to be impossible. Then the Lord asked, "Narada, what brought you to Me when I was so sick?"

Narada: "I had come with an acute grievance against You and when I found You groaning with pain I didn't have the heart to talk to You about it."

The Lord: "You must put it to Me now."

Narada: "I only requested one child for the king and You refused. Then You have another saint passing by the palace and granting the same king four children. When those children were not in the king's destiny, how was he blessed with them?"

The Lord: "He who can give his liver can give anything; he is not bound by the laws of destiny."

If there is such a devotee he can get everything from the Lord, and the Lord becomes a slave of that devotee. That is just one way of putting it. It is the devotee who, by the force of his devotion, is able to get everything from the Lord. Tukaram says, "The great saint whose only object of sense pleasure is the Lord, whose senses receive gratification only from the Lord, rises to such a level that even the Lord begins to follow him. He is walking to meet the Lord, but the Lord is following him in the hope that the dust from his feet will sanctify Him." Such is the power and the glory of true devotees.

GLOSSARY

abhanga : devotional verse in the Marathi language.

ahamkara (ego) : the factor of individuation; the consciousness of separation.

ajana vriksha (or : yogavali) : the tree of yoga; sacred tree growing at Jnaneshwar's samadhi shrine in Alandi, Maharashtra.

Alandi : location of Jnaneshwar Maharaj's samadhi shrine in Maharashtra.

arati : worship of a deity accompanied by the waving of lights.

asana : seat or mat for meditation; yogic posture. *See also* : Ashtanga Yoga.

ashram : abode of a guru or saint; spiritual community similar to a monastery.

Ashtanga Yoga : the eight-fold yoga expounded by Patanjali in his *Yoga Sutras*, which is the authoritative text on Raja Yoga. The eight limbs are : (1) yamas (the practice of five moral virtues : non-violence, truthfulness, continence, non-stealing, and non-covetousness); (2) niyamas (the practice of five regular habits : purity, contentment, austerity, study, and surrender); (3) asana (posture); (4) pranayama (the regulation and restraint of breath); (5) pratyahara (withdrawal of the mind from sense objects); (6) dharana (concentration, fixing the mind on an object of contemplation); (7) dhyan (meditation); and (8) samadhi (meditative union with the Absolute).

Atman : inner Self or soul; also denotes the supreme Soul, which, according to Advaita Vedanta, is one with the individual soul.

avadhoot : a renunciate who has risen above body-consciousness, duality, and conventional standards.

Ayurveda : ancient Indian science of medicine.

Baba : term of affection for a saint or father.

Bahinabai (seventeenth century) : woman poet-saint of Maharashtra who received initiation in a dream from Tukaram Maharaj.

Bhavartha Ramayana : Eknath's rendition of Valmiki's *Ramayana*, composed in the Marathi language.

Bhagavat (or : *Bhagavatam*) : *See* : *Shrimad Bhagavat Purana.*

bhajan : devotional verse or hymn.

bhajiya : Indian snack made from gram flour, spices, and vegetables fried in oil.

bhakta : a follower of the path of bhakti, divine love; a devotee.

bhakti : devotion and love for God; the spiritual path of devotion.

Bhakti Sutras : the classic scripture of Bhakti Yoga attributed to Rishi Narada.

Bhartrihari : poet-saint; king of Ujjain who renounced his kingdom and retired from public life; his poems, divided into three sections, are called the *Satakas of Bhartrihari.*

bhastrika : a rapid breathing exercise; a form of pranayama.

black light : *See* : four bodies.

blue light : *See* : four bodies.

Blue Pearl (*neel bindu*) : the abode of the inner Self, a vision of which comes in the higher stages of meditation.

brahmachari : a celibate; one devoted to the practise of spiritual discipline.

Brahman : the absolute reality; the universal Self; all-pervading consciousness.

brahmin : first caste in Hindu society, the members of which are by tradition priests and scholars. *See also* : caste.

caste : ancient Indian society was organised into four *varnas*, divisions or castes, for efficient performance of various functions : brahmins (scholars, priests, and preceptors); kshatriyas (rulers and warriors): vaishyas (business and agricultural classes); shudras (menial workers).

causal body : *See* : four bodies.

chakra : any one of the six lotuses, or centres of consciousness, in the shushumna nerve through which the Kundalini rises.

Chandraloka : the subtle world of the moon.

chapati : unleavened Indian bread.

Chiti (*or* : Chitshakti, Kundalini, Kundalini Shakti, Mahamaya, Parashakti, Shakti) : divine conscious energy; female creative aspect of Godhead, referred to as a goddess.

Chitshakti : the power of universal consciousness.

Chitshakti Vilas (*lit.* : play of consciousness) : Baba's spiritual autobiography which has been translated and published in many languages.

Dassera : a ten-day festival celebrating the victory of Goddess Durga over the demons. Nine nights, called *navaratri*, are spent in worship, and on the tenth day, called *vijaya dashami*, celebrations take place, and the idol of Goddess Durga is immersed in water.

Dattatreya : a great avadhoot who is considered to be an embodiment of Brahma, Vishnu and Shiva; author of *Avadhoot Gita.*

dharana : concentration. *See also* : Ashtanga Yoga.

dhoti : common dress for men in India; a cloth tied around the waist.

dhyan : meditation. *See also* : Ashtanga Yoga.

diksha : initiation given by the Guru usually by imparting a mantra; the spiritual awakening of the disciple by Shakti-pat.

Dronacharya : great archer and teacher of Pandavas and Kauravas in the *Mahabharata*.

Durga (*lit.* : hard to conquer) : a name of the Divine Mother who was created by the power of the gods to overcome and destroy evil tendencies and remove obstacles that block our progress. She rides a lion and carries weapons in her eight arms.

Duryodhana : eldest Kaurava brother and chief rival of the Pandavas in the *Mahabharata*.

eight-fold yoga : *See* : Ashtanga Yoga.

Eklavya : tribal boy who mastered the art of archery by worshipping and practising before an image of Dronacharya. Cited as an example of an ideal disciple; *From* : *Mahabharata*.

Eknath Maharaj (1528-1609) : poet-saint of Maharashtra, a native of Paithan; his Guru was Janardan Swami.

Eknathi Bhagavat : Eknath's commentary on Book Eleven of the *Shrimad Bhagavat Purana*, which describes the teachings of Lord Krishna to his disciple Uddhava. *See also* : Eknath Maharaj.

Ekadasi : the eleventh day after the full or new moon, which a devotee spends in full or partial fasting and worship.

four bodies : the four bodies are contained in the physical body : (1) the physical body, experienced in the waking state; (2) the subtle body, experienced in the dream state; (3) the causal body, experienced in the deep sleep state; (4) the supracausal body, experienced in the state of meditation. The four lights associated with each body, which can be seen in meditation, are : red light—physical body; white light—subtle body; black light—causal body; and blue light —supracausal body.

four states : the four states of consciousness : waking (*jagrat*); dream (*swapna*); deep sleep (*sushupti*); and transcendental (*turiya*).

Ganesha : elephant-headed god; son of Shiva and Parvati.

Ganeshpuri : an ancient sacred spot; site of natural sulphur springs, where Swami Nityananda settled, and where Shree Gurudev Ashram of Swami Muktananda is situated, in Maharashtra State.

ganja : an intoxicating drug, like marijuana, made from cannabis.

ghee : clarified butter used in Indian cooking and in worship.

Gita (*or* : *Bhagavad Gita*) : a sacred, very popular scripture narrating the teachings of Lord Krishna to Arjuna.

God-realisation (or : Self-realisation) : the final goal of yoga. The realisation that "God dwells within you as you"; enlightenment.

Goloka : celestial abode of Vishnu.

Gopis : the milkmaids of Vrindavan; companions and devotees of Sri Krishna.

Gorakhnath : one of the nine Naths of the Nath tradition who received initiation from Matsyendranath.

Govinda (lit. : Master of the cows) : name for Sri Krishna.

gross body : See : four bodies.

gunas : the three basic qualities of nature : sattva—purity; rajas—activity; tamas—dullness.

Guru : a spiritual Master who has attained oneness with God and who initiates his disciples and devotees into the spiritual path and guides them to moksha, or liberation. In the Siddha tradition the Guru is the grace-bestowing power of God who initiates disciples through Shaktipat diksha.

Gurubhakta : sincere devotee and lover of the Guru.

Guru Gita : a Sanskrit text chanted each morning at the Ashram in which Lord Shiva expounds the mysteries of the Guru principle to his consort, Parvati.

Gurukripa : Guru's grace.

Guru Om : a mantra of the Guru.

Guruseva : service to the Guru.

Hanuman : a monkey devotee of Lord Rama known for his great strength and devotional service to Rama. From : Ramayana.

Hari (lit. : the one who removes miseries and sorrow) : a name of Vishnu; God.

Hari Giri Baba : Siddha from Vaijapur, Maharashtra, who bestowed great love and affection on Baba during his sadhana.

Hatha Yoga : a yogic discipline which involves gaining mastery over the body and its functions through postures, breathing exercises, and other means.

Indra : king of heaven in Vedic mythology.

Indraloka : the subtle world of heaven, presided over by Indra.

Jamuna : a sacred river of India on the banks of which Krishna sported with the Gopis.

Janabai (thirteenth century) : a woman saint who was the disciple and house servant of the Maharashtrian poet-saint, Namdev. Because of her devotion, it is said that Krishna Himself came to help her with her household chores.

Janaka : saint who ruled the kingdom of Mithila in ancient

India; father of Sita; his Guru was Yajnavalkya.

Janardan Swami (1504-1575) : warrior-saint and spiritual preceptor of the famous Maharashtrian saint, Eknath Maharaj, who lived at Devagiri; his Guru was Narasimha Saraswati.

japa : repetition of the divine name, or mantra.

jnana : Knowledge.

jnani : an enlightened person; a seeker on the path of Knowledge.

Jnana Sindhu : a work composed by the Siddha, Sri Chidananda, containing a dialogue between Parashiva and Kartikeya on the theme of the ideal worship of the Guru.

Jnaneshwar (1275-1296) : a great saint of Maharashtra whose commentary on the *Gita*, written before he was twenty, the *Jnaneshwari*, is one of Baba's favourite books. He took live samadhi in 1296 A.D. and his samadhi shrine is at Alandi.

Jnaneshwari : *See* : Jnaneshwar.

Kabir (fifteenth century) : great mystic and poet-saint who lived in Benares and was a weaver by trade. His Guru was Ramananda.

Kailas : a peak of the Himalayas regarded as the sacred abode of Shiva.

Kali Yuga (*lit.* : the dark age) : the last of the four yugas (cycles of time); the present age.

Kannada : a language of South India, Baba's native tongue.

karma : action ; force or effect of one's accumulated past actions.

Kashi : name for Benares or Varanasi.

khichari : an Indian dish prepared from rice and lentils.

Krishna (*lit.* : the dark one) : the Lord who attracts irresistibly, the eighth incarnation of Vishnu ; his life is described in the *Bhagavat Purana* ; His major teaching on yoga is contained in the *Gita*.

Krishna Suta : poet-saint of Maharashtra who is well-known for versifying the *Gita* and *Panchadasi* into the Marathi language.

kriya : yogic movement or process.

kumbhaka : voluntary or involuntary retention of breath.

Kundalini (*lit.* : the serpent power) : the spiritual energy which lies coiled at the base of the spine of every individual and, when awakened, begins to rise upward purifying the body and initiating spiritual processes.

lila : divine play ; creation is often explained in Hinduism as the lila, or divine play, of God.

Mandaleshwar : title conferred upon well-known sannyasis who head an ashram or monastery.

Madhavacharya (thirteenth century) : leader of a Vaishnava sect who founded the doctrine of dualism (*dvaita*) based on the *Vedanta Sutras* ; born near Udipi, north of Mangalore.

mahut : elephant keeper.

mantra : sacred words or sounds invested with the power to transform and protect the individual who repeats them ; name of God.

Mathura : birthplace of Sri Krishna.

Matsyendranath : the first Guru of the Nath lineage, who, while hiding in the form of a fish, received initiation from Lord Shiva by overhearing Him give instructions to Parvati.

Mahabharata : famous Indian epic which tells of the war between the Pandava and the Kaurava brothers, from which the *Bhagavad Gita* comes.

mahasamadhi (*lit.* : the great samadhi) : the conscious death of a yogi.

Maha Yoga (*lit.* : the great yoga) *See* : Siddha Yoga.

Mirabai (1433-1468) : a Rajasthani princess and saint famous for her poems of devotion to Krishna.

mudra : a symbolic position of the body held for a length of time ; a state of consciousness.

muladhar : the chakra at the base of the spine where Kundalini Shakti lies dormant.

nada : divine music or sound ; the various inner musical sounds heard during advanced stages of meditation.

nadi : subtle nerve channel for the flow of prana ; there are 72,000 nadis in the human body.

Narada : a famous rishi, or seer, who is the author of the *Bhakti Sutras*, the main scripture of Bhakti Yoga ; acted as a messenger of the gods in the *Puranas*.

Narayana (*lit.* : the one whose abode is water): an epithet of Vishnu ; that aspect of Vishnu who reclines in the ocean on the serpent Sheshnag and dreams the creation.

Nataraja (*lit.* : the king of dance): an epithet of Shiva, referred to as the dancing Shiva.

Nath : (*lit.* : lord) : an epithet of Shiva ; cult of yoga mendicants who elaborated a yoga practice in which Kundalini is awakened thereby attaining mystic realisation. Originally there were nine Naths, Matsyendranath being the first who received initiation from Lord Shiva. *See also* : Matsyendranath.

Nityananda (*lit.* : eternal bliss) : famous Siddha saint and Guru of Swami Muktananda.

Nivrittinath (1268-1294) : the elder brother and Guru of Jnaneshwar Maharaj ; he was initiated by Gahininath, one of the nine Naths.

niyamas : *See* : Ashtanga Yoga.

Om : the primal sound ; the Word from which the entire cosmos emanates. It encompasses all sounds, words and languages, all things, and all creatures. It is the innermost essence of all mantras.

Om Namah Shivaya : a mantra meaning "*Om* I bow to Shiva."

oondhiya : a special preparation of mixed vegetables.

pakoras : vegetables deep fried in a batter.

Panchikarana : Vedantic treatise by Shankaracharya discussing theoretical aspects of the one reality and the practical way of realising one's identity with it, and the significance of the syllable *Om*.

Pandharpur : a place of pilgrimage, and the centre of worship for devotees of Vitthal in Maharashtra state.

Parabrahman : the supreme absolute.

Parvati : daughter of King Himalaya ; the consort of Shiva, She is regarded as an incarnation of the Divine Mother.

Patanjali (second century) : sage and author of the *Yoga Sutras*, the classical exposition of Raja Yoga. *See also* : Ashtanga Yoga.

Prahlad : a great child devotee of Vishnu, his devotion angered his demon father, Hiranyakashipu, who tried several times to kill the boy, but by the strength of his devotion, Prahlad was saved by Vishnu ; *From* : *Bhagavat Purana.*

prana : the vital force of the body and universe which sustains life. •

pranayama : regulation and restraint of breath. *See also* : Ashtanga Yoga.

prarabdha : the results of past karma, or action, which are experienced in the present life ; destiny.

Pratyabhijnahridayam (lit. : the heart of recognition) : a work on Kashmir Shaivism by Kshemaraja, pupil of Abhinava Gupta.

pratyahara : *See* : Ashtanga Yoga.

pujari : one who performs worship.

Puranas (*lit.* : ancient legends) : traditionally there are eighteen *Puranas*, or sacred books, containing stories, legends and hymns about the creation of the universe and the instructions of various deities, as well as the spiritual legacies of ancient sages.

Rama : seventh incarnation of Vishnu and hero of the *Ramayana* epic.

Ramanuja (1017-1137) : famous saint and philosopher of South India who founded the school of qualified nondualism (*vishishtadvaita*).

Ramayana : one of the two great epics of India relating the life and deeds of Lord Rama, the seventh incarnation of Vishnu ; composed by Valmiki.

rasa : essence or flavour.

rasalila : the mystical play of Krishna with the Gopis (milk-maids) of Vrindavan ; the dance or love-sport of the Lord with individual souls.

Ravana : the ten-headed demon king of Lanka ; enemy of Rama in the *Ramayana*.

red light : *See* : four bodies.

rishi : a seer of Truth ; the term is also applied to the sages to whom the *Vedas* and other scriptures were revealed.

sadhu : a monk or ascetic.

Sadguru : a true Guru, divine Master. *See also* : Guru.

sadhak : seeker on the spiritual path.

sadhana : spiritual discipline.

sahasrar : chakra on the top of the head in the form of a thousand-petalled lotus, where Kundalini Shakti unites with Lord Shiva.

samadhi : state of meditative union with the Absolute ; the tomb of a saint. *See also* : Ashtanga Yoga.

Sankhya : one of the six systems of orthodox Hindu philosophy, founded by Kapilamuni, which recognises two absolute entities of existence : Nature (*prakriti*) and Spirit (*purusha*).

samsara : the world of change, mutability, and death ; the cycle of birth and death.

samskara : past impressions.

samyama : term used for union of the last three stages of Ashtanga Yoga : dharana, dhyan, and samadhi. *See also* : Ashtanga Yoga.

sannyasa : formal vow of renunciation.

sannyasi : a monk or ascetic ; one who has embraced the life of complete renunciation.

saptah : traditionally, seven days of continuous chanting of the name of God.

satsang : a meeting of devotees to hear scriptures, chant, or sit in the presence of the Guru ; the company of saints and devotees.

sattvic : having the qualities of harmony and purity. *See also* : gunas.

Shaiva : worship of Shiva as the supreme Self ; philosophical school describing the nature of reality as the all-pervasive Shiva.

Shakti (*or* : Chiti, Chiti Kundalini, Kundalini, Kundalini Shakti): force, energy ; the divine energy, which projects, maintains, and dissolves the universe ; spouse of Shiva. *See also* : Chiti.

Shaktipat : transmission of spiritual power (Shakti) from Guru to disciple ; spiritual awakening by grace.

Shankaracharya (788-820 A.D.) : the great Indian philosopher who expounded the philosophy of absolute nondualism (*advaita*) ; founder of several orders of sannyasa and author of numerous works.

Sheshnag : the thousand-headed serpent king who dwells in the Nether regions ; in mythology he holds the earth on his mantle and forms a couch on which rests Lord Narayana in the Primal Ocean. *See also* : Narayana.

Shiva : the Supreme Lord, who is transcendent as well as immanent ; one of the Hindu trinity of gods, representing God as the destroyer.

Shiva Mahimna Stotra : a Sanskrit hymn honouring Shiva, chanted nightly at Shree Gurudev Ashram.

Shivasutras : a text Lord Shiva Himself gave to the sage Vasuguptacharya to perpetuate the nondual philosophy, consisting of seventy-seven sutras which were found inscribed on a rock in Kashmir.

Shivo'ham : a mantra meaning "I am Shiva."

Shrimad Bhagavat Purana (or : *Bhagavat, Bhagavatam*) : very popular devotional scripture sacred to Hindus, especially Vaishnavas, containing many legends, stories, and the life and teachings of Sri Krishna ; composed by Vyasa.

Shuka (*or* : Shukadeva, Shukamuni) : the son of Vyasa and disciple of King Janaka ; mentioned in many scriptures but he is most famous as the narrator of the *Bhagavat Purana* to King Parikshit.

Siddha : perfected one ; one who has attained oneness with God and who can, through Shaktipat, bestow His grace on a disciple and initiate spiritual awakening.

Siddhaloka : subtle realm of the Siddhas.

Siddha Purusha : a perfected Being.

Siddha Yoga (*or* : Maha Yoga) : the yoga that is received by the grace of a Siddha, a perfectly realised Master. It is called *maha*, or great, because it includes all other yogas —devotion, knowledge, action, mantra, and meditation. As the Guru's grace begins to work within a disciple, all these forms of yoga are unfolded within him spontaneously.

So'ham (*lit.* : "I am He") the mantra that is the true vibration of the inner Self, which goes on spontaneously within every sentient being.

subtle body : *See* : four bodies.

Sundardas (1597-1689) : a Hindi poet-saint born in Rajasthan who was a disciple of Dadu.

sushumna : the central and most important of all the 72,000 nerves. It extends from muladhar chakra to sahasrar, containing all the different chakras.

swadhyaya : study of Self ; study of scriptures ; scriptural chanting.

tamas : the quality of nature characterised by darkness, ignorance, dullness. *See also* : gunas.

tandra : a state of higher consciousness between sleeping and waking experienced in meditation.

tapasya : penance ; austere or ascetic practice.

Tukaram Maharaj (1598-1650) : the most popular of the Maharashtrian poet-saints ; born at Dehu, he was a worshipper of Vitthal.

Tulsidas (1543-1623) : North Indian poet-saint ; composer of the *Ramacaritamanasa*, the Hindi version of the Ramayana.

Uddhava : devotee of Lord Krishna ; Krishna imparted His teachings to Uddhava in Book Eleven of the *Bhagavatam*, referred to as the *Uddhava Gita*.

Upanishads (*lit.* : sitting near) : the teachings of the ancient seers, forming the end portion of the *Vedas*. There are 108 *Upanishads*.

urdhvareta : perfect celibate whose seminal fluid flows upward.

Vaikuntha : the abode of Lord Vishnu.

vairagi : one who is indifferent to worldly things ; one who has subdued worldly passions.

Vaishnava (*or* : Vaishnavite) : worshipper of Lord Vishnu.

Vasishtha : ancient sage and Guru of Lord Rama ; his teachings are contained in the *Yoga Vasishtha*.

Vasuguptacharya (ninth century) : sage who, through inspiration received the *Shivasutras*, the scriptural foundation of Kashmir Shaivism.

Vedanta (*lit.* : end of the Veda) : one of the six schools of Indian philosophy, arising from the discussions in the *Upanishads* about the nature of the Absolute or the Self.

Vedas : the four ancient, authoritative Hindu scriptures, regarded as divinely revealed : *Rig Veda, Yajur Veda, Sama Veda,* and *Athara Veda*.

vikalpa : imagination ; oscillation of the mind.

viraha : burning agony due to separation from the Lord.

Virochana : an asura (demon) ; son of Prahlad ; he was sent by the asuras to learn the nature of Brahman Prajapati, the creator of the world ; *From* : *Chandogya Upanishad*.

Vishnu : the supreme Lord ; one of the Hindu trinity of gods representing God as the sustainer ; the personal God of the Vaishnavas.

Vishnusahasranama (*lit.* : the thousand names of Vishnu) : the teachings imparted by Bhishma to Yudhishthira on the battlefield in the *Mahabharata*, which forms a chant in praise of Vishnu that is sung every day in the Ashram.

Vitthal (*lit.*: place of a brick) : Krishna went to the house of
Pundalik who, while tending to his aged parents, asked
Him to wait and threw a brick for Him to stand on. This
form of Krishna standing on a brick is known as Vitthal.
His image is enshrined in Pandharpur, a famous place of
pilgrimage in Maharashtra ; worshipped by the poet-saints
of Maharashtra and Karnataka.

Vraj (*or*: Vrindavan) : the district around Mathura and Agra
in northern India where Krishna spent his youth as the
son of Nanda, the cowherd.

Vyasa (*or*: Vedavyasa) : a Vedic seer, compiler of the *Vedas*,
Puranas, and author of the *Mahabharata*, father of Shukamuni.

white light : *See* : four bodies.

yajna : a ritualistic fire sacrifice ; any work done in the spirit
of surrender to the Lord.

Yajnavalkya : a sage whose teachings are recorded in the
Brhadaranyaka Upanishad ; Guru of King Janaka.

Yama : the lord of death.

yamas : five moral restraints. *See also* : Ashtanga Yoga.

yogabhrashta : one who dies before completing his sadhana and
is reborn to complete it.

Yoga Sutras : the scripture of Raja Yoga. *See also* : Patanjali.

yogavali : *See* : ajana vriksha.

yogi : a follower of yoga, who, through the practise of spiritual
discipline, attains higher states of consciousness.

Yudhishthira : eldest of the five Pandava brothers in the
Mahabharata epic.

Zipruanna : avadhoot and Siddha saint of Nashirabad, Maharashtra, whom Baba met and developed a friendship with
during his sadhana.

STORY INDEX

Other publications by and about Swami Muktananda

Books By Swami Muktananda

Play Of Consciousness Muktananda's Spiritual Autobiography
Satsang With Baba (Three Volumes) Questions and Answers
Getting Rid Of What You Haven't Got Introductory Talks
Muktananda-Selected Essays Edited by Paul Zweig
Light On The Path Essays On Siddha Yoga
Sadgurunath Maharaj Ki Jaya Photos and Essays Of The 1970 Australian Tour
Siddha Meditation Commentaries On The Shiva Sutras
Mukteshwari I & II Aphorisms
So'ham Japa Short Essay On The So'ham Mantra
Ashram Dharma Essay On Ashram Life
A Book For The Mind Aphorisms On The Mind
I Love You Aphorisms On Love
What Is An Intensive? Description of Muktananda's 2-day program
Bhagawan Nityananda Biography Of Muktananda's Guru, Swami Nityananda

Books About Swami Muktananda

Swami Muktananda Paramahansa By Amma — Muktananda's Biography
Sadhana Photographic Essay of Muktananda's Spiritual Practice
Muktananda Siddha Guru By Shankar

Other Books

Introduction To Kashmir Shaivism
Siddha Cooking Cookbook
Nectar Of Chanting Sanskrit Chants Transliterated and Translated

Publications

Muktananda Siddha Path Monthly Magazine of S.Y.D.A. Foundation
Gurudev Siddha Peeth Newsletter Monthly Newsletter From India
Shree Gurudev-Vani Annual Journal By Devotees

Books Available In Other Languages

Play Of Consciousness (French, German, Italian & Spanish)
Nectar Of Chanting (French & German)
So'ham Japa (French & German)

(Most of Swami Muktananda's books are also available in Hindi)

These books and Publications are distributed by S.Y.D.A. Foundation and are also available at Centers and Ashrams and by selected bookstores throughout the world. For further information, contact: S.Y.D.A. Foundation, P.O. Box 11071, Oakland, California 94611, U.S.A., Phone (415) 655-8677

Siddha Yoga Centers and Ashrams throughout the world

Swami Muktananda has several hundred meditation centers and ashrams throughout the world and many new ones open each month. The list below was accurate as of March 1, 1978. If you cannot locate a center or ashram listed in your area or you are interested in knowing if one has opened in the intervening time, write to S.Y.D.A. Foundation Headquarters, P.O. Box 11071, Oakland, CA 94611, U.S.A. or to any of the major ashrams or major centers which are identified in bold type below. For information on the ashrams and centers in India, contact: Gurudev Siddha Peeth, P.O. Ganeshpuri (PIN 401 206), Dist. Thana, Maharashtra, India.

UNITED STATES OF AMERICA

Arizona

Tucson
2905 N. Camino del Oesta
Phone: (602) 743-0462

California

Aptos
215 Elva Dr.
Rio Del Mar
Phone: (408) 688-1665

Big Sur
Esalen Institute
Phone: (415) 667-2335

Bolinas
P.O. Box 243
Programs held at:
165 Elm Rd.
Phone: (415) 868-0472

Campbell
430 East Central
Phone: (408) 378-7491
or 268-2130

Cazadero
P.O. Box 221
No Phone

Corona Del Mar
1701 Oahu Place, Costa Mesa
Programs held at:
430 Carnation Ave.
Phone: (714) 979-8727
or 642-9642

Corte Madera
5 Alta Terr.
Phone: (415) 924-3618

Fremont
41764 Chiltern Dr.
Phone: (415)651-3552

Long Beach
6332 Vermont St.
Phone: (213) 598-5366

Los Angeles (Ashram)
605 S. Mariposa
Phone: (213) 386-2328

Los Gatos
16585 Topping Way
Phone: (408) 356-4421

19330 Overlook Rd.
Phone: (408) 354-1109

Malibu
28747 Greyfox St.
Phone: (213) 457-3664
or 277-1711

Mendocino
1085 Greenwood Rd.
Phone: (707) 895-3130

Menlo Park
25 Bishop Lane
Phone: (415) 854-6408

Oakland (Ashram)
1107 Stanford Ave.
Phone: (415) 655-8677

S.Y.D.A. Foundation
P.O. Box 11071
Oakland, Ca. 94611

8573 Thermal St.
Phone: (415) 638-1161

Occidental
18450 Willow Creek Rd.
Phone: (707) 874-3101

Ojai (Ashram)
P.O. Box 994
Programs held at:
15477 Maricopa Hwy.
Hwy. 33, Ojai Valley
Phone: (805) 646-9111
or 646-1289

401 N Ventura St.
Phone: (805) 646-5228

Palo Alto
476 Ferne
Phone: (415) 494-6914

Redwood City
542 Laurel St.
Phone: (415) 364-9971

Sacramento
1616 21st St.
Phone: (916) 442-6425
& 442-6794

San Diego
1214 Sutter St.
Phone: (714) 295-1617

San Francisco
San Francisco State
University—Educational
Technology Center
1600 Holloway Ave.
Programs held at:
Room 13, Education
Building, SF State U.
Phone: (415) 469-1010

795 Elizabeth St.
Phone: (415) 285-8213

San Rafael
101 Bayview St.
Phone: (415) 456-8511

Santa Cruz
149 Hammond Ave.
Phone: (408) 429-1046

Colorado

Aspen
307 Francis St.
Phone: (303) 925-4560

Boulder
1355 Chambers Dr.
Phone: (303) 494-1186

2895 E. College #19
Phone: (303) 449-4689

Denver
58 Washington St.
Phone: (303) 733-0360

Pikes Peak
P.O. Box 6311
Colorado Springs
Programs held at:
3 S. 8th St.
Colorado Springs
Phone: (303) 633-3929

Connecticut

Cornwall
210 Riverside Dr. #5G
New York NY
Programs held at:
Jewell St.
Phone: (203) 672-6498
& (212) 866-3734

Greenwich
52 Riversville Rd.
Phone: (203) 531-9310

New Haven
44 Sycamore Dr.
Middletown, NY
Programs held at:
Dwight Hall
Yale University
Phone: (914) 343-8903

Weston-Westport
144 Goodhill Rd.
Weston
Phone: (203) 227-3481

Delaware

Wilmington
5009 Pines Blvd.
Pike Creek Valley
Phone: (302) 239-4290

District of Columbia

Washington D.C.
2900 Connecticut Ave. NW
#326
Programs held at:
4815 Broad Brook Dr.
Bethesda MD
Phone: (202) 244-3319,
483-4849, (301) 530-1109,
& 530-4325

Florida

Anna Maria Island
P.O. Box L
Bradenton Beach
Programs held at:
2107 Avenue A
Bradenton Beach
Phone: (813) 778-1464

Boca Raton
341 W Camino Real #304
Phone: (305) 368-9258

Clearwater
2625 SR 590 (at US 19)
Coachman Creek Apts.
#2221
Phone: (813) 726-2207

Fort Walton
419 Corvet St.
Phone: (904) 242-5751

Gainesville (Ashram)
1004 SW First Ave.
Phone: (904) 375-7629

1622 NW 52nd Terr.
Phone: (904) 373-5683

Indian Rocks Beach
116 11th Ave.
Phone: (813) 596-5794

Jacksonville
2130 Dellwood Ave. #1
Phone: (904) 641-3597

Miami
8264 SW 184th Terr.
Phone: (305) 253-3336
& 253-3337

Pensacola
2377 Olive Rd.
Phone: (904) 477-0527

Sarasota
620 Corwood Dr.
Phone: (813) 351-2147

Tallahassee
1639 Fernando Dr.
Phone: (305) 224-4282

West Palm Beach
719 Executive Ctr. Dr.
#210E
Phone: (305) 689-9247

Georgia

Atlanta
P.O. Box 76584
Programs held at:
Chattahoochee
Plantation
4445 Papermill Rd.
Marietta
Phone: (404) 971-1710

1647 N. Rocksprings Rd.
N.E.
Phone: (404) 874-2351

Macon
605 Poplar St.
Phone: (912) 745-6310

Hawaii

Honolulu
5660 Haleola St.
Niu Valley
Phone: (808) 373-4881

34 Gartley Pl.
Phone: (808) 595-7073

Kauai
RR #1, Box 223A
Lihue
Programs held at:
2737 Apapone St.
Lihue, Kauai
Phone: (808) 245-4576

Lanikai
151 Lanipo Dr.
Phone: (808) 261-0411

Maui
P.O. Box 1813
Phone: (808) 878-1430

Waikiki
2545 Ferdinand Ave.
Phone: (808) 947-1886

Illinois

Chicago
5848 N. St. Louis
Programs held at:
7920 Cressett Dr.
Elmwood Park
phone: (312) 453-7237
& 539-1407

2422 N. Drake
Phone: (312) 486-6595

468 W. Deming
Phone: (312) 549-5195

Des Plaines
7843 W. Lawrence
Norridge
Programs held at:
750 Cavan La.
Des Plaines
Phone: (312) 453-1186
& 825-0011

Glen Ellyn
571 Lowden Ave.
Phone: (312) 858-8688

Tamaroa
General Delivery
No Phone

Indiana

Indianapolis
5427 Seneca Dr.
Phone: (317) 251-9526

South Bend
733 W. Washington St.
Phone: (219) 287-6147

Kansas

Topeka
7523 Adams RT2
Berryton
Phone: (913) 862-2509

Wichita
3434 Oakland
Phone: (316) 685-5886

Kentucky

Louisville
817 Lyndon La.
Phone: (502) 425-1606

Louisiana

Baton Rouge
3299 Ivanhoe
Phone: (504) 343-6156

New Orleans
5608 Arlene St.
Metairie
Phone: (504) 455-3053

Maryland

Baltimore
P.O. Box 3290
Catonsville
Programs held at:
101 Newburg Ave.
Catonsville
Phone: (301) 788-6997
& 747-5236

Catonsville
1906 Rollingwood Rd.
Phone: (301) 744-0652

Massachusetts

Andover
45 Whittier St.
Phone: (617) 475-0966

Boston (Ashram)
301 Waverley Ave.
Newton
Phone: (617)964-3024

Brookline
15-rear James St.
Phone: (617) 566-6704

Cambridge
44 Larchwood Dr.
Phone: (617) 661-1584

Haverhill
1 Arlington Pl.
Phone: (617) 373-1963
& 372-8492

Northampton
25 Franklin St.
Phone: (413) 584-8167

Pepperell
32 Tucker St.
East Pepperell
Phone: (617) 433-9230

Wenham
3 Meridian Rd.
Phone: (617) 468-1311

Michigan

Ann Arbor (Ashram)
902 Baldwin
Phone: (313) 994-5625
& 994-3072

Milan
12925 Whittaker Rd.
Phone: (313) 439-8249

St. Clair
315 Orchard Rd.
Phone: (313) 329-9178

Missouri

Kansas City
5615 Harrison St.
Phone: (816) 363-5276

St. Louis
4154 Enright Ave.
Phone: (314) 652-3374

Montana

Bozeman
804 S. Black
Phone: (406) 587-8825

Nebraska

Scottsbluff
87 Michael
Gering
Phone: (308) 632-2917

New Hampshire

Mt. Washington
Valley
Birch Hill
North Conway
Phone: (603) 356-2421

New Jersey

Freehold
412 Woody Rd.
Phone: (201) 780-9150

Jersey City
413 Bancroft Hall
509 W. 121st St.
New York NY
Programs held at:
91 Lexington Ave.
Jersey City NJ
Phone: (212) 865-8475

Madison
17 Madison Ave.
Phone: (201) 377-3349

Middlesex
119 Prospect
Phone: (201) 469-8428

Upper Montclair
489 Highland Ave.
Phone: (201) 783-9261

Warren
6 Casale Dr.
Phone: (201) 647-5769

Whippany
9 Handzel Rd.
Phone: (201) 887-1483

New Mexico

Las Vegas
Rt. 1, Box 421 F
Phone: (505) 425-7315

Santa Fe
156 Rendon Rd.
Phone: (505) 983-7652

839 Don Diego
Phone: (505) 982-9529

Rt. 4, Box 50 C
Phone: (505) 988-3639

New York

East Hampton
11 Milina Dr.
Phone: (516) 324-0950

Jamestown
40 Wescott St.
Phone: (716) 485-1428

Mahopac
22 Putnam Professional
Park
Phone: (914) 628-7597

Middletown
44 Sycamore Dr.
(914) 343-8903

Poughkeepsie
2 Barclay St.
Phone: (914) 473-3307

Purchase
Box 1786
State Univ. Purchase
Programs held at:
Room 1021, H & M Bldg.
State Univ. Purchase
Phone: (914) 428-8689

Rochester
291 Pond Road
Honeoye Falls
Phone: (716) 624-3437

Syracuse
865 Ackerman Ave.
Phone: (315) 475-1837
& 422-2890

Yonkers
30 Locust Hill Ave.
Phone: (914) 965-3461

New York City

Brooklyn
169 Greenpoint Ave.
Third Floor
Phone: (212) 389-6058

Manhattan (Ashram)
324 W. 86th St.
Phone: (212) 873-8030

233 W. 83rd St.
Phone: (212) 787-4908

65 E. 11th St. #5G
Phone: (212) 260-6482

115 E. 96th St. #19
Phone: (212) 348-8413
or 628-6094

87-89 Leonard St.
Phone: (212) 925-4718
or 349-2851

10 Stuyvesant Oval #6F
Phone: (212) 777-9219

110 West End Ave. #3E
Phone: (212) 595-2958

Queens
117-14 Union Tpk.
Programs held at:
22 Kew Gardens Rd.
Phone: (212) 268-2248

68-20 Selfridge St. #5F
Phone: (212) 261-9792

Riverdale
4901 Henry Hudson Pkwy.
#5E
Phone: (212) 884-7940

Staten Island
148 Daniel Low Terr.
Phone: (212) 273-6460

Ohio

Cincinnati
157 Ridgeview Dr.
Phone: (513) 821-3629

Columbus
173 E. Tompkins
Phone: (614) 268-6739

Oklahoma

Norman
1501 Parkview Terr.
No Phone

Oklahoma City
3 S.W. 33rd St.
Phone: (405) 632-1366

2733 NW 15
Phone: (405) 947-6060

Oregon

Eugene
2010 Fairmont Blvd.
Phone: (503) 344-7594

Portland
2525A SE 118th
Phone: (503) 244-5509

Salem
2850 Hollywood Dr. NE
Programs held at:
4694 Harcourt NE
Phone: (503) 393-9334
& 588-1357

Pennsylvania

Erie
3525 Windsor Dr.
Programs held at:
3253 Pine Ave.
Phone: (814) 833-8894

Meshoppen
RD 2 Box 45
Phone: (717) 833-2794

Philadelphia
2133 N. Melvin
Programs held at:
302 Schoolhouse La.
**Phone: (215) 877-6910
& 848-0332**

Rhode Island

Providence
64 Standish Ave.
Phone: (401) 272-8237

South Carolina

Columbia
314 S. Bull St.
Phone: (803) 771-4036

South Dakota

Rapid City
1916 Hillview Dr.
Programs held at:
1525 Forest Court
Phone: (605) 342-6109

Tennessee

Oak Ridge
712 S. Main St.
Clinton
Phone: (615) 457-2203

Texas

Austin (Ashram)
1505 West Lynn
Phone: (512) 477-5156

Dallas
14706 Overview Dr.
Phone: (214) 233-7315

Dripping Springs
Star Rt. 1-B, Box 92
Phone: (512) 858-7045

Houston
2220 Rutland
Phone: (713) 862-8411
& 443-6587

811 Branard St.
Phone: (713) 529-0006
& 667-2241

Vermont

Chester
P.O. Box 22
Phone: (802) 875-3412

Virginia

Louisa
P.O. Box 545
Phone: (703) 967-0274

Norfolk
749 W. Princess Anne Rd.
Phone: (804) 625-9379

Roanoke
3534 Hershberger Rd. NW
Phone: (703) 563-5905

Washington

Bellingham
2908 Lincoln St.
Phone: (206) 676-0543

Bremerton
2509 E. Phinney Bay Dr.
Phone: (206) 377-2046

Burton
Vashon Island
Box 41A, Route 2
Phone: (206) 463-9225

Mercer Island
2815 67th S.E.
Phone: (206) 232-1575

Richland
2304 Enterprise Dr.
Phone: (509) 946-7573

Seattle
414 E. Mercer #2
Phone: (206) 325-2642

15709 25th S.W.
Phone: (206) 242-1151

6006 2nd Ave., N.W.
Phone: (206) 782-2027

Wisconsin

Madison
518 E. Johnson St.
Phone: (414) 922-6518

Wauwatosa
7810 Harwood Ave.
Phone: (414) 476-1718

AFRICA
South Africa

P.O. Box 42282
42a Clare Rd.
Fordsburg, Johannesburg
Programs held at:
4631 Lily Ave.
Extension 3 Lenasia

ASIA

Israel

**42 Henrieta Sold St.
Holon Israel**

Shenkin 46, 3rd Entrance
Givataim Israel 53304
Phone: 03-281221, 281222
& 281223 (At work)

Philippines

PSC #1 Box 2295
APO San Francisco CA
96286 USA
Programs held at:
Building 275
Clark Air Force Base
Angeles City Philippines
Phone: 20119

Australia

Armidale
Puddledock Rd.
Armidale NSW 2350

Bung Bong (Ashram)
P.O. Box 77
Avoca VIC 3467

Canberra
5 Mackellar Crescent
Cook, Canberra ACT 2614
Phone: 512 803 (after
6 pm) & (work) 062 89 6379

Ferny Creek
Wondoora, School Rd.
Ferny Creek, Melbourne
3786 VIC

Hawthorn
313 Auburn Rd., Hawthorn
Melbourne VIC 3122
Phone: 82 1985

Kalamunda
54 Kalamunda Rd.
Kalamunda 6076 WA

Melbourne (Ashram)
66 George St., Fitzroy
Melbourne VIC 3065
Phone: 419 6950

Narnargoon
Olsen Rd.
N. Narnargoon VIC 3812
Phone: (STD) 059 42 8206

Perth
P.O. Box 158
Cottesloe WA 6011
Programs held at:
9 Allie St.
Peppermint Grove WA
Phone: 384-4600

Sydney
33 Walker St.
North Sydney NSW 2060
Phone: 929 5431 &
(work) 290 2199

Townsville
5 Morehead St., Flat #1
S. Townsville QLD 4810

New Zealand

Dunedin
82 Gladstone Rd.
Dunedin, South Island

Canada

Malton
7566 Wrenwood Crescent
Malton ONT L4T 2V7
Phone: (416) 677-3301

Mississauga
6789 Segovia Rd.
Mississauga ONT L5N 1P1
Phone: (416) 826-4512

Montreal
745 Decarie
St. Laurent QUE H4L 3L4
Phone: (514) 744-5266
& 744-1247

Ontario
110 Dundas St.
London ONT N6A 1G1
Phone: (519) 471-6001

Ottawa
1300 Pinecrest #1605
Ottawa ONT
Phone: (613) 828-7214

Richmond
10051 4th Ave.
Richmond BC V7E 1V4
Phone: (604) 274-9008

Timmins
107 Pine N.
Timmins ONT P4N 6K8
Phone: (705) 267-5776

Toronto (Ashram)
48 Dundonald St.
Toronto ONT M4Y 1K2
Phone: (416) 923-5402

Vancouver
P.O. Box 2990
Vancouver BC V6B 3X4
Programs held at:
1811 W. 16 Ave., Rm 204
Vancouver BC
Phone: (604) 274-9008
& 838-2032

Victoria
1050 St. David St.
Victoria BC V8S 4Y8
Phone: (604) 598-2173

EUROPE

England

Bristol
43 Picton St.
Bristol 6
Phone: 02-72-42118

Clapham
91 Taybridge Rd.
London SW 11
Phone: 01-228-0969

Eastborne
30 Oakhurst Rd.
Eastborne, Sussex
Phone: Eastborne 37028

Hersham
33, Claremont Close
Hersham, Surrey
Phone: Walton-on-Thames
44228

Hounslow
15 Ivanhoe Rd.
Hounslow West, Middlesex
Phone: 01-572-3432

Ilford
358 Thorold Rd.
Ilford, Essex
Phone: 01-554-8112
01-552-2200

London
47 Maclean Rd.
Forest Hill, London SE23

32 Grosvenor Rd.
Finchley Central
London N3 2EX
Phone: 01-349-0557

United Kingdom
91 Taybridge Rd.
London SW 11
Phone: 01-228-0969

Lowestoft
28 Southwell Rd.
Lowestoft, Suffolk
NR33 ORN
Phone: 05-026-0793

Surrey
Coxhill House
Chobham, Surrey GU24 8AU
Phone: Chobham 8926

France

Nice
30 rue Marceau
Nice 06

Paris
8 rue Freycinet
75116 Paris France
Programs held at:
146 rue Raymond
Losserand
75014 Paris
Phone: 720-8430

14, Domaine de Seignelay
22, Sentier des Torques
92290 Chatenay-Malabry
Programs held at:
14 rue des Sts. Peres
Paris 75007
Phone: 350.41.78

Saint Etienne
Mail:
Bonnie Parker
% Maison des Eleves
20 Boulevard A-de-
Fraissinette
42030 Saint Etienne

Vesoul
26 Bld. des Allies
Vesoul 70 000

Italy

Rome
Via E. Filiberto 29
00185 Rome
Phone: 731-4891

Via Ara Delle Rose, 290
00188 Prima Porta
Rome

Netherlands

Soest
Ereprijsstraat 49
3765 AD Soest

Spain

Barcelona
% Ramon
c/ Torres y Bages 98-100
1o 2a

Sweden

Malmö
S. Forstadsgat. 102a 3v
S-214 20 Malmö
Phone: (040) 130862

Stockholm
Surbrunnsgatan 6
S-114 21 Stockholm
Phone: (08) 435709

Switzerland

Bern
Brunngasse 54, 3011

Geneva
49, Cure-Baud
1212 Grand-Lancy/Geneva
Phone: 94 79 56

West Germany

Bitburg
Box 465
APO New York 09132 USA
Programs held at:
11 Bornweg
5521 Holsthum

Frankfurt
Fischergasse 5
6050 Offenbach 8
Phone: 0611861260

Munich
Lieberweg 12
D-8000 Munchen 45

Mexico

Coyoacan
Miguel Angel de Quevedo
320
Mexico 21 DF Mexico
Programs held at:
Cerro dos Conejo 12
Mexico 21 DF
Phone: 554-1316
&554-0938

Guadalajara
Av. Americas 1485
Guadalajara 6
Phone: 41-11-35

Mexico City (Ashram)
Apartado 41-890
Mexico 10 DF
Programs held at:
Euclides 9
Colonia Nva. Anzures
Mexico 5 DF
Phone: (905) 545-9375

San Jeronimo
Cerrada Presa 28
San Jeronimo 20
Phone: 595-0980

Tepic
Guerrero 74 Ote.
Tepic, Nayarit
Phone: Tepic 2-27-52

SOUTH AMERICA

Curacao
P.O. Box 807
Curacao Netherlands
Antilles
Phone: 35251, 12213,
&11769

Kwartje 39 Sta. Rosa
Willemstad, Curacao
Netherlands Antilles
Phone: 38880

Trinidad
Union Village, Claxton
Bay
Trinidad West Indies

INDIA

Andhra Pradesh — 1

HYDERABAD

Shree Gurudev Center
Shri Rameshchandra Sanghani,
Shri Bakul Seth,
"Muktashram"
% Shri Pravinchandra Modi,
6-3-344 Jubilee Hills,
Hyderabad — 34

Delhi — 3

Siddha Yoga Dham,
Shri Balram Nanda,
Shri Ramesh Kapur,
M-11, Mukta Niwas, Green Park Extn.
New Delhi — 110016

Siddha Yoga Dhyan Kendra,
Shri Santram Vatsya,
K-47, Navin Shahdara, Delhi — 32

Shree Muktanand Dhyan Mandir,
Smt. Urmila Saxena,
Shri Parmama Shanker,
193-E, Dev Nagar,
New Delhi — 110005

Gujarat — 20

AHMEDABAD

Shree Muktanand Dhyan Kendra,
Shri Shirishbhai Desai,
Kum. Bhavna Dhora,
424, Hariniwas, Ashram Road,
Opp. La Gajjar Chamber,
Ahmedabad — 380009

Shree Gurudev Dhyan Kendra,
Shri Niranjan Mehta,
Shri Mahendrabhai Shukla,
15 August Bunglow,
Near Old Police Chawky, Maninagar,
Ahmedabad — 380008

Shree Gurudev Dhyan Mandir,
Smt. Kokila J. Parikh,
5B- Motisagar Society,
Narayan Nagar Road, Paldi,
Ahmedabad — 380007

Shree Gurudev Dhyan Kendra,
Shri Shriram Modak,
A/2 Minita Apartments, Near Swati Soc.
St. Xaviers High School Road,
Navarangpura, Ahmedabad — 380014

ATUL

Shree Gurudev Dhyan Kendra,
Shri Surendra H. Bhatt,
Shri Ramnikbhai Raval,
Room No — 26, A type Colony,
Atul, Dist.-Valsad

VALSAD (BULSAR)

Shree Gurudev Dhyan Kendra,
Dr. Ratubhai Desai,
Sandhya, Shree Buddha Society,
Halar Road, Valsad

Shree Gurudev Dhyan Mandir,
Shri Dilipbhai Desai,
Smt. Darpanaben Desai,
Hanuman Bhagda, Valsad.

Shree Gurudev Dhyan Mandir,
Dr. Jitubhai Parekh,
Kum. Laxmiben Prajapati,
Gangotri, Dhobivad, Valsad

DAHOD

Shree Muktanand Dhyan Kendra,
Shri Gopaldas K. Panchal,
138 'L' Satrasta, Opp. Dayanand Hindi
School, Freelandgang, Dahod
Dist.-Panchmahal

HIMATNAGAR

Shree Gurudev Dhyan Kendra,
Shri Kishorilal Sharma,
Smt. Chandrakantaben Jani,
Kum. Maya Mehta,
Sharma Cottage, Polo Ground,
Near L.I.C. Office, Himatnagar - 383001

KUKARWADA

Siddha Yoga Dham,
Dr. Gangadhar Patel,
Mahant Prempuriji Maharaj,
Kukarwada, Taluke — Vijapur,
Dist.-Mehsana

MOTA JOOJVA

Shree Gurudev Dhyan Kendra,
Shri Babubhai C. Patel,
Shri Dayaji D. Patel,
Shri Thakur D. Patel,
Mota Joojava, Dist.-Valsad

MOTA PONDHA

Shree Gurudev Dhyan Kendra,
Shri Prabhubhai D. Patel,
Mota Pondha, Via- Vapi,
Dist.-Valsad

PARNERA PARDI

Shree Gurudev Dhyan Kendra,
Shri Dolatrai G. Desai,
Parnera Pardi, Dist.-Valsad

SAMANI

Shree Gurudev Dhyan Mandir,
Shri Ghanshyambhai Patel,
Smt. Vidyaben Patel,
At/Post- Samani, Tal.- Amod,
Dist.-Bharuch

SURAT

Siddha Yoga Dham,
Shri Bachubhai Wadiwala,
Smt. Urmila Jariwala,
Shree Nityanand Bhavan,
Kelapith, Surat

UKAI

Shree Gurudev Dhyan Mandir,
Shri Jayantibhai L. Desai,
3A/32 Bhuriwel Colony
Ukai, Dist.-Surat

VAPI

Shree Gurudev Dhyan Mandir,
Shri Krishnarao Dhonde,
Rang Kripa, Zanda Chowk,
Vapi — 396191

DAMAN

Shree Gurudev Dhyan Kendra,
Shri Chunilal Patel,
Bhardwaj Kutir,
Ramji Mandir Compound, Wadi Falia,
Nani Daman, Via- Vapi

SELVASSA

Shree Gurudev Dhyan Mandir,
Shri Madhubhai Patel,
Matruchhaya, Muktanand Marg,
Selvassa, (Dadra Nagar Haveli)

Madhya Pradesh — 3

INDORE

Siddha Yoga Dhyan Kendra,
Shri Basant Kumar Joshi,
89, Emli Bazar (Lal Makan),
Indore — 452002

MHOW

Swami Muktanand Bhakta Mandal,
Shri Balwantrai Sharma,
Bunglow No. L/4A. Rly. Colony,
Mhow, Dist. Indore

RATLAM

Shree Sadguru Bhakta Mandal,
Shri Chunilal Rathod,
Shri Jaisinh S. Pol,
Sadguru Dhyan Kutir,
Nagar Nigam Colony, Block No. 316,
Gandhi Nagar, Ratlam

Maharashtra — 14

AURANGABAD

Muktanand Dhyan Kendra,
Shri B.S. Patil,
Smt. Rajani Patil,
Mukteswari, Prabhat Colony,
Aurangabad

BARAMATI

Shree Gurudev Dhyan Kendra,
Smt. Lila Kale,
Kale Wada, Baramati,
Dist.-Poona

BHUSAWAL

Shree Gurudev Mandir,
Shri Sudhir Rajabhao Kulkarni,
Muktanand Bhavan, Ram Mandir
Bhusawal, Dist.-Jalgaon

BOMBAY

Siddha Yoga Dhyan Kendra,
Kum. Bharati Dicholkar,
New Liberty Co. Op. Housing Society,
Guru Kripa, Block No. 9,
Liberty Garden Cross Road No. 4,
Malad, Bombay — 400065

Nityamukta Siddha Yoga Dham,
Shri Pranubhai Desai,
A/17 Madhav Apartments,
Shimpoli, Borivli, (West) Bombay

Siddha Yoga Dhyan Kendra,
Kum. Lalita Parasarmani,
Guru Chhaya, 62/1 Mulund Colony,
Mulund, Bombay — 400082

DOMBIVALI

Shree Sadguru Muktanand
Swadhyaya Mandal,
Shri Vasantrao Malpathak,
Khot Kaparekar Bldg.,
Agarkar Road, Dombivali (East)
Dist.-Thana

FAIZPUR

Shree Gurudev Dhyan Mandir,
Shri Shamlal Varma,
Shri Rajendrakumar Varma,
Faizpur, Dist.-Jalgaon

KOLHAPUR

Siddha Yoga Dhyan Kendra,
Smt. Jayashree Kori,
Smt. Vijaya D. Ligade,
Prabha, Rajarampuri,
14th Street, Kolhapur — 416001

MANMAD

Shree Gurudev Dhyan Kendra,
Smt. Kusumatai D. Deshmukh,
Railway Colony, R.B. 2-629A,
Yeola Road, Manmad

NAGPUR

Siddha Yoga Dhyan Kendra,
Shri Vasantrao Ghonge,
Mukta Niwas, Gopalnagar,
Nagpur — 440010

POONA

Shree Gurudev Dhyan Mandir,
Prof. G. H. Sujan,
44 Connought House,
12 Sadhu Vasvani Road,
Poona — 411001

Siddha Yoga Dhyan Mandir,
Smt. Pragna Trivedi,
"Kamal", 479/2 Harekrishna Path,
Shivaji Nagar, Poona — 411016

SAPTASHRING

Shree Saptashring Gurudev Ashram,
Swami Prakashanand Saraswati,
Saptashring Gadh,
Post- Nanduri, Tal.-Kalvan,
Dist.-Nasik,
(Residential Ashram)

Rajasthan — 4

JAIPUR

Shree Muktanand Dhyan Mandir,
Smt. Bhagvati Mukta,
B-222, Janata Colony, Agra Road,
Jaipur — 302008

Shree Muktanand Dhyan Mandir,
Shri Nandkishor Varma,
Shree Muktanand Niketan,
Gator Road, Brahmapuri,
Jaipur — 302002

NAGAUR

Siddha Yoga Dhyan Kendra,
Shri Sitaram Soni,
Katharia Bazar, Nagaur

TONK

Shree Muktanand Dhyan Mandir,
Shri Gopalsimh Bhati,
Abdul Qayum's House,
Barmor Darwaja, Tonk

Uttar Pradesh — 2

AGRA

Siddah Yoga Dhyan Kendra,
Dr. Chandrapal Singh,
Ram Niwas, 32 Heerabag Colony,
Swamibag, Agra — 282005

TENTI GAON

Shree Muktanand Dhyan Kendra,
Shri Ramshankar Lavania,
At/Post- Tenti Gaon, Dist.-Mathura

West Bangal — 2

CALCUTTA

Muktanand Dhyan Kendra,
Shri Balkrishna Agarwal,
11 Pollack Street, 1st Floor,
Room No.-3, Calcutta — 700001

Muktanand Dhyan Kendra,
Smt. Shukla Lal,
Shri Shadi Lal,
Flat No. 15, 8th Floor,
8-B, Alipur Road, Calcutta - 700027